The Secret Life of Chief Namakagon

James A. Brakken

Badger Valley Publishing

BadgerValley.com

The Secret Life of Chief Namakagon

James A. Brakken
Badger Valley Publishing
45255 East Cable Lake Road
Cable, Wisconsin 54821
treasureofnamakagon@gmail.com
715-798-3163

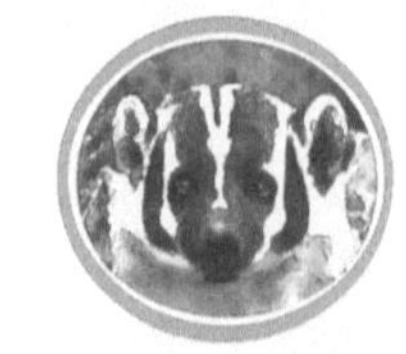

BadgerValley.com

If you enjoy reading this book as much as I did writing it, please tell your local school and community library and your friends to visit BadgerValley.com.
Thank you for supporting independent authors.
James Brakken

James Brakken's books, study guides, discussion questions, maps, and more available at BadgerValley.com where you will find secure, online credit card ordering, excerpts, and special discounts.

Every attempt has been taken to make this book a down-to-earth reflection of 19th century life in the Western Great Lakes States and, in particular, the life of Shaw-shawwa na-baysay, later known as Mikwam-mi-migwan or Ice Feathers, the hermit chief of Lake Namakagon.

The author expresses sincere gratitude to Upper Michigan's Chippewa County Historical Society and the Bayliss Public Library in Sault Ste. Marie for assistance with research for this story. This novel could not have been written without aid from the Manitoba Historical Society, the Wisconsin and Minnesota Historical Societies, the Sawyer County Historical Museum, the Ashland Historical Society, and the Cable-Namakagon Historical Museum.

Assistance and encouragement from my wife, Sybil Brakken, friends and colleagues who reviewed the original manuscript, and indispensable support from my critique group, the Yarnspinners, helped bring this story to life.

The Anishinabe terms used and their English translations are approximations based on the writings of Dr. Edwin James in 1828. As such, they may not reflect present language trends. No content within is meant to disparage or insult any culture or people. This fictional account of actual occurrences is not meant as historical documentation. Rather, it is a guide to the reader's further research. A suggested reading list can be found in the appendix.

This novel is dedicated to my grandson, Wiley, named for the pristine northern Wisconsin lake beyond the windows of my home in Bayfield County. I hope he will one day grow to become an observant, hearty outdoorsman, that he may enjoy and help conserve the woods and waters of the north and the rich history they hold. Wiley, this story is for you.

The Secret Life of Chief Namakagon

The Chapters

The Secret Life of Chief Namakagon

Preface

If it waddles like a duck and quacks like a duck …

This book offers insight into Chief Namakagon's legendary lost silver mine in northwest Wisconsin. Of greater significance, it finally solves the mystery of the identity of Namakagon prior to his arrival at the lake that shared his name.

When, in 2008, I began my first historical fiction novel, *The Treasure of Namakagon,* I did not intend to write a sequel, much less a series of three. However, research for the 1883 lumberjack tale led me to these two conclusions:

1. Chief Namakagon knew where to obtain silver but refused to disclose the location.
2. His demise involved foul play.

I was and am certain of both. Therefore, to share what I'd learned about the location of his silver mine and the many suspicious facts surrounding his death, I felt it essential to write book 2, *Tor Loken and the Death of Chief Namakagon,* a murder mystery.

Research for that novel sent me in another direction. I found myself wondering why, in the 1840s, this man came to a remote lake in far northern Wisconsin to live a hermit's life. Why would he isolate himself in this distant, uninhabited place?

I imagine the November 1880 arrival of the Omaha Railway turned life on end, especially when the newspaperman, George Francis Thomas, stepped off the train and sought out the only English-speaking, long-time resident of the area. The reporter's interview helped answer my questions: According to Namakagon, he'd come from Sault Ste. Marie, Michigan decades earlier. Why? Because a vision had revealed a fire and a death. This dream, he told George Francis Thomas, made him fear he would be executed for murder—a murder we now know he did not commit.

By itself, this dream, this vision, shed no light on my search for his previous life. But a trip to the Soo and deeper investigation revealed that a murder *had* occurred there. Moreover, it happened following a fire and coincided with the time Namakagon arrived in Wisconsin. Two men stood accused. One fled, fearing execution for a murder he did not commit—*a statement almost identical to that given by Namakagon to George Thomas!*

More information and a host of convincing coincidences caused me to continue my research. I exposed many more clues and details you will find within this story. But my final proof came while scouring the old land records, looking for the location of his silver mine. *The official, county land records, buried for decades, disclosed the former identity of Chief Namakagon.* Eureka! I'd solved a 168-year-old mystery—the solution to the 1846 disappearance of an innocent man wanted for a cold-blooded murder. The hermit of Lake Namakagon was that man, a fugitive who hid for forty years in the Wisconsin wilderness.

Of course, some will dispute this. However, the sheer number of clues, statements, and coinciding facts provided by professional historians, along with the official government land records, are clear evidence. They offer compelling, reliable verification—proof far stronger than any existing claims to the contrary.

So research for my fact-based murder mystery, *Tor Loken and the Death of Chief Namakagon,* led me to this—the story of Namakagon's early life, a fascinating, wilderness adventure and a close reflection of his first five decades. It is based on his own words and those of historians—historians, by the way, who know only the first half of his colorful life. My three "Chief Namakagon" books shed light on his intriguing final forty years.

Yes, this is fiction. But it is base on his own memoir. It's a window into the world of a woodsman with an amazing history, an adventurer who evaded death many times, a celebrated author forced to turn fugitive and become Ice Feathers, the legendary hermit of Lake Namakagon.

Take pleasure in sharing his journey and learning his story, *The Secret Life of Chief Namakagon.*

Several original 19th century letters and excerpts from documents are included in the text. They have been left precisely as written to suggest the flavor of writing by various characters in this novel. The errors within these letters and documents are those of the original authors.

An extensive glossary for the Chief Namakagon trilogy, including many Anishinabe terms, local jargon, and lumberjack slang, begins on page 207.

Post Script: Two years after publishing *Secret,* I stumbled on the 1892 memoir of Ben Armstrong, a Madeline Island fur trader who, I am certain, knew Chief Namakgon. In his writing, Armstrong tells of an old Indian who gave him silver from his secret mine. He took Armstrong to see the mine but turned back, not wanting to disturb the Great Spirit. These and other clues I found in Armstrong's memoir convinced me that his friend was Chief Namakagon. I annotated and re-published the Armstrong memoir, as the few original copies are either in disrepair or lost. See the end pages for information on the annotated 1892 memoir of Benjamin Green Armstong.

The Secret Life of Chief Namakagon

James A. Brakken

Prologue
June 1, 1966

A pair of loons called from the bay as I finished cleaning out Grandpa and Grandma's home. Once again the old lodge by the lake, the former headquarters of Grandpa Tor's lumber camp, sparkled inside and out. Although most of their belongings went to the church or the local museum, I'd spared those items that evoked fond memories of my grandparent's years here in far northern Wisconsin. I also saved one that had me baffled—a diamond-shaped silver medallion found hidden inside the old clock on the mantle. With the lodge all set for summer, I needed to satisfy my curiosity about an old Indian's secret—a legendary lost mine known in these parts as Chief Namakagon's treasure. I felt determined to unravel Namakagon's mystery and find that treasure.

I drove into town and headed for the library where I hoped I might learn more about this Indian hermit who, seventy-some years earlier, had shared his knowledge with Grandpa Tor—knowledge of wood lore, of living in harmony with nature, of living the Anishinabe way of life.

Tucked in my back pocket, I carried the silver medallion. From Grandma and Grandpa's stories, I knew the medal belonged to Chief Namakagon before he died in 1886. What puzzled me were the letters J and T scratched into the back. I believed this piece of silver proved Chief Namakagon's secret silver mine was more than a legend. Convinced it was real, I planned to find it.

Velma, the Forest Lodge Library's librarian, knew little about Chief Namakagon, but shared an old map of the silver mines to the north, the area I suspected hid the old hermit's lost mine.

"Mister Loken, I'd say your best bet is the land records office up at the County Courthouse. Now, you just tell them Velma sent you and they will take good care of you. Let them know that you and I spoke and I said that they should show you the land records from the old Marengo silver mining region. Remember, Mister Loken, you tell them Velma sent you, hear?"

I thanked Velma, left Cable, and arrived as the courthouse clock struck eleven. Though the clerk had not the slightest idea who Velma was, she showed me to the records library, stacked floor to ceiling with huge books, each filled with page after page of documents. I soon felt overwhelmed, elbow-deep in deeds, abstracts, and mining claims from the 1880s.

Hours later, dog-tired and thinking this a waste of time, I found it——a transfer of ownership record showing the initials J T on one side and a signature on the other—Jas. Tanner.

"J T!" I exclaimed, startling the clerk who chirped in surprise. "I found it!"

She stepped from her desk to look. There, at the bottom of the deed for a forty-acre parcel on the Marengo Trail, was the Tanner signature. Whoever he was, his initials matched those on the medallion owned by Chief Namakagon. My fatigue turned to delight. With the turn of a page, I'd gone from dog-tired to being as wound up as a puppy in a mud puddle. I'm sure I was beaming when I said to the clerk, "You have no idea how this pleases me!"

"What is it?"

"Oh, part of a family puzzle, I suppose. Where is this property?"

She pulled a small booklet from a top shelf. "This is the 1898 plat book. First one our county made." Wearing gloves, now, she carefully opened it to Marengo, then followed the trail with her finger. "Let's see. Hmm. Here it is. Marked J. Tanner, plain as day. I can give you a county map that shows how to get there."

"Who owns the land now?"

"You do."

"Me? What?"

"We all do," she said with a smile. "Long ago the government took his land and the land of many others for non-payment of taxes. In those days, things were done that way. Once the pine was cut and the mines played out, the owners would abandon the property, let the land go back to avoid the property tax. That parcel is now part of the Chequamegon National Forest."

The plat book showed the Brunsweiller River and the Marengo Trail cutting right through the forty. I knew Chief Namakagon, sometimes called Old Ice Feathers, would have walked this trail many times during his four decades here. We checked the plat book again. This was the one and only parcel in the silver fields held by someone bearing the initials J T. Moreover, the name "Tanner" on the original 1898 county plat map matched the name on the deed. I'd found it! A man named John Tanner owned this forty-acre parcel, a piece of land smack-dab in the middle of the Marengo silver diggings. The medallion must have once been his. Delighted with my discovery, I replaced the record books, thanked the clerk, and left the county courthouse as the clock struck five.

Top down, I cruised south toward Lake Namakagon again, the radio in my Pontiac blaring out *California Girls* by the Beach Boys.

That evening, I caught a dozen bluegills off the end of the dock. Sacrificing a bottle of Leinenkugel's for the beer batter, I soon enjoyed a nice supper while watching the final episode of *The Dick Van Dyke Show*.

Dishes done, my energy spent, I rested my feet by the fire and drifted off to sleep in Grandpa Tor's overstuffed chair. I dreamt of days past, of another Loken who warmed his feet by a fire long ago. I dreamt of a cold winter morning in a birch wigwam on a nearby island.

Chapter 1
The Second Reason
1887

Tor Loken sipped wild rose and sorrel tea, brewed over the coals of the fire in Diindiisi's lodge. Diindiisi, the Blue Jay, an old woman dressed in a blue buckskin dress, passed him a piece of smoked venison. The young lumberjack stretched out his long legs to let the fire warm his feet. Wrapped in a bearskin robe once owned by his friend, Chief Namakagon, Tor acknowledged the gift of venison with a smile and a nod. Blue Jay, her hair in a single, grey braid, spoke as the February wind howled outside.

"Do not grieve for him, Tor Loken. He would not approve. Like all else in life, his death is but a change from one state of being to another—from one world to another—from one life to another. He has had many. Mikwam-mi-migwan will always be with us, Tor, just as Wenebojo the teacher will always be with us. So, too, Gitchee Manitou, the greatest spirit of all."

"I know. Still, I cannot help but miss the old fellow. What about you, Diindiisi? Don't you grieve? Don't you miss him?"

"Not so much. I know he is where he wishes to be. Besides, I am accustomed to being away from him more than with him."

"Not me. For the last three years, he has been almost like a second father and rarely but a canoe paddle away. Now, he has gone away and left me with too much time to ponder. I must tell you, Blue Jay, I cannot make heads or tails of it all."

"Perhaps, young woodsman, you have questions for which no answers exist." She blew on her tea. "Tell me, what is it that has you so unsettled?"

"Many things, I suppose. Maybe what bothers me most is this." He pulled a diamond-shaped silver medallion from his mackinaw. "His emblem—the symbol he wore for all to see."

"Yes. I know it well," she replied. "He wore this with pride all the years he lived here. I am pleased it is now with you. I am sure he is pleased, as well. It came from the cave of silver, you know."

"Yes. He kept it stitched onto his buckskin shirt. Always with him, always there to see. But, what troubles me are these letters on the back. The J and the T make no sense. Not a lick. Is there anything you can tell me? Anything?"

Diindiisi studied the medallion, considering the question.

"Young woodsman, there are things in life we share with all others—things such as our appearance, our manner of speaking, laughter, and perhaps our stories. Then there are some feelings, ideas, concerns we share only with our closest friends, our companions, those we hold dear. What remains, Tor, is that which we keep only to ourselves—certain personal thoughts, knowledge, perhaps things from our past we feel best belong within our hearts only—things meant for us alone. It is the right of every person to hold certain things deep within, to tell no one, not even those nearest. My father was no exception."

"Your father? No, you mean your husband."

"Husband?" Diindiisi chuckled. "No, Tor. The man you knew as Ice Feathers was my father."

"But ..."

"Tor, listen to me. The one you call Chief Namakagon, Mikwam-mi-migwan, Ice Feathers, was my father—husband to my mother who died long ago."

"Mikwam-mi-migwan was your father?"

"Yes. His blood flows within my veins and my love for him remains in my heart."

"But, I thought ..."

"Many others thought the same. No, I am not his wife. It is an easy mistake, I suppose. He was old. I, too, am old. I have been here many decades, but three less than him." She sipped her tea. "So many winters."

"But, he called you 'Woman.' You called him 'Old Man.'"

"Yes?"

"Diindiisi, I had no idea that ..."

"He saw no reason to explain, I suppose. That was his way."

"But, this does not explain the J and the T on the medallion."

"I will tell you, Tor Loken. I will tell you his story. He is gone, now. His past life can no longer come back to harm him. I doubt that he would mind. Of the secrets kept by him, one soared far, far higher than the others."

Diindiisi reached over to pet Makade, the black, husky mix, then looked at Tor. "My father was not who you think—not who anyone thinks. That newspaperman, the one who seems unconcerned about writing the truth, had much to do with this."

"George Francis Thomas?"

"Yes. Thomas. He came here by train from Chicago in 1882 to write about this land. My father was the only man who lived here many years and who also spoke English. Although he never lied to Thomas, my father allowed him to draw conclusions that were wide of the mark. Thomas did not seek the truth, only a story. His words, his newspaper writings helped my father hide. You see, Mikwam-mi-migwan did not wish for others to know who he truly was."

"Why? I mean, why hide who you are? Why live alone out in the wilds?"

"You ask why someone would choose to live the life of a hermit? A life far out in the woods? Away from others? I know only two reasons. One is a deep dislike of people. Who cannot comprehend this after standing in the midst of a busy city with people rushing here and there, often for no good reason? But this was not the way with my father. He enjoyed the company of others. You saw this many times when he visited your camp, you and Ingman and Olaf."

"Then, why, Blue Jay? Why did Mikwam-mi-migwan live the life of a hermit way out here in the woods?"

"Yes. This is the second reason—to avoid the past. My father stayed far away to conceal what went before, to avoid something that plagued him. It haunted him like a ghost from a dream. It drove him from his earlier home, made him come to this place, caused him to hide here for over four decades— hide almost until sent off to his next life."

"Your father's heart was full of courage. What could possibly make him hide?"

"Murder."

Tor stared into Diindiisi's eyes. "Murder?"

"Father was sought by the United States Army."

"The Army? But ..."

"Yes. For the slaying of James Schoolcraft, brother to Henry Schoolcraft, the Indian agent in Sault Ste. Marie."

"But, murder?"

"In 1846. Summer. At Fort Brady in Michigan. James was the Sheriff there."

"Your father? Ice Feathers? He wouldn't murder ..."

"No. He did not. James Schoolcraft was shot and killed, but not by my father. Another man, a soldier named Gibsen. I will not forget the name. Lieutenant Bryant Gibsen of Fort Brady. Both Father and Gibsen were accused. Henry Schoolcraft pointed his finger at my father. His hatred for my father blurred his judgment like clouds hide the sun before a storm. Schoolcraft made others at the Army post blind to the notion that an Army officer would slay James Schoolcraft, a white man and a sheriff. Had Father not left, not run far away, had not come here to hide, he was certain to hang for this other man's crime.

"Father's flight from there made them suspect him more. He knew Schoolcraft and the soldiers would hunt for him, hunt for him forever. He had no choice. He flew like a fast bird, a falcon. My father came here, made a new life, discarded the old, discarded his true name, discarded even his family, his friends, all things from before—discarded everything."

"All these years? Forty years?"

"No. Not all. They say, after the war with the Mexican Army, this soldier, this Gibsen took part in another murder. One night, Gibsen and other soldiers were celebrating, drinking, maybe drunk. They robbed a store looking for more whisky. The storekeeper heard them. They shot him dead. All were caught. Found guilty. Sentenced to hang. They say the Army general freed Gibsen because he was an officer. The others they hanged. Gibsen turned to whisky. Drank himself sick. On his deathbed, he confessed to slaying James Schoolcraft."

"But then, why did your father …"

"By the time word reached him, he was an old, old man. His new life here seemed better than his past. He chose not to return. He would remain Mikwam-mi-migwan, Old Ice Feathers, Namakagon."

"How did you find him?"

"Oh, he found me. I lived far west of here near Rainy Lake in Minnesota. Father came one day to tell me his story. Since then, we remained close, though apart more than together. I had my family there. He grew old. I grew old. When my man died and my children all left, I came here to care for Father. It seemed right."

"Diindiisi, how was he known before he came here?"

"What name? Yes. My father's first name. The answer, Tor Loken, begins with a boy eight years of age, a boy captured by Shawnees and raised by the Ottawas—a boy who grew to be more an Indian than a White, grew to become a great and respected Ojibwe warrior, a chief among them. He also became a friend to other great men—white men. He had many adventures. But later, his life was destroyed by the arrogance of a different White, the Indian agent, Henry Schoolcraft, who is now long dead."

"Blue Jay, you have me so confused. I must know more."

"Yes. It is right. Father has told me so in my dreams. I will tell you his stories—the stories of my father who had many lives, many names. One of these is Shaw-shawwa na-baysay. It means fast swallow. I will tell you the story of this man who many knew as White Swallow when he was young and Wewiib gekek Waabishki, White Falcon much later. I will begin in the middle. I will begin with the dark, rainy day he met the man who changed his life forever. Changed it for better, then for worse."

Diindiisi lifted the copper kettle from the coals and poured more steaming tea into the two tin cups. She sat again, both dogs near and the diamond-shaped silver medallion in her weathered hands. With February's frigid wind howling beyond the birch bark walls, Diindiisi, daughter of Chief Namakagon, began.

Chapter 2
The White Indian
June 1822

Henry Schoolcraft leaned over the hearth, tapping his briarwood pipe on the andiron. Its ashes, caught in the draft, drifted onto the hot coals. As he turned back to his large, oak desk, something far beyond the windowpane caught his eye. He stepped to the window, rubbed away the condensation, and peered across the Fort Brady parade grounds. In the penetrating Sault Ste. Marie drizzle, a tall man secured four packs and three children below the

cover of the branching limbs of a large spruce. Henry watched as the man huddled the children together next to an Indian woman. Taking off his coat, he shielded the four from the rain before walking across the muddy field directly toward him.

Schoolcraft waited, then swung open the heavy door to see the lean, pitiful misfit standing before him. Henry, a broad-shouldered, plump, bearded man, stood there, hands on hips. "Yes? What is it? What do you want?"

"I seek audience with your master, Mister Henry Schoolcraft. I was told I would find him here. Can you direct me?"

"Who are you?"

"I am an interpreter looking for employ. I go by the name Tanner. Might I step out of this weather, sir?"

"What makes you think Henry Schoolcraft needs an interpreter?"

"I was told such by a fellow named Boyd. Colonel Boyd. I am recommended by him and by another named Cass. May I speak with Mister Schoolcraft?"

"Cass, you say?"

"Lewis Cass. From Detroit."

"Lewis Cass? Governor of Michigan Territory?"

"Yes. Governor Lewis Cass, sir. Now, may I speak with Mister Schoolcraft?"

"How do I know you speak the truth?"

"I beg your pardon?"

"How do I know you speak the truth? How do I know you are an interpreter looking for employment?"

"Why would you suppose I am not? I did not travel months with my wife and our three offspring to be questioned, nay, interrogated by a plump doorman. Nor do I seek an audience with President Martin Van Buren. I wish only to speak with Henry Schoolcraft and only for a brief moment."

"I, sir, am Henry Schoolcraft."

"You? Come now! You are Schoolcraft? Schoolcraft the explorer? I doubt this is so. You have not the frame for it."

"Doubt as you wish, sir. I am Henry Rowe Schoolcraft, the man you seek."

"And, how do I know *you* speak the truth?"

"You, a vagabond, dare doubt *my* truthfulness?"

"One minute on your front stoop and already we seem to have come to loggerheads."

"So it seems. Now, perhaps you should leave."

The rain-drenched traveler reached in his pocket. "If it is true that you are Henry Schoolcraft, then you will recognize this." He handed him a letter.

"Hmm. Says you are, indeed, John Tanner. And, to be sure, it bears the scribble of our governor, Lewis Cass."

"Now, how do I know you are the Henry Schoolcraft I've journeyed so far to meet? How do I know you are no more than a simple doorman?"

Schoolcraft scowled at the dripping-wet visitor. "I will attribute your insolence to the weather, intolerable as both may be." Schoolcraft read the letter. "Governor Cass is a close friend. I served with him against the English in 1812. Yes, I see this letter seems to be in order. Come in out of that bothersome drizzle, John Tanner. And do wipe your feet."

The man stepping out of the rain did not look like a government interpreter. His wet, worn buckskin shirt and britches, his muddy moccasins, braided black hair hanging below his coyote-skin hat, and a thick, unkempt beard did not fit the part. He stomped some of the mud from his feet and entered the foyer, dripping puddles onto the hardwood floor.

"So, Mister Henry Schoolcraft, might you have work for a wayward interpreter?"

"Parlez-vous français?"

"Français? Oui, monsieur. Je parle beaucoup …"

"But, I already have a man who translates French, and quite well, I must add."

"And, Ojibwe? Does your man speak French, English, *and* Ojibwe?"

"You speak Ojibwe?"

"And Ottawa, sir. Thirty years I spent with them."

"You may be of some use after all."

"And Menomonee? And Sioux?"

"Sioux, you say?"

"Sioux, Ojibwe, Menomonee, Winnebago, Blackfoot, Shoshone, Cree, Iroquois …"

"Say no more, sir. I see now why the Governor offered you this letter," Schoolcraft said, returning it. "Yes, I can definitely use you. Pay is thirty cents a day, room and board included. Now, tell me about the woman and children I saw with you."

"James, is my eldest. Nine years. My daughters are seven and six. Martha and Marie. Their mother, Therezia, is Ojibwe. Eighty-five cents a day, sir."

"My wife, Jane, is also Ojibwe. Thirty-five cents."

"This woman, Therezia is my second. I have another three children by my first wife. They live near the Rainy River with many relatives in their village. Eighty cents, sir. 'Tis a fair wage."

"Eighty? Never. Perhaps fifty cents in a year from now if you show your mettle. For now, forty a day and I will see to it the children are enrolled in our post school."

"Seventy-five, sir. I will secure my own lodge and you will provide schooling for my offspring and meals twice daily. Know, too, that one day I will bring my first family here to live."

"More mouths to feed? I am beginning to wonder if I am getting more than a translator, Mister Tanner. Forty cents a day is damn good pay."

"Lord Selkirk paid me ninety, Mister Schoolcraft, though I did find myself dodging the occasional musket ball when we rousted the Nor'Westers from their posts."

"Selkirk, you say? Of Hudson's Bay Company?"

"One in the same, sir."

"I met him as he journeyed west to Fort William. Quite the adventurer, that Selkirk."

"Quite." Tanner handed Schoolcraft another letter.

"My word! Says here you were his chief translator, scout, and guide."

"I was, sir."

"This letter is authentic? You'll swear this?"

"It is and I will, sir."

"Selkirk's interpreter. Then, you must be the man who brought the Sioux to the table? The one who helped quash the wars between the Sioux and the Ojibwe?"

"And others, sir."

"And you led the attack on Fort Douglas? Routed the Nor'Westers?"

"'Tis true, sir."

"Then … you must be the man they call … the White Indian?"

"I am, sir. Shaw-shawwa na-baysay. John Tanner, at your service."

"My word! Tanner, if I should engage in an expedition to the Mississippi River headwaters and beyond, you would travel along as my interpreter?"

"And guide, sir. I know the country betwixt here and Lake of the Woods very well. I know the fastest route to the Mississippi. Much faster than beyond Fond du Lac. Have we returned to ninety cents?"

"Eighty, Mister Tanner."

"Would you have it known that the Englishman, Selkirk, pays more than the American, Schoolcraft?"

"Hmm."

"Even now his Hudson's Bay Company pays me a dollar-a-week and always will, sir."

"My word. You are under his employ, then?"

"I was. The monthly pension is his way of showing his appreciation for work done and lives saved, sir."

"Fascinating."

"I shall see to it that you get your money's worth when we reach Rainy River country and encounter the Sioux, Cree, and Blackfoot there."

"Blackfoot? I've heard chilling tales about the Blackfoot."

"They come eastward in the summer following the buffalo herds. I know them. They know me. You will have trouble with neither Blackfoot nor Sioux. Ninety cents, sir?"

"Ninety cents? No sir! Henry Rowe Schoolcraft will not be outdone by some pompous English lord. Dollar-a-day, John Tanner. Done, sir?"

"Done, sir."

Schoolcraft grinned, stroking his chin. "My goodness! Wait until that old windbag, Louis Cass, learns I have retained the services of Lord Selkirk's own interpreter, the man who led the attack on Fort Douglas!" He turned, shaking Tanner's wet hand. "You may sleep in the post livery until you find better lodging. There you will find clean oat straw for your bedding. I shall instruct the mess sergeant that we have need for five more plates. Your young ones may eat with the other Fort Brady children. You, Tanner, will share my table. I will seat you next to Major Quimby. He is sure to benefit from your experience. Now, sir, before your poor wife and children are beset upon by consumption, fetch them over to the chapel that they can shed the chill of this April rain. The women of the church will put the lot of you in dry garments and fill your bellies with hot soup. Then, John Tanner, return here that you may tell me the full tale of your adventures."

Chapter 3
The Abduction

Pipes lit, brandy glasses in hand, John Tanner and Henry Rowe Schoolcraft sat in upholstered wingback chairs before the fireplace.

"Now, tell me your story," said Schoolcraft. "From the beginning, then."

"As you know from the Governor's letter, Mister Schoolcraft, I am John Tanner. I am a Kentuck by birth but not by choice. For as white as I may appear, I am a Chippewayan."

"No, sir. I do not believe you. You are not …"

"In my heart, I am, Henry Schoolcraft. And in the hearts of my people, the Ottawas and Ojibwes."

"I see."

"My mother was French, though her I recall dimly for I was told she died of the pox in 1783 when I was but a babe. My father, an Englishman who also bore the name John, was a minister and farmer. I know not why he struck out westward when I was but eight years of age, a journey that resulted in my abduction in the year 1789."

"Abduction, you say?"

"Yes, when just a boy, I was stolen away from my white family by Shawnee warriors, Manito-gezik and his blood-thirsty son, Kish-kau-ko. Many times during my time with them these shiftless rogues wanted to kill me and would have, if not for the wife of Manito-gezik who is called Ne-keek-wos-ke-cheem e-kwa or Otter Woman. She caused me to be torn from my family and spirited away to live the life of the Ottawa. I will tell you now, although I harbored deep hatred for the men in this family, I would not trade my time with the Ottawas and Ojibwes for that of the white man.

"My life has been a great adventure, aided by my protector and guardian, Wenebojo, the spirit-man who sees all things. Like the holy one you call Jesus, Wenebojo shares a lodge with the red man's Great Spirit, Gitchee-Manitou. Long ago I learned how to summon him—how to share thoughts with him. It is Wenebojo who saved me many times throughout my adventurous life. He made me a wise mashkikiiwinini, a medicine man. It is Wenebojo who sits alongside me now, even as I speak."

"But, Tanner, you must tell me of your abduction."

"I am often asked about my capture. Although four decades past, this memory I cannot purge from my mind nor my heart. My father, John Tanner the elder, was slave to strong drink. As a boy, I was beaten often, as were my sisters. Many times, I cried out that I wished so to run into the woods and live with the Indians. My wishes, one spring day, were fulfilled, but to my dismay and great distress, then, later, to my great benefit and education.

"My white family had traveled two days by wagon to the gentle Ohio where Father traded our two wagons for three rafts. One held our family and furniture, the second our horses and cow, the third my father's Negroes.

Three-day's journey down the river, our raft struck bottom and was bound to sink near a land they called Cincinnati. Father took this sinking as a call from the Lord and soon had us safe and sound in an abandoned cabin across from the confluence of the Ohio and Miami Rivers. Father soon learned that hostiles had killed the former inhabitants. No matter. He wanted to stay. He, with his Negroes, surrounded the log cabin with a strong picket, then, began preparing the nearby field for the planting of corn.

"In spite of Father's orders that I must remain in the house with my sisters,

I chose to climb a nearby hickory tree to help father watch for hostiles. Though forty years have passed since that day, I clearly recall hearing a crackling in the nearby brush as I began my climb. My wrists were next seized by two men, one old and very tall—the other short and thick. My shouts of protest brought a sharp crack from my father's rifle and the short man let go a holler and dropped to the soil, shot in the neck. Another hostile immediately took his place and I was dragged off into the nearby brush, down the bank and across the river. In mere minutes, we stood on the far side of the Ohio, looking back at Father and my sisters on the opposing bank. Kish-kau-ko gave a victory cry before my captors spirited me off into the woods, never again to see my father alive."

"Never, you say?"

"Never. He is long since dead as is my sister, Martha. Of my family then, only my sister, Lucille, and my brother, Ned, remain alive in spite of attempts by these evil men to murder them."

"Please, go on with your story—your kidnap."

"For the next nine days, I was forced to run to keep up with Manito-o-geezhik, and his son, Kish-kau-ko. A strap made of braided deer sinew kept me tethered by the neck to Kish-kau-ko's wrist and he often showed his scorn for me by yanking on it, throwing me to the ground. This he did over and over again, much to the delight of his father. During one rare stop along the trail while they rested, I worked the tether over my head and slunk into a cattail marsh. My trail must have been manifest, for soon the shadow of Kish-kau-ko lay upon me. His tomahawk was raised above his head and I plainly understood, from the expression of his face and his manner, he was directing me to cast my eyes Heavenward for the last time, for he was about to kill me. I uttered a hasty prayer as I looked to the Lord. But, as you can see, I am still here today for his father, Manito-o-geezhik, caught his arm even as it fell. I believe both my abductors wanted to kill me then and there and would have, were it not for the wishes of Otter Woman, the mother of one and wife of the other. It soon became clear to me that Manito-o-geezhik's fear of her was greater than his hatred for me.

"My punishment for my brief flight was immediate and unjust. My shoes were torn from my feet and thrown far into the cattails. Thenceforward, I was forced to keep up with my captors with my feet bare, bruised, and bloody as we ran down woodland trails. That night we traveled by light of a half moon and, by dawn, my feet were cut and swollen—so much so, that the abductors found it easier to drag me along rather than try to make me run to keep up. I endured this seven days until we reached the village at Sau-ge-nong."

"Sau-ge-nong?"

"Whites know it by Saginaw."

"Saginaw, yes. Along the shore of Lake Huron. I have encamped at Saginaw on my journeys to and from Detroit."

"Then, Mister Schoolcraft, our paths have crossed."

"Perhaps I have seen you without knowing."

"No. My abductors always kept me far from the eyes of any White for fear I would be rescued and they would hang for their misdeeds."

"I see. Go on."

"At Sau-ge-nong, my new Ottawa mother was pleased to receive me, offering embraces and kisses throughout the day as well as dried venison and rock maple. She treated my bleeding feet with mud and nettle sap. During the next fortnight, she offered kindness and friendship, as did her daughters. Not so, Kish-kau-ko and his father, who remained abrasive and cruel toward me.

"While I lingered with them at Sau-ge-nong, I saw white men but once and was kept far distant when they neared. Perhaps you were one they secreted me away from, sir."

"Perhaps."

"While there, I soon learned the tongue of my new family as well as the habits, skills, and beliefs. Gitchee Manitou, the Greatest Spirit, often came to me, as did Wenebojo. I welcomed them into my heart and they gave me the ability to see the future and know the ways of the midewinin, the healer of body and spirit. But, even while he helped me, Wenebojo also took from me my white man's language. Years later, when I had grown to be a man, I encountered an English exploration party. I found I could not speak with them. I could not exchange words sufficient to explain my situation. They took me for a savage. I quickly saw I was in jeopardy of giving up my scalp so I retreated into the forest, returning to my village. I chose then to live with my red family rather than die by the hand of the whites. This decision led me on many adventures."

Henry Schoolcraft poured more brandy and stirred the fire, realizing the tale of John Tanner had only begun.

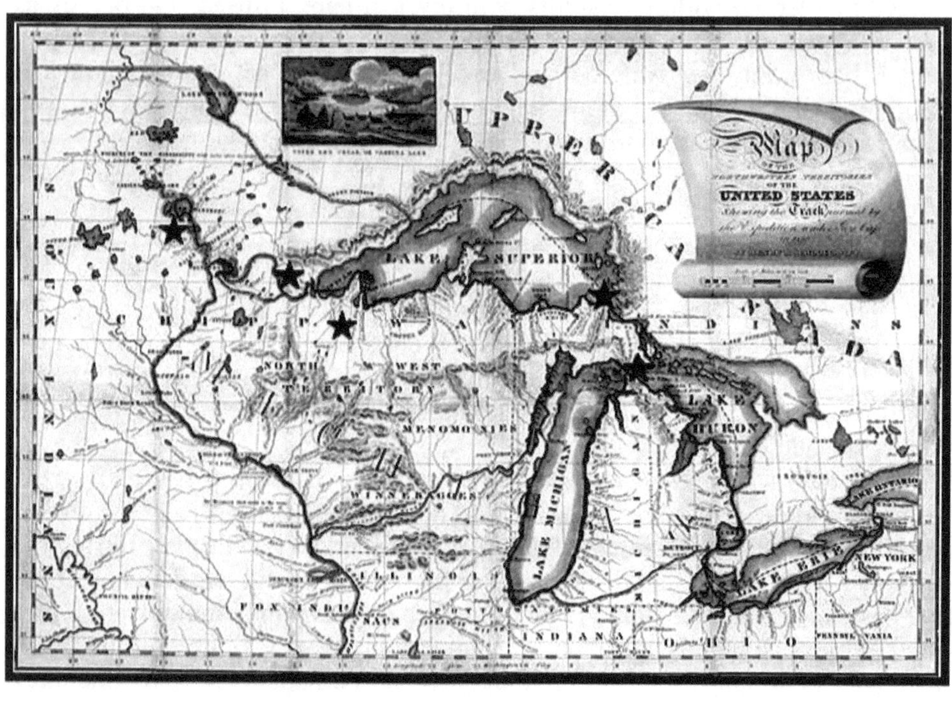

"Within months of being taken from my family and home on the Ohio, I grew accustomed to my new life, though the bad treatment from Manitou-o-geezhik and Kish-kau-ko continued. In spite of this, I gathered skills in tending the small gardens in our village. The corn, beans, pumpkins, and squash grew faster and larger than those my father had grown the years before. I learned to skin animals and to prepare the pelts. My sisters showed me how to make the hide of a whitetail into the soft deerskin needed for our shirts, britches, and moccasins. We mashed the brains of deer then mixed oak ash and a tea made from boiled acorns, soaking the hides for days before preparing the hides by rubbing between two stones. We chewed the hides to give the final softening before the women stitched the hides into clothing. They taught me to use smoke and salt to dry venison and bear meat, beaver, and fish. From the men in our small village, I learned how to carve pipes from stone and how to make stone tools, spear points and arrowheads, and how to build a strong bow.

"I accepted my new life and would have even enjoyed it, if not for the harsh treatment I still endured from Manitou-o-geezhik and his son. It seemed every attempt I made at helping them or making their day better was met with angry rebuff. One day, Manitou-o-geezhik asked me to watch over a net he laid in a nearby stream. After hours of observing I fell asleep. I later woke to the voice of Otter Woman, standing over me. My head throbbed with pain and blood flowed in my eyes and onto my shirt. Manito-o-geezhik found me asleep and had bashed my head in with his tomahawk, then threw me into the stream to die. He then went to her, telling her I was useless and he had rid the world of me. She somehow found me and rescued me and scolded him for his foolishness, saying if I were dead he must then capture another boy from the whites. The scar from his weapon I still bear on my head and the scar from his hatred of me on my heart. But he is now long dead and his bloodthirsty son, Kish-kau-ko, is in prison in Detroit for murdering a white man. He will hang. Kish-kau-ko is a good-for-nothing. Not even his mother will shed tears.

"My life at the Sau-ge-nong changed little during the next years. Otter Woman and her daughters were my salvation. I am certain Wenebojo sent them to protect me from Kish-kau-ko and Manito-o-geezhik. When Kish-kau-ko fell sick with fever, his father blamed me and beat me even more severely. I, in turn, explained as he whipped me that this fever came to his son due to the wrath of Wenebojo who came to protect me from his unjust treatment. I told him Wenebojo had come in the form of fire—the same fire that heated his lodge and cooked his food. I said the heat from the fire was now inside the belly of his son and would remain until he stopped beating me forever. Manito-o-geezhik laughed at me and refused to believe this and he beat me even more as his son suffered day after day.

"One morning, a hunting party returned to our village with many deer. While I helped a woman skin one of the deer, I used a hollow gourd to collect blood from it as it dripped onto the ground. Manito-o-geezhik knew not that I poured the blood in the moccasins of Kish-kau-ko as he laid suffering. I then sang a chant summoning Wenebojo. Manito-o-geezhik laughed at me and scorned me until Otter Woman saw the blood oozing from the moccasins of her son. I then told my family that the fever suffered by Kish-kau-ko was cast on him by Wenebojo and other spirits to repay their treatment of me. I pointed to my feet and the scars from my capture. I told them, in my dreams Wenebojo said only to me that this evil fever would take the life of Kish-kau-ko unless he and his father took me into their hearts, as had the mother and sisters and all the women in the village. Again, Manito-o-geezhik scorned me but Kish-kau-ko's fever soon broke and passed. Never again did I endure beatings and scornful treatment from either of them. Curiously, never again did the feet of Kish-kau-ko ooze blood."

"Mister Tanner, your resourcefulness, your cunning deserves applause. Tell me, what age you were you when all of this took place?"

"Age? Hmm. Eleven, perhaps. I cannot say with certainty. Age is an odd idea. Means little. These people showed no interest in measuring the occasion of my birth. Nor did I."

"Do you know your age today?"

"I believe I was born in the year 1781. If so, I must be forty-one-years."

"Then you spent over three decades with the savages?"

"Savages? No. I spent those thirty-some years with the Ottawa and Ojibwe people. It is true a few had a savage temperament. But are there not savage Whites? Those who place no value on others' lives?"

"Yes. I suppose. Please, go on with your story."

"There came a time at Sau-ge-nong when the British called for a great council to take place at Fort Mackinac on the island that overlooks the Straits of Michilimackinac. Many traveled long and far to attend. The Sioux, the Winnebagos, the Menomonees came as did the Ojibwes and the Ottawas and others. I soon learned that Manito-o-geezhik had met his kinswoman, Net-no-kwa, at this council. In spite of being a woman, Net-no-kwa was a great chief among the Ottawas. She had lost her son, a boy of about my age. When she learned of me, she wished to purchase me to take his place.

"My old Indian mother, Otter Woman, protested, saying, "My son has been dead once. My heart cannot bear to again lose him." But her pleas had no bearing on the decision of Manito-o-geezhik, who had grown tired of me since learning I could summon the man-spirit, Wenebojo. For my exchange, Net-no-kwa offered him a large measure of powder and shot, blankets, tobacco, and a ten-gallon keg of whisky. Although Manitou-o-geezhik sought more, his objections to the trade were softened after the keg had been sampled. When another ten-gallon keg was offered, I was given over to Net-no-kwa.

"This woman was more pleasant than Otter Woman. After she had completed the bargain with Manito-o-geezhik, she took me by the hand, and led me to her own lodge. Here, I was treated quite well. She gave me plenty of food, good clothes, and, rather than toil away, she told me to play with her own sons. After these days at Mackinac, we embarked on a journey that took me far away by hickory bark canoe. We traveled day and night, arriving at Shab-a-wy-wy-a-gun, far up river. There, we left our canoes and, traveling over land, encamped three times before we came to the place where we met Taw-ga-we-ninne, her man. He was a hunter, seventeen years younger than Net-no-kwa, and had turned away a former wife to be married to her. Taw-ga-we-ninne was kind to me, treating me like an equal and calling me his son. To me he was even more a father than I had before known.

"For many days we walked. Taw-ga-we-ninne then built a great birch canoe that took us many miles to Rainy Lake where we made our home. By this family, I was named Shaw-shawwa na-baysay. It means Swallow. It is a name I wore with pride during all my time among the Ottawa and Ojibwe. Net-no-kwa, and her husband cared for me far better than my former Indian family and even more so than my true father. Still, I was given tasks shared by the other boys of my age. I was made to cut wood, bring water, and perform other services. I was treated with so much kindness that I was far more happy and content. And, though Net-no-kwa sometimes whipped me if I misbehaved, as she did her own children, I was not so severely and frequently beaten as I had been before.

"Taw-ga-we-ninne let me join him in the hunt one day, offering to let me shoot his pistol. Though it set me back onto the ground and made my ears ring, I killed two pigeons with my first shot. When Net-no-kwa learned of this, she gave me a long gun, shot, flint, and powder. I soon learned to hunt and often brought back more game than did my elders. From that time forward, I had the respect of the village and was never again beaten or shunned. In my heart, I know it is not I who squint down the barrel at the target. It is Wenebojo. He is strong in me even now.

"As I grew older, word of my skills found its way to the ears of the commander of Fort Daer. He sought me out and hired me as a hunter to provide meat for his soldiers and others at the fort. I learned I could trade my hunting, trapping, and fishing skills for blankets, flour, and other supplies. They also gave me money, although I thought this money to be a worthless thing and threw it away. One day a soldier who was my friend showed me how to trade it for items of value. He opened his heart to me, teaching me some of the words I had lost years before. Slowly, Wenebojo allowed my White tongue to return."

Henry Schoolcraft splashed more brandy into his glass, then the glass of his guest. "Fascinating! Was that when you began your work as an interpreter?"

"Yes. Because of my ability to speak with the Ojibwe, Sioux, Ottawa, Cree, and other tribes, the Hudson's Bay Company hired me to speak with these people to try to get them to live together peacefully, to guide them and help them accept the many Scotsmen who came there to live. They hired me to listen and speak to both Indians and Whites."

"As I have hired you."

"Yes. And because of my work there as a translator and my experience in trading pelts, I soon traveled from Lake of the Woods through Rainy Lake and as far away as Saint Paul on the Mississippi River and La Pointe on Madeline Island. My knowledge of language all the while growing, I experienced many new adventures and saw many places, many rivers and lakes seen before only by Anishinabe travelers."

"Might you, one day, be able to help me map the ancient Indian trade routes and trails from Lake Superior to the Mississippi?"

"I can show you the way. I carry my map in my heart, not in a pocket."

A clock in the hallway chimed. Henry Schoolcraft stood, slapping his pipe against his palm to empty the ashes.

"Your tales intrigue me, John Tanner. I look forward to hearing more. Perhaps you would be willing to join me tomorrow at the dinner table? Your wife, your children as well, of course."

"My children? Sir, I fear they may not be as clean as your wife might like after our long journey."

Schoolcraft laughed. "You underestimate the enthusiasm of the women of the church who care for them at this very moment. By now, I'll wager your three offspring are scrubbed to the bone, spit-polished, and ready to be tucked in for the night—after a full volume of prayers, of course."

"Prayers? My children? It will take volumes to get them caught up. I've only been able to offer my own Chippewayan songs, though perhaps the result is the same."

"The same? I wonder. You will accept my offer to dine, then?"

"Yes. I accept with thankfulness, Henry Schoolcraft. You are truly a generous, kind fellow."

Chapter 5
Life in the Wilderness

Although the families of Henry Schoolcraft, Major Quimby, and John Tanner surrounded Henry's dinner table, Tanner's tales dominated the conversation. He told of a life filled with adventure. At times, those around the table shuddered when told of buffalo stampedes destroying encampments and killing all in their way. And, in the frozen plains, harrowing struggles to survive starvation when a village of his people ran short of food during the coldest months of winter. Next, he told of spring hunts when he and a handful of men filled a thousand donkey carts with salted buffalo meat and hides bound for England. When Major Louis Quimby asked about the lands near Lake Winnipeg, Tanner offered his experiences there.

"I spent many months at the Fork, Major."

"The Fork?"

"Where the Red and the Assinneboin Rivers meet. You would enjoy being there in summer. In winter, the Fork changes. Many have died there from cold and sickness and starvation."

Henry poured more wine. "John, what is the land north of the Fork like?"

"Between Lake Winnipeg and Hudson's Bay, most of the land is muskeg swamp. Too wet to grow potatoes and rutabaga and corn. Many cranberries though. It is the perfect home for the caribou. As a young man, I often ventured there each spring with a handful of other hunters. We stayed until the October snows drove us south with our bundles of hides and barrels of salted meat. These we sold to sutlers at Fort Douglas and Fort Frances. I always kept enough meat to abide my family until spring. Hudson's Bay Company gave us plenty of blankets, sugar, and flour in trade for the hides. Shot, flint, and powder, too. And many silver coins."

"Were other hunters as successful?" asked Major Quimby.

"I met some hunters in the muskeg swamps west of Hudson's Bay but none stayed more than a few weeks. They left too soon, fearing they would be lost in a snowstorm. But we stayed. I shot many caribou and moose. Many."

"My word!" said Henry. "How did you get the bounty to the merchants?"

"We used carts."

"How so?" asked the Major.

"We built two-wheeled carts and used mules to deliver the bounty to Fort Douglas. From there, we took it by canoe up the Rainy River to the Grand Portage and Fort William where we would float down to Gitchee Gumi—the lake you call Superior.

"Thousands of these mule-driven, two-wheeled carts can be seen from March through July in the lands west of Fort Frances. Especially when the buffalo herd comes there in summer. Most of the hunters left too early. My plan was different. We did not haul my bounty during the hot weather. Instead, we salted the meat and hides and waited.

"In early October, right after the swamps froze solid, I began. The cold weather was easier on the mules, the muskeg froze solid enough to cross, and I neither froze in the snow nor burned under the sun. In three weeks time, we made four trips back to Fort Douglas. By the last trip, we had fourteen carts delivered, each with a thousand pounds of meat and hides. My village prospered that winter but it did not matter. Most got the small pox and died. After that, the rest were afraid to go hunt the caribou. They thought the caribou had a god who was seeking vengeance. They were foolish so I left them and I went to another village.

"One year, our last journey took place in late October. I knew not of an early winter storm coming soon. We were a hundred miles into the wilderness north of Winnipeg when it fell on us. We knew we were in trouble. All eighteen men in our company and many women and children who came to skin and butcher had to settle in until the storm passed by. Seven days later, it left. During that time, I lost as many mules, some good dogs, and one old woman who wandered off into the storm to die. We made snowshoes and pulled seven of the carts ourselves. We were able to bring back two thousand pounds of elk and venison so our journey was not so bad after all. Though we never saw the old woman again, we knew this nokomis would want us to leave and survive and sell the game to the sutlers at Winnipeg and Fort Douglas. Some say they have seen her wandering in other snowstorms looking for her mule and moaning like the winter wind over Lake Winnipeg."

"Dear me," Jane Schoolcraft said. "Henry, the children. They'll have nightmares if he continues."

"Nonsense! They need to learn such things. Please, John, go on."

"Madam, I will temper my tales as not to disturb the young ones."

"Thank you, sir."

"Spring found us spearing fish at the rapids below Lake Winnipeg. We filled many barrels until the trading post there ran short of salt. When the sutler raised his price, we began smoking our walleyes and carp. We had so many Ojibwe and Assinneboin Sioux fishing there that the smoke from our fires drove many from their homes in Winnipeg. The Jesuits at the mission told me they would have plenty of salt the next year so we would not drive them out. I have heard that, on rainy days, the mission still smells of smoke and fish from that time."

"What's it like to live out in the wilds of Prince Rupert's Land?" asked Edora Quimby.

Major Quimby grinned. "Are you planning on making a new life there, Edora? Perhaps wedding some Métis trapper and helping him skin muskrats?"

"Papa, one never knows where life will take one."

Tanner turned to the young woman. "You will need to study up on your trapping skills, young lady. No woodsman there wants a woman who cannot run a trap line. Some lines are short—only ten or fifteen miles. Most are not. One fellow I met has a trap line that takes him over sixty miles in six days, though his woman does it in five. As soon as she returns, he trades her peltries and meat, then she begins anew. This is not a life for most, but that young doe can do it with ease."

"Is it dangerous?" asked Elsie, Edora's younger sister.

"Dangerous? No. There are but three animals the trappers seek to avoid. All will steal the game caught in your trap and often take the trap along for good measure. One is the ma'iingan—the wolf. Another, makwaa—the bear. For these looters, an animal caught in a trap is an easy meal. There are many wolves and bear in the woods there."

"Here in the Sault, as well," said Schoolcraft. "Can't keep the blasted bruins out of our garden."

"Find a good dog," said Tanner. "Makwaa hate dogs and stay far away."

"You say a bear will steal a trap, Mister Tanner?" asked Edora.

"A big makwaa can easily break the chain used to anchor a wolf trap or any trap that is smaller. The Makwaa does not get caught in small traps, though. He is too smart. He comes for the animal caught in the trap. He thinks the trapper put it there for him."

"What do you do when a bear stands betwixt you and your game, Mister Tanner?" asked Henry.

"Some have tried to shoo the bears away from the traps as though they were horse flies. Sometimes this works. Other times, the bear will fight if hungry. This is why all the trappers carry a musket while working their trap line. Many have hoped for otter, raccoon, or a beaver in their trap just to find a bear finishing his meal. Many have come home with no mink or fisher but, instead, a bear skin and three hundred pounds of meat."

"Mister Tanner," said Edora, "You mentioned three animals that trappers dislike."

"Oh, yes. The other animal that trapper loathes is the trap thief. Whether red or white, a clever renegade can steal a week's pay in one day. He takes game from the trap, and, like the makwaa, steals the trap, too. A clever thief will follow a trapper one day to see where the traps lie. Then, on the next, he will go out ahead of a trapper, stealing both game and traps. The remedy for this is the same as for the bear—a musket. The only difference is that, unlike the makwaa, there is no market for the hide and the meat flayed from the trap thief's bones is good only for the dogs."

Laughing, Henry said, "You don't expect us to believe that the trap thief is fed to the dogs, now, do you?"

"Nothing is wasted."

"Oh, my!" said the Major's wife. "And I thought life here in Michigan Territory was harsh!"

"None of my people think life is harsh. They think life is life."

"A good attitude, I say," said Schoolcraft. "Please, John, continue."

"Setting the trap is different for every type of animal. Muskrat and beaver traps are laid under water where the trapper thinks the animal will swim. Mink and weasel trappers favor the edge of a pond or a creek. Fox, fisher, and martin traps are set on a game trail, often under some leaves and with rotten meat for bait. All these traps must be free from human scent. Many trappers boil their traps like soup bones. Some carry along a pouch filled with moose or buffalo droppings and use this to wipe down their hands before handling the trap."

"I believe I will leave the trapping to the trappers," said Edora.

Tanner continued. "Every trap must be chained to a sound stake or stout tree lest the animal itself become the trap thief. Wolf traps need special attention, as wolves are very cautious. And, because bear traps are large enough to catch a man, the trapper skins the bark from a nearby tree to warn men away. Sometimes trappers forget this and catch a man. This is not good."

"They catch a person?" asked Elsie, eyes wide.

"Sometimes they even catch themselves. If you are alone when you step into a bear trap, you will not get out."

"You won't? What do you do."

"You go to your next life."

"Whatever do you mean, sir?" asked Edora.

"Unless someone comes to check the trap line in time, you die."

"Oh, my! Have you ever stepped into a bear trap, Mister Tanner?"

"Not yet. I once found a man who did."

"Were you able to free him?"

"Yes, but it mattered not. Wolves found him first."

Major Quimby stood. "On that pleasant note, Mister Tanner, I believe I will escort my wife and daughters home. I do hope you will call on us one day and share more of your charming wilderness tales."

"I have many to share, Major. Each one as true as the flight of my arrow. When next we meet, I will tell you of a day when a sutler for the North West Fur Company tried to cheat me out of two bundles of beaver pelts. It is a story I will long remember, as will he."

"Yes. When we next meet, Mister Tanner," said the major. "Until then, we bid you all goodnight. And may you have the most pleasant of dreams—and not those of being caught in a bear trap, facing a pack of hungry wolves!"

Chapter 6
Nor'West Greed

John Tanner dropped two tethered bundles on the table in the trading house. The sutler's eyes widened when he untied the leather thong and three dozen silvery beaver pelts splayed out before them.

"I see you have had success with the beaver, Tanner. But I have plenty. Take them and go."

"What? Take them and go? You may have beaver pelts a-plenty, Mister Wells, but you surely do not have many silver beaver, if even one. These are worth a pretty penny in England. The gentry covet them."

Wells stroked the soft fur of a silver beaver pelt. "Three pounds in trade."

"Three pounds, sir? A fraction of their worth! Winter's coming, Mister Wells. And with it the height of the trapping season. I need enough credit to carry me. I will bring you a hundred more like this. My word is my bond."

"Tanner, the North West Fur Company no longer wants your business. The Hudson's Bay Company seems to have your allegiance. Take your peltries to them. You will no longer trade in my house."

"You know well the closest Hudson's Bay house is a hundred miles north."

"Not my concern."

"Wells, this bickering between you Nor'Westers and the Hudson's Bay merchants is senseless. We hunters and trappers spend our days making you and your overseers wealthy. You both salute the British flag, do you not? Why, do not the whole lot of you stem from one or two families? Can you and your cousins not make amends?"

"Take these and depart, Tanner," Wells said, pushing the pelts onto the floor. "Nor'West wants not your business any longer."

Tanner gathered and tied the pelts and left, the bundles slung over his shoulder. By canoe, he crossed the Rainy River to the home of an old friend, Pierre La Fans.

"Entrez, mon ami!"

"Pierre, my old friend, have you a corner where this weary trapper might rest for the night?"

"Oui, Jean Tanner! I see few visitors these days. After all, who wants to share stories with an old fellow like me? Stay, s'il vous plaît! Stay as long as you like."

John set the two bundles of pelts down. He sat on one as Pierre poured tea.

"But *your* tales," said Pierre, "that is different. Your tales are full of a young man's adventures. I will listen to yours for hours and hours. Mine? My stories have not changed for many years. My wife has grown weary of hearing my stories again and again, although she never seems to tire of jabbering herself."

John peered beyond the window to see three men approach. "Monsieur, if we are to tell stories at all, we need to make them short, for here come visitors."

As Pierre opened the door, they pushed him in. He fell back onto the floor and lay there looking up. The largest of the three men spoke.

"We are here to confiscate the hides you stole from the North West Fur Company house."

"What's this?" said Tanner. "These pelts belong to me. What makes you think …?"

The large man pulled a pistol from his belt, pointed it at Tanner's chest, and cocked the hammer. The other men each hoisted a bundle.

Tanner made nothing of the threat. "I trapped, skun, and stretched those pelts one by one. Wells will not have them without due payment. Now put that pistol away and go tell your master that."

"I will tell Mister Wells. But the hides go with us."

"Then first you must pull that trigger, if you've the courage. Know before you do that all my Ojibwe and Sioux friends will know of it before the setting of the sun. You and your family will suffer, sir, as will your friends here who hold my pelts in their hands. You know, in some of the Indian villages, the hands are often hacked from the arms before a thief dies that he not steal in the next life."

Both bundles immediately dropped to the floor, each with a thud.

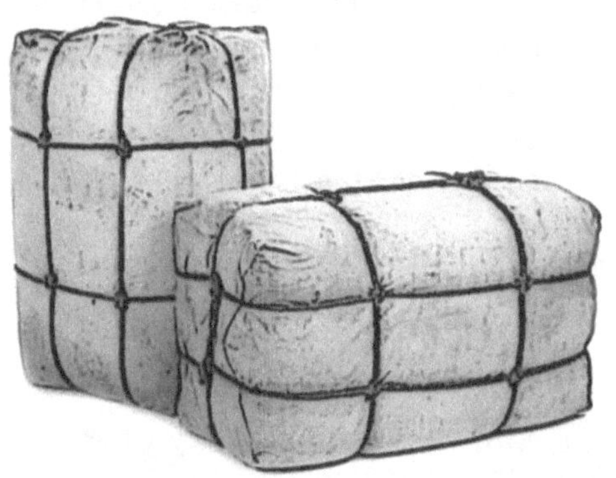

"Fools! Pick those up," shouted the man with the pistol.

Tanner grinned. "So, here you stand aside your two cowards with your pistol at my heart but not courage enough to pull the trigger." He grabbed the muzzle, twisting the pistol from the ruffian's grip. "You are as much a coward as your friends. You should have shot while the opportunity existed." He turned to the other men. "Now, be off! The last man to leave will feel the ball from this pistol in his backside!"

Three men scrambled through the doorway and down the path, Tanner and Pierre on the stoop, laughing. As the Nor'Westers reached the gate, Tanner fired the pistol high into the air. All three ducked, then ran even faster. "Tell Wells he is a fool to think he can steal from John Tanner! Tell him!"

Chapter 7
A Whisper of Rebellion

A week after driving off the two Nor'West thieves, John Tanner entered the Hudson's Bay Company trading house at Rainy Lake. "Mister McSween!" said Tanner, "How good to see you again."

"Well now, John Tanner!"

Tanner plopped his bundles onto the floor. "When we last met at Fort William, it seemed you so enjoyed it there. I doubted we'd again see you in these faraway lands."

"Trust when I tell you my presence is not of my choosing. I am assigned here to lay plans. Seems Lord Selkirk seeks to re-establish Hudson's Bay's authority from Lake Superior beyond Lake of the Woods to the fork of the Assinneboin and the Red Rivers. Prince Rupert's Land, as they call it."

"I have heard talk of this plan. By your word, it is true? Does Selkirk intend to bring a thousand Scotsmen to the lands surrounding Winnipeg Lake?"

"That he does. And knowing the stubbornness of his character, he will. A thousand Scots to hunt, fish, trap, and farm for him. Many have already arrived and now make their homes there. Others are coming. Moreover, if this first colony prospers, Selkirk's plans call for others. Imagine, Scottish colonies from the Rocky Mountains to Saint Paul—all loyal to the Hudson's Bay Company, mind you."

"How many of these innocents will suffer the fate of those ambushed last year? Twenty-two murdered by the Nor'Westers, they say."

"Precisely why the North West Company must be driven from the fort and expelled from the district by one means or the other—every Nor'Wester banished evermore."

"Fine by me. Nor'Westers be damned, I say."

"In fact, John, Lord Selkirk has charged me with a challenging task. He is now at Fort William with a large company of settlers and De Meurons soldiers—Swiss mercenaries he engaged after the Treaty of Ghent ended the war. He intends to embark westward down the Rainy as soon as the ice leaves. As he ventures out, he will build fortified trading houses along the route."

"In spite of the Nor'West posts standing in his way?"

"They are small, lightly guarded if at all. Selkirk will have his De Meurons regiment to rely upon. Each fort will fall to with little resistance."

"Until he reaches the river fork betwixt the Red and the Assinneboin, a hundred miles upriver."

"Yes. There he will face a test."

"And your task in all this?"

McSween lowered his voice. "Selkirk has it in his mind to storm the fortification there."

"The North West Company post?"

"Shh. Mustn't speak of it too loud, my friend."

"He will never do it. That fort hosts the heaviest stockades of the lot. Blockhouses bearing cannon, too. It sits out in the open like a ship on the sea. No general alive would risk his men in a run on that fort. This Lord Selkirk, is he a fool?"

"No, John. Ambitious. And, by the Lord's graces, he will surely make a name for himself if he can do this. He has solicited me to plot the siege by first calling together a meeting of compatriots—men who have experience in these events."

"Mister McSween, I see, now, why our voices are low."

"John, no white man knows this country, these swamps and rivers, as do you. And, safe to say, nobody knows the Indians here like you, either. Will you join us in this quest?"

"Me? I hardly think so. Should the North West Company get word of this, the conspirators would swing."

"Those Nor'West buzzards have too long run roughshod over this country. Not even John Astor and his American Fur Company can get a fair share. Moreover, Nor'West is known to burn homes and trading houses in their way. They steal and murder to get what they want. Selkirk must put a stop to it before the good people in his colonies become slaves to the Nor'Westers. What say you, John Tanner, will you help us?"

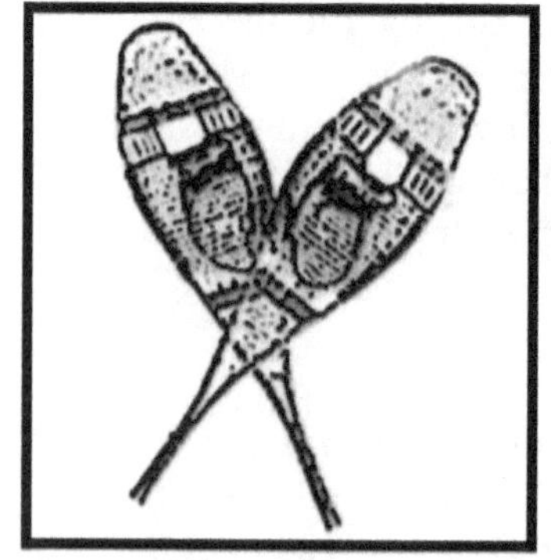

"Now, see here, sir. I have nay but disdain for the North West Fur Company. I would not be in your presence today were it not for Wells himself casting my business aside. Tried to steal my peltries out from underfoot, besides. However, I dassn't get caught up in this family squabble betwixt the Hudson's Bay Company and the Nor'Westers. I shan't stir this hornets' nest. I spend plenty of time looking over my shoulder as it is."

"I understand, John." McSween stepped to the fireplace, put a twig in the fire, then used it to light his pipe. "Might you consider eavesdropping?"

"Speak plainly, Mister McSween."

"Lord Selkirk has sent ahead a number of his men. Captain D'Orsonnens and two other officers will meet with Chief Peguis to consider all of this. Sit with us, my friend. Offer your thoughts. Would you do that for us, John? Do you dislike the North West Company enough to attend when we make our plans tomorrow evening?"

"Perhaps, Mister McSween. Perhaps. Will there be whisky?"

"Lord Selkirk's own, Mister Tanner, all the way from Scotland."

Chapter 8
The Wisdom of Peguis

Seven men met in a trapper's cabin beyond the edge of town. Peguis, an Ojibwe leader and foe of the North West Company, sat at the head of a rickety table. Mister McSween and Captain D'Orsonnens sat near the fire. Moore and MacDonnell, two of Selkirk's officers, sat between Tanner and Louis Nolin, an interpreter and trusted friend of Tanner's.

"Gentlemen," said the Captain, "my military training says we bring the entire brigade upriver come spring. Once near the post below Lake Winnipeg, we mount our attack front on, our ranks of riflemen supported by the two cannon I command. Meanwhile, Peguis and the other savages attack from the rear, using ladders. The siege won't last more than a few days."

Nolin translated for Peguis, substituting *warriors* for *savages*. Tanner laughed, patting Peguis on the shoulder.

"No need to roll the Captain's words in the sugar bowl, Louis. Peguis is proud that his warriors are feared for their savage appearance. 'Tis far easier to win a battle when your enemy's aim is shaken off the mark by fright."

Nolin translated this and Peguis howled with laughter, saying in his words, "Only a fool waits until winter to harvest blueberries." Nolin translated.

All but the Captain laughed. "What does Chief Peguis mean by this? Does he dare insult an officer in His Majesty's service? By what …"

Tanner interrupted. "Captain D'Orsonnens, you need to understand that the people who live here, who feel they have lived here forever, do not think as we Whites think. He means no insult. He is making a point and that's the lot of it."

"And the point he makes is …?"

"You should attack when they do not expect an attack. If you do, you will spare the lives of your men, Captain."

"The Crown is prepared to lose some soldiers, Tanner."

"Even when not necessary? When you have had enough whisky from the jug, do you pour the rest on the ground? No. Peguis is correct."

"When, then, do we attack?"

Nolin translated, Peguis replied, and Nolin said. "Now."

"Now? We have no army now. No cannon. A fool's game!"

"Peguis has won many battles," said Tanner. "Trust in his wisdom. Surprise will be our cannon."

McSween grinned. "A wilderness attack during the throes of winter, Captain. Imagine the notice you will receive—and the medals."

"We have enough men, Captain," said MacDonnell.

"And enough supplies," offered Moore.

"Tanner," said D'Orsonnens, "you know this country. Can my men make this journey and be able to fight when they arrive at the Assinneboin?"

"There is a way, Captain."

"Then we go."

Plans laid, the meeting ended, each man carrying away a bottle of Scotch whisky in each pocket. Tanner met Nolin outside after the others were gone.

"Peguis was right, Louis. The time to strike is midnight on the coldest night of the winter. The sentries will be huddled against the cold if not inside by the fire. Peguis's braves, a handful of Selkirk's soldiers, you and I could do this. We'd have it done and the Nor'West officers in shackles four months before Selkirk finds his way west."

"John, I thought you wanted no part."

"Ah, yes, Louis, but that was before I saw the great adventure this. And I do so wish to rub the wine-reddened, bulbous noses of the Nor'Westers in their own dung, especially that of Wells and his master, Harshield."

Chapter 9
No Man is to Die

John Tanner led Captain D'Orsonnens and his contingent of eighty armed Scotsmen north through the wooded wilderness. Louis Nolin and Chief Peguis's band of Ojibwe braves joined the party north of Rainy Lake. Eight sled teams, each with six dogs, pulled food, tents, and rifles. Their destination was the North West Company's Fort Douglas at the fork of the Red and Assinneboin Rivers.

Encountering chest-deep snow, the party stopped to make snowshoes at Rush Lake. From there, to avoid discovery by Nor'West trappers, Tanner avoided the conventional route. Instead, his band of liberators followed caribou trails through the frozen muskeg, skirting the winter encampments.

Fair weather and night skies lit by bright northern lights allowed the party to hike long into each night, shortening the fifty-day tramp to forty-four.

On the thirty-ninth day, they marched through a thick spruce swamp to the banks of the Assinneboin River, two miles above their intended prize. Tanner and Nolin went ahead to plan their approach. They soon returned.

"Peguis," said Tanner, "to scale the stockade, we will need four ladders. Each must be thrice my height. Have your men find spruce saplings with stout limbs and prepare these." He turned to D'Orsonnens. "Captain, please insure every rifle and pistol is dry, primed, and ready to fire. Eight men shall scale the wall, each with two pistols in his belt when we move tonight."

"Tonight, Mister Tanner? Then you believe your assessment to be true—that we few can overtake the fort?"

"Can and will, Captain. Nolin and I were close enough to see there are few men in the fort. Nolin and I noticed but one man at the gate and one more on the wall. They have no reason to expect more than the occasional hawker of hides or peltries, and then only during daylight hours."

"Then, Mister Tanner, tonight it is!"

"Yes. We attack well after dark, after the chill of night has them all inside, their bellies full of pudding, and their wits muddled with wine. The soldiers will be asleep in their barracks, the officers in their rooms. If we are able to approach undetected, Lord Selkirk will have his fort and the dawn light will see a Hudson's Bay Company flag waving o'er the river fork."

"You say eight men, Tanner? Only that?"

"Eight over the wall. They shall then thrust open the gates that your rifles may enter and overwhelm. Go, now. Tell your men to prepare, Captain. Tonight is our night. Selkirk's prize is at hand."

All fires were buried in snow before the sun set. The men waited, bundled in blankets against the exceptionally cold January 10, 1817, evening. No man lit a pipe, fearing the flicker of a match might reveal their presence. At last twilight, Tanner and Nolin left the camp to again spy on the fort. They returned at midnight. Peguis and Captain D'Orsonnens heard their report.

37

"'Tis time, my friends," said Tanner. "The lanterns in the cabins outside the gate are dark. Louis and I could see no sentry on the wall."

"Not even in this frigid air could we hear as much as the bark of a dog," added Nolin. "We believe the lot of 'em, every man, woman, child, and dog, to be soundly asleep."

"Captain, our first action must be to secure the few, occupied cabins outside the gate. I'd suggest Corporal Miles and one other be assigned this task. He need only knock on each cabin door, one by one. Upon answer to this beckon, the Corporal should explain that Indians have been lurking about. Caution the occupant to remain inside until the hostiles are turned away. He must also warn them not to fire on anyone lest they strike a noble soldier or unleash a battle with the red men. Then post several men in plain sight that they may send any brave soul who steps out from a cabin back inside."

"And the rest of my men?"

"They shall steal their way to the gate to await your signal."

"Peguis," said Nolin, "your ladders need be placed against the south wall, the wall away from the gate. This is beyond sight of the barracks. Two men are to steady each ladder. "D'Orsonnens, Moore, Tanner, and I will first scale the wall, then four of your braves. Captain, if shots are heard, four more men, your best marksmen, are to come next, for all will be lost if we inside are captured before we can throw open the gate."

Tanner grinned. "Fear not, Captain. That gate will swing wide before any Nor'Wester stirs. Nolin and I will then lead you to the barracks where you will quickly overpower the soldiers. Peguis, MacDonnell, Nolin, and I will then seek out the officers, disarming and placing each in our custody."

"Friends," said Nolin, "stand by this plan and we will have our morning tea and biscuits with our feet warming on the hearths of Fort Douglas."

"As Peguis told us, surprise is our best weapon," added Tanner. "We must catch them unaware, socked away snug for the night. No blade is to be bloodied, no shot fired unless we find ourselves in peril."

"This is not right," said Peguis. "My people starved because of North West Company greed. Many have died. My warriors lost family. Now you say they cannot take revenge. I say the Nor'West men shall die like my people died. Long Knives' holy man has words for this. Eye for eye."

"Peguis, my friend," said Tanner, "what the North West Company did was wrong. But killing these men and women will not bring your people back. If those inside die, many more soldiers will come. We will lose not only the fort but our lives and the lives of others. Have patience, Peguis. There will be another time, another way."

"No, John Tanner." demanded the chief. "Eye for eye."

"An eye for an eye leaves both blind, my friend. Let not murder shame the legacy of Chief Peguis. Show your people you are better, stronger, wiser than your Nor'West enemies."

"I will tell my men no man is to die."

In the light of a half-moon, John Tanner and Louis Nolin led the band of liberators to the fort. The dreary howl of a wolf drifted through the frigid air as the ladder bearers struck for the south wall of the stockade. Corporal Miles made for the cluster of small cabins and shacks outside the front gate. One by one, he knocked and warned those inside to remain inside. Four Scots posted within sight of the cabins while another waved the all-clear.

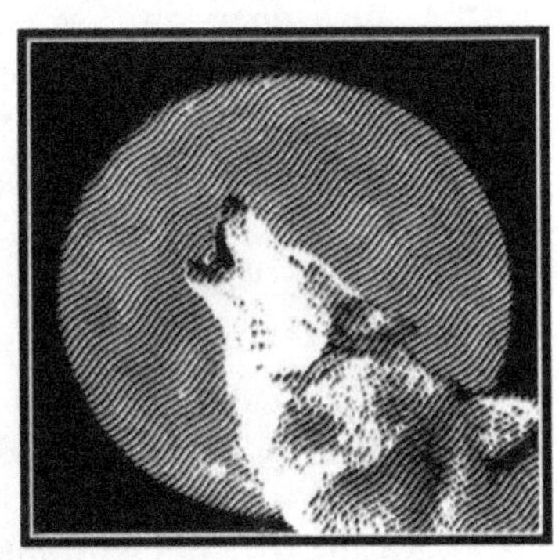

"To the wall, then," whispered Tanner, "for justice and the honor of Selkirk."

Silently, the men climbed the ladders and scrambled over the wall. Below, the roof of the blacksmith shop aided their descent to the snow-covered ground. Staying in the shadows, they circled the fortress to the front gate."

"Who goes there?" came a shout from above the gate.

"It is I, Commander Harshield," shouted Nolin. "I've come to ask why you sleep on duty."

"Sleep, sir? I do not …"

"How is it, then, I was able to cross this wide yard without detection if you were not sound asleep?"

"I assure you, sir, I …"

"Come down here that I can see the man who shirks his duty."

The sentry sheepishly scampered down the narrow steps into the arms of Nolin and an Ojibwe man. A swift blow to the head sent him to the ground while others unbarred the gate, throwing it wide. Like locusts over oat fields, a rush of Scottish soldiers and Ojibwe braves quietly fanned across the grounds. Door-by-door, they rousted drowsy clerks, cooks, and clergy. Louis Nolin led Captain D'Orsonnens to the North West Company barracks.

D'Orsonnens gave the order. "The time has come. Arms ready? Pile in!"

The soldiers' quarters quaked as the Hudson's Bay boots tramped in. Corporal McDonnall shouted, "We are fellow Englishmen. Raise not your arms against us and you will be safe."

"We mean no harm to you," said D'Orsonnens. "We have come to claim this fort for Lord Selkirk, your new employer who offers you higher pay and better food. Who leads you?"

All but one of the Nor'Westers remained in their bunks, eyes wide.

"I am Sergeant Cooper," said the man climbing out of the last bunk.

"Sergeant," said D'Orsonnens, "we have taken this fort tonight in order to spare you and your men from facing a full military siege and severe loss of life. It would do well for you to order your men to remain in their bunks."

The room fell silent. Then, "Men, we've been undone," said the Sergeant. "Remain in your beds. We shan't risk our lives for the sake of the Nor'West merchants' purses."

"A wise decision, Sergeant," said Tanner. "You have our assurance you will remain safe and be treated well—no doubt better than you have been."

"Captain D'Orsonnens," said Nolin, "I suggest your men confiscate all firearms and knives. And post three men at the door to each cabin to contain our new friends."

"Sergeant," said Tanner, "keep your men at bay. There are those among us who would savor an excuse to even the score with the North West Company by the taking of a scalp."

The sergeant looked at his men, then to Tanner. "Rest assured neither my men nor I will stand against the Hudson's Bay Company, though I cannot speak for the officers who may be blinded by ambition or glory."

"I will tend to them, Sergeant," said Captain D'Orsonnens. "We have yet to fire a shot tonight and will not unless first fired upon."

Tanner, Nolin, and a squad of men led by Captain D'Orsonnens worked their way room by room through the fort. They found one door locked, the bedroom of Commander Harshield. Ten Hudson's Bay marksmen raised their rifles as the door was bashed in by the blacksmith's anvil.

"We are Hudson's Bay Company men and have taken the fort, Commander. Surrender yourself and no harm will come."

"I'll do no such thing!" replied Harshield, stepping into the light, brandishing two pistols.

"Commander," shouted D'Orsonnens, "lower your firearms. Your fort has been taken. Your men are in our custody. We mean you no harm, though I fear I may not be able to restrain Chief Peguis's warriors if you do not surrender. Your choice is to yield to me or die at the hands of the Indians whose village you knowingly starved. What say you?"

Harshield, his trembling pistols raised against a dozen rifles, said nothing.

"Commander, we have taken this post without firing a shot. Will yours be the first?"

Harshield lowered his weapons. "No, Captain. As much as I loathe your Hudson's Bay Company, I surrender this fortress. You are welcome to it."

Dawn's first glow showed the flag of the Hudson's Bay Company flying above Fort Douglas. In the mess hall, the Tanner party sat at tables for the first time in over a month. Before them, roast pork and fresh biscuits, boiled potatoes, squash, tea, and a dram of North West Company brandy.

"Gentlemen," shouted Nolin. "Raise your glass to the Hudson's Bay Company and the success of our endeavor. Long live the King."

"And same to good Lord Selkirk," added Tanner. "May he see to it we each fare well under his just and honorable treatment."

"Hear, hear," replied Nolin. "To good Lord Selkirk!"

By mid-afternoon, the liberators had assumed the affairs of the post and the Nor'West soldiers now swore allegiance to Lord Selkirk. Their names and the names of the other post employees now appeared on the Hudson's Bay Company roster. Chief Peguis and his men, eager to return to their lodges, began their trek to Rainy Lake. The gates opened to settlers the same day and the trading post resumed business.

John Tanner remained at Fort Douglas through March, when his restless nature arose and the post's supply of meat dwindled. Accompanied by six other hunters equally impatient for spring, he led the group north beyond Lake Winnipeg in search of deer and elk. Finding neither in quantity, they turned west, hoping to encounter buffalo returning to their summering grounds.

One April evening, shortly after sunset, a guard on the wall above the Fort Douglas gate gave a shout. "Campfires! Campfires on the horizon! Close the gate and apprise Captain D'Orsonnens at once!"

D'Orsonnens climbed to the catwalk, followed by Louis Nolin. Beyond, fires flickered between the trees far beyond the banks of the Red River. The captain put a brass telescope to his eye and studied the horizon.

"I count nine, nay, ten fires, Louis," he said as he handed the telescope to Nolin. "You know this country and its people better than I. What do you make of it? Are these Assinneboin Sioux?"

"No. Not Assinneboin. These fires are too big. Only the Whites make such campfires this big. I see white tents, too. Captain, this is a military force."

"Military? Perhaps the Nor'Westers have raised a force to retake the fort."

"Captain, could this be Selkirk? This early in the spring?"

"I will send a man to find out. If Nor'Westers, we need to know—to prepare for a siege."

"Captain, let me go. An interpreter walking into their camp will be less menacing than a man in uniform."

With thirty rifles guarding the Fort Douglas stockade walls, Nolin left the post, armed with only a letter of introduction from Captain D'Orsonnens. Fording the river by canoe, he soon walked into the unknown camp and found himself escorted by two armed guards to the tent of the commander. With the eyes of many soldiers on him, Nolin watched as a tall, uniformed officer carefully place a feathered, silver coronet on his head, then stepped out.

"And who might we have here?" he asked.

"Louis Nolin, interpreter for the Hudson's Bay Company."

"Nolin, you say? And, do you come from Fort Douglas?"

"Aye, sir."

"And Captain D'Orsonnens—he and his men are there—in command of the fort?"

"They are."

"This is the best of news, Nolin. The best of news! We must share a toast. Come into my tent that I may hear your story."

"I would first like to know whose tent I enter, sir."

"Hmm? I thought you knew. My apologies, Nolin. I am Thomas Douglas, the Fifth Earl of Selkirk."

"Lord Selkirk, sir?"

"One in the same, Nolin. Now come share a dram of Scottish whisky to toast the fact that my army shan't need to lay siege to the post."

Selkirk and Nolin exchanged toasts and tales of the taking of both forts, William and Douglas.

"Mister Nolin," said the Earl, "it appears I owe you for the success of the mission. Let me reward you." He placed a fifty-pound coin in Nolin's hand.

"I thank you deeply, sir. But know that there is another, a brave hunter, even now afield, who shouldered more responsibility than I."

"And who is this man?"

"John Tanner. Some know him as the White Indian. Others as Shaw-shawwa na-baysay or Swallow. This is the man who led us through the muskeg, past the Nor'Westers, and o'er the stockade. 'Tis Tanner you need thank, milord.

"Then fifty pounds for him, as well."

"Tanner spared you many soldiers, cannonballs, and the need to lay siege to the fort. If not for him and Chief Peguis, our January assault would not have been considered, the company would not have made it to the forks, and the walls not been breached. If not for them, this fortress would not be yours. Tanner need be properly compensated and Chief Peguis honored in some fashion."

"What do you recommend, Nolin? That I make this Tanner, this buffalo hunter, a Scottish Duke?"

"No, sir. But reasonable recompense would be in order."

"The fur trade affords us a bottomless treasury, Nolin. What would you suggest?"

"A pension, sir. Give Tanner two pounds a month that he need not again wonder if he might slip into destitution and dismay."

"Two pounds? Nay, I'll make it four that he will enjoy a nog now and then without dismay. And, Louis, the same for you."

"Me, sir? I thank you, sir, and tip my hat to you."

"And what might be reasonable reward for this Chief Peguis?"

"Honor him with a ceremony at the fort, sir. And bestow upon him gifts for the families of his men. Blankets, copper pots, and such. Now, if I may, I need to return to tell Captain D'Orsonnens and the others the good news. They'll be pleased to know they do not need to powder the cannons and ready the muskets for a siege. We shall look for you on the morrow, then?"

"Tomorrow it is, Louis. Tomorrow it is."

Chapter 11
Selkirk's Plan

Lord Selkirk's army remained encamped on the Red River while Selkirk and several others moved into officers' quarters in the fort. Two weeks passed before John Tanner's hunting party returned, hauling their game through the gate in hand-drawn carts. Within minutes, news of Tanner's return sparked Selkirk to invite the hunter to his quarters.

"Milord," said D'Orsonnens, "I present to you the man who led your soldiers through the wilderness and over the wall, John Swallow Tanner."

Selkirk studied the hunter, clad in his buckskin and buffalo hide clothing "So, you are the white Indian I have come to learn about?"

"And you are the Scot who intends to have colonies across this land?"

"From Lake Superior to the Rocky Mountains, Mister Tanner. Thousands of Scots making a new life in the wilderness. Now tell me of your hunt. Were you successful?"

"The cooks have plenty of moose, elk, and buffalo to salt, sir. Venison and bear, too. No man, woman, child, or dog need go hungry."

"Wonderful! I again seem to be in your debt."

"Again?"

"Louis Nolin and Captain D'Orsonnens tell me I am beholden to you for sparing me the trouble of taking this fort by siege."

"We spared more than trouble, sir. We spared lives."

"Yes. Many lives. John, would you consider joining me in my quest to establish Scottish colonies here? I will pay you well."

"What makes you think the Sioux, the Cree, and the Blackfoot will allow your colonies in their hunting grounds?"

Selkirk laughed. "Prosperity, Mister Tanner. I will give them wealth in trade for the furs and the buffalo meat they provide. The Red River Valley is ideal farmland. I will show them how to irrigate and harvest grain for profit. They will soon speak and dress like Englishmen—a far better life for them."

"Your Englishman's boots make noise and blisters. Moccasins are soft and silent. This is but one small difference between the Indian and the White. I have lived as both. Many here will not trade the simple life of the Anishinabe for the constant toil for power and property of the Long Knives."

"Is it true, sir, that you were stolen from your family as a child?"

"I was. I remember it too well."

"And you've not seen your family since?"

"My family? I lived with my family many years. My life with them was one of joy. I was called Shaw-shawwa na-baysay."

"My apologies, sir. I meant to inquire of your earlier family."

"My white family. I see. I was eight years when last I saw them."

"And, you do not wish to again see them?"

"My mother died of the pox in 1783 when I was but a babe of two years. My father was a minister and farmer. I remember two sisters and two brothers. I was told by the Shawnee dogs who stole me away that my brothers and father were killed so they would not seek revenge."

"And, all this time you have not tried to find out if they live?"

"The man who stole me showed me scalps. He said I would not see my family again in this life. I wondered if the scalps were from my family but chose to not make my heart heavier by finding out they were killed."

"Then, there is a chance they live? My God, man! Are you not curious? Would you not like to reunite with your first family? Live a civilized life?"

"My life dwells not in years past. I have tried to live as a White. It is no longer my way, no longer my life. My white father, brothers, sisters are far behind now. What would I say to them? How would I even find them?"

"Mister Tanner, you have done me, my people, and our Hudson's Bay Company a great service. You have saved the lives of my soldiers that they may join their families one day. In turn, sir, I shall scour the land for news of your kin that you may, one day, call on them. This I must do. I insist."

Early the next morning, Selkirk called Captain D'Orsonnens to his office.

"Captain, what are your thoughts of this white Indian in our midst?"

"My thoughts, sir?"

"This tale he tells of abduction from his family as a lad, his decades living an Ojibwe's life, preferring it to ours. What do you make of it?"

"I've no reason to doubt him, sir. Tanner is an honorable man, in spite of the way of life he chooses to live. His skills on the trail are a great asset, as is his knowledge of the various dialects of the tribes. What brings you to ask?"

"I am quite fascinated with this, how do you say it, Shaw-shaw-wah nay-bay-say? This White Swallow. I intend to ask him to accompany my southbound expedition next month. I believe he will be of use as I map out lands for our next colonies. He has hunted there and knows the people."

"I see no fault with your thinking, sir. I would do the same."

"I also wish to locate his family, his white family, should any remain alive. He has been separated from them for decades. I believe it is time that John Tanner renewed his bond with his blood relatives. Considering all he has done for me, I see this as a small favor."

Lord Selkirk removed a letter from his desk. "Captain, can you read?"

"Sir?"

"Can you read, man?"

"I dare say, sir."

"Good. I intend to post this notice, penned only this morning. I would like you to read it back to me."

Taking the letter, D'Orsonnens held it in the light from the window and read:

Regarding one named John Tanner:

A quest is now afoot to find the family of John Tanner, my loyal supporter and aide. In the year of our Lord 1789, at eight years of age, this boy found himself seized from his home by Shawnee Indians. His father, the Reverend John Tanner, thence dwelt nearby the confluence of the Ohio and Miami Rivers.

The circumstances that Mr. Tanner mentioned of his family are that he had a brother called Ned, and two sisters previously married to his being carried off. Also that his father was a big lusty man. Mr. T. also said that old John Tanner had been settled in Kentucky several years before 1790, but that possibly he might have removed at that date, by river, from some other part of the State. The young Tanner told me that his father had changed his residence a very short time before he was carried off and had been settled on the banks of the Ohio only about ten days when the attack of the Indians took place. He mentioned particularly his having come down the river in a large boat or float with horses or cattle. He also mentioned that at the place where his father lived previous to his removal, there was a brook running in a cavern underground where they used to go with a candle to take water.*

With promise of due reward, I beseech they who know of any living member of the family of my aide, John Tanner, to post written notice to me at Fort Douglas on the Red River that a reunion may occur.

Lord Thomas Douglas, the Fifth Earl of Selkirk.

"Captain D'Orsonnens, I ask you to see to it that this notification is soon posted in every newspaper along the Ohio and Mississippi that one of his kin might stumble upon it."

"Every newspaper? That will take some doing."

"Too long has Mister Tanner suffered removal from family, Captain. No military leader could ask for a more loyal servant. 'Tis my intention to assist Tanner—to cultivate this reunion of kith and kin. Are you up to the task?"

"I will prepare copies to be sent by courier today, sir. Will there be anything else?"

"Yes. Inform Mister Tanner I wish to see him. I will ask if he will accompany me on the southbound expedition as my interpreter and guide. Captain, I'll invite him to travel in our canoe and dine in my tent that we may hear of his many wilderness adventures."

*Center paragraph reflects Selkirk's precise wording.

One evening, late in his expedition to the Mississippi River, Lord Selkirk shared supper with his friend, John Tanner. He also shared some information.

"John, a courier arrived today with news of your white family."

"Last night I dreamed this would occur, Thomas. This news he carried, is it news I wish to hear?"

"I believe so. 'Tis a message from your brother, Ned. He desires to meet you."

"He wishes to see me?"

"He does. In Kentucky, if you are willing to make the journey."

"Are there others? My father? My sisters?"

"Sisters, yes, and another brother, James. Your father passed not one year ago, so says your brother."

Tanner turned to the window. "I have seen this in many dreams lately. I know now that I must find them."

"John, I will arrange for you to meet Ned, if that is your wish."

"Yes. It is right that I do this. I will go there. I will find him."

"I am delighted in your decision, John. You will carry along a letter of introduction from me. Trust that, upon its presentation, doors shall open. You will travel as my personal emissary and establish trading in cities along the Ohio, if you are willing."

"In light of your endeavors to reunite me with my white family, you ask little of me. I fear I will not find a way to repay you."

"Repay? Nay, John, there is no debt between us, though I would ask a favor before you depart."

"Anything, my friend."

"The hostility between the Sioux and Ojibwe must end. Their skirmishes, though deadly only to each other, have caused many of my Scottish friends and other settlers to become unnerved. Trappers are afraid to venture far from the post. Farmers are reluctant to plow and sow."

"What would you have me do?"

"Gather them that we may foster goodwill. A rendezvous here at the fork of the Red and Assinneboin Rivers may help settle their differences. Speak with them. Will you do that, John?"

"I will, though I see little hope in it. The Sioux and the Ojibwe have been fighting over these hunting grounds for as long as the sun has risen and set. It is all they know. It is how they live."

"It is also how they die. I say we endeavor to end this war. Go to the tribes. Tell them to council here. Tell them the Lord of the Scottish Highlands has gifts. Help me do this, John. Help me end their war."

Seventeen chiefs from the tribes of the Red River Valley and western territories camped near Fort Douglas, eager to hear the words of the Scottish leader. John Tanner interpreted Lord Selkirk's plea.

My children, the sky which has long been dark and cloudy over your heads, is now once more clear and bright. Your great father beyond the waters, who has ever, as you know, nearest his heart the interests of his red children, has sent me to remove the briars out of your path that your feet may no more bleed. We have taken care to remove from you those evil-minded white men who sought, for the sake of their own profit, to make you forget your duty to your great father; they will no more return to trouble you. We have also called to us the Sioux, who, though their skins are red, like your own, have long been your enemies. They are henceforth to remain in their own country. This peace now places you in safety. Long before your fathers were born, this war began, and instead of quietly pursuing the game for the support of your women and children, you have been murdering one another. That time has passed away, and you can now hunt where you please. Your young men must observe this peace, and your great father will consider as his enemy any one who takes up the tomahawk.*

Chief Peguis was first to speak. "My brothers, not one among us can recall a time when we were not at war. Nor can our fathers or grandfathers remember this. Now this Long Knife, Selkirk, offers us a path we have not known. It is my hope that we all take this path and bring peace between us. Too many have died. Many more will die if we do not accept the words of Selkirk today. I lay down my rifle."

An Assinneboin Sioux chief stood. "We know Peguis to be a wise and great warrior, full of courage. He would not lay down his rifle out of fear or cowardice. I say we accept the peace offered by Selkirk."

"But what of the buffalo?" shouted another. "They stay to the west in the land of the Sioux. Are we Ojibwe not allowed to hunt them? We will starve."

"No." said Selkirk. "The Hudson's Bay Company will provide buffalo for the Ojibwe in trade for peltries. You will have plenty. You will also have the elk, moose, deer, and bear in your forests."

Tanner stood. "I have lived with Ojibwe, Ottawa, and Cree. I have hunted for Nor'West and Hudson's Bay. I have come to trust Lord Selkirk. His word is my word. It is time for peace. This I know. This you must do."

"My people have long wanted this," said another chief. "My knife will remain in my sheath."

"Is there any chief here who will not accept this peace?" shouted Tanner. No one spoke. "Then it is done. Go to your people. Tell them to embrace their children and know those babes will grow to become elders one day."

The council ended after sundown. Thirty-two tribal leaders left, most grinning and carrying gifts of American tobacco, copper pots, and English blankets.

*Lord Selkirk's precise words.

"Well, Mister Tanner," Selkirk said, raising a glass. "I would say this was a most rewarding assembly. Not only does it appear we mended the wounds between the Ojibwe and Sioux, but I believe we have won them all to the side of the Hudson's Bay Company, wouldn't you say?"

"This talk was good, yes, for a time."

"Then, you do not believe we resolved their mutual loathing?"

"This hatred has too long been part of their nature to be ended with a few words from an Scotsman."

"Surely, though, you heard what they said. Were they not forthright?"

"Their words were true, just as the wind is true. But the wind often changes. So, too, will their words."

As Selkirk poured the third round, Corporal Miles burst into the room.

"Lord Selkirk, it's the horses. I'm afraid they are all gone."

"Gone? What on earth do you mean, soldier?"

"Stolen, sir."

"What? Impossible."

"No, sir. Gone to the last."

"How so?"

"I fear the Indians took them."

"All of them?"

"Every last horse, two milk cows, and at least four goats, sir."

"After all I've done for them! Those thieving dogs!

"Gifts," blurted Tanner.

"What?"

"They saw your horses as gifts—gifts to them in trade for peace."

"I don't follow, Mister Tanner."

"These men are wise. They know peace will bring the Hudson's Bay Company even more profit than before. They chose to take their share of the bounty now, in trade for their pledge of peace."

D'Orsonnens stood. "I will form a party to retrieve our stock, sir."

"Like the wind," repeated Tanner.

Selkirk laughed. "Captain, let them go. Consider the horses a goodwill gesture—a gift to the Ojibwe and Sioux. I agree with Tanner that they see it as such. Perhaps the wind will now blow in our favor." Lord Selkirk tipped up his glass. "Those thieving dogs. Those clever, thieving dogs."

Tanner and eleven soldiers departed Fort Douglas in the early morning hours by canoe. The three-week journey took them to Fort William where Tanner found passage to La Pointe on Madeline Island before setting out by canoe to Sault Ste. Marie. There, he booked passage on a southbound schooner. A three-day sail took him down Lake Huron and into Detroit.

Shouldering a sea bag, Tanner strode into the city. He passed shops and offices, dodging the people, horses, and donkey carts that crowded the narrow streets. His eyes widened when he heard his name called.

"Shaw-shawwa na-baysay!"

Tanner turned. Seeing no familiar face among those in the street or on the boardwalk, he continued.

"Shaw-shawwa na-baysay!"

He turned again. An Indian, arms outstretched, ran toward him.

"Shaw-shawwa na-baysay!" yelled the Indian as he threw his arms around Tanner. "Do you not see who I am? It is me, your friend, Kish-kau-ko!"

Tanner pushed away. "You? You are Kish-kau-ko from thirty years past?" Tanner studied him. "Yes. I know you. Why dare you call me friend? Is your mind so weak that you forget our first encounter? Do you not remember how you and your father stole me away and treated me worse than your dogs?"

"I am not the same as I was then."

"Not the same? Am I to believe that?"

"The Jesuits have mended me."

"Jesuits? Kish-kau-ko, are you so daft that seeing me now does not bring to mind your past? Was it not you and your father, Manito-o-geezhik, who long ago plucked me from the field of my father, beat me, fed me little more than scraps if at all? Did you not beat me, too? Now you call me friend?"

"I wish it would be so."

"I should plunge my blade in your heart a thousand times and then a thousand times more!"

Kish-kau-ko lowered his head. "You are right. My evils were many. My wickedness runs too deep to be forgiven." He pulled his knife from its sheath. "Here, take this. Have your revenge."

Tanner pushed the knife aside. "Where is your father? He is the rabid dog who should suffer most."

"His suffering is done. He is dead five years."

Tanner looked at the humbled man before him. "Three decades I have been away from my white family. Now I am on my way to find the last of them, lost to me because of your father's wickedness."

"Then I must help you."

"You? A snake who slithers in the dark to snatch eggs from a bird's nest? Do you think I wish for you to be near me? I would rather sleep in a cave with a score of skunks."

Tears in his eyes, Kish-kau-ko looked up. "Tell me what I must do to make you my friend."

"Kish-kau-ko, Kish-kau-ko. First you steal me from my family and my life. Then you beat me and treat me in ways unspeakable. Now your tears and remorse rob me of my ability to hate you for it."

"I wish to help you. I wish to repay you by being your friend."

"Yes, I will let you help me find my family."

"I will carry you to them on my shoulders if you ask."

"No need for that. If I am able to find Governor Lewis Cass, I will have a better way to travel. Can you take me to him?"

"I can show you the way, but they will not let us near his house."

"In my rucksack I carry a key sure to unlock his gate. Take me there."

Kish-kau-ko led Tanner beyond the city market to a row of brick mansions, the largest protected by an iron gate. A soldier answered Tanner's

call.

"I am John Tanner. I wish to speak with the Governor of Michigan Territory."

The guard huffed. "I dare say the Governor wishes not to see two common Indians. Be off with you."

"I carry a letter from Lord Thomas Douglas, the Fifth Earl of Selkirk."
Tanner held the letter high.

"Poppycock! Away with you rascals before ..."

"Corporal, who are these men?" came a shout from the porch.

"Two roughs, sir. Come to beg for food, by the looks of 'em."

Tanner shouted, "I have a letter from your friend, Lord Selkirk, sir."

"Corporal, bring the letter."

Within minutes, they sat on the terrace and Tanner's story flooded the ears of the statesman.

"Mister Tanner," said Cass, "as my friend Selkirk suggests, you shall have provisions and passage to the Ohio. You will also carry along my own letter of introduction. I hope it helps you on your quest."

"Governor, I know not how to repay you."

"Repay me? Nonsense. But when next you see Lord Selkirk, tell him I am still waiting for the whisky he owes me. Will you do me that, sir? Those Scots do make a fine spirit."

"I will relay your words. Let's hope he has not traded it all for peltries and pemmican."

"Scottish whisky for pemmican? My heart sinks at the mere thought."

Kish-kau-ko and John Tanner left Detroit on foot, bound for the Ohio River. There, they parted, Tanner continuing toward Kentucky and his reunion with relatives. Weeks on the trail left him with no food. Famished, he stopped at a farmhouse and knocked on the oak door.

A man poked his head out of a second floor window. "What do you want, half-breed?"

"Let not my buckskin fool you, sir. I am John Tanner, on my way to find my Kentucky relatives."

"There's no Indians here. Off with you."

"My provisions are used up, sir. Might I ask for a scrap of bread?"

"Bread? I give no handouts to wayward fools. Be gone or I'll set loose my dogs on you, Indian."

Three miles and four farmhouses later, Tanner's lack of food made him dizzy. Hot, tired, and weak, he lay in the shadow of a maple and soon slept.

"Boozhoo."

Tanner looked up to see an Indian woman on horseback. "Boozhoo," he replied.

"I thought you were dead."

"I might well be if I cannot find something to fill my stomach. Have you any food?"

"I do."

"Might I ask for a bite?"

"It is at my lodge where I am going. You are welcome to come. I am Ah-koo-nah-goo-zik."

"I am Shaw-shawwa na-baysay."

"You are Anishinabe?"

"Not in my blood, but in my spirit—in my soul."

"You say you are Shaw-shawwa na-baysay?"

"Yes. John Tanner. On my way to Kentucky to find my family."

"You are weak. Come. Ride my horse. I will walk. Your belly will soon be full."

Tanner gathered his blanket and bundle. He mounted the horse. "Wenebojo will smile on you."

"You are a White but you know of Wenebojo?"

"He is watching over me now. He is why I am riding not walking and will soon eat."

"Maybe he is why you have no food in the first place," said his friend. "He is full of tricks."

Tanner ducked through the entrance and into the lodge of Ah-koo-nah-goo-zik. There, next to an extinguished fire, was stew in a copper pot. "I could lift the stew to my mouth and empty it."

"Wait. I will make a fire, heat the potage. Then we will eat."

"It is so hot today, the stew will be better cold."

"Not wise," she said. "It should be hot."

"Cold," insisted Tanner.

She scooped a bowl of the cold venison, potato, and corn stew and handed it to Tanner who lifted it. Using fingers to push it into his mouth, he gulped it down and held out the bowl for more.

Four bowls later, Tanner laid back. "Ah-koo-nah-goo-zik, you have given me strength to continue my tramp." He reached into his rucksack, pulling out a half-pound twist of tobacco. "Take this, my friend."

"I have pemmican and hens' eggs for your journey. But you should stay until morning."

"No, I am close now. Soon I will meet my family. I must go."

"Then good travels to you, Shaw-shawwa na-baysay."

In the cool of the evening, John Tanner walked along the Ohio River. He rested by the shore, drank his fill of water, then walked again as a full moon rose. Mile after mile he shortened the distance between himself and his family. Then, as the eastern sky offered its first morning blush, he felt pain inside. Within minutes, he lay by the road, doubled by the agony in his gut.

"Aagh! Wenebojo, why do you do this to me? Are you in my belly with a spear?" He rolled side-to-side, grimacing. "What must I do to pacify you, to appease you? What did I do to make this happen? Was it the stew? Do you punish me for not allowing my friend to boil it?"

Travelers, seeing Tanner alongside the trail, moved to the other side of the road. Most hurried by. One man stopped.

"Indian."

Tanner looked up.

"You'd be smart to sleep off your fire water beyond sight of the road 'fore someone robs you or worse."

"I'm unable to move. I have wildcats fighting deep in my belly."

"What cause?"

"Stew served cold, I fear. Or water from the river. Or the spirit, Wenebojo. I know not which."

"Let me help you off the road."

"Megwitch. I am John Tanner, traveling to Kentucky to find my kin."

"Tanner? I know well an Ed Tanner of Lexington."

"I have a brother called by Ned."

"Ned? I have heard him called this. But he is white."

"I am white."

"You? You mean you are mixed blood?"

"I am white by both father and mother and their fathers and mothers. I have only white brothers, James and Ned, and sisters, Lucy and Agatha."

"Then I would suppose the Ned I know is one in the same. His son tends my wife's garden."

"Can you take me to him?"

"Not as you are now, pilgrim. But, upon my arrival in Lexington, I will inform your brother. Perhaps he will come to your rescue."

Tanner watched the man ride off, wondering if anyone would care enough to come for him. He lay in the woods, ill with fever for the next three days before curiosity about his family drove him to resume his trek. He ambled slowly along, still avoided by passersby. One man did not avoid him.

"Git off the roadway, Injun! You're sickly and bound to spread the pox to the lot of us," he yelled, striking Tanner with his walking stick.

Tanner splashed into the muddy ditch.

"Dang Injuns have no right to walk a white man's trail."

Tanner stood, ankle-deep in muddy water. "First, sir, the Injuns, as you call them, have walked this trail for thousands of years prior to the curse of your birth. Second, sir, I am as white as you, even though I prefer the comfort of buckskin to starched wool breeches."

"Come up here and say that, Injun. I'll thrash you good."

"As weak as I am from my travels and torments, you are not man enough."

His walking stick held high, the man lurched forward. Tanner stepped aside, pushing the man down into the ditch. As the man struggled to stand, Tanner snatched the stick from his hand, beating him until the man buckled.

"Stay down, sir," shouted Tanner, "lest I beat you more with your own staff." He looked in his rucksack to find his pemmican covered in mud and his eggs broken, then climbed to the road and pulled from the man's pack a meat pie and two apples. "You, sir, have made a poor trade today. For your pie and apples, I give you muddy pemmican, eggshells, and an insult to your honor. I hope you apply better sense in your future trades."

The man struggled to his feet and turned, brandishing a pistol.

Tanner grinned. "You would shoot a man over a pie? I doubt you have the courage."

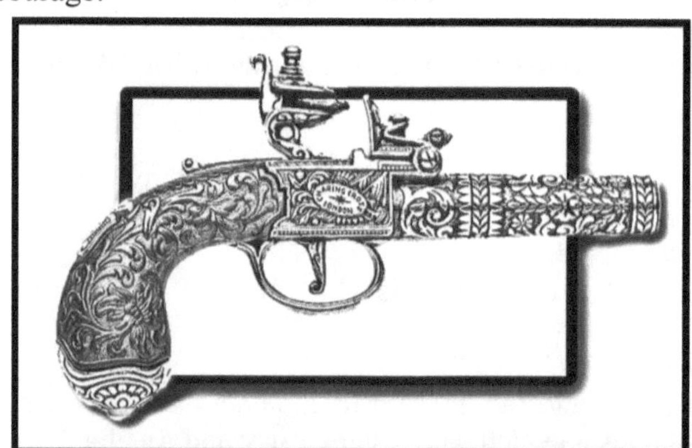

The man took aim at Tanner's chest.

"Know, Mister, that if your aim is off, I will pummel you with your staff until your family no longer recognizes the hideous face of their kinsman."

The hammer clicked as it came back.

"Twice before I have had muzzles tight to my chest. Twice before has the hammer failed to fall, the men having no courage. I can tell you are the same."

"Replace my food, Injun, or feel my ball pierce your heart."

"You will not kill a white man and face the noose, coward."

"You are no white man."

"He is!" came a shout from down the road. "He is my Uncle John. He is as white as you and me."

Tanner looked up to see a young man running toward him.

"I don't believe it, boy," said the man with the gun.

"Then, coward, if you have the pluck, shoot me."

With a *clack* the hammer fell, the flint striking mud in the pan.

Tanner jumped into the ditch, tore the pistol from the man's hand, and climbed the bank to the road. "All that spares you from being beaten bloody is the presence of this boy." He heaved the horse pistol into the river. "My nephew and I will leave, now. Follow and you will feel your staff on your head."

As the muddied, angry man struggled out of the ditch, Tanner and the boy hiked down the dusty road toward Lexington. Eager for news of his family, Tanner quizzed the boy as they walked.

"What is your name, Nephew?"

"John Tanner. Like you."

"Then it is good my red family gave me another name so we can tell each other apart."

"You have an Indian name?"

"Shaw-shawwa na-baysay. It is Ottawa. My name means Swallow. Some call me White Swallow. Others know me as White Indian. And you are the son of my brother, Ned Tanner?"

"Only Ma calls him Ned. Others call him Ed or Edward. He says that's what he wants on his stone."

"Stone?"

"When he dies. His tombstone. Edward Tanner."

"Is he dying?"

"Are we not all dying?"

Tanner stopped and turned. "How long does my brother have to live?"

"Pa? Oh, thirty, forty years, I s'pect."

"Then he is not ill? You talk like the hawk flies—in circles."

"No, Pa's not ill. I s'pose he talks about it because we buried Grandpa not long ago."

Tanner stopped again. "Father to your father? Reverend John Tanner?"

"Yep. Grandpa got struck down by the grippe, least that's what the doctor said."

"I came so close to seeing him, yet so far."

"Will you miss him?"

Tanner pondered the answer. Then, "Three decades ago, those who stole me away told me they had killed my father and brothers. They showed me scalps and said I would not meet them again in this life. All the years since I believed them to be dead. Now my memory of them is clouded and I remember little more of my father than the smell of his pipe and the sting of his razor strop."

"He missed you."

"How is it you know this?"

"Sometimes in his Sunday sermons, tears would come to his eyes when he mentioned his little boy who was taken by the savages, never to return."

"I wish now I had known he was alive. Perhaps I would have …"

"He would have come to find you if he knew where you lived. My pa would have come, too."

"Good they did not. They would surely have been killed. My brother, James. Do you know of him?"

"Uncle James? He is eager to meet you. Pa says he was but a babe when you were stolen."

"I remember him in his crib that day, bawling and bawling. Your Aunts, Lucy and Agatha could not quiet him. That is when I went against my father's wishes and played in the field near the house. That is when the Shawnee dogs stole me away."

"Did they hurt you?"

"Not at first. Not until I tried to escape from them. They caught me and beat me. One man tried to kill me but another stopped him before his tomahawk fell. This I remember well, lying at his feet, looking up at the tomahawk held high over my head. I dream of it often. My sisters, are they alive?"

"They are. Others, too."

"Others?"

"Grandpa outlived three wives. You are one of sixteen children."

"Sixteen?"

"His farm was very large."

"Sixteen!"

"The farm made him very wealthy. When he passed, Pa got paid a fine sum. Now we live in the city. Pa calls it the high life. I liked the farm better."

"I doubt I would like this high life."

"No need to ponder that. Pa told me Grandpa did not leave you a penny. They thought you dead."

"A just decision."

John Tanner and his nephew entered Lexington after dark. They walked into the city under flickering lamplights suspended over Broadway. Reaching the center of town, they entered a brick home. Three decades and three months after his capture by Manito-o-geezhik and Kish-kau-ko along the Ohio River, John Tanner was home. He would not stay long.

It was only a matter of days before the Tanner brothers' exchanged words.

"John," Ned began, "please do not misunderstand. We enjoy your company and you can remain here as our guest as long as you wish. But, for Lord's sake, our neighbors are talking.

"Talking is good."

"No, you do not understand. They are talking about you ... your ... appearance."

John raised an eyebrow.

"John, you must cut your hair. Your Indian braids look a fright."

"Cut my hair?"

"How long has it been since you bathed?"

"Bathed?"

"And, John, I am concerned about the brocade upholstery on our chairs. I am afraid I must insist on you discarding your buckskins and wearing civilized clothing at the dinner table. I've given you some of my old suit coats and trousers—civilized attire."

"Your *civilized* clothing makes my skin itch worse than the stab of the mosquito. Your collars choke me and your boots bring pain to my feet. Brother, my buckskin breeches and shirt do not have me scratching like a dog plagued by fleas. Civilized clothing? If by civilized you mean uncomfortable, then I grasp what you say. Nay, 'tis buckskin and buffalo hide for this Tanner."

"Then John, I must ask you to take your meals in the kitchen with our hired folk. It pains me to do this, John, but I feel ..."

"I will pitch my tent in the woods and take my meals there. Perhaps I will be of less embarrassment to you and your wife. I sleep better on the ground than on a sagging mattress."

"In the woods? I won't have a guest of mine living in the out-of-doors like a heathen."

"Nay, not a heathen, my brother, a man of the woods. I have spent months on end in the forest, never with regret. Yet, here in your brick house, nary a night passes when I do not lie awake, my ears straining to hear the sounds of nocturnal creatures in the moonlit forest, the hooting of owls, and leaves quivering in the breeze. Sleeping in your house makes me ill. I will take to the woods where I can live a free life."

"Take to the woods? People will think I cast you out. I would be ridiculed throughout the city. John, I fear I cannot tolerate such thoughts."

"Ned, if that is so, I believe it is best I depart."

"Depart? No! John, you misunderstand. We want you to remain with us here, in Kentucky, your new home. I must insist, though, that you ... well, let's say, *present* yourself better."

"Ned, the woodlands and waters of the far north call to me. There, among my red brothers and sisters I can live without the burden of what you call luxury. There I can live without being barricaded within walls of brick."

"I won't hear of it. Nor will Agatha or Lucy or James or any of your other kin."

"In that case I must open their ears that they understand. Before I embark, I will call on each one to say adieu and wish them happiness. I wish the same to you, Brother, and to your wife and son, John. He is a fine young man. I hoped to teach him the Indian way. Perhaps in a later life."

"We named him after you that we never forget the boy stolen from us so many years ago."

"That little boy is who you must picture when you hear my name. He is the one you long for. I am no more than a lost man."

"Come, now. You? Lost?"

"Brother, I am neither a White like my father and mother nor an Indian like those who reared me. I have no true family, no family of any color. I cannot seem to dwell in Kentucky or Michigan or even in Minnesota among the Rainy Lake people. And believe me when I say life among Lord Selkirk's soldiers is hardly for me. No, I must find another."

"Another?"

"A place where I fit. A place where I can discard my past and start anew. Until I find this new home, this new life, I will wander, my heart heavy with emptiness."

"Go if you must, John. I wish you all the best. And may God go with you."

"God? No, Brother. Know that Gitchee Manitou guides me and Wenebojo protects me. I am now in their hands."

John Tanner left Lexington by canoe, bound for a meeting with Governor Clark of Missouri. As he traveled, he met with merchants on behalf of Lord Selkirk. Tanner descended the Kentucky River to the Ohio, then the Ohio to the Mississippi. Here he turned north, slowly making his way upstream toward St. Louis. News of his arrival preceded him. Greeted with fanfare at the docks, he was escorted to the governor's mansion.

"Excellent! exclaimed the governor. "Excellent! Welcome, Mister Tanner! I received word from Detroit that you would be coming. Governor Cass holds you in high regard, sir. Very high regard, indeed."

"I am humbled by these words."

"So, too, my comrade, Lord Selkirk. Did you know, his meanders brought him here this summer?"

"I did not, sir."

"Thomas Douglas claims you to be an astute conspirator when it comes to military plotting."

"Conspirator? No. I am not …"

"Fret not, Mister Tanner. It is considered treason only when you conspire for the *other* side," he said, huffing with laughter. "Selkirk told me of your rescue of Fort Douglas. Goodness, such a tale he told. Yes, Thomas Douglas, the Fifth Earl of Selkirk, speaks very highly of you. Indeed, he warrants you to be the greatest adventurer he has come to know."

"Adventurer? Yes, I suppose others might see me that way. As for me, I do not …"

"Balderdash! Your travels only this past year are more than most men see in a lifetime. Tell me, did you find your white family?"

"I did, Governor. I found them happy and well. Now, with our acquaintance rekindled and friendships renewed, I have chosen to return to the north—a journey in search of my next quest."

"Oh, how I envy you, John Tanner. I once aspired to voyages, explorations, escapades like yours."

"You, sir? Why, you and Meriwether Lewis are widely known and highly regarded for your trek to the Pacific shores."

"Perhaps, but that was another time. Now I sit, day after day, listening to complaints about this and that, quarrelling with windy officials about nothing in particular, and signing paper after paper, most never to be again seen by any person of import. Unlike you, instead of fighting off hostiles, I fight off only rival politicians and I dare not do so by sword and pistol," he said, huffing with laughter again.

"Life sends us on curious journeys, Governor. It offers many paths. Rarely can we see beyond the bend where any one path might lead. Yet, journey we must."

"Yes, journey we must," replied Clark. "Mister Tanner, how might I help you on yours?"

"My canoe descends rivers with greater ease than it ascends. I fear I may not reach Lake Superior before winter. If passage north could be arranged ..."

"Done, sir. Excellent! Up the Mississippi you'll go! I have a fine Mackinaw boat soon to depart for Fort Snelling. It's manned with three oarsmen on a side and another on the tiller. You will be in St. Paul in a fortnight, sir. Sooner if the wind is with you and they can raise the canvas. In addition, you will have a hundred in silver, a letter of commendation from me, and provisions enough to carry you up the St. Croix to its headwaters. Gitchee Gumi is just beyond, as you well know."

"I know this route, Governor Clark. But I know not what to say."

"Say only that you will dine with my friends and me every evening until you embark upriver so we can hear tales of your adventures. Will you say that, John Tanner? Will you?"

"'Twill be my pleasure, Governor Clark—a meager amount to pay for such generosity."

"Tell me, Mister Tanner, how should I herald you on the dinner invitations I intend to post to my associates?"

"Post only this, 'Shaw-shawwa na-baysay, the White Swallow.' Let them wonder."

William Clark laughed. "Excellent!"

Chapter 14
Again into the Wilderness

Traveling alone, John Tanner left Fort Snelling in his canoe. He followed the Minnesota River to the Mississippi, then headed up the St. Croix. A week later, with leaves beginning to fall, he skirted Lake Superior's south shore, bound for the St. Mary's River. Days later, his canoe slid onto the beach above the rapids called Sault Ste. Marie, breaking the thin ice along shore. Tanner lashed his paddles and rifle to the thwarts, slung his pack onto his shoulders, then hoisted the canoe overhead. Before him lay the trail to Drummond Island. Beyond, Fort Mackinac, his destination.

"Mister Tanner? Mister John Tanner?" came a call from the trail.

He looked out from below his canoe. A young soldier ran his way.

"Are you John Tanner?"

Tanner eyed the boy.

"If you are, sir, I have a letter for you."

"A letter?"

"From John Astor of the American Fur Company. Are you Mister John Tanner?"

"I am, Private." He lowered his load to the ground. "Can you read?"

"I can, sir."

"Read it. Tell me what it says."

The young man broke the seal and unfolded the paper. "My Dearest Mister Tanner," he began, "I am writing you on the recommendation of your friend and mine, Louis Nolin. He tells me you are most familiar with the woodlands and waters near the upper reaches of the Mississippi River. I wish to travel there and hereby solicit your services as both my interpreter and guide. As such, I will pay you twice over. This is double the rate of most of my men. Please reply by courier by the end of October, as we will soon thereafter embark. With kindest of regards, John J. Astor, Esquire."

"How long has this letter waited for me, soldier?"

"A good three months, sir. Maybe longer."

"Has the American Fur Company boat departed?"

"No, Mister Tanner. She lays at the docks taking on provisions as we speak. Wish you to reply?"

"No, not at this time. I must first see Colonel Boyd who has promised me another post—one that will keep me out of Sioux country."

"Very well, sir. I can accompany you to the post, if you wish."

"I would like that, young man. In return, I will teach you a valuable skill."

"Sir?"

"Are you right-handed?"

"Yes, but …"

"Good. Pay heed. Grab hold of the gunnels. Now, with a twist, hoist her up overhead."

The soldier lifted the canoe.

"Nicely done, Private. Now rest the thwart on your left shoulder, then raise the bow so you can see the trail ahead and off you go."

"Like this, sir?"

"Precisely."

Tanner followed the soldier down the portage trail to Lake Michigan where they rested before putting in. An hour later they rounded Drummond Island to see before them Fort Mackinac. Tanner's military guide soon had them at the door to the fort headquarters.

"Is Colonel Boyd in?" the soldier asked the company clerk. "A Mister John Tanner comes to call."

"Tanner?" came a voice from the next room. A tall officer stepped out. "Why, so it is! Tanner, for Lord's sake, where have you been keeping yourself? Must be three years since we last met."

"I dare say, Colonel. But I've arrived at last to accept your offer."

"Offer?"

"You once told me to call at any time and you would employ me as your interpreter, did you not?"

"John, years have passed since then. I have two interpreters on my staff at present and I fear no room for a third."

"But ..."

"I will list you as next in line, my friend, but that is the best I can offer. You might wish to consult the church. Reverend Bingham often needs help speaking with the Indians. In fact, I believe he may wish to translate the scriptures into Ojibwe. It would keep a man busy for years."

"I fear I may not be a good fit for such work, Colonel. I know little of your Bible. He turned to the young soldier. "Private, I believe I ought book passage on the American Fur Company boat if they will have me. Colonel Boyd, I will thank you to keep my name on that list for I now plan to make my home at Mackinac. It is my intention to fetch my children and, if willing, my wives. Look for us when the south winds bring spring and the geese return."

"I will, sir. Until then may the winter treat you well. Good travels to you, John Tanner."

Tanner guided the John Jacob Astor party to the upper reaches of the Mississippi River by way of the Namekagon and St. Croix Rivers. Astor established several trading posts along the way and they reached the American Fur Company post at Rainy Lake in time for the early winter hunt. Tanner stayed on, guiding others on hunting and trapping expeditions until deep snows in late December and frigid temperatures in early January sent the hunting parties back to the posts. They spent the remainder of the winter working trap lines, then skinning, stretching, and curing pelts for the tanneries and furriers in New York City.

Seven months after arriving at Rainy Lake, two small canoes came down the Mississippi toward St. Paul beneath flocks of northbound Canada geese. In the lead canoe, John Tanner and his daughters, Martha and Marie guided the craft downstream with the current. Tanner's wife, Therezia, and their son, James, followed close behind. At the confluence of the Mississippi and the St. Croix Rivers, they turned north, following the St. Croix to the Namekagon River.

Now shaded by mile after mile of majestic white pines, the Tanner family ascended the Namekagon, making camp each night. Five days later, they reached the big rock portage, ninety miles upstream from the St. Croix. There, they followed the Indian trail northward, portaging to long, narrow Lake Kagy-nogum-aug. From there they portaged again to the Waabishki River, eventually finding their way to Lake Superior. They paddled east for a fortnight, finally arriving at Sault Ste. Marie. Tanner immediately sought an audience with his friend, Colonel Boyd, commander of Fort Brady.

"Though I may not be able to hire your services, Mister Tanner, I've good news," said Boyd. "I hear the Indian Agent, Henry Schoolcraft, has need for an interpreter with skills such as yours. Seek him out, John. When you do, tell him you come with my recommendation."

John Tanner and his family now made their home in a one-room log cabin at the edge of Sault Ste. Marie. Behind, a lean-to made of culled boards from a local sawmill shielded the family cow and a dozen chickens from the Michigan weather. Therezia cooked their meals and heated water for bathing and washing in the small stone fireplace. At night, James, Martha and Marie shared a straw mattress on the only bed while buffalo hides separated their parents from the dirt floor. A single whale oil lamp provided evening light for reading. During the day, oiled parchment sufficed for glass on the only window. John closed the shutters each night and barred both window and door from within for safety's sake.

Tanner's profound knowledge of the Anishinabe language and various dialects of Indian tribes in the western Great Lakes States soon placed him in demand. His abilities as interpreter had him working both for Henry Schoolcraft, the Indian agent at the military post and for Reverend Abel Bingham at the Baptist mission. The Tanner children enrolled at the mission school where their father often translated both lessons and scripture.

As weeks became months, Tanner spent more of his time at the Mission. There, his work with the children caused him to miss three of his own—the three he left with his first wife at Rainy Lake. One day, with a warm, March wind melting the snow, Tanner took his concerns to his employer.

"Mister Tanner," said Schoolcraft, "though I feel sympathy for you and understand your want to have your children join you here, I fear I cannot give you the leave of absence you request. I hired you to work here for me, not scamper off on another one of your adventures."

"I must do this, Mister Schoolcraft. My heart weighs too heavy having left them. I'll not suffer to be apart from my children another year."

"I pay you a dollar a day to work for me, Tanner. If you leave, know that your job will go to another and it will not be here upon your return. And the nine dollar monthly housing allowance that I pay keeps you and your urchins in your hut. Where will they go when your money runs out?"

"My journey will be swift. My paddle will have me back by mid-summer. I have salted away my wages. My wife, Therezia, and our children shall endure my absence with ease."

"And after your return? How will your family endure then? You will have no employment. The post will not carry you. No one will."

"You forget that I lived in the wilderness some forty years. Wenebojo and Gitchee Manitou provided for me then and will again if need be. There are pelts a-plenty to harvest and trade, fish to spear, and game to snare. I refuse to be caught up in the trap you and others like you lay. No man should be slave to another in order to earn his livelihood."

"You and your family will be cast out by winter. See how they enjoy crowding into a chilly birch bark lodge, huddling together in a bearskin under a blanket of snow whilst the wind whistles within and without. Abandon this idea now, sir."

"I will not. If you choose to deny me this request, then I must resign."

"I will not have it, Tanner. Forget not who I am. I employed you to work for me, not to gallivant into the western wilderness and certainly not to work for that Baptist minister, Abel Bingham. You will remain here and you will do my bidding. I insist."

"Insist all you like, Henry Schoolcraft, but not to me. I am no longer in your employ. Good day."

Cold and weary from his journey to Prince Rupert's Land, John Tanner entered the Fort Garry headquarters, leaned his musket against the fireplace, and dropped his bundle on the large hearth. The tied pack of martin and mink pelts made a fine seat.

"Captain Bulger," he said, "I've nearly exhausted my ways with these people in trying to get them to return my three children. Last spring, when I left them in the care of their mother and the village, Chief Giah-ge-wa-go-mo assured me I could collect them in a year's time. Now, upon my return, they discard every plea I make to have my children restored. This, even though I have consented for my son, the eldest of the three, to remain here if he pleases. Captain, I have even offered to give them these peltries, hides they could easily trade for food or blankets or whisky. Before I choose violence to loosen my other two children from their grasp, I felt I should offer my circumstances to you that you might intercede."

"Good you did, too, John Tanner," replied the Captain. "The United States Army has, for the most part, succeeded in keeping peace with the Ojibwe people. You would answer dearly if you caused that peace to be upset."

"Then, tell me, Captain, is there another course? I know of none."

"I will speak with them on your behalf, Mister Tanner. I believe I know a way to pose the request in such a way that they will surrender the children. Will you allow me that opportunity, sir?"

"Allow you, Captain? Oh, my. Yes, indeed!"

Chief Giah-ge-wa-go-mo and eleven men from his village sat at the end of the Fort Douglas entrance hall. Captain George T. Bulger and John Tanner sat flanked by Lieutenant Forsythe and three other soldiers.

"Chief Giah-ge-wa-go-mo," said the captain, "you have heard the request made by John Tanner, to have his children returned to him, have you not?"

The chief responded only with a nod.

"Tell me, then, what is the reason you do not allow him to take his children from your village?"

The chief considered the question, then spoke. "This man abandoned his family. He no longer has a right to them. That is my decision."

Tanner bristled. "That is not the bargain we had last spring. Did you leave your honor with your women? These children are not …"

Captain Bulger interrupted. "Giah-ge-wa-go-mo, my friend, our law and your law are the same on this. John Tanner has the right to take his wife and children at any time, does he not?"

"I have consulted the midewinini-shaman who told me the spirits wish for these children to not leave our village. That is my decision."

The Captain paused, then, with a wave of his hand, Lieutenant Forsythe and his men laid before the chief supplies in trade for the Tanner children. Bulger then offered the following words:*

> Chief Giah-ge-wa-go-mo, I have now placed before you here, a pipe full of tobacco, not because I am willing to have you suppose I would purchase from you a right for this man to come and take what is his own, but to signify to you, that I still hold you by the hand, as long as you are ready to listen attentively to my words. As for this man, he comes to you not in his own name only, and speaking his own words, but he speaks the words of your great father who is beyond the waters, and of the Great Spirit, in whose hand we all are, and who gave these children to be his. You must, therefore, without venturing to give him any further trouble, deliver to him his children, and take these presents as a symbol of the goodwill that subsists between us. Here, then, I offer you twenty blankets for your people, ten pounds of salt, these copper pots that you may cook the meat from the next two horses we send to our butcher, and this keg of whisky. What say you now?

Chief Giah-ge-wa-go-mo motioned to his companions who leaned toward him, listening. They whispered at first, then their voices became louder as the anger of some also increased. In time, the chief responded.

"Captain Bulger, my people thank you for these gifts but some of us wonder if they will not soil our honor as the horses you offer soil their own stalls. No more should you insult my people. The children will remain. That is my decision."

Captain Bulger jotted something on a slip of paper and handed it to Lieutenant Forsythe. The lieutenant left the room, all eyes on him.

The captain spoke again. "Chief Giah-ge-wa-go-mo, I know you to be a friend and a wise and strong leader of your people. Surely you know nothing good can come from this decision of yours. I do not wish to make it appear to your people that you are weak. To show how strong you are, I will double what I have offered. Your people will be pleased at your skill in dealing with the white men."

*Precise words spoken by Captain Bulger to Chief Giah-ge-wa-go-mo.

"I have made my decision."

The sound of soldiers marching along the building widened the eyes of the chief and his fellows. A squad of twenty passed by the windows, marching up the steps. The double doors to the hall opened. Forsythe's men quickly encircled the chief and his men.

"Parade rest," ordered the Captain. The men stood erect, their muskets by their sides. "No need for concern, my friends." He smiled reassuringly. "Chief Giah-ge-wa-go-mo, I ask you again, will you honor me and reward your people by accepting this offer you have so skillfully caused me to make?"

The chief stood, his men rising with him. Captain Bulger shot a glance to Lieutenant Forsythe who whisked his sword from its scabbard. His twenty men snapped muskets to shoulders and immediately bore down on Chief Giah-ge-wa-go-mo and his men. Twenty musket hammers came back with as many metallic clicks. The warrior nearest the chief pulled his tomahawk from his belt. Before it could be raised, a rifle butt slammed against his jaw, sending him to the floor. Tension high, the room fell silent, all waiting for the next man to move.

"Chief Giah-ge-wa-go-mo," the captain said, "your people will be proud of you for your courage and for insisting that all of these gifts and provisions come to your village in trade for the children of John Tanner. You will be respected from Gitchee Gumi to Lake Michigan for your cunning and clever way. Your people would much rather have these gifts than more mouths to feed. Will you honor me by accepting these prizes and ridding your people of John Tanner and his family?"

"I see no reason to keep the children from their father. He may take them but also must take their mother, Red Morning Sky, so her weeping and complaining falls not on my ears. That is my decision."

"You, Chief Giah-ge-wa-go-mo, are a great and wise leader. My men will escort you to your village and return with the family of John Tanner who will depart at first light. When I hear they have embarked for Gitchee Gumi in their canoes, my men will deliver your rewards. Now, go tell your people of your victorious negotiation."

As soon as the chief and his men left, Captain Bulger turned to Tanner. "John, you will be wise to immediately prepare for your journey. When my men return, gather your family and go in haste—not tomorrow, but today. No doubt I have angered Giah-ge-wa-go-mo. Be wary. He might take revenge on you. Watch your back trail."

"Be sure of it, Captain," replied Tanner as he slid his bundle of pelts over to the captain. "And thank you for interceding. My methods would have been far less civilized."

"Of that, John Tanner, I have little doubt."

Chapter 16
Ome-zhuh-gwut-oons

Three days after leaving the fort, John Tanner and his younger daughter, Lucy, ascended the Maligne River in the evening twilight. Red Morning Sky and Sunshine, Tanner's older daughter, lagged far behind in a second canoe. He put in to shore and built a small fire where others had built campfires for a thousand years before him.

Along the shore, Tanner found a waterlogged oak limb. Using his axe, he cut the limb into three pieces, then placed it in the fire, setting two dry logs on top. This drew a quizzical stare from Lucy. Before she could ask, he said, "This will keep the mosquitoes away for a time. If you find yourself stabbed by their beaks in the middle of the night, put more wet oak in the fire."

Soon, the second canoe nosed onto shore. Red Morning Sky and Sunshine joined them by the fire.

As Tanner passed around some pemmican, a third canoe bearing a lone Indian rounded the bend. Musket in hand, Tanner met the young man.

"Boozhoo," called John Tanner's wife from the camp.

Tanner turned. "You know this boy?"

"He is Ome-zhuh-gwut-oons, from my village. He has helped me much while you were away. He is like a son to me."

Speaking in Pottawatomie, John said, "Come into our camp, Ome-zhuh-gwut-oons. I am about to boil water for tea. Join us. Share our food."

The young man pulled his canoe onto the shore, grabbed his rucksack and musket, and ran up to the camp. As he approached the campfire, Lucy and Sunshine moved away. He laid a slab of dried meat on a flat rock. In Pottawatomie, he said, "John Tanner, boil this in your kettle when your tea is over. It will become a good breakfast and help us paddle throughout the day."

"Megwitch," Tanner replied. "I will simmer it through the night. Now, tell me, why are you so far from your home and your people?"

"My home? I have lost my home. I was as foolish as the loon. I complained to Giah-ge-wa-go-mo, our chief that he too soon gave in to the Army captain called Bulger. I told Giah-ge-wa-go-mo he was weak and had not the heart and courage of a woman child. This angered him so, that he cast me out of our village. I had nowhere better to go than to follow my friends, Red Morning Sky, and your daughters and you, my new family."

"You thought my daughters should remain in your village?"

Ome-zhuh-gwut-oons stared at Tanner, making no reply.

"Are you fond of one of my daughters?"

Ome-zhuh-gwut-oons said nothing, drinking his tea.

"You came here to take them back with you, didn't you?"

The young man remained silent.

"Ome-zhuh-gwut-oons is my friend, my helper," Red Morning Sky said in English. "Do not badger him. He means no harm."

"No harm? He is here to steal my children. How do I know he does not intend to kill me first?"

Red Morning Sky did not answer.

"So, dear wife, is that your plan? To have this boy kill your husband, kill the father of your children so you can go with him? Go back to your village?"

His wife remained silent.

Tanner turned to the young man. Speaking in Pottawatomie again, "Ome-zhuh-gwut-oons, I know you came to kill me and steal my daughters."

"I have no such plan. Your mind is muddled with fear and suspicion."

"Suspicion? Yes. Fear? Not of you. I do not fear a boy who hides behind a woman—shames himself with lies and deceit."

Ome-zhuh-gwut-oons stood. "I do not lie for your old, withered woman. You insult me. I will leave now. Look for me no more. The meat you now simmer is yours to keep. Think of this injustice you have done to me while you chew it in the morning, John Tanner."

The boy grabbed his pack and musket.

Tanner sprang to his feet, stepping close to the young man, assuring he could not raise the weapon.

"Husband," shouted his wife in English, "this young man means no harm. You are a fool to drive him off. A suspicious fool!"

"Woman, it is better to be suspicious and alive than trusting and dead."

"Ome-zhuh-gwut-oons," she said in Pottawatomie, "there are many Sioux in these lands. Do not allow your scalp to be their trophy—one more to hang on the belt of a bloodthirsty warrior. Give no heed to my suspicious husband. Stay with us here, I beg you."

"Daughters," Tanner said in English, "Do you wish for Ome-zhuh-gwut-oons to remain?"

Fear in their eyes, the young women looked at their mother saying nothing. The youngest began crying.

"Daughters, what is this? Why do you cry?"

Neither would speak. Lucy, the youngest, rushed to her father, throwing her arms around his waist. He pushed her away.

"Your eyes show fear and shame. What is it? If you do not tell me, I will think the worst."

"Our daughters are daft when in the presence of young warriors."

"Daft?" snapped Tanner. "You are not telling me all of it." He turned. "Lucy? Sunshine? What is the reason for all these tears and your cowering? Tell me now."

"I will tell you," said Ome-zhuh-gwut-oons. "They fear me."

"Have you beat them?"

"No. This I would never do."

"Then ..."

"I want them for my wives. I have said this to them. They are not ready to accept me as a husband."

"And you, Woman? Did you know of this?"

"Ome-zhuh-gwut-oons is a good young man. He would be a good husband to them. They would soon have babes to warm our hearts."

Rage replaced John Tanner's astonishment. "Ome-zhuh-gwut-oons, leave my camp this minute," he demanded, arms folded before him. "Never let my eyes fall upon you again. Go."

The young man turned toward the river, his pack in one hand, his musket in the other.

"Husband, you are a fool to drive him off. What of the Sioux? Would it not be better for us to have one more rifle to defend us?"

"Defend us?" Tanner asked, watching Ome-zhuh-gwut-oons push off, heading upstream. "Or to use against me when my guard is down? Do not think that I cannot see your plan. You could not stay in your village with our daughters so you had this boy come to kill me. Is that not true?"

Red Morning Sky stood mute.

"I thought as much," Tanner said. "You would sooner steal the life from the father of your daughters and remain in your village than to be with your true family. You had Ome-zhuh-gwut-oons follow us so he could kill me. I know this, now. Admit it."

His daughters whimpering, Red Morning Sky remained silent.

Tanner stepped close to her, pulled her knife from her belt and shouted, "Was Giah-ge-wa-go-mo behind this? Did he come to you? Did he tell you he would send this boy to kill me?"

Red Morning Sky said nothing.

"Yes. Now it all becomes clear. Giah-ge-wa-go-mo, this cowardly leader of your village, could not prevail over Captain Bulger. He could not get his way by honorable means. He chose to take the gifts offered by Captain Bulger, then take the life of John Tanner so you could return to your village. Yes. He sent Ome-zhuh-gwut-oons to kill me and take you and my daughters back."

Red Morning Sky turned away. "Your suspicious nature has you blind and senseless, John Tanner. You imagine too much. I had no such meeting with Giah-ge-wa-go-mo. He does not care if I remain in his village. Now I see why your daughters seem daft now and again. You gave them this gift." She sat before the fire. "Now I suppose you will use my own knife to kill me?"

Tanner threw the knife on the ground at her feet. "Sunshine, you will sleep under the canoe with your mother. Lucy, you will sleep next to me under my canoe. Red Morning Sky, know that I will sleep lightly and not hesitate to sink my knife into any vile creature who comes to murder me."

"Husband, do not let wild ideas muddle your brain. I have done nothing. Ome-zhuh-gwut-oons has done nothing. It is only you who has imagined this. Do not allow this trickle of water to grow into a river that floods your senses."

"Tonight, in my dreams, I will see the truth and find our way. Tomorrow I shall continue upstream. How many will travel with me, I know not."

Chapter 17
Ambushed

Midnight brought heavy rain and lightning to the woods surrounding the John Tanner party. The storm quickly passed, but the rain had extinguished their fire. With no smoke from the smoldering wood, mosquitoes invaded. Thousands swarmed over the canoes. Below, the Tanners defended themselves from the winged blood-thieves only with blankets. When the high-pitched whine of the mosquitoes grew louder than the sound of the rippling river, John Tanner rose in disgust. Dry tinder from his pack and a spark from his flint and steel soon rekindled the fire. Low-hanging smoke sent the insects off in search of better hunting grounds and Tanner climbed under his canoe, his knife slipping from its sheath. He drifted off with thoughts of Red Morning Sky, Ome-zhuh-gwut-oons, and the devious Giah-ge-wa-go-mo swirling from his mind to his heart and back. As the soft glow of morning broke through treetops, he woke, knowing what he must do.

After breaking camp, John loaded the supplies into his canoe, his musket last. "Wife, you and our daughters will share a canoe and follow me upstream. When we reach Fort William, we will part. I will find you safe escort back to Rainy Lake and your village. My daughters will travel upriver with me and across Gitchee Gumi to Sault Ste. Marie."

"But Giah-ge-wa-go-mo has cast me from my village. He will not let me return. It would show weakness to allow a woman to upset his decision."

"No. Giah-ge-wa-go-mo will have little to say about this. You will hand Captain Bulger a letter from me. When he sees the path of treason taken by Giah-ge-wa-go-mo, all will change. I will write the letter at Fort William before you depart. It will guarantee your safety and a good home in your village for the duration of your life. That is my decision. Now we are off."

Bright sun warmed the river valley as the Tanner family ascended the Maligne River. Steam rose from the forest floor and drifted from the leaves and needles of the trees as the rainwater evaporated. John Tanner shed his shirt and hat, soaking in the sunlight. With his wife and children trailing behind, he rounded a river bend in time to see something appear in the mist, far ahead. "A canoe?" he said to himself as the misty air hid the apparition. It appeared again for an instant before rounding the next bend. "Do my eyes play tricks?" he wondered aloud. "Wenebojo, is this your work?"

Minutes later, Tanner's canoe rounded the bend. Again, he saw the ghost-like canoe far ahead. And again it vanished up the twisting river. He shifted his weight for sake of more strength. His paddle now violently cut into the river water. Stroke after sun-splashed stroke shortened the distance between the canoes. His muscles burned as his birch craft came nearer the place where he last saw the apparition. A red-tailed hawk, soaring far overhead, screamed a warning. With the roar of the whitewater rapids looming ahead, John Tanner never heard.

An amazing beauty resides in a wilderness river, its clear water coursing between rocks and over windfalls, its magical ripples and riffles chattering soft songs. Below thrives an infinite hodgepodge of remarkable life. On shore, a marvelous assortment of plants provides for birds, mammals, reptiles, and insect life, as though a continuous, ever-changing carousel of artfully crafted and brightly painted carnival horses. Perhaps the greatest thrill of a river journey is the mystery of what lies beyond the next bend. Whether another soothing, aquatic feast of delight or the nerve-testing challenge of whitewater rapids, the voyager's fate is cast. Tanner was committed to continue—to catch up with the mysterious canoe ahead—if indeed a canoe at all.

With his wife and daughters lagging behind, Tanner pushed himself, every muscle tense, forcing his canoe around the river bend. With the early morning sunlight glistening from his bare, wet skin, he knew he would catch the mysterious ghost-canoe now. His musket lay near him, should that traveler have other than peaceful intentions. He made the turn, then rested his paddle. Again the red-tail's sharp cry came from above. The ghost-canoe was not there. Instead, a field of large boulders lay before him, water roaring around and between granite—a challenge he was accustomed to, like most travelers of these wild woodlands. On he went.

He paddled fast, cutting deep into the coldwater stream and deftly guided the small watercraft around this rock and that and over others submerged. The flexible birch bark canoe, a canoe he built, rode out the rapids with ease. He reached the top of the rapids, seeing only one final challenge—a large, flat rock ahead, midstream. Faced with a final choice of left or right, and the left being somewhat obstructed by a windfall, he chose right, making his way upstream.

What followed next did so with such immediacy that Tanner scarcely understood, even though he was precisely in the violent midst of it. Three simultaneous events, abrupt and spontaneous, broke the morning peace. A piercingly loud crack-flash of a musket from the nearby bushes, the whiz of a ball past Tanner's right ear, and the crash of a second ball through his raised, right forearm and into his chest. The impact of the second ball sent the paddle from his grip and twisted his torso so violently, he fell into the canoe. Yet, knowing another round might come from a second assassin, he raised up and reached again for his paddle. Tanner then realized his right hand was of no use. Splinters from one of the two bones in his forearm protruded from the skin at the elbow.

Drawing near the flat-topped, midstream rock, Tanner rolled his body over the canoe's left gunnel and splashed clumsily into the stream, kicking for the far side of the stream, away from his assailant. He tried to pull the canoe with him but the shock of the attack, the pain in arm and chest, and the confusion of the incident caused him to let it slip away. Staying low in the water, he made his way to the flat, midstream rock. Tanner hid behind it, peering around. Seeing no one, he looked downstream to see his canoe floating crosswise in the river, along with his gear, food, and musket. As he stared, another shot shattered the quiet morning and two musket balls tore through the hull, splashing beyond the canoe. He looked across the stream to see a cloud of gun smoke rise from the bushes. "One assassin," he whispered.

Seconds after being ambushed, Tanner, lay in the cold river near the midstream boulder. Shot in both arm and chest, he watched his blood flow downstream. Across the river his assassin hid, concealed in tag alders. From downstream, his daughters and wife came up the rapids, looking for the source of the two musket reports. Eyes now locked on Tanner's floundering canoe, they came within a few yards of him. He suppressed his urge to call out for help, knowing this might make a target of his children. Red Morning Sky turned their canoe toward his. Lucy and Sunshine, seeing their father's diluted blood sloshing in the empty canoe, screamed in terror. Then, paddling furiously downstream, they rounded the bend below.

Bleeding from arm and chest, Tanner waded to the shore behind, keeping the rock between himself and his assailant. There, he hid in the cattail reeds. Looking downstream, he saw his canoe slowly go under, pierced through both sides by the two musket balls. With the red-tailed hawk watching from high above, the birch canoe rolled, emptying his gear into the river. As the canoe went down, so, too, sank John Tanner's heart.

He then turned to himself, to his wounds, finding one of the two bones in his forearm shattered. Scraps of bone protruded from skin. His eyes went to his chest, torn open by the same musket ball now lodged against his breastbone. Blood flowed from both wounds. He felt dizzy, weak. He tried to stand but fell to the bloody, muddy, weedy water.

Again, the red-tailed hawk cried. Raising his head, Tanner saw movement across the stream. A man, musket to his shoulder, skulked along the shore, stepping rock to rock. "Ome-zhuh-gwut-oons," Tanner whispered to himself. "How foolish was I to not see this coming? Now here I hide, bleeding, slowly dying. I was a fool to deny my suspicions."

"Ome-zhuh-gwut-oons," he shouted across the stream. "You have shot me in arm and chest and now I lay here bleeding and dying. If you are any man at all, you will show mercy by finishing me now."

Ome-zhuh-gwut-oons did not reply.

"You are a pitiless coward to not cross this stream and end my life. I am already a dead man. I beg you, do not leave me here to suffer. Please! Come finish me quickly."

Still, the assassin remained mute.

"I ask you again, Ome-zhuh-gwut-oons, come take my life. It is the only manly thing to do. I have no musket, no pistol. I offer no threat, no challenge. Come end my life!"

Ome-zhuh-gwut-oons walked upstream along the shore, then vanished into the woods. Soon, he pushed his canoe from the bushes into the stream, stepped in, and floated toward the place of the ambush.

"I see you coming, Ome-zhuh-gwut-oons," whispered Tanner to the murmuring waters. "When you pass, I will muster my last remaining strength and have you."

The young warrior approached. Tanner reached for his knife, finding the sheath empty. The canoe came closer. Tanner forced himself up to a crouch. He could now hear the paddle slice the water. He commanded his muscles to tense. The canoe was almost within his reach when he sprang from the cattails with a blood-curdling scream.

Ome-zhuh-gwut-oons, stunned by the surprise attack, raised his paddle in defense. Tanner grabbed the spruce blade with his left hand and pulled. But, weak from loss of blood, Tanner lacked strength enough to upset the canoe. The assassin reeled back, pulling the paddle free, then struck Tanner in the head, sending him to the streambed.

Shocked and terrified, Ome-zhuh-gwut-oons raced downstream, not looking back. Tanner watched him disappear around the bend. Then, tumbling and splashing through the shallows, he dragged himself onto the flat rock that lay midstream. The red-tailed hawk landed in a nearby tree as Tanner collapsed face down on the rock in the bright morning sun. His legs still submerged, he gasped for breath, certain he would die slowly if not finished by wolves.

Chapter 18
John Tanner Lives!

The hot mid-afternoon sun warmed the river valley and the rock where John Tanner lay wounded, hearing only the roar of the rapids and a faint call from the red-tail. The hawk's cry woke him, his back burning from the sunlight, his feet cold from flowing water. But his tremendous, parching thirst distracted him from all else. Throat dry from loss of blood and his long sleep in the bright sun, he slid down the rock, supporting his shattered right arm with his left. Cool water on hot skin refreshed him as he slid deeper and deeper, until submerged neck-deep. Turning aside, he drank and drank, then boosted himself onto the rock again, feeling stronger.

An otter with three pups, working their way upstream, passed close by, sniffing and snorting, investigating but keeping their distance. "I must be something to see, Mother Otter," he whispered. "Here I sit on your eating-rock, invading your hunting ground, scaring your children. What a sight I must be, burnt red on one side, white on the other, broken, bleeding, and scarred."

The otter moved upstream, her pups behind. Tanner watched as they dove and dove, searching out each scour hole for a meal. Finally, one of the pups brought a fine trout to the surface. The other, jealous, snapped it from him. As Tanner watched, the mortally wounded trout fell free. Seeing the fish float downstream, both pups raced for it until a sharp bark from their mother stopped them short. The trout floated directly to John Tanner who reached out with his good hand and secured his dinner.

"Whether you are simple otters or, perhaps, Wenebojo," said Tanner, "I offer you my highest gratitude." He bit into the tender meat along the back of the fish. "Mother otter, in years past I have trapped and killed many of your brothers and sisters for their pelts and my stewpot, but never again. You may have saved my life and, for that small act, I pledge to never take the life of another of your kin."

The three otters climbed onto a nearby rock and watched Tanner finish their trout. He flipped the severed head to one pup and sent the entrails floating. The second pup slipped into and under the surface and soon popped up downstream. Tanner watched as the innards quickly disappeared down the otter's gullet. "Young pups, I hope what little I left for you gives you as much strength as what you gave me. This meal you sent my way may be enough for me to find my next. To live, that is all we need, is it not? One dinner leading us to the next?"

The otters dove, re-appearing farther upstream, and looked back at Tanner, now standing on the rock. They dove again and vanished.

Tanner looked at his arm, then downstream to his overturned canoe lodged, now, between windfalls and rock. Stepping into the stream again, he leaned back, letting the current take him to his craft.

Now waist-deep, Tanner unwound a length of spruce root lashing from the bow thwart, then used it to create a sling for his wounded arm. He struggled to pull the canoe onto shore. Rolling it bottom-side-up, he realized the holes from the musket balls could be repaired. He waded downstream to find his deerskin pack and soon spread the contents atop the canoe to dry. He removed a knife from the pack and slid it into the sheath on his belt. A sopping-wet Hudson's Bay wool blanket came next, a valuable prize. He hung it on a limb to dry as the red-tail, wings set, glided silently above. Tanner unwrapped a small, tightly tied, oilcloth package. The letters within, perhaps his most valuable possession, remained dry. He whispered a chant of thanks to Gitchee Manitou. Tanner knew he could use the oilcloth to create a bandage for his arm. In silence, he pushed protruding bones back in place as best he could, grimacing from the pain, but knowing a scream would not reduce the agony. With deer sinew, he tied the oilcloth around his arm before replacing the sling.

Tanner next looked to his chest wound. He found that the ball, slowed by traveling through his forearm, had lacked enough energy to puncture ribs. Entering from his side, Tanner saw that it skidded between skin and ribs before lodging in his breastbone. Although his forearm was shattered, those bones had saved his life, at least for the moment. The ball in his chest would need be removed to afford him a return to fair health. The wound seeped watery ooze, but like the arm, little blood. And though each breath brought acute pain, this pain he could endure.

Realizing the musket ball had not pierced his lungs, he grinned. "Ome-zhuh-gwut-oons," he whispered, "you have not killed me after all—at least not yet. Though I surely shall die from these wounds when fever and rot set in, I might live long enough to see your deceitful, conniving corpse sprawled at my feet before I, too, fall. If you have even the sense of a lowly river snail, you and Red Morning Sky will flee to the farthest corner of the land, never again to show yourselves. Still, I will hunt you. Not for hatred and revenge, but to rescue my daughters. This is my pledge."

Strength slowly returning, John Tanner waded the river again in search of more of his supplies. He found one of the three canvas bags given him by Captain Bulger. The dried, salted beef and beans inside were soaked, but food, nevertheless. He also recovered his musket, though no flint remained, the powder was wet, and the lead musket balls were lost to the river. The ramrod was there, equipped with a screw that would allow him to pull the loaded ball and dry both powder and bore. The flint from his fire kit would suffice, giving him one shot with the musket. One chance to fire a deadly ball. The thought brought a smile replacing his grimace of pain. "If tomorrow's sun is as hot as today's, my powder will be dry by midday and I'll soon have you ready to fire, old friend," he said to his rifle. "One shot—all I need."

Tanner inspected his rescued provisions, satisfied he could now survive if his health did not fail. He had his fire kit, a simple flint and steel. His shirt was gone but, with his arm in a sling, he would not be able to pull a deerskin shirt over his head and torso. The blanket, when dry, would suffice. The small knife and his trading ax were his only hand tools. His musket aside, they would also be his only weapons, should weapons become necessary. He hoped they would.

As dusk approached, so did the mosquitoes. Their bothersome, high-pitched whine, their sting, and itch had Tanner scratching in misery and pain while searching the riverbank for help. A patch of horsemint was his salvation. With his good hand, he gathered a dozen plants, green and lush, carrying them to his overturned canoe. The woodsman rubbed them between his hands to release their pungent oils. He daubed these oils on face, arms, neck, chest, and other exposed skin as best as he could. More horsemint soon hung around his small camp from boughs and branches. The worrisome whine and sting ended abruptly, though the itch did not.

Tanner supped on pemmican and river water, getting stronger by the hour. As night fell, he repacked his salvaged belongings, securing the packs below the canoe. He then followed them under, wrapping himself in his blanket, eager for morning. By midnight, a half moon floated above the river. The scream of a faraway bobcat woke him, answered by other night sounds and odd animal chatterings. Tanner left his makeshift shelter, hoping to hear better and identify the source of the sounds. Minutes later, these strange calls came again, clearer now, downstream. Several minutes of silence was followed by more of these peculiar sounds. They became louder, more pronounced, exceeding the roar of the rapids above.

"Voices," he whispered. "A man and a woman … working their way upstream in the moonlight."

With his left hand, Tanner quietly rolled the canoe upright, placed his gear inside, and dragged it beyond sight of the river. He returned with axe and musket, secluding himself behind a windfall.

In the dim light of the moon, John Tanner watched as a birch canoe slowly rounded the bend, two paddlers fighting the upstream current. In the bow, a woman pushed the craft away from logs and rocks, paddling when she could. In the stern, a man stroked feverishly. They soon passed Tanner, who remained hidden on shore.

"This is the spot, the place where I killed him."

"No," she said. "Where is his canoe? We are not there yet. Keep going."

"That rock ahead is where I shot him—where he fell. I am certain."

"Then where is the canoe, Ome-zhuh-gwut-oons? Where are the supplies? Where is his musket?"

"Thieves must have stolen them."

"What thieves? We have been downstream. No one passed by."

"That rock is where I killed him, Red Morning Sky. I know this. That is where he fell. Where he called out, 'You have killed me. I am dead.'"

"Ome-zhuh-gwut-oons! You told me you killed John Tanner. You did not say he spoke to you after. Don't you see? He was the one who moved the canoe. John Tanner is still alive!"

"His arm was raised with paddle in hand when struck by my musket ball. The other went deep into his chest. I saw this from close by. I saw him fall. I heard him beg for me to finish him. I saw all the blood in his canoe. No, Red Morning Sky, John Tanner is dead."

"Perhaps his spirit moved the canoe?"

Close now, the bobcat screamed again. The chilling scream, like a woman tortured, startled all. Shocked, Ome-zhuh-gwut-oons, dropped his paddle. It floated downstream toward the windfall concealing Tanner.

Red Morning Sky whispered, "Ome-zhuh-gwut-oons, grasp your blade as we near it. We are leaving. If John Tanner lives, we are in danger." The paddle floated within feet of Tanner. Their canoe followed. "Now," said Red Morning Sky. "Grab it now."

As the young man reached for the floating paddle, Tanner sprang, axe in hand, screaming a terrifying war cry. He landed a sharp blow on his enemy's forehead. It glanced off, tearing skin and hair. The woman screamed. The warrior jerked back. The canoe rocked, sending both traitors into the river.

Tanner pulled the warrior's musket from the canoe just as the current dragged the craft downstream. With his left hand, he aimed the muzzle at Ome-zhuh-gwut-oons, now floundering in the stream between Red Morning Sky, ahead, and the birch craft, behind. The musket's hammer fell onto flint and a blinding flash lit the night. The crack of the rifle shattered the night air. Two musket balls blasted water high into the air near the fleeing warrior.

Tanner screamed another war whoop, then fell back onto the shore, exhausted. Struggling to his feet, he cupped his hands around his mouth and shouted downstream, "You failed, Ome-zhuh-gwut-oons. John Tanner lives! John Tanner lives!"

A note from the author ...

Unlike writers who choose to publish through traditional "brick and mortar" corporations, independent authors rely upon their readers to help spread the word about their books. If you enjoy this novel, please let others know by recommending BadgerValley.com where they can read excerpts, view illustrations, and enjoy free shipping.

And please consider ordering a Badger Valley title as a gift for a friend. Every book sold at BadgerValley.com helps generate more stories from the great north woods. Thanks for your help.

James Brakken

Chapter 19
Tanner is Coming!

With the words "John Tanner lives" echoing down the river valley. Ome-zhuh-gwut-oons floundered in the current. Trying to keep his head above water, catching a breath when he could, he struggled to gain footing. His canoe, sideways and empty, came from behind, pushing him under again. As he surfaced he heard Red Morning Sky shout, "I have it! I have the canoe, Ome-zhuh-gwut-oons. Where are you?"

Caught by the current, he cried, "I am … I am here."

"Come to my voice," she replied. "Swim this way. This way!"

The young man, blood streaming from the wound on his forehead, thrashed and splashed, tumbling into a fallen tree that extended into the stream. He stretched far, grabbing the wet, slippery treetop but lost his grip in the force of the rushing water.

"This way, Ome-zhuh-gwut-oons," came another call.

The injured warrior struck a midstream boulder. Driven to survive, he wrestled and strained, grappling his way onto the huge rock and collapsed, all energy spent.

"Do you hear me, Ome-zhuh-gwut-oons? Where are you? Come this way. Ome-zhuh-gwut-oons," cried Red Morning Sky. "Ome-zhuh-gwut-oons!"

John Tanner now lay under his overturned canoe, his arm pounding from pain and his chest wound bleeding again. He wrapped himself in his blanket and lay on his side in agony, his swollen, musket-shot arm throbbing.

"Yes, Ome-zhuh-gwut-oons, you should have killed me yesterday when I begged you. Now, though the dawn light may fall upon my dead remains, you will forever wear the scar I gave your face. Forever, may your hideousness take the breath away from all you meet. May each man, woman and child who sees you run from the sight of you, Ome-zhuh-gwut-oons, and may that be worse than death."

For hours, Tanner lay under the canoe, his pain preventing rest. "Wenebojo," he begged, "why, do you not give me peace? Sleep or death—either would relieve me of this misery. Let me go to the land beyond the great river. I have done enough here. What use will I be without this arm? Let me go so I might be whole again in the next life. I beg you, let me go now."

John Tanner's eyes closed, his words heard only by a thousand mosquitoes swarming far above and Wenebojo, the spirit, who lay there with him, sharing his pain, absorbing it, saving it for another time, another tale.

As the faint, pink light of morning outlined the treetops to the east, a ghost-like figure moved on a midstream boulder, downstream.

"Ome-zhuh-gwut-oons," came a woman's call from shore. "Ome-zhuh-gwut-oons, I see you there. Wake up. Wake up!"

Blood dripping from his wounded face, the young warrior, lifted his head, then lowered it, too exhausted, too cold to move.

"Ome-zhuh-gwut-oons, hear me," cried Red Morning Sky. "I have the canoe. We must go. We must escape. John Tanner may come hunt us any minute. Wake, Ome-zhuh-gwut-oons!"

He turned his head, his blood-washed eyes focusing enough to see the silhouette of Red Morning Sky. She stood knee-deep on a spit of sand extending into the river, the canoe alongside and upright.

"Ome-zhuh-gwut-oons, can you see me? Raise your hand if you see me."

A hand rose a few inches, then fell to the rock.

"You can make it. The current will pull you to this sandbar, just as it pulled me. Roll off the rock toward me. Ome-zhuh-gwut-oons, you will make it," she cried.

He lifted his head. Seeing her again, he rolled toward her. Splashing into the water, he let the river take him now, not caring if he lived or died. As the woman foretold, the current carried him her way. Steadying herself with a paddle, she stepped deeper and deeper. Catching him by his hair, she dragged him to shallow water.

Coughing and spitting river water, the warrior crawled near shore and collapsed. "You should have left me for the ravens, Red Morning Sky."

Straddling his body, she lifted him, dragging him onto land. "We must go," she said, running to the canoe. She pulled it into the stream next to him. "Ome-zhuh-gwut-oons, muster your strength. You must get in. Now."

With her help, he slowly rose, then rolled over the gunnel, falling with a loud grunt to the bottom of the birch craft.

Looking upstream for Tanner, Red Morning Sky climbed in. Pushing off with her paddle, she said, "Perhaps he sleeps. I do not see him."

"Or, perhaps he is hiding—waiting with my musket—waiting to kill us."

"That is a chance we must take. We cannot stay here. We must return to our camp, pick up my daughters and flee."

Using the current to propel the canoe now, Red Morning Sky steered with her paddle. She looked down at the wounded young man before her. Tanner's hand axe had skinned a palm-sized patch from the man's forehead, leaving a v-shaped notch in the bone, showing white in the morning light. Blood seeped from the surrounding skin.

Ome-zhuh-gwut-oons opened his eyes enough to see her staring. "What do you see when you stare at me so? How homely has the axe of John Tanner made me? Tell me."

"He cut you, that is all. You will heal. This will be like wind on the fire that makes the flames of revenge in your heart grow stronger. You will kill John Tanner. Of this I have no doubt."

"They say the spirit of Wenebojo is strong in him. Maybe he is beyond killing. Maybe John Tanner will live to be an old, old man. Maybe it is I who will die if I return to kill him."

"You speak the words of a coward. Are you a coward, Ome-zhuh-gwut-oons? Or are you the young warrior who has pledged to rid me of a bad husband, a bad father of my daughters? I promised you those daughters as wives if you killed him. I still promise them. Now, you bear a fine trophy. On your face you wear a scar that shows your bravery in the face of John Tanner. Kill him and you will have your two new wives to honor you—the daughters of White Swallow. Is this not what you want?"

"It is. Yes. I will kill Shaw-shawwa na-baysay that I may have your daughters to keep my lodge, to have my sons and your grandsons."

"We will flee now, Ome-zhuh-gwut-oons, but only until your heart nearly bursts for revenge. Soon, you will seek out my husband and kill him. This time, you must take his scalp as he tried to take yours. That is my wish."

The pain within Tanner's swollen, broken arm pried his eyes open. He pulled the blanket away to see his chest wound had stopped bleeding. Wincing, he rolled out from under the canoe and sat, leaning against it. The pounding in his right arm prompted removal of the bandage. Slowly loosening the sinew that bound it, the pain subsided some. He opened the oilcloth wrap. There, the bone fragments he pushed back into place a day earlier, protruded again. He tried pressing them back in, but the pain would not allow. Tears welling in his eyes, he pulled them out one by one, dropping each bloody bone splinter into his medicine pouch. Blood flowed, flushing away bits of flesh, skin, bone, and hair. Tanner laid yarrow leaves over the wound, then wrapped the oilcloth around his arm, tying it as before.

Tanner placed his hand on his breastbone, feeling the musket ball lodged there, eight inches from where the ball had entered under his arm. He shook his head in dismay, knowing the ball must be cut out. The muffled bark of a river otter caught his attention. He looked up to see the mother otter and her two pups out in the river.

"You left before I could convey my appreciation for the fine meal you served, Otter. I may not have lived were it not for you. Are you here to bring me another trout?"

She dove, her pups dove, then all three climbed the river bank, watching him from a distance. The morning sun now warming the sand under them, the otter pups rolled and rolled, throwing sand over their shiny coats, then shaking themselves clean again. The mother sat, staring at Tanner, unwilling to play.

"You have no need to fear me, mother otter. I have pledged to never again hurt you or your kind. I am an honorable person. I keep my promises, like my promise now to seek out Ome-zhuh-gwut-oons and the woman-turned-evil, Red Morning Sky. I will punish them both. I promise, too, to find my daughters and keep them well, provide for them until they find husbands who will care for them. I pledge all this before you and your pups, before the river and the woods, the sun and the sky.

"If my wounds do not kill me, I will keep this pledge until it is fulfilled or I am dead." The sandy otter pups slithered and slid across the shore to the stream, then, clean again, popped up in the river. "Let the wind and the river carry my promise of revenge to the ears of Ome-zhuh-gwut-oons and Red Morning Sky that they know I come for them. Otters, if you pass them on the water, tell them this woodsman, this hunter, keeps his word. Tell them John Tanner is coming."

For two more days, John Tanner suffered from his injuries, hiding aside the river. With birch bark and pine pitch, he patched the four bullet holes in the canoe, anticipating the day when his right arm would be strong enough to journey downstream. Now and again, he loosened the bandage, pulling out more emerging bone fragments before washing the wound in the river. To accomplish this, and to spare further distressing his chest wound by bending, he waded waist deep into quiet water The cool stream flowing over his wounds gave temporary relief, prompting him to return often.

On the third day after being shot, as he rinsed and soothed his wounds, Tanner heard voices above the rapids. "Fur traders?" he said to the wind. "Am I rescued?" The voices grew louder.

As the first of two canoes, each carrying four men, rounded the bend, he dropped to his knees. "Sioux!" he whispered. With only his head above water, he worked his way near the windfall, hiding from them as they ran the rapids and passed by, unaware. When out of sight, he stood, rapidly bandaging his arm before retreating to his makeshift camp. He checked his musket, then the musket taken from Ome-zhuh-gwut-oons. Loaded, primed, ready to fire, he next hung his hand axe on his belt, securing it with a cord made from woven buckskin. "John Tanner might die," he said defiantly, "but, if by the hands of rogue Sioux marauders, then he offer them his best fight."

Red Morning Sky guided her canoe downstream past some rocks, over others, through whitewater rapids, around bend after bend. In the bottom of the black spruce and birch bark craft, Ome-zhuh-gwut-oons, head wound oozing and throbbing, woke. He sat up, wiping blood and watery fluids from his eyes, wincing from pain when the tip of a finger touched his skinned forehead. The pain angered him and he tore the paddle from the hands of the woman, then violently sliced into the water.

"Your anger," said Red Morning Sky, "fuels fires of vengeance in your heart. But this is not the time. We must not let our wish to see John Tanner suffer and die be our undoing."

"I will finish what has begun. I will kill John Tanner."

"Yes. But not today. Not soon. We must flee. Later, we will seek him out when he is not expecting us. Do not let your hatred cloud your direction."

The failed murderers, having retrieved their few supplies from their encampment, helped Tanner's daughters into the two canoes. They pushed off downstream, soon putting in at Kettle Falls and the village of Chief Wa-wishee-gah-bo, brother of Ome-zhuh-gwut-oons.

The morning of the fourth day of Tanner's recovery again found him waist deep in the river, washing his wounds. The roar of the rapids upstream hid the sounds of four canoes, rounding the bend. Tanner looked up, then dove for safety, but surfaced when he realized these were not more Sioux warriors. He waited until the first canoe came through the rapids, then stepped from his hiding place.

"Bonjour, mes amis!" he yelled, waving his good hand. Bonjour, bonjour!"

The lead canoe came about and four of the eight men aboard raised muskets, aiming at his chest. The others searched the shore and woods for would-be slayers waiting in ambush.

"No, no my friends," Tanner cried, "I am a friend, alone, and in distress. I've been badly wounded and need your rescue."

The second and third canoe joined the first in the quiet water near shore. More muskets appeared. "Who are you?" came a shout in French.

"I am John Tanner of the Red River and Rainy Lake. I am victim of ambush by Ome-zhuh-gwut-oons, a murderous savage."

The fourth canoe joined the others. "Mister Stewart," came a call from an Englishman in a white cotton suit and hat, "why are we delayed? Who is this scoundrel? Dare you hold up our journey for this rogue?"

"He claims to be victim of an ambush. And it appears he is gravely wounded."

"Shoot the hopeless blaggard. 'Tis clear he's near death and bound to die. End his misery that we may be on our way."

"Mister Grant," shouted Tanner, "do you not know me? I have hunted for you and the Hudson's Bay Company many times. I have fed your men, saving some from starvation. Sir, you have employed me to speak with the Sioux and Ojibwe on your behalf. Now you would leave me here to fill the bellies of the wolves and ravens?"

"Bah!" came the reply. "I know him not, Mister Stewart. Either finish this savage out of mercy or leave him to his own providence. We must be off."

"Mister Stewart, surely you recognize me. You bought my peltries and those I won in trade for you. This axe I wear you gave me in trade for a buffalo hide. Do you not see who I am, sir?"

Stewart gasped. "By the Lord! Tanner? Is that really you? Rest your rifles, men. This is John Tanner, the one called the White Indian. He is a friend!"

"Imposter!" shouted Grant. "John Tanner is tall and hearty."

Tanner waded to shore. "I admit, monsieur, my appearance is rude and vulgar in my bloodied, wet clothing, wounded and mosquito-bit, and my face has not felt a straight-razor for a month. Yet, I am he, John Tanner, the one you call the White Indian, and I am in dire need of medical attention. I have papers, sir."

"Papers, you say?"

"A letter from Governor Lewis Cass of Detroit, sir. And another Governor Clark of Missouri Territory. Yet another from Lord Selkirk, himself. As I recall, you know his Lordship quite well."

"Mister Stewart, you say you recognize this man?"

"I do. I will attest he is who he says. John Tanner, one in the same."

"Have you a surgeon in your party?" asked Tanner.

"I am a surgeon, monsieur," came a shout from the second canoe. "What service might I provide?"

"I carry a lead ball in my chest. It wholly disturbs me. So much so that I will gladly pay to have it extracted, sir."

"Pay? If it is true that you are the White Indian also called John Tanner, I'll accept no award, sir. My pay will be the tale I shall tell to my grandchildren about cutting a ball from the chest of the White Indian."

"If ever you see them again, Docteur," came a gibe from the next canoe.

"Mock me if you will, my friend, I will gladly ply my skill in trade for a good story."

"Enough delay," shouted Grant. "Tanner, fetch your goods. Let us be off."

Four canoes carried twenty-eight men and supplies downstream, a smaller, fifth canoe tethered behind. They camped before nightfall, boiled water for tea and dined on boiled beaver. Before turning in, the surgeon cleaned Tanner's injured arm, doused it with whisky, applying a clean, cotton bandage and a sling.

"Now, let us see about that chest wound," said LeBlanc.

With Tanner lying on the ground, the surgeon poked and probed the wound. "You are right, Monsieur Tanner, the ball must come out. However, I am not the one to do this. I worry that it is too close to your heart and one slip of my knife would be the end of you."

"If not you, Doctor, then who? No one else has your touch or knowledge of such things."

"No, sir. I cannot. I will not. Forgive me."

"Mister Stewart? Can I call on you? It should not take long."

"Me? Have you not heard that our surgeon has refused?"

"Come now. Only hours ago you ordered me to be shot. Surely this small task could not result in a worse end."

"No, John Tanner. I'll not have a hand in dispatching the White Indian."

"And, Mister Grant?"

"Nay, sir."

"Is there any man here willing to cut this evil metal morsel from under my hide?"

No man spoke.

"Then I shall have to do it myself."

"You know, John Tanner, you may die if your knife goes astray," advised the surgeon.

"And I will die if I do nothing about it, will I not, Docteur LeBlanc?"
LeBlanc's silence answered Tanner's question.

"Docteur, might I use your scalpel?"

The doctor handed the scalpel to Tanner who now sat cross-legged before the fire. All eyes watched in silence as John Tanner sliced into his chest above the breastbone. Blood running, he worked the thin blade between ball and bone, then twisted the knife. With a snap heard by all, the blade broke, lodging under the bullet. Tanner winced as LeBlanc blotted the blood, applying pressure. One of the others offered a folding pocket knife. Tanner accepted, working the blade under the ball. He pried again. The blade snapped.

"My hunting knife was lost to the river when I fought the warrior, Ome-zhuh-gwut-oons," Tanner said. "Will any man here loan me his?"

A Frenchman leaned toward him, extending a glistening ten-inch blade, handle first. "Monsieur, if your life this knife saves, you may keep it and know you owe me a favor in return one day. But, Tanner, should you die, I will carry it that I can tell others mine was the blade that killed the White Indian."

Tanner accepted the stout-bladed knife with a nod, stuck the tip under the ball, and twisted, screaming in agony. The ball flew across the fire into the lap of a Frenchman. Tanner dropped the knife, falling onto his back as the surgeon pulled the broken knife blades out and placed a clean cotton rag over the hole in his chest, leaning on it to slow the bleeding.

"John Tanner," he said, "it appears you have a new hunting knife and owe a favor to Monsieur Clairet, no?"

"Oui, Docteur," he replied, "Now, if there's whisky left in that jug, I would be grateful for enough to help me sleep. I have two daughters to seek out and vengeance to claim, all at first light."

"Docteur LeBlanc, fill a tin cup for this brave soul," ordered Stewart. "Never have I met a man who is more worthy."

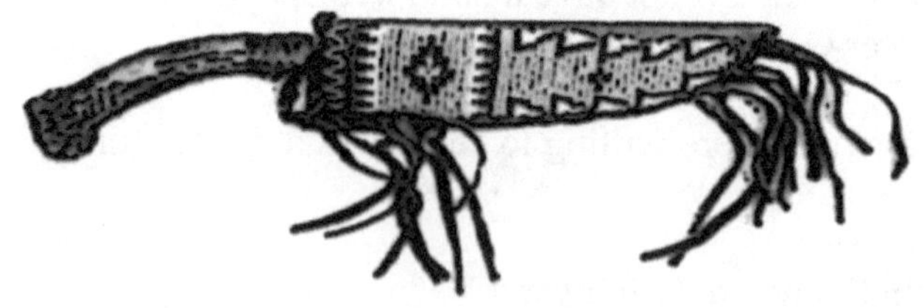

John Tanner woke at first light of dawn. Seconds passed before he realized he was in a camp, safe and among friends, not alone waiting for the wilderness to claim him. He tried to sit up. A sharp stab of pain from the bullet wound in his chest abruptly laid him back. Closing his eyes, he focused all thoughts on his two daughters, imagining them forced into horrific and unholy submissions by Ome-zhuh-gwut-oons, Tanner's would-be assassin. He envisioned their mother looking on, willing to trade their flesh for a chance at a new life with this young, robust rogue—the cowardly assassin who shot him, leaving him to suffer a slow death on the riverbank four days earlier.

Grimacing from pain, Tanner pondered the urgent need to rescue his daughters and wreak vengeance on his assailant. Subdued rage now driving him, he stood, supporting his shattered right arm with his left hand. The woodsman struggled to slip into his moccasins, then inspected the bandage on his chest. With the slightest wince, he peeled the blood-soaked cotton rag from the wound, tossing it into the fire ring, now cold. The whisky jug sat near Docteur LeBlanc. Tanner raised it, pulled the cork, and poured a splash into his palm, wiping it into the bullet hole near his sternum. Before the sting had time to subside, Tanner guzzled four swallows of the spirit, then socked the cork in place.

He looked to his throbbing arm, refitting the sling offered the night before by the surgeon. Silently enduring the pain, he managed to pull his buckskin shirt over his head and left arm. He stepped outside and soon heard others in the small, riverside camp begin to stir, preparing for another day's paddle toward the fort and the comfort and security it provided.

"John Tanner," came a shout from the tent behind him. "I see you survived the night."

"I believe so, Mister Grant, for if you can see me stand and hear me speak, then I am scarcely a ghost, sir."

"And your wounds, Tanner, how are they? Are you fit to travel?"

Tanner grinned. "Fit or not, I will be off with the first paddle. I have kin to tend to and a wildcat to skin."

"John, if I may, I would like to suggest you nary make haste in your pursuit of the savage who shot you. By your own account, he is a fit young man. Moreover, he seems to lack caution and might spring upon you at the most inconvenient time. Let my men tend to him."

"Were I in better health, I'd scoff at your suggestion. But, yes, if your men are willing, I welcome their help. Should he be captured, I would be forever in your debt, sir."

They broke camp as the sun appeared above the treetops to the east. The party of twenty-seven floated downstream, accompanied by the suffering gunshot victim.

The advance canoe held Mister Stewart and eight men, each carrying muskets loaded with buckshot and ball, the standard military round. Silently, they rounded each bend in the river, rifles at the ready, watching for the assassin, Ome-zhuh-gwut-oons. An hour later, they pulled onto a sandy shoal to light their pipes.

"Mister Stewart," offered Tanner, "you won't find this wildcat standing in the sunshine where he might be an easy target for your marksmen."

"I beg your pardon, sir?"

"Ome-zhuh-gwut-oons may be a young buck, reckless and rash in his ways, but he is not so foolish to be easily found. You must look for him in the shadows. Look for him where you least expect him. He is less apt to be surprised when your men come 'round a bend than he is to be the one who surprises you."

"So, John Tanner, what would you have me do?"

"You have four large canoes and my smaller craft tethered behind. Send three of your canoes ahead. He will think this is only a few soldiers moving from fort to fort. He will not be threatened. Then, well behind in my canoe, one man, your most courageous, clad in buckskin. Finally, let your last large canoe follow at some distance. If Ome-zhuh-gwut-oons has not already fled downriver, he will be hiding in the shadows. He will watch your three canoes pass by. When he sees my canoe he will not be able to resist an opportunity to finish me. When he tries, your rank of riflemen will be close at hand."

The party left the shoal as Tanner suggested. Mile after mile turned neither a sign of Ome-zhuh-gwut-oons nor John Tanner's daughters and his deceitful wife. Then, near sunset, the vanguard of three canoes descended a small rapids. Tanner felt eyes watching them from the dark side of the stream. Minutes later, another canoe, small, bearing one man, entered the rapids, descending quickly, bobbing and bouncing over submerged rocks.

Caught by surprise, the assassin raised his rifle, muzzle following the buckskin-clad paddler. Hammer snapped back. Trigger tripped. Hammer fell. Flint struck steel. A deafening blast and blue-grey smoke filled the evening air. But the shot went high.

Tanner's surrogate jammed his paddle into the rocky riverbed, sending the canoe to the riverbank. Rifle in hand, the soldier jumped onto shore, then ran through the woods toward the smoke. Ome-zhuh-gwut-oons fled mere seconds ahead of the armed impostor.

Upstream, paddles thrashing water, the remaining riflemen quickly reached shore. They vaulted from the canoe and fanned out into the woods.

Ome-zhuh-gwut-oons fought his way through the underbrush. Now racing upriver for his life with the soldier close behind, he burst from the thick brush into the rank of support soldiers. He stopped, drew his knife, and two rifles discharged, sending one musket ball through his thigh and another, along with two buckshot pellets, deep into his shoulder. Bound and bleeding, he soon lay in the bottom of the Hudson's Bay Company's canoe.

The canoes met downstream. Tanner looked on as the Hudson's Bay Company men lashed Ome-zhuh-gwut-oons to a birch.

"Where are my daughters?" asked Tanner.

The young warrior said nothing.

Tanner pulled his knife from its sheath. "I ask again. Where are my daughters?"

Ome-zhuh-gwut-oons remained mute.

Tanner held the blade to the wounded man's throat. "Tell me!"

"I am dead, John Tanner," he said. "Finish me."

"Did you give me the same respect, the same sympathy when, like you, I begged to die? No, Ome-zhuh-gwut-oons, I will not kill you. You may die, but know you die by your own doing, not by my hand. Now, where are my daughters?"

With twenty-seven soldiers watching, Tanner stared into the eyes of his would-be assassin. Seconds passed. Tanner lowered the knife, slipping it into its sheath again.

"Mister Stewart, Mister Grant, many years past, my father taught me no man should take another's life. This man sees himself as a warrior. He will tell us nothing. We should go."

"And leave him? Leave him to try to kill you again, Mister Tanner? I think not."

"He knows I have spared his life. His honor, his heart will not allow him to again try to kill me. Mister Stewart, I ask you to spare his life that he may long remember his encounter with John Tanner."

"Sergeant," said Stewart, "I'm less trusting than Mister Tanner. Fetch the renegade's knife, musket, powder, and shot before you loosen his bonds."

The moon now rising, the soldiers and Tanner pushed off, paddling downstream toward their next camp with John Tanner wondering if he would ever again see his daughters.

Chapter 22
On to Fort Frances

At twilight, the Hudson's Bay Company band pulled onto the shore at Kettle Falls and the village of Wa-wishee-gah-bo, brother of Ome-zhuh-gwut-oons. John Tanner lay hidden in the second canoe. Mister Grant approached the chief, arms wide.

"Chief Wa-wishee-gah-bo, I bring greetings from the Hudson's Bay Company elders who wish you good health and prosperity."

A boy wearing only a loincloth translated Grant's words.

The old Indian smiled, nodding in approval.

"Wa-wishee-gah-bo, we hope you will help us. We are seeking three travelers, a woman and her daughters. We believe they came here from upriver."

The elder said nothing.

"Tell me, my friend, do you have these visitors here?"

"We have no visitors."

"The woman I speak of was accompanied by your brother, Ome-zhuh-gwut-oons. Did he not stop here with them?"

"We have no visitors."

"Wa-wishee-gah-bo, do you not know your brother shot a white man not far upstream from here? Do you not know he plucked from this man his beloved daughters?"

Wa-wishee-gah-bo hung his head.

"Tell me where these daughters are now, before the blood on your brother's hands comes to be on your own."

The chief stared at the ground as he said, "My brother came to this village four days ago. With us, he left two young women. He returned upstream with their mother to claim the rifle and goods of a man he fought with and killed after the man attacked him."

"Ome-zhuh-gwut-oons lied to you. No one attacked him. He plotted with the woman to kill the man by surprise."

"My dreams told me this was so. My brother shames us with all his killing. We live in fear for he brings the threat of vengeance on our village. Who was this man he killed?"

"Your brother set a trap for John Tanner."

Wa-wishee-gah-bo looked up, eyes wide. "Shaw-shawwa na-baysay?"

"Yes, Shaw-shawwa na-baysay. John Tanner."

"I knew this man. He had powerful medicine. Wenebojo was strong in him. Rode in his canoe, walked with him on his hunts. Now my brother has killed him? My people will never be safe."

Tanner rose from the canoe, clutching his injured arm. "You need not fear, Wa-wishee-gah-bo. There will be no revenge taken on you or your people. This I swear."

"You live, John Tanner? Then, my brother, Ome-zhuh-gwut-oons, he is no more?"

"As the wise leader of your village, you know that we must choose our trails wisely. Wa-wishee-gah-bo, your brother, chose a foolish path, a path he thought was short and easy to walk. But he was wrong. It went astray. Now he is far away, so far that he will never again return. Perhaps he will do better in the next place."

"John Tanner, can I tell my people we are safe from revenge for what he has done to you?"

"Will you tell me where I will find my daughters?"

"Their mother took them by canoe only this morning. Look for them near Fort Frances."

"Wa-wishee-gah-bo, you and your people need not fear my revenge. Your brother's deed was not your choice, not your doing. You may always call me your friend."

"Then camp here tonight, John Tanner. We have a wise mash-kikii-kwee. She has strong medicines to help your wounds. And I have fresh pemmican from the Americans, not the tainted fodder offered by the English."

"I beg your pardon," groused Grant.

Wa-wishee-gah-bo grinned. "No need to beg like dogs, we have enough pemmican for you, too."

The party's descent to Rainy Lake was brief, the current in their favor. Crossing the lake to Fort Frances proved long and arduous for all but John Tanner. His injuries spared him from the paddle. Though he would have preferred pulling his own weight, Tanner's only tasks were to rest and tend to his wounds. Cedar leaves, sweet grass, powders, and tonics given him by the medicine woman at the village of Wa-wishee-gah-bo offered some relief.

By day's end, Tanner and the twenty-seven Hudson's Bay Company voyageurs spied the trading house of Donald McKenzie on the great island named for him.

"McKenzie," shouted Grant from the lead boat, "have you time to tell us some of your lies, sir?"

"Aye," came a call from shore, "and enough rum to make you believe every word, Mister Grant. Come ashore! Make your camp, sir. I'll not turn away any Hudson's Bay man as long as his purse jingles with British silver."

Tents readied and campfire kindled, the men rested near McKenzie's store. Trout speared from a nearby stream provided supper. In McKenzie's largest copper pot, a stew of dried buffalo, wild rice, and blueberries simmered. Bowls were soon filled. McKenzie poured rum into wooden cups, emptying the keg. He vanished into the woods, returning in minutes with another.

"Queer," said Stewart, "that you store your spirits in the woods and keep wood in your store. Seems to be upturned, does it not?"

"I fear the Sioux have caused this, Mister Stewart. Not the lot, mind you, merely the younger of 'em. They are at odds with the Ojibwe again. I trade with anyone who has goods fit for England, including their enemy, the Ojibwe. The Sioux know this and do not take to it well. Last week, a half-dozen of these young bucks stole four kegs of rum from me. This, sir, is why I've taken to the woods with the remainder."

"And, how many kegs lay in hiding?" asked Tanner.

"Eighty-two, by my last count."

"I see why you cannot risk having them in plain view."

"Foolishness," scoffed Stewart. "No way to run a trading house. Mister McKenzie, let me know if you'd like to see these marauders brought to justice. The gallows at Fort Frances are there for a purpose."

"Heavens above, speak not these words, Mister Stewart! Would you have the entire Sioux nation upon me? There must be no retribution against these red hooligans. Dear me! My scalp would soon swing from the belt of some galloping savage."

"He is right," said Tanner. "Hang one renegade and McKenzie's life would be forfeit before the crowd of onlookers dispersed the gallows. 'Tis far better to exchange pelts for blankets than arrows for musket balls."

Stewart laughed. "McKenzie, I say again, this is no way to run your trading house. No Hudson's Bay overseer would tolerate this."

"I am not a Hudson's Bay man. I am with Nor'West and I do a fine bit of business for them, Mister. Should I lose a bit of rum here or the odd twist of tobacco there, it is all in the best interest of the company—and my scalp."

"And take note that McKenzie still has his," added Tanner. "Some less tolerant traders hereabouts cannot say the same."

"Aye," said McKenzie, "being in the grave, they can say nothing at all."

"Mister Tanner," countered Stewart, "this behavior, nay, intimidation must be met face-on. We cannot let a few savages dictate our commerce. If we should, our trading posts will be done, sir, for no hunter, trapper, or trader would dare venture westward."

"They come because the pelts of the animals fetch a good price and are plentiful," said Tanner. "Plentiful as stars in the night sky and highly prized in England and France. As long as the peltries can be traded for gold and silver, men will come west. Man's greed overpowers his good sense."

"And will for all time, I dare say," added McKenzie, driving the cork in the keg.

The first blush of morning light found the travelers breaking camp and shoving off on the final leg to Fort Frances, twenty miles west. Two pipes later, they met two eastbound canoes, each bearing three Sioux braves. The canoes passed each other without event other than the mutual nod of respect one voyager offers another.

"It appears our good trader, Donald McKenzie, will have some business this morning," Grant said.

"I saw no peltries or trade goods in their canoes," said Tanner, "only weapons. Perhaps these are the young troublemakers he spoke of."

"Say, Tanner," said Stewart, "you know these Sioux. You can speak their tongue, can you not?"

"Well enough, sir."

"Wouldn't it be a fine feather in the cap of the Hudson's Bay Company if we again brought the Ojibwe and these Sioux together for talk of peace betwixt them? Tanner, you did this once for Lord Selkirk, did you not?"

"I did."

"Why not again, then?"

"The Sioux and Ojibwe live different lives, Mister Stewart. Those different lives cause them to cross paths in search of buffalo, deer, and rice. Other than this, they keep to their own. When men keep to their own, trust never grows between them."

"Is there nothing to be done to bring them together?" asked Grant. "Nothing we can do?"

Tanner grinned. "My friends, you are already doing it."

"Explain yourself, Tanner," said Stewart.

"I once saw two crows fighting over a dead trout. A buzzard watched from a tree limb above, waiting for the crows to drive one another away. They fought and pecked and screeched, but neither would give up the prize. When the buzzard tired of this, he flew down for the trout. Gentlemen, I watched as those two crows took after that buzzard with zeal, each diving on him, pecking and pulling his feathers out. Off he flew with the two crows close behind, taunting and striking him even as he flew well away."

"We are talking about Indians, Tanner," snapped Stewart, "not some feathered scavengers. What nonsense is this?"

"Nonsense, Mister Stewart? The crows are like the Sioux and Ojibwe."

"And the buzzard?" asked Grant. "Is he representative of the Caucasians? Is that your point, Tanner?"

"The Whites come here to take away wealth, kill the game, even kill those Indians who interfere. Yes, the Whites are the buzzards who will feel the sting of the beak when the tribes band together."

"Balderdash! Neither Mister Grant nor I have done anything but good for these people. Nor have any of the Hudson's Bay Company merchants."

Tanner laughed. "Can you say the same for those who head the company? Those who sit in velvet chairs back in London? How do you suppose they would respond if you told them their profits were declining because of problems with the Indians? What would they do? Would they send food and clothing?"

"Tanner's right," Grant said. "They would send King George's soldiers—and by the thousands."

"Perhaps, my friends, it is best to watch the crows peck at each other than it is to interfere as did the buzzard."

The Hudson's Bay men rounded Birch Point to see the tall stockades of Fort Frances and the Northwest Trading Company store. Soon, a greeting came from the pier.

"Messers Grant and Stewart, welcome!" cried Simon M'Gillevray, the North West Company overseer. "How good to see you have arrived." He watched as the canoes approached. "Your quarters await. I fancy you might enjoy a bath and a meal?"

"We would, Mister M'Gillevray," replied Grant as the canoes slid onto the beach. "More than you know."

"Mister Stewart, your men may use the soldiers' quarters for a time, as Major Delafield is off on another of his adventures."

"Simon, we will need lodging for one more," Stewart said. "We stumbled onto this fellow who'd been ambushed far upriver. He was on his way here with his wife and daughters. Poor fellow found himself shot and left to die in the woods by a wicked rogue, a brigand known as Ome-zhuh-gwut-oons."

"A renegade," added Grant.

"Heavens! I have heard of the butchery of this man."

"Monsieur M'Gillevray," said the soldier, Clairet, "with his own hand the White Indian pried the assassin's ball from his breastbone using my knife."

"White Indian? No. You must be mistaken."

"John Tanner," said Grant.

"But the John Tanner I knew left here long ago. I recall that Lord Selkirk himself sent him off on some adventure. Why, last I heard, he was on the Ohio River and bound for Missouri River country to be with family. I venture he would not return here. Not John Tanner."

"I beg to differ, Simon," came a voice from the third boat. Tanner stood, using his musket as a crutch.

"John, is it really you? I doubted I would lay eyes on you another time. Come! Rest and repair under my roof. You must tell me of this and all your adventures."

"Simon," replied Tanner, "your hospitality is met with deepest gratitude. My greatest need, though, is to recover my two daughters, then seek their mother, Red Morning Sky. She is responsible for the attempt on my life."

"John, a woman who appeared unduly agitated and upset arrived at this post with her two daughters only this morning."

"I must find them."

"My men will seek them out. Come, John. Llet us tend to your wounds."

"Tell them to use caution, Simon. Red Morning Sky is not above treachery."

Canoes ashore, the men tended to the cargo, then found their bunks. Stewart, Grant, Doctor LeBlanc, and John Tanner stowed their packs in the overseer's house. After Tanner's dressings were changed, they heard a call from the trading post yard.

LeBlanc helped his injured friend to the door, Tanner looking gaunt and tired, his arm in a sling. Before him, hands tightly bound, stood Red Morning Sky. She looked at him, then hung her head.

"My daughters—tell me where they are," demanded Tanner.

The woman stood mute.

"John," said M'Gillevray, "both daughters are safe and well. My housekeeper has taken them to the chapel. They will be washed, fed, and cared for until you call for them." He turned to the other men. "Messers Grant and Stewart, it appears this woman duped the ruthless savage, Ome-zhuh-gwut-oons, into attempting the slaughter of Mister Tanner. I recommend we minister to this vile woman the same as we would any assassin. What say you?"

"And what might be the consequence of her treachery?" asked Stewart.

"The customary punishment, sir. Subsequent to a fair hearing, the prisoner will be found guilty, then beaten to death or hanged, whichever Mister Tanner prefers."

"No," said Tanner. "Though I wish to never again lay eyes on this wicked wasp, the fact remains that she is mother to my children. I ask only that you put her out with nothing. Send her on her way into the forest with only her guilt and shame to comfort her. Gentlemen, should you choose to honor my wish, I am confident she will never again cross my path."

Grant looked at M'Gillevray, then Stewart.

"Agreed?" asked Grant.

"Agreed," replied Stewart.

M'Gillevray hesitated. "Gentlemen, I prefer she face her maker now and we be done with it. However, I shall, with reluctance, defer to Tanner's remedy." He turned to the woman's captors. "Remove this woman."

John Tanner watched as the two men led his wife away. As they did, she looked over her shoulder at him. Tanner turned away that she not see the tears welling in his eyes or know the heaviness of his heart.

Chapter 23
So It Shall Be

John Tanner spent the next twenty-eight days on his cot convalescing from his wounds. Though he'd removed the musket ball from his chest five weeks earlier, it had fractured his ribs and breastbone, making each breath painful. The same ball also shattered his right forearm. In spite of a makeshift bandage and the natural medicines gathered by his daughters, the wound remained open and, day after day, bits of shattered bone emerged. One morning, while changing the dressing, he saw something other than bone protruding. Tanner winced as he pulled a five-inch-long object, finger-thick and green in color, from his wound. His daughters washed the wound, applied clean rags, and wrapped his arm.

"Father, this is the magic of Ome-zhuh-gwut-oons, said his eldest. "He talked of this. He told us he bored holes in both musket balls and threaded his black medicine, a strand of deer sinew, through both. He put more of his medicines on them before he loaded his rifle. Ome-zhuh-gwut-oons knew this might stay in you even if the lead balls shot through."

Tanner shook his head. "So, this is why my arm has not healed. Even now he tries to kill me. The coward Ome-zhuh-gwut-oons knew this would slowly poison me if his unsure aim did not. Daughter, did your mother know of this medicine?"

"She knew."

"And even after she was captured, she said nothing? Perhaps M'Gillevray was right. Perhaps she should have been sent to the next life."

"Father, when we learned Ome-zhuh-gwut-oons had not killed you, our hearts were made light. You know this. But know, too, that we love our mother."

"Your love for her saved her life."

"After her heartless, murderous plotting, your mother knows to not let me cast eyes upon her. And should she come here, Simon M'Gillevray would certainly see her swing.

"Father, this is why we must leave. We must find her and know she is safe and well. When we learn this, we will return."

Tanner motioned for his pipe. His youngest stuffed it with tobacco and lit it for him, drawing in a deep breath of the smoke. Tanner puffed on the pipe, then said, "Daughters, your desire to see your mother is perplexing. You watched her cast her clever wiles on young Ome-zhuh-gwut-oons . You saw how she planned my death, how she plotted even against you. You know now that she hid her dark motives from you and from me. Now you wish to help her? She sways you like no other, wins over your hearts that she may induce you to deny me your company. Now you long to find her? Nay, I cannot grasp any wisdom in this."

"Father, as confounding to us as her deceitful devices have been, and as much as we honor and adore you, Red Morning Sky remains our mother. We need to know she is safe and well."

"Daughters, travel here is not wise for young women. Every bend in the trail, every rock in the river might conceal danger. The Sioux walk these woods as often as the Ojibwe. You would make fine slaves for them. No, you must not leave."

"But, our mother …"

"Your mother has wiles. She will find men to care for her. Those who do not, she will abandon along the trail, though I doubt they will carry in their chest the extra weight of a musket ball. No, daughters, you will stay here among friends who provide for us."

"Father, we must go."

Tanner drew on his pipe, then blew smoke rings into the air. "Do you remember how once you so enjoyed seeing the rings of smoke come from my pipe? Oh, how happy we were with such simple things." He blew another smoke ring. "Do your minds drift back to days when you, your brother, your mother, and I were like one? I often do. My daughters, hold fast to those memories, for all things too soon change. The moon and the stars wait not. Visions you carry in your heart are yours alone. So, too, your memories. Do not hurry to find your mother. You will again cross paths, I know. I will not forbid this. However, now is not the time. Should you go now, then suddenly find yourselves in a bear trap, how could I, a man suffering so, come rescue you? Tell me. No, my daughters, you must remain with me until I become strong enough to protect you once again. I have decided. So it shall be."

Chapter 24
Major Long's Offer

John Tanner woke to the voice of his friend, Simon M'Gillevray.

"Rise, Mister Tanner. You have a guest, sir."

Tanner sat up. "Could it be the boy with fresh, loose straw for my mattress, Simon? This ragbag I lie upon day and night feels as though it's been trodden by a thousand fat buffalo."

"Bah!" snapped Simon. "These are not the words of a man who prefers sleeping on bare earth to a Boston featherbed. John Tanner, meet Major Stephen Long, passing through by way of his return from a western expedition."

"Good day, Mister Tanner," Long said. "M'Gillevray, here, tells me you've suffered some trouble."

Tanner glared at the uniformed Army officer. "I suffer only from choosing a deceitful wife. A condition shouldered by many others, Major."

Simon laughed. "Major Long, trust me when I say that Tanner's disposition is not always as such. Often, it is far, far worse."

"Mister Tanner, I dare say you have every reason to grouse, your arm damaged as it is. However, Simon tells me you are nearly fit to travel. If such is the case, I welcome you to accompany me to the Sault and beyond."

"The Sault?"

"If that be your wish, sir."

Forgetting his injuries, Tanner sprang to his feet, then winced, saying, "Major, your offer stirs me from beak to tail feathers. And, though I will miss the joy of hearing my friend Simon's never-ending yarn-spinning, I accept."

"My men make camp as we speak. Two days hence, we will break at dawn to depart for Fort William. Then we press south and east to La Pointe on the Isle called Madeline where we again encamp. You know La Pointe, sir?"

"Quite well, Major. I have rested there often on my travels."

"At dawn, my men paddle from La Pointe. By way of the Keweenaw, we cross to the east, and another camp. Next day, we skirt the southernmost shore of Superior for the post at Sault de Ste. Marie, a two-day's paddle, weather and fatigue notwithstanding. At the Sault, we restore our bodies and supplies. Your final leg, sir, will take you a day south to Fort Mackinac where you may then hang your coat and hat."

"And my two daughters? May they trail behind by my small canoe, Major?"

"Trail they may, Mister Tanner."

"Simon, might you ask them to come here? I must advise them."

"I will. John, I will miss your presence here."

"Miss my presence? I have been nay but a burden to you Simon. I should think my departure a gift. Your ears will no longer be filled with my grousing and mine with your stories."

"True, John. But then, I wonder to whom I shall spin my yarns and offer my far-fetched recollections, not knowing others quite as gullible."

Exhaling a laugh that turned to a cough, Tanner dropped onto his cot again. "Gentlemen, this news dizzies me. I will take my rest, if you please."

"Mister Tanner," said Long, "are you certain you are up to this travel? As well you know, it is a most rigorous trip."

"My wounds have improved these last few weeks, Major. Should I need assistance, my daughters will be at my side."

"Our expedition surgeon, Doctor James, will assist you as well."

"Major Long, you may have every confidence that I shall endure."

"Then it's done," said Simon. "John, I will summon your daughters directly."

Two hours passed. The anticipation of his return to the Sault and Fort Mackinac kept John Tanner awake. He wrapped, unwrapped, then wrapped again his few belongings, stuffing each oilcloth-covered package in his pack. When he finished, a tattered book of poems entertained him until someone knocked a loud knock.

"No need to break it down," shouted Tanner.

M'Gillevray entered, saying, "John, I spoke with your daughters who told me they would come to you. However, I fear, I was duped for I am now told by the women in the chapel that both your daughters have deserted you. They stole away into the woods that they not suffer a journey to Michigan."

"My daughters are gone?"

"John, would that they could, I know they'd wish you a safe voyage."

"Gone, you say?"

"They are young. Perhaps they do not see matters as you and I might. I am certain they will do fine. My friend, you should go with Major Long. I will send my son to find your daughters. I will make certain they are safe, whether back here or at their next abode. Meanwhile, John, tell me what I can do to assist you prior to your departure."

"Only this. In my absence, please watch over my daughters."

"As they are my own, John. This I pledge."

"Simon, my friend, since the day I appeared on your doorstep, bloodied and in need of rest, you stood by. You befriended me and aided me in all ways. Now, you continue to assist, even in my absence, knowing I cannot reward you. Simon, you are a true friend. I will miss your company."

"And I yours, John."

Tanner sat in the bottom of the twelve-man birch canoe cradling his arm. He stared at the dark, overcast sky, watching treetops float by as the paddlers pressed up the Rainy River. Between him and the stout, spruce ribs of the birch canoe lay a straw mattress, a departure gift from his friend, Simon M'Gillevray.

In spite of the fresh straw in the mattress and the cushion of water below the canoe, each bump from a submerged rock and every rattle across a whitewater rapids caused Tanner great pain, pain he endured with no verbal complaint. His appearance, however, betrayed him, revealing his torment. When Major Long's party put in for their first pipe, Tanner could scarcely walk from boat to shore.

"Mister Tanner, let me help," offered the Surgeon. "You look a fright, sir."

"Perhaps, Doctor James, I was too hasty in my desire to return to Mackinac, too eager for the medical care I need. My pain is more than I expected."

"We are but two hours into this leg of our voyage. It is not too late. I am certain the major could have a man return you to the care of the North West Company."

"I'd say yes, Doctor, but there I would receive neither doctoring nor medicines. I fear the worst might happen with my arm. I am a hunter and guide by trade and have no other. One arm will not do. No, Doctor, I will ride out the journey."

"Sir, I say again, it is not too late for you to return to Rainy Lake."

Tanner sat, grimacing. "Ask again after one more pipe, Doctor James. If, by the next wayside respite, I feel I cannot endure, I will succumb to your suggestion and return to Fort Frances where I will leave my well being to chance."

"One more pipe it is, Mister Tanner."

As they prepared to embark on the next leg, rain fell, quickly becoming a downpour. The men scrambled into their boats, pulling oilcloths from their packs. They sat in the rain, draped with dark, wet shrouds, waiting it out. After the cloudburst subsided, they pulled their huge canoes onto shore. Ten men to a side, they tipped them up, water washing over the gunwales.

Tanner stood by, trying to shake some water from his soaked mattress with one arm. His moccasins wet, he slipped, falling on his injured arm. He rolled on his side, suppressing a scream.

Both Major Long and Doctor James saw Tanner fall and the torture in his eyes. "Mister Tanner," said James, "I know well your heart wants to press on. Clearly though, the rest of you is not fit for this journey."

"Tanner, I fear that you will not make it to Fort William and I may well be forced to set you off somewhere. Rather than risk slowing the progress of my men and further danger to you, I must insist, with deepest regret, that you return to the North West Company."

"So be it, Major," replied Tanner. "I thank you for trying."

John Tanner did not speak on his return trip to Fort Frances. He collapsed on his bed and slept into the midday before Simon M'Gillevray knocked.

"John, I fear this may be the last dinner I will bring you. Seems there has been some talk among the officers regarding your allegiance to Hudson's Bay Company. They were pleased you had left. Now, upon your return, they have decided you should be turned out, that perhaps you should appeal to Hudson's Bay for your room and board."

"My allegiance to Hudson's Bay? Simon, I have no such allegiance."

"Nevertheless, in spite of my ardent objection, I've been told you are to be sent away. John, I regret I have neither power nor position to override. I am under orders to cast you out by the time the sun sets."

"My daughters—do we know where they are that they can help me?"

"No word, I am afraid."

"Do you have a man who might help me across the river?"

"I can find a good fellow."

"Then, fetch my hat and help me to the door. I am off to speak with John Astor's men. Perhaps they will see me through this inconvenience."

John Tanner left the North West Company post and crossed to the United States side of the border. He passed through the American Fur Company gates, bound for the quarters of the post superintendent, Major George Davenport.

"I have heard of your plight, Mister Tanner. As much as I would like to help you, I cannot."

"Major, I am in dire need of your mercy. You know well that I came to the aid of your company in the struggles against the Nor'Westers. Why, John Astor himself approved my employment to hunt buffalo and elk for your winter stores. Why, then, can you not help me in my time of need?"

"Mister Tanner, I've no doubt you deserve our kindness. However, we are a business, not a charity. Shall I let slip our competition with Nor'West? Astor would have my hide if I gave you as much as a handful of beans."

"Astor be damned. Tell me, Davenport, how would it interfere with your commerce should you give me a place to sleep—even as much as a space in your livery?"

"Here's your answer, woodsman. There is not one Indian within a hundred miles who does not know you have been shot and left for dead by one of their own. According to their customs, you are now bound to avenge yourself. If it be learned that you are housed at the American Fur Company house, few Indians would trade to us their peltries."

"I have pledged no vengeance for what Ome-zhuh-gwut-oons has done. They are my brothers. I would not harm even one. Nor could I."

"Be that as it may, Tanner, their furs will cross the river to the Nor'West Company. I cannot risk that."

"Mister Davenport, your decision, like that of the Nor'Westers, will leave me to fend for myself in the wilds with no provisions. Fall and winter approach, sir. In short, your words herald my death for I am not fit to survive winter by my own means. Am I doomed to suffer and die by your decision?"

"Please believe how dreadfully sorry I am, Mister Tanner."

"Major, not many years ago I was hired to secure meat for men and women encamped along the Red River that they not starve. And starve they would, had I not killed four fat buffalo cows for them. Other American Fur Company men did nothing for them, falling back here for their own safety. My loyalty remained with this company and I risked all, nearly starving myself, yet saved the people in that camp."

"I know the story well, sir. Still ..."

Now angry, Tanner stared at the plump post superintendent. "I regret, Davenport, that I cannot accept your decision. Either you accommodate me, or I will spend the balance of my days outside your front gate. There, I will wither and die, sir. However, until I do, no man will cross into this trading post lest he hear my tale. Furthermore, be certain I will send every red man carrying peltries or other goods across the river to your competition."

"For that, sir, I could have you shot."

"Yes, you could. But tell me, Davenport, where would that put you? You, a young man on the rise in the house of John Astor and his American Fur Company. Dear sir, how do you suppose John Astor might take the news that you, little more than a mere clerk in a fat man's uniform, posted here in the wilderness, has signaled my doom? Me, the White Indian—the man who, by dark of night, took, secured, and held Fort Douglas? Stole it away for Lord Selkirk, himself? Me, the man who brought peace between the Sioux and the Ojibwe so all the fur companies could prosper in safety? How might Astor feel, knowing this wounded hunter, the man who saved his camp from starving, the man who secured his American Fur Company's position in the fur trade business all along the border ..."

"Enough, Tanner. Enough. Suffer me no longer. I will provide you a stout tent with stove, cot, and blankets. Pitch it where you will, as long as it is not within sight of my gate. My men will bring you firewood and water that you not need fetch these. This, John Tanner, is all I can do."

"A mattress for the cot, Major. One well stuffed with fresh straw."

"Not too much to ask. I will see to this last request."

"Am I expected to cut poles and erect the tent with only one arm?"

"Hmm. I suppose I could send a man to help with that. No more, mind you."

"What do you suppose I shall eat, Davenport? You can see I am unable to hunt or trap in my present circumstance."

"Our provisions are short. Seek your vitals elsewhere."

"The North West Company will not assist me. Hmm. The Ojibwes, perhaps—yes. I shall make mention you steered me their way."

"No, no, please. Not the Indians. Perhaps our pantry can accommodate after all, at least until my hunters arrive with game from the fall hunt. Until then, the Rainy River teems with fish, as you know. Perhaps you can cajole someone to spear the occasional sturgeon for your table, much as you've wheedled me to supply you better than I have some of my own trappers."

"Major, although you drive a hard bargain, I will accept your offer. I shall keep my name distant from that of the American Fur Company, so neither to spoil your commerce nor your sleep. Please have your man bring the tent and other trappings outside the gate."

"He will be there shortly."

"Oh, Davenport, be so kind as to ask him to bring a tin pot and a pound of tea. That should hold me for a while. Good day, sir."

"Tea?"

"English tea, if you please."

"Very well. English tea and teapot. Yes. Now, please! Good day!"

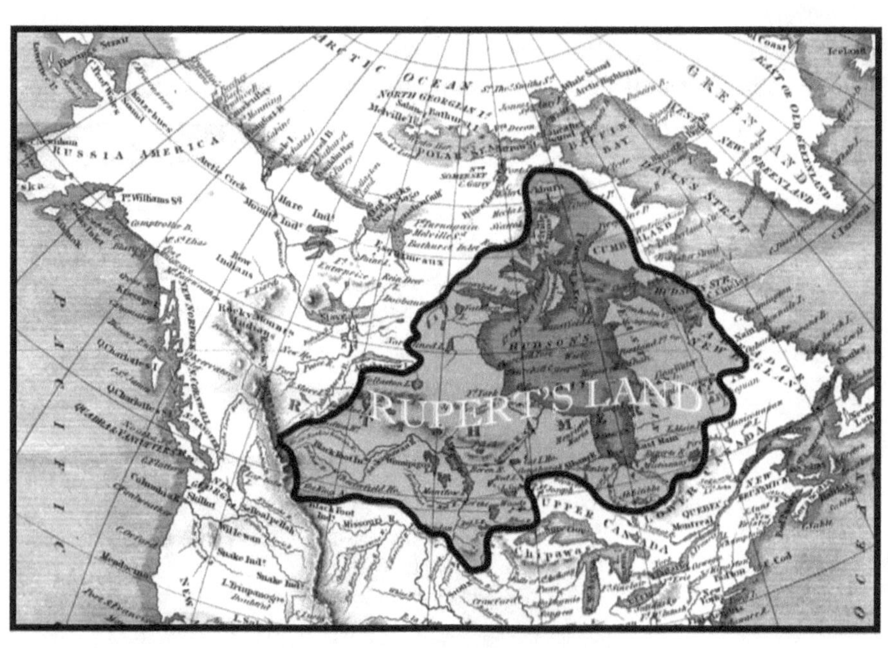

RUPERT'S LAND
HUDSON'S
ARCTIC OCEAN
RUSSIAN AMERICA
GREENLAND
BAFFIN BAY
NEW GREENLAND
PACIFIC OCEAN
UPPER CANADA
QUEBEC

John Tanner chose to make his camp on the British side, across the river from the American Fur Company. Here, he could call upon an acquaintance, a Doctor McLaughlin. In addition to harboring very basic medical knowledge, the doctor was a man with influence in the North West Company—and a fair barber. Although aware that the success of his post in the winter's trade would be injured by Tanner tenting nearby, McLaughlin consented. Occasionally, he brought Tanner a bottle of wine and a loaf of freshly baked bread in exchange for no more than friendly conversation.

By early winter, Tanner's wounds had healed well enough that he could load, lift, and fire his musket, using his left hand. After some practice, he found himself able to shoot accurately, bringing home several rabbits, a raccoon, and a wildcat. The hides went to the good doctor for a liberal amount in trade.

Then, on New Year's Day, Doctor McLaughlin received word Tanner needed help after slipping on ice and falling. His fragile right arm broke again as did his collar bone. He struggled to return to his tent and collapsed in pain outside. The doctor helped him to his cot, administered several drams of whisky, and inspected the wounds.

"John, though painful, your collar bone will heal well before spring. Your forearm is another matter. Thus far, you have tended to your injuries yourself with only fair success. If you consent, I will apply my skills from here on in."

"I managed before. I shall manage again."

"I have no doubt you can manage, my friend. The question, however, is not whether you can manage, it is how your arm will serve you for the rest of your days. This morning, your arm looked to be as crooked as a king's tax collector. The very fact that it now lies broken again may be a godsend, for now I will straighten it, then apply splints. Let me do this and you will no longer suffer the mockery of the children playing in the town square, John."

"Bah! Think you that I care a fig about children mocking me?"

"The reward, John, would be a straight and strong arm, an arm able to support a musket. By way of it shall come the capacity to shoot straight, spear a fish, lift a canoe—tasks lost to you—tasks I can restore, but only on your say-so."

"Then so I say, Doctor McLaughlin."

The doctor poured more whisky, gave Tanner a rag to bite and, with both hands on his right arm, twisted and pulled, straightening the warped limb. Tears flowed from Tanner's eyes though he made not the slightest whimper. The doctor held the arm with one hand, using the other to wrap it with a cotton bandage. He reached in his bag, pulling out two flat wooden paddles, each a quarter-inch thick and the length and breadth of Tanner's forearm. More cotton bandage secured the splints and bound the wound.

"John, I will fashion a new sling for you. Not for your neck, mind you. We will hang this from the tent pole that your arm may remain well above you while you rest. This will help quell the incessant throb of pain a bit. I have some herbs here for you to suck on when the pain keeps you awake. No more than one at a time, though, and not with whisky, rum, or wine or you will lose all your senses."

"One-by-one it is, Doctor. Say, shall I ever play the fiddle again?"

"I see no reason you will not, once healed."

"Then, dear doctor, you truly work miracles, for I've never even held a fiddle, much less attempted to play."

"I see the whisky has distracted you from your discomfort. Another dram, my friend?"

"Only if you lift one with me, Doctor."

"John Tanner, it would be my pleasure."

With the American Fur Company supplying buffalo meat, grains, and other staples from one side of the river, and Doctor McLaughlin providing bread, sausage, and spirits from the British side, John Tanner slowly recovered from his injuries. Pension funds in arrears from his days with Lord Selkirk arrived by a courier in March, along with a letter of appreciation from Thomas Douglas, the Fifth Earl of Selkirk himself. Tanner placed it with the letters from Governors Clark and Cass, and wrapped them in oilcloth for safekeeping.

By the time the snow left the ground and the backcountry traders arrived from their wintering grounds, Tanner's injuries had healed well enough to allow him time outdoors again. A trap line occupied his days, plans to return to Mackinac his evenings. He sought out his daughters, locating them in a nearby village. There, by choice, they would remain at least until their father's next sojourn to Rainy Lake.

Three weeks later, he learned a canoe bearing six Frenchmen and eight hundred beaver skins had room for him, his pack, and his musket. In return, they asked only that he translate for them upon meeting the Ojibwe, Sioux, and Englishmen they expected to encounter. Tanner agreed. The journey to Fort William and Fond du Lac went without event. The party pressed on to La Pointe, then eastward along the south shore, beyond the Keweenaw, and soon to Sault Ste. Marie.

Chapter 27
Doctor Edwin James

John Tanner arrived at the Sault on a rainy June morning. Following the main road, he soon walked up to his cabin door. Returning empty-handed after a year's absence, he lifted the latch and stepped inside.

"Who is it?" came a strange voice. "Who's there?"

"The tenant of this house."

"Tenant?"

"Yes, tenant. And who are you?"

"Doctor Edwin James, the rightful occupant of this cabin."

"James? The surgeon who accompanied Major Long on his expedition to the Rocky Mountains?"

"Tanner? John Tanner, is that you?"

"It is, Doctor."

"I see you've recouped. Considering the condition in which I last saw you, I did not think we would again cross paths."

"Only the generosity of several friends made my recovery possible."

"Your arm, does it function well?"

"Well as can be expected. Painful at times, though it is still mending. And, how is it, Doctor, that you now live in my house?"

"I rent this from the new proprietor, Sheriff James Schoolcraft, brother to Henry. He purchased this land last fall after your wife and children were turned out."

"I should have expected as much. I was delayed a year while tending to my health. Can you tell me where I might find my family?"

"The mission took them in. Your wife now works there in exchange for room and board."

"And my possessions?"

"All sold."

"Sold?"

"In order to settle your debts, I believe."

"By James Schoolcraft?"

"Yes. By both the sheriff and the church when your kin were turned out. You may wish to ask Reverend Bingham. I believe the money was needed for your children's schooling and keep."

Tanner spent little time traveling the final leg to Mackinac Island. He pounded on the door to Reverend Bingham's study. Bingham soon appeared.

"Well, John Tanner! I see you finally chose to return. Have you tired of your wanderings, my son?"

"I am here to retrieve my family."

"I fear that is not possible, Mister Tanner. You see, Therezia, has been baptized a Christian. She disavowed her Indian marriage. She is no longer your wife."

"Bah! I will thank you to deliver my wife, children, and the remains of my possessions at once."

"Did you not hear me? You no longer have a wife. She now resides here at the mission as my employee. Your children will remain here with her. As for your few goods, they were sold off to pay some of your debts. You will receive a bill for what's left."

"You did this, Abel Bingham! You and the others here wanted my wife to remain—to work for you—a servant of the Church."

"She chose this life, John, as did your children, also now baptized as Christians. They desire to remain here with us."

"I wish to see Therezia and my children that I can hear from their mouths what life they prefer."

"My son, even if the Devil should make them proclaim a desire to go with you, I could not allow it. You see, John, their stay here has cost the mission quite a sum. Unless and until you are able to purchase their debt, they are indentured to me—to the Church."

"Indentured. I thought as much. Call them here at once. I command you!"

"Here, my son, we only recognize God's commands."

"Reverend, I once served you, translating your sermons for months on end with nary one request for a penny of pay. I translated three books of your Holy Bible into Ojibwe. Now you treat me as a stranger? You take my family? You turn me out like a buffalo herd shuns a sickly calf?"

"If you wish to continue your work on the Bible translations, I welcome it, my son. It will not result in a renewal of your Indian marriage arrangements with Therezia, nor a return to the sinful life you left. And your children will remain here, under my care and the watchful eyes of this mission."

"I wish to see my children."

"I regret they are not available for a visit at this time, my son."

"Reverend Bingham, the laws of this territory give me the right to determine where my children reside, as does your Bible."

"I am sorry if the church has disappointed you, my son."

"I leave now. But know that our conversation is not over. I will have my children."

Tanner returned to Sault Ste. Marie and sought out Henry Schoolcraft.

"Help you?" answered Schoolcraft. "After you all but deserted me two years past? I think not."

"First I suffer from being shot and nearly killed. Now, because of this attack on my life and the long recovery it caused me, I have lost my family and home. All here now seem to conspire against me, even you, the overseer of this region. I see little recourse than to enlist the help of a friend."

"What friend might you, a wayward woodsman have?"

"Governor Lewis Cass. You will recall he has assisted me before."

"Do what you will, Tanner."

"The governor and all others who hear my complaints will wonder why the great Henry Schoolcraft has not come to my defense, not helped with the rightful return of my children. Some will wonder what other plots and ploys might this family of Schoolcrafts have bubbling away in their porridge pot."

"Dare you threaten to besmirch the name of Schoolcraft? Threaten me, the literary explorer, statesman, and agent of the territorial government? Bear in mind that Lewis Cass is also a friend of mine and a fellow officer against the British in eighteen-twelve. 'Twas he who appointed me to this post."

"All the more reason he needs be made aware of your underhanded handling of affairs, your devious and scheming manipulations."

"Bah! None will take heed. You will become the laughing stock of the territory."

"I care not who laughs. I will have my family back with your help or without. The Governor knows me. I carry his letter and those of William Clark, Governor of Missouri Territory and Lord Thomas Douglas, Earl of Selkirk. When Lewis Cass hears of the abuses taking place in your office, he will have much to say." Tanner turned toward the door.

"Now, let us not be too hasty, John. I am certain we can find a solution satisfactory to one and all. I will sleep on this quandary. Come back in the morning for my answer. Perhaps ..."

"By morning I will be on my way to Detroit."

"Tanner, I warn you ..."

"Warn as you wish. I have been wronged and so, too, the people you pretend to represent. I dare say the governor will be interested to learn you have appointed your brother James as Clerk of Court, Register Probate, and Sheriff. With you conveniently situated as both Indian Agent and Territorial Judge and then deliberately ignoring my well-grounded grievances against the mission, well, I would care not to be in your place. Hellfire will rain from the heavens. Add to the stewpot your decision to deny me employment here in spite of his say-so. Why, when he learns of this injustice ..."

"All right! Enough!" shouted Schoolcraft. "I will intercede on your behalf. I have no love for Abel Bingham or his Baptist Mission. I abhor his stranglehold on the funds intended to civilize this territory. His spending is all for his own promotion and benefits little the settlers and Indians. I will send him a letter demanding discharge of all debts and encumbrances against you and deliver to you your family."

"And you will immediately reinstate me as interpreter at my previous wage if not more. It is only right."

Brow furrowed, Schoolcraft glared at Tanner. "Do not provoke me, John Tanner. Remember who you are dealing with."

"Housing allowance and meals as before."

"Humph. Would you also ask for a golden carriage? A dozen white horses? A driver? And a stable boy to tend the lot?"

"A fine idea. Instruct the post livery that I am to have use of a horse at my will. The carriage and driver you propose will not be necessary. However, I thank you for the offer." Tanner again turned toward the door, saying, "Henry Schoolcraft, you will not regret this bargain."

As soon as the door closed, Schoolcraft whispered to himself, "You will, John Tanner. I'll see to it."

Four days later, a letter arrived from Reverend Bingham.

"Mister John Tanner,

It is with heavy heart that I relinquish to your care your children, Martha, Marie, and James. I so do only because the laws governing Michigan Territory require it of me. However, as for Therezia, your former wife only by Indian custom, the choice to remain at the mission or reside with you are hers alone. She has informed me that she no longer wishes to abide by the Indian marital ways and will not be part of your household. You may call for your children tomorrow. May God be with them and with you.

Reverend Abel Bingham"

Chapter 28
A Book, Mister Tanner!

In spite of their complaints about leaving the Baptist mission school at Mackinac Island, John Tanner brought his three children to the Sault. Together, the Tanners constructed a birch lodge at the edge of town and resumed living what he referred to as his Chippewayan way of life.

The children attended classes at the Fort Brady school in Sault Ste. Marie while Tanner worked in an office within the post infirmary translating volumes of Michigan territorial law into Ojibwe and Ottawa languages. An Army scribe attempted to record each word as Tanner sounded them out. Progress was slow, the work tedious, tiresome, and often interrupted by patients waiting to see the physician, Edwin James.

Fascinated by his stories, Doctor James often invited Tanner to his home. One evening, following a dinner of roast duck, squash, and red wine, James listened to another adventure, then unveiled an idea.

"John, tell me, these accounts of your life, your abduction, your time with the Ottawa, Sioux, and Chippeway, your adventures with Selkirk, all the rest, have you ever known anyone to not be captivated by them?"

"Captivated? My ramblings?"

"Am I the only one who thinks your escapades are thrilling?"

"Those who hear me often ask for more. Lord Selkirk and both Governors Cass and Clark begged me to continue even when I grew too tired to speak."

"John, I have watched as you translate documents for Schoolcraft. I say it is time you translate for another."

"Another? I am satisfied working for Henry Schoolcraft, this in spite of my contempt for him and his brother. Who would you have me work for, if not Schoolcraft?"

"Yourself."

"Edwin, I fear the wine has muddled your brain."

"Think of it! The Travels and Tales of Shaw-shawwa na-baysay, the White Swallow."

"Mating loons make more sense than you make now."

"A book, Mister Tanner! John, deep in my heart I believe there are many others who would enjoy your stories. Why not let me write them down for you that others can share them. Once compiled, your stories could be presented to a publishing house back east. Many copies of your book could be printed and sold across the land."

"And, if no one agrees with you that my stories are worthy?"

"If you allow me, I have yet another idea."

"Another. Is it better than the first?"

"We divide your book in two. Part one is the story of the White Indian, Shaw-shawwa na-baysay—your adventures—your triumphs, if you will."

"And, part two?"

"Ah, John, part two. There is the key. Part two will all but guarantee your book will find its way into the pocket of every traveler, every clergyman, teacher, and military man west of the Cumberland Gap. Part two will be a guide to translating English words and phrases to the various tribal dialects and vice versa. No person venturing into Indian country or doing business in this land will be without a copy. Every scholar of language, American culture, and geography will want one. John, every schoolboy will beg his grandmother for your book. Think of it! A translation ... nay, an interpretation of Algonquin speech. It is sure to be a most desired item and bound to make us wealthy, wealthy men. Will you do this with me? Will you hazard to allow me to put your stories down in ink that the nation may benefit?"

"Am I then to become a book peddler, traveling village to village, begging for people to read my stories for a penny or two?"

"The publisher will arrange for your adventures to be spread far and wide. Perhaps even across the sea. Pennies will grow into dollars, dollars into a fortune, if we succeed. Will you do this?"

"Surely there are other books people can buy. I doubt my stories would be of interest."

"Oh, I disagree. Your adventures are wonderful. People are thrilled to read tales of the wilderness. Other writers have done quite well with such stories. James Fennimore Cooper and Nathanial Hawthorne come to mind. Even Henry Schoolcraft has books on the shelf."

"Schoolcraft?"

"He has published the chronicles he wrote while on his travels. Most eastern libraries and institutions now have his journals in their collections."

"Schoolcraft."

"Yes."

Tanner paused, sipping his wine. Then extended his hand. "I will, Doctor. But you must tell no one until it is finished and ready to travel. If Henry Schoolcraft learns of this ..."

"I agree. Save for you and me, no one must know. No one shall."

"When do we begin?"

Edwin James opened his writing desk, pulled the cork from the inkwell, and selected one of several pens. "When? What say you we begin this moment?" The Doctor pulled a sheet of paper from a drawer and dipped the pen tip in the ink, daubed it on a blotter, and spoke as he wrote. *A narrative of the captivity and adventures of John Tanner (Shaw-shawwa na-baysay) the White Indian known as Swallow, during thirty years residence among the Indians in the interior of North America.* He blotted the page and held it closer to the whale oil lamp. "We are on our way, my friend."

The collaborators finished the cover page of the manuscript and prepared a list of episodes and adventures they might include in the story of John's life. Work on the text began the next evening and carried on every evening for seven weeks.

Both men worked late into the night and, on occasion, until morning's first light. The memoir quickly grew. Night after night Tanner told his stories as the doctor recorded his words. Entry after entry filled page after page, their progress proving far better than Tanner's daytime translations of the territorial laws. The two men carried on until, one autumn evening, Edwin James wrote two simple words: *The End.* He pulled the cork from a bottle of wine, filled two tin cups, and shouted, "Shaw-shawwa na-baysay, on to part two!"

The second half of the book began with an explanation of feasts, fasts, dreams, and ceremonies and the importance of these to the Anishinabe culture. Next came a catalog of plants and animals found in Ojibwe country with the English translation of each entry. Tanner began with metik-goak, the trees. The doctor made scores of entries.

"Next heading will be weah-gush-koan, Doctor James."

"Please, John, call me Edwin. Now, what is meant by weah-gush-koan?"

"These are the many small plants."

Hundreds of grasses, herbs, and weeds filled column after column followed by Ah-wes-sie-ug, the animals.

Tanner listed as many as he could recall with James writing as fast as the pen and ink allowed. An hour later, Doctor James put the cork in the inkwell.

"You quit so early, Doctor. But I do not hear the Cha-ta-mei-met kwa calling."

"Mourning dove?"

"Yes. Very good. Mourning dove."

"We've made good progress tonight. But, John, I am tired to the bone. I fear I cannot write another word."

"Tomorrow, then?"

"Tomorrow it is!"

The next entries began the following evening with the doctor listing hundreds of insects and their translations, followed by a section on the fishes. Whenever possible, he added clarifying comments at the bottom of the page before blotting the ink and adding the page to the ever-growing stack.

Tanner's understanding of Ottawa, Ojibwe, and Cree totems came next. They followed this with an eight-page section on astronomy and the origins and interpretations of the stellar bodies and constellations. At the doctor's suggestion, the next section was a comparison of numbers in five Native dialects: Ojibwe, Ottawa, Dakota Sioux, and Algonquin. "This will help with trading," he told John. "Merchants need such instructions as they travel westward."

"If such be the case, we must present this in more than five dialects. I will offer what I know of the other tongues."

Tanner added Winnebago, Muskogee, Pottawattamie, Choktaw, and Shawnee. He recited the numbers for each as Doctor James scribbled away. With ten more pages added to the pile, the second section was finished.

Section three, Anishinabe culture, would be different. It would take more time to explain. They chose to do so with Native music and poetry. The pace slowed. Doctor James offered an idea.

"John, you must trust me here. Tell me your thoughts and I will do my best to compare your visions of Anishinabe culture to the cultural practices of the Europeans. After all, it will be descendents of Europeans who are most likely to carry your book in their pocket, will it not?"

"Write what you think best, Doctor. I'll not object as long as it is forthright and honest and reflects my beliefs."

"That, sir, is my goal. I'll have you singing like the miskoh-muh-kuk ke."

Tanner stared at the doctor. "I think you mean miskoh-be na-say, the cardinal. Unless you wish me to sing like a red toad."

James flipped through his pages. "Oh, yes. Kuk-ke is the toad, na-say, the bird. So many terms. So much to learn."

The section on Indian culture shifted from music and poetry to the use of images of animals, objects and signs as written language. The doctor described the pictographs, but found it difficult to clarify their meaning.

"Edwin, if we use the pictures to sing the songs, it will all come clear. I will show you. We will begin with songs of medicine for hunting." Tanner drew a deer showing its heart pierced by an arrow, then chanted, "Neen-go-te-naun ke-da-ne, ne-miz-zho-taun ke-da-ne, ah-wis-sie ke-da-he, ne-miz-zho-taun ke-da-ne. This means, 'I will shoot at your heart. I hit your heart, oh animal, your heart, I hit your heart.' Edwin, this is mere boasting by the hunter. He is wishing in his song that this will all come true in the next hunt. The song is sung with much gesture and grimace of sadness for the animal."

"Good, good," said Doctor James. "Go on, give me another."

Next, Tanner drew a bear lying on its back. "Makwaa-yah-na hah-che-maun-duk ha-yo-ta-he. I hunt a bear, his heart I take."

"What does it mean?"

"These words show respect for the bear, his heart, his blood. It also tells us the hunter understands the great sacrifice of the makwaa that must give his life so the hunter's family will not starve."

"Wonderful, John. More!"

"I danced and sang these Cree war songs before battles with the Sioux. These songs kept me safe." With his finger, Tanner traced an image in the air between them. "Kagsa-ween mowwie-may zeekaa. It means 'Do not mourn, my women, for me who is about to die.'"

"Rather pessimistic, don't you think?" asked the doctor as he sketched the image onto his page. "Have you a rosy thought to go with it?"

"Hah-me-ge-neen a-na-ne-mo-e-yahn a-beech e-nin-neeng a-na-ne-mo-kwain ah-me-ge-neen a-na-ne-mo-e-yan," chanted Tanner.

"And this means ...?"

"If any man is a great warrior, I think myself as great a warrior."

"Yes, John! That's what we need. Substance such as this will spark the fire of the reader. More, John!"

Tanner's songs and chants, along with their corresponding images, filled forty-eight pages. He devoted the next ten to a discussion of the Anishinabe language. In addition to the origin of certain words, they explained such things as accentuation of syllables, long and short vowel sounds, and verb conjugation. Though not certain of the precison of the writing, Tanner and James knew their effort far exceeded any previous attempts at such a book.

"Be sure, Doctor, that you do not make me sound the fool.

"Not to worry, Mister Tanner. Any future scholar wishing to dispute the opinions of the author and his scribe are welcome to do so. In fact, such inquiries are likely to spread the word about the book and encourage sales."

"Yes, sales would be good. But accuracy is utmost. I would rather be known as an author poor in the pocket than one poor in the mind."

The writing continued with a seven-page comparison of words and phrases in the dialects of the Ottawa and the Menomonee.

"Why only these two?" asked Doctor James.

"The language of the Ottawa, Ojibwa, Cree, and Pottawatomie is similar. It is the same with tribes to the south. Many speak much like the Menomonee. Each page should have three columns with the English words in the third. This, my friend, will be understood by the greatest number."

An English to Ojibwe section followed, listing words and phrases in alphabetical order and the Ojibwe translation. And valuable to those who wished to communicate with almost any Indian in the Upper Midwest. By flipping to the back of the book, a conversation could be quickly initiated.

Doctor James laid his pen on the desk and blotted the last page of the section. "John, I believe we have reached the end."

"No. Not the end."

"What could be left? Have we not exhausted every avenue?"

"Since coming here, I have spent much time at the mission. I have seen the light in the eyes of those who first hear the words from your Bible. Plunge your pen tip, Doctor. There is more to write."

James pulled another leaf from his desk, dipped his pen, and listened.

"Ko-se-naun, (Our Father,)" he began, "o-wa-nain, (who,) ish-pe-ming ain-daut, (liveth above,) mah-no-ti esh-she-wa-but, (what you wish to be done,) wah-e-she wa-be-to-e-yun. (let it be done.) Kaw-taw-paw-pish zhin-dah-zeem. (Let us not play with thy name.) Mah-no-be-zhe nah-zhe-yun nah-gah-muk sa-ne-guk. (Let thy great power come.) Me-zhe-shin-naung ka-me-je-yaun noong-goom ge-zhe-gut, (give us our food this day,) me-zhe-shin-naung o-ma-ze-naw-o-mon-aung, (forgive our debts,) a-zhe-ko-te-bah-mah-tink. (We will forgive our debtors.)" Tanner waited for Edwin to write. "Are you with me Edwin?"

"Truly amazing words, no matter the language. You are right, this needs to be in your book. Please, John, continue."

"Ka-go e-zhe-wizh-zhis, zhe-kaun-gain mi-ah-nah-tuk. (Do not lead us into bad things.) Kun-no-wa-no mish-she-naung mi-ah-nah-tuk. (Keep us from bad things.) Naw-gau-ne-zit ta-ba-ne-mut, (Power belongs to thee,) gia mash-kaw-e-zeet, (and strength,) kau-gin-neek. (forever.)"

"Wonderful!" The doctor reached for his Bible. What say you we give them some more? I will simply read book, chapter, and verse, you give the interpretation, and I will write."

"How large is our book to be?"

"Hmm. Yes. Perhaps we should give them a mere taste, then direct them to seek more from the church." He opened the book. "Give them Genesis 1."

Tanner recited it from memory. "Wi-azh-kut Man-e-do wa-zhe-toan mahn-dun Ge-zhik gia ak-ke."

"Excellent! Verse two?"

"Gia pa-bunk ak-ke at-tah go-bun gia kah-ga-go at-ta-sin o-go-bun, gia tib-be-kut o-kit-te-beeg, gia man-e-do o-pug-git-to nah-mo-win o-mam-mah-je-mug-gut o-kit-te-beeg."

"John, I had no idea you were a scholar of the Bible. Your father would be proud."

"Which father?"

"Forgive me. Reverend John Tanner, your birth father."

"He despised all red men. He would not be pleased."

"Perhaps you could have changed his opinion."

"Perhaps. Perhaps not. Though I was very young, I remember that he was very stubborn. It is a gift he gave me for I, too, am hard in the head."

"I believe you mean hard-headed, John."

"Yes. Hard in the head."

On they wrote, Tanner listing all thirty-one verses. Below the last, Doctor James took pleasure in adding the last two words in part two, "The End."

"We've done it!" he exclaimed, blotting the final page. Your manuscript is ready for the publisher to turn it from a rough stone to a polished gem."

"And how do we find this publisher?"

"New York. That's where you will venture first. I know a fellow who is sure to see its value. If not, there are other publishing houses there. I shall send letters ahead. You will need to leave at your first opportunity."

"Henry Schoolcraft will not be amused."

"Yet, you must go. Surely, being a published author, he will understand."

"I wonder if he is too proud, too arrogant to allow me to pursue this. Me, a savage in his view. Lacking his brand of culture. Unable to read. Unable to write little more than my name. I must change that."

"I'll help you learn, John—upon your return from New York City."

Chapter 29
A Book, Mister Tanner?

The next morning, John Tanner crossed the Fort Brady parade grounds to the home of Henry Schoolcraft and rapped the brass door knocker against the plate.

"Tanner! Come in. Come in. How fortuitous you should call. I have news for you."

"News? For me?"

"Good news, I must add. Come, have a chair." The two men entered Schoolcraft's office.

"John, after a decade of trying, I may soon receive approval to venture westward on a journey of exploration and good will. It seems the War Department is paying heed to my warnings about the fighting betwixt Sioux and Ojibwe. I hope to win over many of the tribes along the Mississippi and northward into Prince Rupert's Land."

"The Red River Valley?"

"And beyond. Far beyond. I feel Washington will soon agree with me that we must befriend the aboriginal people. In the event of invasion by Britain, the Army needs the tribes to serve as our allies."

"Better they be allies than foes."

"We shall also endeavor to inoculate the savages against small pox."

"Savages?"

"Yes. Well, the Indians."

"They will be suspicious of your doctor's attempt to shine brighter than theirs."

"Nevertheless, my expedition, though it may be a year hence will be twenty-seven strong and you will act as my interpreter and guide."

"Me? I hardly think so. My work is here—interpreting for the post by day and translating the scriptures for Reverend Bingham each evening."

"Tanner, you test my patience. I find you lacking respect and disagreeable. Were your skills on the trail not so valuable, I would not offer this. Think this over carefully, Mister. Do not be so foolish to deny me. Now, tell me what brought you here."

"I need to tend to some business. I wish a furlough."

"How long a furlough? A day? A week?"

"Perhaps two months, maybe three."

"What? Never! My Lord! What business might you have that would take you away so long?"

"Personal business."

"In that case, furlough denied. Why should I extend you the courtesy of a furlough if you will not tell me the nature of your business?"

"I am in need of a publisher for my book."

"What? A book, Mister Tanner?"

"A manuscript now. A book soon."

"You? Preposterous! You have no such abilities, no skills, no …"

"When published, its pages will number four-hundred and twenty."

"Four-hundred and twenty? Humph. And the content of this … book?"

"My life among the Ottawa and Ojibwe."

"Fancy that. John Tanner, an illiterate savage writing a book that no one shall read."

"Doctor James would disagree. He served as my scribe."

"Edwin James served you?"

"I believe the term he used is collaborated. My manuscript is finished. I now need a furlough."

"And I need you here. Furlough denied."

"I am not one of your military subordinates. I will leave with or without your approval."

"I shan't put up with this. Do as you will, but know you, John Tanner, this time you will have no employment upon your return."

"So be it, Henry Schoolcraft. So be it."

Tanner booked passage on the next schooner bound for the east. They sailed down Lake Huron to the Port of Detroit where the vessel put in for an exchange of cargo. While they did, he hiked to the Ottawa village beyond the rush of the city and approached an old woman sitting outside a small cabin.

"Boozhoo, old mother. Can you tell me if you know Kish-kau-ko?"

"I had a dream someone would ask me this today. My dreams are seldom wrong."

"Then you know this Kish-kau-ko?"

"The Shawnee dog that casts shadows on all of us?" she asked as she stitched a sleeve onto a buckskin shirt. "Do not mention his name here. It is madji mushkeeki. Bad medicine."

"Nokomis, what can you tell me of him?

"He once stayed in this village. He is gone. Six, seven, eight years. I do not know."

"Gone?"

"Long Knives took his breath away."

"What did he …?"

"The Jesuits could not wash out his hatred, could not rid him of his evil spirits. Many candles they burned for him. No good. He killed some Whites, stole their money and horses. We no longer speak his name," she said with a sigh. "You must not either."

"Then he is dead?"

"Hanged from the White Man's gallows."

"I knew him long ago. He and his father stole me from my white family when I was a small boy. On my head I still bear the scar where he struck me with his tomahawk. They sold me to Net-no-kwa, chief of the Ottawas. She offered him blankets, tobacco, ten gallons of whisky."

"I know of Net-no-kwa. A great leader of our people. Fair-minded. Evenhanded. Respected still." She studied Tanner, then asked, "What is your name?"

"Shaw-shawwa na-baysay."

The old woman jumped to her feet, dropping the shirt and her needle. She stepped back. "Are you a spirit? Have you come for me? I have had this dream often," she said, half-crying. "Do I now set out for the next life without my grandchildren to see me away? You are unfair to take an old woman without first letting her see her …"

"Nokomis! Your dreams deceive you. I am not here for you. I am not a spirit."

The woman sat, taking up her stitching again. "My dreams trick me. Are you sure you are not dead?"

"Why would you think me dead?"

"Shaw-shawwa na-baysay is your name?"

"It is one of my names."

"I have heard this name often. Shaw-shawwa na-baysay waa-bishki. Many stories are told of White Swallow. One story tells how you died at Rainy River. Shot. Left for the aandags. Are you certain you are not a spirit returned to take this old woman to the next life?"

"Fear me not, old woman. Though I have come close many times, I am not yet dead. Each time Death came, Wenebojo brushed him aside. Wenebojo is strong in me."

"Perhaps Gitchee Manitou has a purpose for Shaw-shawwa na-baysay waabishke. Perhaps there is somewhere you must go, something you must do before you pass. I have seen this in my dreams."

Tanner boarded the schooner with the words of the old woman fresh in his mind. He watched the City of Detroit fade into the distant mist as the ship descended the Detroit River toward Lake Erie. The captain sailed east to New York's Port of Buffalo where Tanner again disembarked, his sea bag over his shoulder.

He immediately booked passage on one of the many canal boats serving the new Erie Canal. A teamster walked the towpath on the north side of the canal, his team hitched to the sixty-foot, twenty-passenger packet boat. The horses towed the canal boat from lock to lock. Day and night, the boat floated the canal toward the Hudson, locking through the eighty-three locks. The three-hundred-sixty-three mile trip took Tanner ten days and cost him ten dollars, but saved him twenty days of overland travel.

Upon reaching the Hudson River in Albany, he boarded a riverboat bound for New York City where Tanner found lodging. Dressed in buckskin and drawing stares from those he passed on the streets, he made his way to Broadway. Struggling through throngs of people on the street, he found the Carvill Brothers Publishing Company. He knocked on the large, oak door of the office.

"You, sir, must be John Tanner," said the man who answered the door. "Doctor James told me to watch for you. Said I'd know it was you. Please, come in."

Tanner stepped into the stylish office, brushed past Carvill, and plopped down on a velvet-clad settee. He rubbed his hand across the velvet, then looked up with a grin."

Laughing, Carvill replied, "My wife chooses the furnishings. Frankly, I would prefer beaver. And you?"

"Muskrat is softer."

"Doctor James said in his letter that you carry his latest manuscript."

"Not his. Mine."

"Yours? No. Edwin has published with us before. I believe you brought his second book."

"Not his. Mine. My stories. My words but Edwin's ink. He wrote my words. It is my book."

"May I see it?"

Tanner pulled the manuscript from his rucksack and plopped it on the desk. "My book. Not his."

"Well, now. This seems to be quite the stack of pages. I will need time to review it, appraise its worth. Once I weigh its value, I will contact you to let you know if it is of any use to me."

"Use to you? I believe my book will be of use to many people other than you. The canal that brought me east from Lake Erie to your Hudson River also takes thousands of people to the west. Each traveler will yearn for my book. Read it and you will see. I shall return in two days for your answer."

Two days later, Tanner returned. Henry Carvill invited him in.

"I have looked over your manuscript, Mister Tanner. Though somewhat crude, I feel it could be a worthy endeavor. If I choose to publish this, there will be much work for my editors to do. My expenses will be great and I fear I will make not a penny on your book. Nevertheless, if you are willing to part with your manuscript, I will take the risk. Now, about the terms. I am prepared to offer you … say … two hundred dollars. What say you?"

"I will take my manuscript now."

"Hmm? I don't under…"

"While you were laying plans to swindle me, I met with others who make books. Bring me my manuscript."

"Well, that is not quite how this business works, sir. I have made you a generous offer. Has another publisher bid even a penny?"

"Not yet. They will. Bring me my …"

"All right. All right. I will purchase your book for … three hundred."

"Bring me my manuscript."

"Four hundred?"

"Bring it now."

"Tell me what you want."

"To be treated with fairness. My book will sell many copies. You know this. You will pay me two hundred now and three cents for every copy of my book you sell. You will pay Doctor James the same."

"All right. I will draw up a contract. You will sign it?"

"You know I cannot read."

"My lawyer will read it to you."

John Tanner pulled two letters from his haversack. "These are from Doctor James. They say how much you will pay. One is for you. One is for me. Edwin signed both. I signed both. You may sign if you wish. If not, bring me my manuscript."

"Mister Tanner, you are more a businessman than you let on," Carvill said as he signed. "It is customary to include a portrait of the author in the book. I have already made arrangements for you to sit for the artist, Henry Inman."

"Sit for him?"

"Yes. In his studio down the way."

"I must sit?"

"He will paint you."

"I no longer wear paint. Why must I sit?"

"Actually, you will be standing."

"I see. I will stand while I am sitting for him."

"Yes. Now you have it."

"What do I have?"

"Inman will paint you so we can put you in the book."

"You speak like the loons in the spring. I told you. I no longer wear paint. It scared my neighbors in Sault Ste. Marie. Let him paint your face, instead."

"Oh, he has! He has! Come, I'll show you." They walked into Carvill's study. "There," he said, pointing to a portrait. "Henry Inman painted me."

"Ah, yes. Mazinaazowin-an, like a reflection in a pool. Why did you not say this before? I will let him borrow my face for the book."

"You will need to make yourself look a bit more … presentable. I know of a good barber. My tailor will measure you for a suit and the cobbler next door will put you in something far better than those moccasins of yours."

"I have worn your shiny, stiff shoes. Unless the picture man, Inman, intends to put my feet in the book, I will keep my moccasins. Fewer blisters."

"All right, keep your moccasins. Of course, the cost of all this—the portrait, the suit, the barber—will come from your two hundred."

"Read the letter you signed, Henry Carvill. You are to pay to make this book. Not me. Not Doctor James. You."

"Hmm. I see," said Carvill. "All right. But you will return the suit of clothes to me when the painting is done?"

"With pleasure. What else?"

"What else? Well, there is one more issue we need discuss. Your name."

"Which name? I have several."

"Shaw-shawwa na-baysay. I see the translation means 'swallow.'"

"Yes. I was named this by Net-no-kwa when a small boy. I was fast, hard for others to catch, like the swallow."

"But in reading your memoir, your life story, you seem more like the eagle than a small bird such as a swallow. Rather than call you John 'Swallow' Tanner, I intend to use something stronger. You will be known as the 'Falcon.' Yes John 'Falcon' Tanner."

"Falcon? The bird Englishmen use for hunting small animals?"

"Oh, it fits you well, sir. A falcon is a very sleek and fast hawk. A great hunter. Prized by kings around the world."

"Wewiib gekek."

"What?"

"Fast hawk."

"You will agree, then"?"

"Falcon, swallow, no matter as long as you send the money."

"You can trust me, John Falcon Tanner."

"I know I can." Tanner crossed the office, opened the door and turned back. "I know of an Ottawa hunter who owed another man a dog. He had many but could not bear to part with any so he decided to not give away the dog as he had promised. The other man came to his lodge, knocked this Ottawa hunter to the ground, bit off one of his ears and took the hunter's best dog. Henry Carvill, I see you have both your ears. This is good. I know I can trust you."

Chapter 30
The Fast Hawk, Doctor

The John Tanner who sat in the studio of Henry Inman hardly resembled the John Tanner who had come to New York a week earlier. Clean-shaven, his hair cut and combed, and wearing a new suit, he fit in with the many well-to-do men who strolled the New York sidewalks in the warm afternoon sun.

The artist loaded his brush and turned to his canvas. "I must say, Mister Tanner, I have rendered portraits of important politicians, European royalty, wealthy widows, and many others. But never, never have I painted a white man who has lived most of his life among the savages."

Staring ahead and moving only his lips, Tanner replied, "I believe you meant to say 'Indians,' Henry, for savagery is not limited only to red-skinned men. You have plenty in your city."

"Yes. I see your point. Though you must admit, the stories we hear from the west are chilling. Indian attacks on settlers and merchants, women and children killed, scalping, mutilation ..."

"Long ago when I was on a hunt, I came across many, many moose tracks in the snow. I thought this herd to be large. But when I followed, I learned only one moose made all those tracks. You see, just as one moose can leave many tracks, one story can be told many times. I have lived among the Ottawa, Cree, and Ojibwe for five decades. In all that time, I have seen only four scalps and two of those were Pottawatomie scalps on the belt of a Frenchman. Yes, it is true some Anishinabe people resent how the Whites come into their hunting grounds to cut the trees, plow up land, then plant crops. But few answer this with war. Very few."

"But, according to Henry Carvill, even you were a victim of abduction, were you not?"

"Yes. Shawnees stole me from my father in Kentucky. Since that day I have visited many places, lived in many lodges in the wilderness. In all my travels, I never met another White who was taken by Indians. Never have I seen a white man's home in ashes. Never have I heard white men, women, or children cry out in fear of the tomahawk. Only one time did I learn of a white trader who was killed by young Sioux warriors for his whisky. Yet, here in the city, my ears burn from all the stories told of Indians killing Whites. As I said, one moose leaves many tracks."

"The government now talks about reserving large tracts of land for the Indians, then moving them to these places. Would you favor this? Would it help them?"

"It would help them if they were left alone to live their lives as they have for all time."

"Some say the answer is to educate them to the ways of the Whites."

"I am a White who has been taught the ways of the Ojibwe. Perhaps that would be better."

"You know that will not happen, Mister Tanner. White men will not give up the progress we've made over the centuries. Do not the Indians wish to share the prosperity enjoyed by the Whites? Live in nice homes? Own farms?"

"Henry, the idea of staying in one place is strange to many Anishinabe people. They move to their hunting grounds during the hunting moon, travel to the lakes during the fishing moon, to the meadows during the berry moon, to their fields during the harvest moon, to the waters during the rice moon, to the maples during the sugar moon. It makes no sense to stay in one place."

"I wonder if the cultural differences are too great to bridge?"

"People can exist together. Culture is not the problem. Pride is. Once an osprey felt so proud that he could fly that he wanted to share his flight with the fish. He dove in the lake and plucked the fish from the water to teach him how to fly. The fish, out of water, died. Henry Inman, when one people are so proud of their ways that they force them on another people, what should we expect will happen? The first people of this land should be left to live their lives as they wish, as their ancestors have for all time. Ask them. They will tell you this."

After four long afternoons sitting for his portrait, John Tanner was delighted when Henry Inman announced he'd finished. Tanner stood, stretched, reached for his hat, and made for the door.

"Mister Tanner, in four days you have not once asked to see my effort to put your image on canvas in oil. Do you not wish to see how I have portrayed you?"

"Mister Inman, you are being paid by Henry Carvill. Should he not be the one asking to see the picture?"

"Well, yes, I suppose, but … John, are you not curious? Come. Have a look. Tell me how you like it."

Tanner crossed the studio and peered around the easel at the portrait.

"Step back. It looks best from a few feet away. What do you think?"

Tanner burst out laughing. "You made me look like one of your New York bankers. Wait until Henry Schoolcraft sees this. He'll be in a fit for a fortnight."

Tanner changed into his buckskins, bought a horse and saddle, and left New York that evening. His return route took him through the Allegheny Mountains and into Indiana and Ohio, then back to Detroit. There he stopped at the Woodworth Hotel for the night. He told the story of his stay in New York City to old Ben Woodworth and a pleasant, fair-haired woman who worked at the inn.

"Sir," she said, "the very thought of visiting New York and having someone pay an artist to capture a likeness seems a world away from life here. It is the stuff of fairy-tales, certainly not life as I know it. You must be so proud."

"Proud? Hmm. 'Twas an odd thing to do and an odd place to be. The city is not for me. I much prefer my birch lodge, the company of my children, and the call of the loon on the river."

"There is romance in that, as well. I would love to live the free life, wander where my heart takes me."

"The waters and woodlands of the Red River Valley are where my heart wishes to be," said Tanner. "However, my work keeps me in Michigan."

"Michigan?" asked Ben. "Near Detroit?"

"Nay, far up Lake Huron on the St. Mary's River."

"You mentioned your children. You have a wife as well?"

"No longer. She's run off with another."

"Oh, my, sir!"

"I fear the mission on Mackinac Island is her true love now. I imagine it is for the best. She seems content." Tanner turned to the woman. "And you? Have you a family?"

"Me? No. Like the mother of your children wedded to the church, I seem wedded only to this inn. My father sees to it. One day that will change and I will have a husband and little ones of my own. Where I will live, I know not. Nor when, for that matter." She filled his cup with cider. "Are you to be in Detroit long?"

"Tomorrow I must sail for the Sault. Say, do you know of anyone who might wish to buy a strong mare and fine saddle?"

"What's your price, friend," said a man from across the room.

"Ten for the horse, four for the saddle, same as I paid in New York only last month."

"New York? Do you mean to say you took near to a thousand mile ride on the nag and expect to get the same money as you paid?"

"No. I mean I fed the horse well and exercised her daily. She's far more fit now than when I first saw her. Are you looking for a horse?"

"No, but I am forever on the lookout for a bargain."

"In that case, I will sell the mare for twenty and the saddle for eight."

"Now, just how do you figure that to be a bargain?"

"Oh, it's not. But to you, friend, I'll sell her for half price. Ten and four. Now, that's a bargain!"

The next day, John Tanner booked passage for himself and his horse on a ship bound from Detroit to the Sault. After a four-day sail on Lake Huron and up the Saint Mary's River, he disembarked and then rode to the home of Doctor James.

From his saddle, Tanner called, "Boozhoo! Edwin, come out and hear the news from New York City."

Edwin James opened the door and stepped into the afternoon sunlight. "Shaw-shawwa na-baysay! Are you a published author, my friend?"

"I am! We are! Come. I will buy us a bottle of wine to celebrate."

"Thank you, but I fear you better save your ten-cent piece."

"But, are we not soon to be as wealthy as the fur merchants of London?"

"John, you have no employment. Henry Schoolcraft hired his brother-in-law to serve in your place as interpreter."

"Bah to Schoolcraft! I knew he would do this. I care not a fig. Come! Let us share a pint, Edwin. Then I am off to see my children. I have missed them so. My being apart from them these months has left my heart nearly empty."

"Then I am delighted to report they are happy and healthy and eager for your return, John."

"You will join me at the tavern?"

"One moment while I fetch my hat, White Swallow."

"Nay, no longer a swallow, Doctor. By the stroke of Carvill's magic pen, Shaw-shawwa na-baysay has become Wewiib gekek."

James looked puzzled. "A few months ago, I could have told you the translation."

"The Fast Hawk, Doctor. The wise and industrious Henry Carvill now calls me 'Falcon.'"

Chapter 31
Balderdash!

With his daughter at his side, John Tanner knocked on the door to Reverend Abel Bingham's office. Twice. Then three times.

"Papa, he must be away."

Tanner knocked again. The door finally opened.

"Martha!" said Bingham, "You brought your wayward father to see me?"

Tanner ignored the remark. "Reverend, I have returned from my sojourn to New York City with pleasing news."

"News?"

"The publisher, Henry Carvill, intends to print my book. They expect to sell thousands upon thousands."

"Hmm. Well, that is wonderful, my son. I congratulate you. May I have our cook fetch us tea and biscuits to celebrate?"

"Tea? No. I was wondering if, until my payment arrives, you might be in need of an interpreter."

"John, we at the mission all agree your skills are many and much desired. And, in spite of our past differences, I welcome your service. In fact, you may start at once! Unfortunately, there is no money in the church account for you at this time. However, I *can* offer you a place on my staff if you will agree to work for no pay."

Tanner stood silent, then, "How long think you I might serve without pay, Reverend? A month? A year?"

"I am sorry, my son. I have no control of such decisions."

"Reverend, I might help you under the condition that you write the Baptist Board of Missions and request I be employed as your main translator."

"I can inquire, but cannot predict the results. In the meantime, the mission serves many Ojibwes who could profit greatly from your skills. I invite you to volunteer. Help share my sermons with them. You may also continue your work on the Bible translations. These acts would demonstrate your good intentions and may stir the board to offer employment."

"*My* good intentions? And what of *your* intentions? Do you not recall how you have treated me in the past? How you purloined my wife and children from me? How you sold my possessions? My good intentions, indeed! If I decide to assist, know my choice will be for the good of the people and not your church, Reverend."

"In God's eyes, are not the good of the people and the church the same?"

"That, Abel Bingham, is a question you might ask yourself at the dawn of each day," Tanner said as he left.

The following morning, he stood before a scowling Henry Schoolcraft.

"If, Tanner, you came here to beg to be reinstated as my translator, you are wasting both your time and mine."

"I've no such plan. I came only to offer my congratulations."

"Congratulations?"

"Yes, Henry. You have succeeded in employing all of your family without having been called to task for it by our governor. Everyone I know regards this as quite an accomplishment."

Schoolcraft did not respond.

"Or, could it be that Lewis Cass is unaware of your mischief? Yes. That must be it. However, no need to fret. My letter to him did not mention it."

"What letter?"

"You failed to pay me for the last three months of my employ. I have written him, asking to be paid."

"Tanner, due to the untold evening hours you squandered on your so-called book, your work for me, if indeed it could be called as such, was second-rate. I do not pay for expectations unfulfilled."

"I will mention this when next I write. I am sure Lewis will be interested."

"Lewis? Bah! Do as you will."

"By the by, Henry Carvill is publishing my book."

"Carvill? Of the New York Carvills? Balderdash!"

"'Tis true as the flight of my arrow."

"And just as bound to fall flat."

"Not according to the Post."

"Who?"

"They seem fascinated."

"Who!"

"*The Saturday Evening Post.* Carvill offered them a glance at a few pages. I am told Sam Atkinson begged for more."

"Who?"

"Samuel Atkinson. The editor of *The Saturday Evening Post.*"

"Humph!"

"You know, Abel Bingham has offered to put me on his staff."

"I did not know."

"He sees the light."

"Humph."

"I will let you know what transpires between the governor and myself."

"Two can play at this letter-writing game of yours, Tanner."

"Good day, Henry. And, again, congratulations."

"I'll not be bested by one such as you, a mere swallow among men."

Tanner turned to reply. "Nay, Henry, not a swallow."

"No? Then, what?"

"Henry Carvill has given me a new name. You may call me Falcon."

John Tanner crossed the parade field, fumbling in his pocket, counting his last few coins. Arriving home, he found his rifle, flint, shot, and powder, then struck for the woods. He returned at dusk with a fat doe, two geese, and the determination to survive with no income until his royalties began.

Doctor Edwin James received two letters when the weekly mail boat arrived at the Sault. One contained a bank draft for eighty-eight dollars. Half would go to John Tanner. The other envelope contained a copy of a message written by Governor Lewis Cass to Henry Schoolcraft. The doctor took both to the John Tanner home, a wigwam at the edge of town.

"Good news, twice over, John," said Edwin. "Not only do we now have some jingle in our pockets from the book sales, but you also have this from the Governor." He waved the letter in the air. "Lewis Cass has instructed Henry Schoolcraft, his appointee, I must point out, to pay you in full your back wages. John, in this letter, Cass tells Schoolcraft to do this even if it means borrowing from the bank. Henry Schoolcraft dares not disobey."

"Edwin, your optimism is inspiring. However, I shan't plan to see payment from Schoolcraft anytime soon. I know him, Doctor. Schoolcraft is too proud, too arrogant. He will not admit defeat in these matters, even at the censure of his friend, Lewis Cass."

"John, would he dare tweak the nose of our governor?"

"And anyone else who might chance to step in his way. Schoolcraft sees himself as a great leader, a deity, if you will."

"I will speak with him."

"Talk all you want, Edwin. Henry Schoolcraft will not bend. His pride has been damaged by our success with my book. He will neither reinstate me as his interpreter nor will he pay my back wages. To do so would tear out his heart, if, indeed, he has one."

Doctor James left, intent on convincing Henry Schoolcraft to do the governor's bidding by paying Tanner his back wages. When he told Schoolcraft of the letter he received from Cass, Schoolcraft held up a letter of his own.

"Look, Doctor," said Schoolcraft, "I told Tanner two could play at his letter-writing game. I have here a message I intend to have delivered to the Baptist Board of Missions in Philadelphia. It points out the grave discrepancies between the monies delivered to Reverend Bingham and the amount spent on charitable work. I have no doubt that they will see that Bingham is little more than a swindler of the church, a man who lines the pockets of his friends and stuffs the rest into his own poke. I have little doubt that, on my word, they will immediately denounce him and hold back any more compensation to him and his corrupt staff, including John Tanner."

"Henry, you know quite well that these accusations are not well founded. Why think you that the Baptist Board will fall victim to your ploy? I urge you to cease this folly and simply follow the request of your friend, Governor Cass. Pay Tanner what is due him. Put this matter behind you so that you can move on to more important issues."

"Tanner has been a festering thorn in my toe since you and he wrote that confounded book. Likewise, Abel Bingham has done nothing but annoy me. This letter will kill two birds with a single stone, Doctor. Both John Tanner, the swallow, and Abel Bingham, the would-be songbird of the Baptists, are about to be deplumed."

"Your hatred, nay, your … vengeance, may be your undoing, sir."

"My concern, Doctor James. Not yours. Fix your mind on the ills and aches of your patients."

Troubled by Schoolcraft's words, Edwin James left for his office.

Three weeks later, Reverend Abel Bingham, a letter from the Baptist Board of Missions in hand, confronted Henry Schoolcraft.

"Henry Schoolcraft, this time you have gone too far! You have no right to impugn my character before my superiors. You complained to them only because my position with the mission does not fit with your *perceived* position as sovereign leader of the northwest. You, Mister Schoolcraft, are not God. He, sir, is *my* department. I protest your intrusion, your meddling in my affairs!"

Schoolcraft leaned back in his chair with a grin. "Reverend, I only reported what I saw as a misuse of funds—an abuse of your authority. I realize that you, somehow, persuaded the church to channel the entire territorial grant for the education of the Ojibwe directly into your hands. For that success, Reverend, I tip my hat. I have no idea how you did it. But that does not mean I must sit idly by and watch you squander those public funds according to your every whim."

"'Tis not your place to intrude."

"Not my place? I am overseer of this entire region by order of Lewis Cass, our territorial governor. I serve both the settlers who now call this their home and the Indians who have for centuries."

"Bah! Henry Schoolcraft, you use your office to your own advantage and always have. Now, sir, you have sent a letter intended only to cast dispersions and foster uncertainty in my programs. When it comes to helping the settlers and the winning over of the Indians, you, sir, are more a problem than a solution."

"I have done more for these pathetic people than anyone before me. You and the miserably meager, often trivial efforts of your mission hold no candle to what I do daily."

"Schoolcraft, I pity you. You cannot help but play the fool. You have deluded yourself into thinking you are the servant of the citizenry and savior of the savages. This will surely come back to haunt you."

"I will ask you to leave now, Reverend Bingham. Moreover, I will thank you to not return. Nor should you send your subordinate, John Tanner, to beg in your place."

"Tanner? Hmm. Yes. It all comes clear, now. You see him as the cause for all this disruption. You are insulted by his success. Am I not correct?"

"Such words are an insult to your own limited intelligence, Reverend."

"Tanner is the stone in your shoe. Admit this!"

"He is but a flea!"

"John Tanner is a good man, in spite of your attempts to discredit him."

"He has you fooled, Bingham, but not me. Never me!"

"Henry Schoolcraft, I will see to it that every word of this is explained to both my superiors and yours. I will not stand by while you use your lofty position to manipulate the people of Michigan Territory and line your purse with public monies. Good day!"

Reverend Abel Bingham rushed out, slamming the door. Minutes later, he found John Tanner in the mission school, speaking with the children.

"John, may I see you a moment?"

Tanner joined Bingham in the hallway.

"I've only just now returned from the office of Henry Schoolcraft. Our conversation was unpleasant. It seems he is intent on forcing you out. His obsession with removing you may even result in the loss of funding for my mission. John, I fear I must retract my request that you be paid for your service to the church."

"Retract your request for my pay, Reverend? Because of the ravings of a pompous politician?"

"Seems it is the only thing I can do to save the mission. Should I ignore Schoolcraft's designs, I believe he will find a way to have the monies we depend upon channeled directly to his Territorial Office of Indian Affairs. I am dreadfully sorry, John. You have given your all for us. This is an unfair farewell for such a devoted servant of the people."

"Abel Bingham, the children need the mission school far more than do I. And, although I would much rather stay that I could put a thumb in the eye of Henry Schoolcraft, I will go."

Chapter 33
Monsieur Alexis de Tocqueville

The small pension from Lord Selkirk was not enough to sustain John Tanner and his family, even with the royalties that trickled in from his book. He turned again to the Earth Mother to supplement his earnings but soon found the waters and woodlands surrounding the Sault had been hunted and trapped to excess. His skills, as sharp as they were, allowed him to take barely enough game to feed his children until spring. Then, one sunny morning, the mail boat brought good news. His book had been published in London. Englishmen were now reading his story and his royalties reflected the sales. The following week, the mail boat brought more good news when a man dressed unlike any other at the Sault stepped onto the dock asking a clerk, "Monsieur, where might I find the Falcon, John Tanner?" The visitor soon stood outside Tanner's lodge.

"Pa," said Martha, "There is a man outside who is dressed like a … like a banker."

"Tanner stepped out.

"Bonjour! C'est vous Wewiib gekek? Are you the Falcon, monsieur?"

"Oui, I am John Tanner."

"I have come far to meet you, Falcon. I am your servant, Alexis de Tocqueville."

"I need no servant." Tanner turned toward the door.

"Monsieur, you misinterpret. I came far to meet the great Falcon who

once lived in the Canadian frontier. Like you, I am a writer of books. I only wish to meet the inspiration for my next."

"You wish to write about me?"

"I do. That is, if you will allow me."

Tanner invited de Tocqueville into his lodge to meet his children.

"Jean Falcon Tanner," said the aristocrat, "Long have I waited to speak with you. I desire to share your story with my fellow Frenchmen. Will you allow me this?"

"My story?"

"Tales of the Great White Falcon of the Wilderness. This will be the title, if you will agree. I will pay you well, Wewiib gekek. And these stories I write of your life among the Indians will spark interest in your book as well."

Tanner waited for more.

"I will write about your years in Prince Rupert's Land with your Ojibwe people and tell tales about your struggles against the Nor'Westers, if you will agree, of course."

Seizing the opportunity, Tanner pulled a pinch of tobacco from his pouch and sprinkled it onto the glowing coals. "Perhaps, I should consult the spirits before I answer."

"Monsieur Falcon, please do!"

He chanted softly, occasionally looking up at the Frenchman.

"This song, what does it signify?"

"It means, if you make a fair trade with me for my stories, you will always be safe from the white bear while on your journey."

"The white bear? The great bruin from the far north?"

"My song protects you."

"But, do the great white bears come this far south?"

"No. My songs and my tobacco keep them several month's journey north. My other song keeps the alligator far to the south. Monsieur de Tocqueville, you may travel at ease."

De Tocqueville's laughter filled the small lodge. "Monsieur, for every story I write about you, I will send you ten of your American dollars. C'est bon?"

"C'est bon! It is good."

"And I have another offer I feel you will enjoy. I wish to pay you to allow me to print your book in Paris. Will you offer your consent for this?"

"Paris?"

"Oui. For my compatriots. Oh, they will delight in your story. I can offer you three hundred American dollars if you will agree."

"Alexis de Tocqueville, for three hundred dollars you may print my book, pitch your tent, and eat supper with us for a week."

"Magnifique! Now, please, tell me one of your many stories of the wilderness that I, Alexis de Tocqueville, may share something new with my many readers."

"Oui, oui, monsieur. En Français? Or would you prefer English?"

John, James, Martha, and little Marie Tanner sat around the fire along with their guest. The Frenchman filled a white, ceramic pipe with tobacco. Lighting it, he passed it to John and said, "Jean Falcon, show me the proper way to share this around the fire. I need to know for my stories."

"There are many ways but none better than the other. What is most important is that the pipe is raised in respect of Gitchee Manitou and the trickster, Wenebojo. Other spirits, too. The smoke is from them and for them. When you take it in, you take them in. When you exhale, part of you, your breath, goes to them as well. Do this with much reverence and all who sit with you to smoke will be pleased."

"Is there anything I should *not* do? Any mistake I might make?"

"Only this. Do not drool. It will disgust the others. They will laugh at you and point."

The Tanner children burst out laughing. "Papa," said Martha, "don't be so mean to our guest. Mister de Tocqueville, my father was making a joke on you."

Alexis laughed along with the Tanners, passing the pipe again. As he did, James grabbed it and sucked in a lungful of smoke, then coughed and coughed.

"Oh, yes," said Tanner, "try not to pass the pipe to the young ones. The chiefs will not ask you to return if you do. Now, James, hand the pipe back to our guest and I will tell you all a story from another time when I shared a pipe with an Ottawa chief."

"Beyond the Rainy River lies Rainy Lake. And beyond that is a sheet of water so great it is called Lake of the Woods. I once sat around a fire in the lodge of a great chief there. We shared pipes often. I will tell you how he earned his name.

"This chief traded many beaver pelts to the Nor'West Company and had many blankets, sugar, gunpowder, and other provisions. But, most of all, he had whisky. Many in his village celebrated with him for days.

"Now James, you must pay close attention to what I say. For just as the smoke made you lose control of your breath, whisky will make you lose control of your thoughts. This happens many times and will happen to you if you drink whisky.

"The chief and I were taking some whisky but not too much. We were talking, passing the pipe, when two men and a woman came into his lodge. They were drunk from the whisky he gave them. This chief asked them to sit with us. The woman said she would not sit with me because I was white and should not smoke in his lodge. The chief was angry at these words. He jumped to his feet. One of the drunk men drew his knife from its sheath. I jumped to my feet and pushed the man down and took his knife. The other man pushed the chief. He fell. The man jumped on the chief. They fought like warriors until the man bit off the nose of the chief. The drunk men and the drunk woman ran out, knowing they might die for this. The woman stumbled as she ran, then fell. Running behind her, one of the drunken men stepped on her hand and broke many bones that never healed.

"My friend, the chief, was bleeding from his face. I watched him pick up a hot coal from the fire with his bare hand and push it onto his nose to stop the bleeding. I helped him. I put my medicines on his nose but it did not heal right. After that day, he was known as Chief Peguis. You see, 'Peguis,' in Ojibwe, means, 'split in two.' The Whites call him, 'Chief Cut Nose.'"

"Papa," said Martha, "did Peguis's nose ever heal?"

"No. But he was old and said he did not mind because he was not looking to attract another wife. He said, 'I am an old man and it is but a short time that they will laugh at me for the loss of my nose.' His nose always remained split and scarred from the burn of the hot coal. It made it easy to tell him from the others and once you met him, you would never forget his name."

"Magnifique, my friend! A wonderful start and the first story I will send to my editor."

"Papa, what became of the two drunk men?" asked James.

"The men? They ran away but soon returned to beg Peguis to forgive them for drinking his whisky and insulting him and stealing his nose."

"Did he forgive them, monsieur?"

"Yes. Then he killed them both."

"Why, Pa?" asked James.

"He was a chief. He could not have his courage questioned or be insulted

in such a way. No one expected him to do otherwise."

"Pa, did he kill the woman?"

"No, James. Not the woman. Peguis thought it better to let her live—let her suffer every time she tried to use her broken hand. She did. Probably still does."

"Gosh, Pa, I ain't never gonna drink whisky. Don't think much about pipe smoking, neither."

De Tocqueville laughed. "Young man, although you make a wonderful pledge, you are not the first to say those words."

"Nor will you be the last, my son."

Near the edge of town, along the St. Mary's River, Henry Schoolcraft's buggy slowed to a stop. He tied the reins of his horse to the limb of a white pine overhanging the trail. For a moment, he stood there admiring the wigwam built by John Tanner and his children James, Martha, and little Marie.

Spaced an arm's length apart from each other, an oval arrangement of ash saplings with their broader ends buried in the ground, supported the structure. The tops of these slender ten-foot poles, bent over and lashed to one another with spruce roots, formed a curved roof. Birch bark neatly covered the ash sapling skeleton. Pine pitch sealed the seams, making it similar in outward appearance to Tanner's canoe. The home looked to be nearly twelve feet wide and twenty long. A moose skin hung under a birch bark awning, serving as a door. From the smoke hole in the center of the roof, a thin, feathery shaft of white climbed between limbs of the surrounding pines.

Three rope swings suspended from white pine limbs and a large garden complimented the yard. Near the garden stood a second, smaller birch shelter for a milk cow, the horse, and chickens. Behind hid the privy, built of cedar. Tanner's canoe lay overturned between the house and the river.

"Mister Tanner," shouted Schoolcraft. "Mister Tanner, come out. I have news."

"My ears deceive me," Tanner said to his children. "I think I heard the bellow of a portly hog."

"Tanner, are you there, man?"

The door opened. Tanner squinted, the daylight in his eyes. His children peeked from behind.

"I have news for you, John. Good news."

"What good news could you possibly have for me? Have you and your brother been reassigned to some faraway land?"

"Better! John, after more than a decade of trying, I have finally received approval from Washington!"

"Approval? Approval to what end?"

"To venture west, John."

"Then you *have* been reassigned! Joy to us all!"

"No, no, John, approved to oversee a journey of exploration and good will. You and I spoke of this before. It seems the War Department has finally taken heed of my warnings about the Indians and now wishes me to win over the tribes along the Mississippi and northward."

"Yes. You mentioned this before."

"Washington is now aware of the danger of invasion from the north by Britain. The president wishes to persuade the tribes betwixt here and the Rocky Mountains to serve as our allies in the event of such a war."

"There will be no war with the British."

"What? Is the memory of 1812 not still fresh in your brain? Do you not think London's bankers have their eyes on the fur trade here? My Lord! Why do you think Selkirk has colonized the river fork near Lake Winnipeg?"

"Poppycock! The Hudson's Bay Company already controls all lands west of Montreal. Lord Selkirk is now embroiled in lawsuits stemming from his overthrow of Fort William. His army, skilled as they are, will not act without him."

"And if you are mistaken? If they do invade?"

"The British, without Selkirk, have little hope of surviving another war here. Rather than conspiring to take lands now claimed by the United States, King George should fear more a war of independence with Canada. What has all this to do with me?"

"John, you are to be a part of all this journey. You will be my interpreter."

"You jest! Do you not recall how you replaced my services with those of the wife of your brother? Take *her* into the hunting grounds of the Sioux."

"I jest not, Tanner. You will accompany me, all right. We will be twenty-seven strong including a company of twenty riflemen under the command of Lieutenant Clary. Besides being my chief interpreter, you will serve as our guide. When not engaged as either, you will act as my personal porter across the various portages."

"Porter? You wish me to carry your effects whilst you lumber along empty-handed? No. Your sister-in-law will carry your trappings. Not me."

"John, I cannot find another with your skills to fill this post. I will pay you well. Twice your monthly pay here."

"Three times the pay and I will guide you. I will speak with the people we meet on your behalf. I will tote my own provisions and, with the others, heft a canoe. That is all. I will *not* serve as your valet."

"Done! We embark one week hence. Arrange for your children's care, Mister Tanner, and know that this expedition will consume most of two months if not more."

Within the hour, Tanner met with Doctor James.

"Yes, John. I know of this news. Schoolcraft came to enlist me just as he did you."

"Then you will be with us? Wonderful!"

"No. I told Schoolcraft I had my fill of such wandering through the wilderness when with Major Long in the mountains. Doctor Houghton is personal physician to old Schoolcraft. Let him do it. We will see how much he enjoys practicing his trade out on the trail."

"I'd not think you would turn down such an adventure."

"You and the others can swelter in the summer sun, swat away the deer flies and horse flies by day and the mosquitoes by night. I am content to remain here, read my books, tend my patients."

"And, my three young ones? Would you tend to them in my place?"

"Certainly! I would delight in this, John. I will keep them scrubbed, fed, and tending your garden until your return. Now, tell me, do you know yet where it is you are headed?"

"It appears we will venture west along Lake Superior's south shore till we first catch sight of Madeline Island. We then leave Gitchee Gumi, ascending the Bad River to the White. We follow the White, then seek the portages south to the Namekagon."

"Nameh?" muttered the Doctor. "It means sturgeon, does it not? Sturgeon River? Nameh-kagon?"

"Yes. I have been through there before. Good waters. Good woodlands. Not yet crowded with Whites like Michigan and Rainy River."

"I suppose I should take exception to that last remark."

Tanner grinned. "From the River called Namekagon, we float downstream to the Saint Croix and Mississippi, visiting tribes and villages along the way. Our destination is the Mississippi headwaters, then Sioux country not far from Winnipeg. I know the land and the people well. We will return by the Mississippi, venturing up the Wisconsin to the Fox and Lake Michigan. This will be no gentle journey."

"Take heed of all you see and hear, John. It may lead to another book."

"If I should undertake another, would you again assist?"

"I would be honored."

"Then horde your ink and paper, Doctor Edwin James. And I will do the same with my observations as I watch Henry Schoolcraft stumble through the wilds."

"John, trust that all will be well here. I will await your return in eager anticipation and with your three pups under my wing. Upon your arrival we shall celebrate the next book as you share with us every episode of your wilderness adventure."

Chapter 35
The Mississippi Expedition

Under the leadership of Henry Rowe Schoolcraft, twenty-seven men set out in five long canoes from Sault Ste. Marie in the summer of 1832. With them traveled John Falcon Tanner, serving as interpreter and guide. The mission, funded by the United States War Department, was to befriend the tribes along the way in hope of gaining their support, should the western Great Lakes suffer invasion from Great Britain. A secondary goal was to vaccinate as many Indians against small pox as they would allow. A third was to explore and map the Indian travel route between Lake Superior and St. Paul, then ascend the Mississippi to its headwaters and beyond before returning to Sault Ste. Marie.

Thirteen days after leaving the Sault, they entered the Bad River at the Ojibwe village, Odanah. From there, they struck southwestward up the White River. Three days later, beyond Bibon Swamp, they portaged, then camped. Over the next few days, Henry Schoolcraft entered the following in his log:*

On the 25th we went three *pauses* to breakfast, in a hollow or ravine, and pushing on, crossed the last ridge, and at one o'clock reached the foot of Lake Kagy-nogum-aug, a beautiful and elongated sheet of water, ... about nine miles long.

Lake Kagy-nogum-aug — At nine in the morning, we embarked on the lake in four canoes. Two of the flotilla of canoes were occupied by the military under Lieut. Clary. Its waters were clear; we observed fish and ducks. After proceeding a little less than two hours through a very irregular, elongated, and romantic lake, we reached a portage in the direction of the Namakagun. This portage is called Mikenok, or the Turtle. It proved to be two hundred and eighty yards to a pond, or small lake, named Turtle Lake. About two hundred yards of this portage lies a dry pine ridge, the remainder bog. On crossing this little sheet, we encountered another portage of one thousand and seventy-five yards, terminating at a second lake we named Clary's Lake. About five o'clock the canoes came up, and we embarked on the lake and crossed it, and, striking the portage path, went four hundred and seventy-five yards to a third lake, called Polyganum, from the abundance of plant. We crossed this and encamped on its border.

This frequent shifting and changing of baggage and canoes exhausted the men, who have not yet recovered from the toils of the long portage. Three of them were disabled

*Precise words from Schoolcraft's journal of the expedition.

from wounds or bruises. Laporte, the eldest man of our party, fell with a heavy load, on the great Wunnegum portage, and drove a small knot into his scalp. The doctor bandaged it, and wondered why he had not fractured his skull. Yet the old man's voyager pride would not permit him to lie idle. If he died under the carrying-strap, he was determined to die game.

Namakagun River. — Early on the 27th we were astir, and followed the path 1050 yards, which we made in two pauses to the banks of the Namakagun River. We were now on the waters tributary to the Mississippi, and sat down to our breakfast of fried pork and tea with exultation.

Dead pines cover the ground between Lake Polyganum and the Namakagun. A great fire appears to have raged here formerly, destroying thousands of acre's of the most thrifty and tall pines. Nobody can estimate the extent of this destruction.

The river, where the portage strikes it, is about seventy-five feet wide, and shallow, the deepest parts not exceeding eighteen inches.

About one o'clock the canoes had all come up, and we embarked on the waters of the Namakagun. Rapids soon obstructed our descent. At these it was necessary for the men to get out and lift the canoes. It was soon necessary for us to get out ourselves and walk in the bed of the stream. It was at last found necessary to throw overboard the kegs of pork, &c., and let them float down. This they would not do without men to guide them and roll them along in bad places. Some of the bags from the canoes were next obliged to be put on men's shoulders to be carried down stream over the worst shallows. After proceeding in this way probably six or seven miles, we encamped at half-past seven o'clock. Mr. Johnston, with his canoe, did not come up. We fired guns to apprize him of our place of encampment, but received no reply.

There had been partial showers during the day, and the weather was dark and gloomy. It rained hard during the night. Our canoes were badly injured, the bark peeling off the bows and bottoms. The men had not yet had time to recover from their bruises on the great Wannegum portage. Mr. Clary had shot some ducks and pigeons, on which, at his invitation, we made our evening repast, with coffee, an article which he had among his stores. Some of the men had also caught trout--this fish being abundant here.

On the next morning I sent a small canoe (Clary's) to aid Johnston. Found him with his canoe broke. Brought down part of his loading, and dispatched the canoe back again. By eleven o'clock the canoe returned on her second trip. Finding the difficulties so great, put six kegs of pork, seven bags of flour, one keg of salt, &c., in depot.

Puckwaéwa Village. — At four o'clock we had got everything down the shallows, mended our canoe, and reached the *Pukwaéwa*, a noted Indian village, where we encamped. The distance is about nine miles from the western terminus of the portage, course W. S. W. We found it completely deserted, according to the custom of the Indians, who after planting their gardens, leave them to go on their summer hunts, eating berries, &c. (We saw a) high wooden cross on the south bank. Hence we called it the Lake of the Cross. It is called Pukwaéwa by the Indians.

We found eight large permanent bark lodges, with fields of corn, potatoes, pumpkins, and beans, in fine condition. The lodges were carefully closed, and the grounds and paths around cleanly swept, giving the premises a neat air. The corn fields were partially or lightly fenced. The corn was in tassel. The pumpkins partly grown, the beans fit for boiling. The whole appearance of thrift and industry was pleasing.

A little below we met the chief Pukquamoo and his band returning to the upper village. Held a conference with him on the water on the subject of my mission and movements. He appeared, not only by his village, which we had inspected, but by his words, eminently pacific.

I sent two canoes immediately upstream, to bring down the stores put in deposit. I descended the river, taking along Dr. Houghton and Mr. Johnston, leaving the heavy baggage in charge of Mr. Woolsey, with directions to accompany Lieut. Clary across the portage from the Namakagun to Ottowa Lake. It was half-past five on the morning of the 29th, when, bidding adieu to Lieut. Clary and Mr. Woolsey, we embarked.

About four o'clock the chief of this party hailed us from shore, having headed us by taking a short land route from the Lake of the Cross. He sought more perfect information on some points, which was given, and he was requested to attend the general council appointed to be held at *Lac Courtorielle* (Ottawa Lake). We continued the descent till eight o'clock P. M., having descended about thirty-five miles.

On the 30th we embarked at five in the morning, and reached the contemplated portage to Ottawa Lake at seven. I stopped, and having written notes for Lieut. Clary and Mr. Woolsey, put them in the end of a split pole, according to the

Indian method. At ten I landed for breakfast with my canoe badly broken, and the corn, &c., wetted. Detained till twelve. Near night met a band of Chippewas ascending. Got a canoe from them to proceed to Yellow River, and, after dividing the baggage and provisions, put Mr. Johnston with two men in it. This facilitated our descent, as we had found frequent shallows, in consequence of low water, to impede our progress. Yet our estimate for the day's travel is forty miles.

On the 31st we were on the water at six A. M. Soon passed seven Indians in canoes, to whom a passing salute of a few words and tobacco were given. We landed at ten to breakfast. The current had now augmented so as to be very strong, and permit the full force of the paddles. Stopped a few moments at a Chippewa camp to get out some tobacco, and, leaving Mr. Johnston to make the necessary inquiries and give the necessary information, pushed on.

Their first request is tobacco, although they are half starved, and have lived on nothing but whortleberries for weeks. '*Suguswau,* let us smoke,' is the first expression.

The country as we descend assumes more the appearance of upland prairie, from the repeated burnings of the forest. The effect is, nearly all the small trees have been consumed, and grass has taken their place. The moose is also an inhabitant of the Namakagun. The Chippewas, at a hunting camp we passed yesterday, said they had been on the tracks of a moose, but lost them in high brush. Ducks and pigeons appear common. Among smaller birds are the blackbird, robin, catbird, red-headed woodpecker, kingfisher, kingbird, plover and yellow-hammer.

We frequently passed the figure of a man, drawn on a blazed pine, with horns, giving the idea of an evil spirit. The occiput of the bear, and head bones of other animals killed in the chase, are hung upon poles at the water's side, with some ideographic signs. The antlers of the deer are conspicuous. Other marks of success in hunting are left on trees, so that those Indians who pass and are acquainted with signs, obtain a species of information. The want of letters is thus, in a manner, supplied by signs and pictographic symbols.

Late in the afternoon we passed the inlet of the Tetogun-- one of the principal forks of the Namakagun. The name is indicative of its origin. *Totosh* is the female breast. It describes a peculiar kind of soft or dancing bog. Soon after, we broke our canoe—stopped three-fourths of an hour to amend it—reached the forks of the St. Croix directly after, passed down the main channel about nine miles, and encamped a little below Pine River. We built ten fires to keep off the mosquitoes, and put our tent and cooking-fire in the centre. It rained during the night.*

Henry Schoolcraft found little need for John Tanner's skills as an interpreter until the party of explorers met Chief Pukquamoo downstream from Puckwaéwa Village. Until then, Tanner helped heft canoes, packs, and provisions over each of the five portages between the Bad River and Ottawa Lake, then one more carry to the Namekagon River again.

"Fifty years I have walked this land and now I am but a beast of burden," he muttered as he raised the bow of the canoe.

One of the other four porters replied. "Aren't we all beasts in the eyes of his lordship, Schoolcraft? I've yet to see him carry more than his writing kit."

"Hush, you fools!" came a voice from the stern. "You will soon have us on latrine duty with such talk. Be content to carry a canoe and be paid for the pleasure. Soon we will be on the water again."

"Fifty years," repeated Tanner. "I shall not engage in such labor for the next fifty. Once we return to the Sault, I make my living with my brain, not my back."

Angry, now, the man below the stern of the canoe spoke again. "That's the lot of it, fellows. Purse your lips, watch your step, and let us get this ship to sea."

The sun beating down, the men lowered the canoe, rolled it upright, and slid it into the Namekagon River. As they did, Tanner waded in, knee-deep, then splashed water onto his face and neck. Lieutenant Clary and four others lowered their canoe next.

"Mister Tanner," said Clary, "you say you have been down this river before?"

"Up, not down,

*Precise wording from Schoolcraft's journal of the expedition.

Lieutenant. From the fork of the Minnesota and Mississippi. Near Fort Snelling."

"How far up is the headwaters?"

"Half-a-day's paddle."

"And what might one find there?"

"More of the same until you reach the mouth of the lake. The sheet that feeds the river is worth a look if one has the time."

"Inhabited?"

"Moose, deer, bear, and otter when I went 'round it. Two Ojibwe encampments, but no people in them. Some islands. Pines all around. Pike and sturgeon below. No sign of Whites. A fine place, if solitude be your treasure."

"Tanner, what say you accompany me there that I can add it to Mister Schoolcraft's map of our trek?"

"What of this carry, Lieutenant?"

"My men can complete this work."

"If that be the case, I would much rather have a paddle in my hands than a pack on my back and a canoe as my cap. I will take you to the headwaters. Some shallows in the upper reaches of the river will require some walking. I suggest a small canoe, one not heavy and not burdened with the excess provisions your Army seems to think we need."

"What, then?"

"Musket, paddle, and blanket. No more than these and we will rejoin the others by evening tomorrow."

"You are sure we will find food enough?"

"I am your guide. You will have food."

"Then, White Falcon, away to the headwaters!"

Chapter 36
Goo-koo ko'oo

Clary and Tanner shoved off upstream. Alternating between paddling and wading with canoe in tow, they made the eleven miles to the lake outlet by mid-afternoon. On still water, they skirted the shore under a cloudy sky, then put in on a large island. Before them, lay the remains of several birch lodges.

"We are not the first to stop here," said Tanner. "Others have come and gone for many years."

"Why here?" asked Clary. "There are many places on this lake to encamp."

"None with such a view of all around. No one could catch you unaware from this vantage point."

"Spoken like a military man."

"I lived among the Ojibwe and Sioux when they were at each others' throats even more than now. There were times when both wanted me dead. I learned to choose my lodging in the same way an old buck chooses his bed."

"How so?"

"One eye on the trail behind, nose to the wind, and a sure way to escape."

"Not exactly what we learned at West Point, sir."

"It is the way to stay alive in the wilderness. Indian warriors will tell you this."

Clary built a fire while Tanner explored the island. The crack of Tanner's musket told the lieutenant they would have something to roast over the coals. The overturned canoe shielded the men from rain during the night and, before the sun rose the next morning, they were away. They joined the others in the late afternoon.

"Tanner," said Schoolcraft, "I do not favor this decision of yours to leave our ranks. I needed you to haul provisions."

"I am first an interpreter and a guide. That is why you have me here."

"I have you here, Tanner, to do my bidding."

Clary stepped forward. "I am to blame, Mister Schoolcraft. I required his assistance. His experience aided me immensely."

"No matter," replied Schoolcraft. "His absence was inexcusable."

"As are your priorities," said Tanner. "The War Department sent us here for a reason."

"Mind your place, Mister Tanner. I lead this expedition, not you."

"You are no leader of men. You are but a porcupine gnawing away at the soft bark until the tree is dead—a porcupine without quills enough to stand your ground. You rely on others to do your work while you suck money from the people like the leech sucks blood."

"Enough, Tanner! I will not tolerate another rude insult. Any further contemptuous remark will cost you your pay and position."

John Tanner turned to leave, then turned again. "I will spare you from hearing more from me, Henry Schoolcraft, but know you that my words reflect the thoughts of others who, with you holding their purse strings, are too timid to speak for themselves."

"Lieutenant, see to it this does not happen again or you, too, will suffer."

"Yes, sir."

Tempers cooled over the two-week-long trek down the Namekagon and St. Croix Rivers, then up the Mississippi. Making twenty to thirty-five miles a day while stopping to offer gifts and vaccinations to inhabitants of the Indian chiefs along the route kept the men working dawn to dusk, regardless of weather. They ascended the river to Cass Lake, named by and for explorer, Lewis Cass, Governor of Michigan Territory. A decade before, on another expedition, Cass declared the large lake to be the headwaters of the Mississippi River.

After making camp, Schoolcraft ordered Lieutenant Clary and a few, select men to visit the area villages and convene a council that he could speak with all the chiefs. Tanner accompanied Clary to translate. Upon returning, Clary reported to Schoolcraft.

"The chiefs will meet with us at first light, Mister Schoolcraft. You will have an audience of thirty or more representing a dozen area villages. They seem quite friendly and willing to cooperate. Tanner believes it is because they are tired of the way the British have treated them."

"Precisely what I hoped to hear, Lieutenant."

"We learned something else. Something I believe you will find quite satisfying."

"And what might that be?"

"In his discussions, it seems Tanner gained knowledge of a stream which flows into Cass Lake. A rather healthy course, at that."

"I fail to see the import of such a find."

"We sought it out and ascended several hundred yards with little hindrance other than windfalls in our path."

"Clary, why should I think this trifling find of yours satisfying? This means nothing."

"On the contrary, sir, it means Governor Cass was wrong. It means Henry Schoolcraft will be credited with finding the *true* headwaters of the Mississippi River."

Schoolcraft was silent in thought for a moment. Then, "By God in Heaven, Clary, this *is* good news! Wonderful news! Where is this stream, this river, this torrent? We must plan our ascent tonight that we can be off at dawn."

"Perhaps midday would be better, sir."

"Nonsense! We have a monumental task at hand. Historic! We shall depart at first light."

"If so, you will have thirty chiefs upset with you, Mister Schoolcraft."

"Hmm? Oh, yes. Yes. The chiefs. Blast! We embark after the council, then. Tell the men to prepare for the next leg. And, say, this is wonderful news, Lieutenant Clary. I commend you for it."

"'Tis John Tanner who deserves the commendation, sir, not I."

"Tanner? Well, if you say so. Now be off, Lieutenant. Inform the men."

A hundred Whites and Indians assembled for the morning council. Tanner related Schoolcraft's greetings and interpreted for both groups. Pipes were shared, gifts exchanged, and the expedition proceeded up the river. As they did, the river became narrow, shallow, and obstructed with windfalls. Axes became more useful than paddles. Frustrated with their progress, Schoolcraft ordered half the party to encamp along the stream while twenty men, including Schoolcraft, Clary, and Tanner, ascended the streambed on foot. They reached a natural dam that formed another lake. Three men in a small canoe explored the shoreline. They returned with news of no canoe-worthy waters feeding the lake.

Schoolcraft stood on a fallen log, raised a finger high, and said, "On this day in 1832, we have come to the uppermost stretch of this river. Therefore, as leader of this expedition of discovery and good will, I, Henry Rowe Schoolcraft declare this lake to be Schoolcraft Lake, the rightful headwaters to the River Mississippi! And, by doing so, undo any other claims of such. And ..."

"Sir?" said Clary. "Is there not already a Schoolcraft Lake in Michigan? Will this not confuse future travelers, geographers, even the military?"

155

"Hmm. Point taken, Clary."

"This lake already has a name," Tanner said. "The French called it by Lac La Biche many years ago."

Schoolcraft bristled "The French? I won't have it! I did not come here to kowtow to the French. Let them find their own blasted headwaters."

"But, sir. Did they not already do that?" asked Clary.

"Look. I choose to declare this the headwaters of the Mississippi River and I shall name this lake as I please. The American cartographers will use whatever name I decide upon."

"If not Lac La Biche, then perhaps an Ojibwe word," said Tanner. "Ameek? Named for the beaver here?"

"Mister Tanner, far too many geographical features in this country of ours carry Indian names," said Schoolcraft.

"Or, Nigig. For the otter."

"Too difficult for Americans to learn them all."

"Lac Goo-koo ko'oo," said Tanner. "Lake of the owl."

"No more of your nonsense. I will, instead, call upon my knowledge of Latin."

"Latin, sir?" said Clary, eyebrows raised.

"Yes, Lieutenant, Latin. If, indeed, this is the true headwaters, as I believe it to be, a Latin term be a good choice. Let me see … yes. In Latin, veritas means true. And caput refers to head. Yes! That's it! I shall name this Lake Veritas Caput, the true head. Gentlemen, behold before you Lake Veritas Caput!"

"As long as owls continue to call, Americans would not forget Lake Goo-koo ko'oo," said Tanner. "But they will never remember Lake Veritas Caput."

"Tanner's right, sir," added Clary.

"Hmm. Then I shall shorten it for them. Let me see, now. Veritas. Hmm. All right, I shall take the last four letters from the first word, I, T, A, S, and the first two, C and A, from caput. That's it! I-T-A-S-C-A. Behold, gentlemen, Lake Itasca!"

"Lake Itasca it is, Mister Schoolcraft," said Clary. "Good work, sir."

"Goo-koo ko'oo is still a better name," said Tanner, walking away.

Chapter 37

A Bitter Homecoming

Following a two-day survey of the region, a long, tedious trek up the Red River to Winnipeg, and another Indian council, the company of explorers and soldiers began their return journey. Weeks later they descended the Mississippi to Fort Snelling on the Minnesota River. After resting and restocking supplies, they paddled through St. Paul and down the Mississippi, holding councils whenever and wherever they could. Following one of these councils, Schoolcraft heard disturbing news from his interpreter.

"What is it, Tanner? What complaints do you bring me now?"

"The Sioux are wearing paint."

"Why bother me with this? Many tribes wear paint."

"It is war paint."

"Bah. We have no need to fear the Sioux in these waters."

"They do not wear the paint for war with Whites."

"Who, then?"

"Chief Black Hawk and his warriors have been raiding white settlements. They are pursued by Pike."

"Zebulon Pike? Well, then! Nothing to fear. General Pike is a skilled Indian fighter. No doubt he has the lot of them in the stockades by now. Tell Clary to ready the canoes. We must be off."

"Pike was not able to stop Black Hawk when last they battled."

"What? The United States Army cannot tame a mere handful of renegades? Don't be a fool!"

"More than a handful."

"What, then? A dozen? A score? Two dozen?"

"Twelve-hundred."

"Twelve-hundred? Twelve?"

Tanner nodded.

"Oh, my!"

"The Salk and the Fox. Many chiefs. Many muskets."

"Perhaps we need to reconsider our course."

"General Atkinson is downstream. He has a war boat to protect us if we can reach him."

"And how might we do that with this Black Hawk on the prowl?"

"Black Hawk will not cross the Mississippi into Sioux lands. The Sioux detest his people. We should stay to the west shore. There we will be safe."

"I will need to confirm this with Clary. Meanwhile, Tanner, tell the others to prepare to embark."

Rifles in the lead, the expedition party floated south, passing the outlet to the Bad Axe River. There, Lieutenant Clary saw something ahead. He halted the small flotilla and shouted to the canoe behind.

"Mister Schoolcraft, we have two bodies floating in the backwater here."

The river current slowly pulled the canoes downstream.

"Here's another, sir," he shouted. "And another."

Within minutes, the Schoolcraft canoes were drifting through scores of scalped bodies.

"What do you make of it, Clary?" yelled Schoolcraft.

"The Sioux must have killed them, Mister Schoolcraft. The Army frowns upon the taking of scalps."

"They are Salk and Fox," said Tanner. "Some were warriors. Most are women and children."

"Look there," Doctor Houghton said. "That man on shore appears to be alive."

"Ready your rifles, men," ordered Clary as they floated closer. "Tanner, if he is able to talk, see what you can learn."

The Fox warrior lay before them, clutching his belly. His scalp gone, blood oozed from his head. Tanner spoke in his tongue, translating to the others.

"I am Red Knife," he muttered. "I am gut-shot and will soon die if the spirits are kind."

Tanner opened his medicine pouch. "Here," he said, handing the man some leaves. "This will ease the pain. Tell me, my friend. How did this happen?"

"We showed the Long Knife, Atkinson, we wanted to surrender. We put down our weapons and showed him our white flag. When we began to cross the river to him, the Long Knife boat's cannons began to fire. The Army rifles began  to fire. I made it this far before I fell. From morning to night I heard the Long Knife guns. They killed and killed and killed. Then they came to take our scalps."

"Mister Tanner, ask him how many men are left," said Clary.

"Did *any* of your people make it across?"

"Some. Maybe a hundred. They were met by the Sioux and butchered. We are no more."

"Was Black Hawk captured?"

"Black Hawk is no fool. He knew this might happen. He left two days past with White Cloud."

"Tanner," said Clary, "he must be wrong about the scalps. Surely it was the Sioux who took them."

Translating, Tanner replied, "No, Lieutenant. It was the Long Knives. He says they will trade the scalps to peddlers who come to the settlements."

"Doctor Houghton," said Schoolcraft, "is there anything to be done to save this poor soul?"

"Only this, sir," replied Houghton. "I can give him enough laudanum to make him sleep through to the end."

"A merciful act, Doctor. Administer it now that we may be on our way."

Tanner carefully lifted the mortally wounded warrior's head, allowing him to drink the sedative. "Drink, my friend, and soon you will dream of the next life, a better life than this one of war and pain and suffering. With my songs I will ask the spirits to guide you that your journey will be swift and pleasant."

The men of the 1832 expedition continued down the Mississippi, John Tanner chanting softly and Henry Schoolcraft feverishly scribbling notes of the event in his journal. Arriving at the confluence of the Wisconsin River, they changed course, leaving the Mississippi and ascending the Wisconsin.

Days later, they portaged again, following the ten-thousand-year-old trail of the Original People to the Waagoshkagan or Fox River. They soon reached Oshkosh, staying to the west shore of Lake Winnebago beyond the villages of Nee-naah and May-nay-shay to the river mouth and descended to Green Bay. There, strong winds delayed them three days. On the forth, they set out for Fort Mackinac and home.

A south breeze eased the effort needed to make the two-hundred-mile trek. Six days later, a three-cannon salute announced their arrival at Mackinac Island where Colonel Boyd, commander of Fort Mackinac, hosted a celebration in honor of their successful expedition.

"So, Henry," began Colonel Boyd, "did you jot enough notes in your journal to warrant another book?"

"More than enough, Colonel. Though I detest the task, I will need to trim the fat before any publisher sees it. Half or more, I expect. Still, it should reach two hundred pages in all."

"And you, Mister Tanner, I hear your recent book is quite popular. Do you intend another?"

"Humph!" Schoolcraft bristled.

"Another book, Colonel? If truth be told, yes. Doctor James and I settled on this months ago. I will offer our readers a description of this journey I now complete."

"You, sir?" blurted Schoolcraft. "You will do no such thing! I commissioned you as guide, interpreter, and porter. I gave you no orders to record the expedition. This was not your duty."

"But is it not the duty of each to share what they learn?" Tanner replied. "If not, then how may the state of mankind ever hope to improve?"

"This is marvelous," Boyd said. "We will be able to compare both versions and see the expedition from two points of view—two gentlemen vying for the best tale!"

Schoolcraft shook with rage. "Tanner, I forbid this! I will not have you or any other subordinate of mine interfering with my work."

"Dear me!" said Boyd. "Do I hear correctly? Are you, Henry Rowe Schoolcraft, standing in the way of our nation's constitution? Interfering with a man's legitimate right to put on paper his thoughts and feelings? You, sir? Indian Agent and Territorial Judge? Why, you could lose both appointments! I say! Dare not deny John Falcon Tanner his rights, sir."

"Tanner? Tanner has no rights. He is no American. He lived in Prince Rupert's Land most of his life. Thus, he is a subject of King George."

"Nevertheless, Henry, he has …"

"I am no king's subject!"

"Mister Tanner, as long as you remain in my employ, I shall have say over what writing you will and will not do."

"To blazes with you!" yelled Tanner. "You may think yourself the biggest toad in the pond, but no man born to woman will tell me what I can and cannot do!"

"You give me no choice. As of this moment, I dismiss you from your duties. You are no longer part of this expedition. Further, I will not need your services as interpreter in the future. Tanner, you have lit the flame that burnt your own pudding. Now see how it tastes!"

Chapter 38
The Second Book

In a small boat rowed by one of Colonel Boyd's men, Tanner crossed the Mackinac Straits to the mainland. He collected his pack, blanket, and walking stick, thanked the soldier, and followed the portage trail north.

"Papa is home!" Marie cried, as her father walked up the path to the home of Doctor James. "Martha, James, come see! Papa is home!"

Tanner dropped his pack on the path and ran, meeting the children. Edwin watched their reunion from the doorway.

"John!" he shouted over the noise of the children. "Welcome home!"

"How good to see you, Edwin. I have longed for this moment since the day I departed. Oh, how I've missed these pups of mine!"

"Come in, then! I was about to serve up a stew. Sit with us that you may share news of your adventure."

"After this long time, Edwin, I thought you might beg me to drive my herd of kid goats to their rightful house."

"Nonsense, John. Their presence in my home these few months has been my joy and delight. Your two daughters have been more help than hindrance. And what can I say about your son, James? He is a spirited one, an adventurer like his father. We have had the best of times."

"Your account seems a bit sugary," Tanner replied as he mussed his son's hair. "What are you leaving out?"

"You will hear not a word of regret or complaint from me, John. In all honesty, I enjoyed being with your children so, I am now considering taking a wife and raising my own small herd."

"Taking a wife? What good news! But whose wife do you intend to take?"

"Whose wife? Oh, dear me, John! You take me too literally. I have designs on two who have yet to marry."

"Then who, Doctor? Do I know them?"

"Both are daughters of Major Quimby."

"Lewis Quimby? I once shared a dinner with the Major at the table of the old frump, Henry Schoolcraft. He seemed to be a good fellow—Quimby, certainly not the toad, Schoolcraft."

"You must join us for a meal one day that you may meet the entire Quimby family. His daughters are charming. Quite charming, indeed."

"And pretty," said Marie. "Yellow hair."

"They get to wear white dresses to school," added Martha. "Wish I had a white dress and yellow hair."

"Nothing can be done about your hair, daughters, but when old Schoolcraft pays me my back wages, I will buy you each a white dress, but only if you agree to save it for Sunday church meetings. Our home is not the place to wear white."

"Unfair," whined James. "What do I get, Pa?"

"Why, you can have a white dress, too, son."

"Don't want no dress!"

"Then, how about a powder horn, a flint, and a pouch of lead balls?"

"For what? You won't let me shoot your rifle."

"James, you are now old enough. I will see to it you have one soon."

"You are mocking me, Pa. Ain't you?" James waited, then realized, "You ain't! You ain't! I'm gettin' my own dang rifle!"

Edwin muttered, "Oh, my. No creature 'twixt here and town will be safe!"

Work on the new book began three evenings later in the home of Doctor James. Tanner dictated several events recalled from the expedition as Edwin filled six, then seven pages with text.

"John, it sounds as though you and Henry were at odds on this journey more than not."

"At odds? Yes. He was a blustery wind, blowing away, bellowing his orders, orders that seldom made much sense. The others said little, not wanting to stir his wrath."

"Meaning that you did not tolerate him?"

"I ignored him all I could until we made Fort Mackinac."

"And, then?"

"The pompous porcupine ordered me to not write this book we now cultivate. Seems he intends to do the same. He fears competition."

"As he should. His writing is dry, a mere report of day-to-day developments. Tell me, how did you respond to his order?"

"With my usual frankness, Doctor."

"I see. Hmm. You no longer have employment then?"

Tanner grinned. "I am no longer his to command at will and want."

"Ha! A fine reply. Not to worry, John, Your royalties will cover you. The mail boat brings enough each week to survive until the next. I have squirreled away a nice pile of coins for you. A nice pile, indeed."

"Schoolcraft owes me for the expedition, too."

"Do you mean, John, that you have not yet been paid?"

"Paid? Not a penny thus, Doctor."

"Odd."

"How so?

"I believe all the others have. Perhaps Schoolcraft's intentions are ..."

"To hold back my wages? To keep them for himself?"

"I know not, John. He may be writing the voucher as we speak."

"I doubt this. Schoolcraft is a wily one. He thinks he can twist the knife and make me obey his wishes. If he does not pay me, dash it all, I will again write to the governor. If Lewis Cass cannot make Schoolcraft recompense me my due, I will write to President Martin Van Buren himself."

"Heavens! John, I may not be able to help with such letters. My position as the post surgeon could be jeopardized."

"No matter. My Martha can read and write. She will help me."

"Yes, your Martha is a bright one."

"She will help me write, I know."

"John, while you were away, she spent many evenings reading books to James and little Marie."

"Books? What kind of books?"

"Oh, fairy tales, fables, adventure stories, all from the library of Major Quimby. He keeps his daughters surrounded with literature."

"One day, I wish to read."

"Have Martha teach you."

"Martha. Yes, I have thought about this."

"She would be proud to be your teacher, John. Do give her the chance. Now, before the hour glass runs out."

"And, Doctor James, before *our* lamp runs out, let us get on to the next episode of my book."

Across town, the Schoolcraft brothers retired to the study after supper. James struck a match and lit both his and Henry's pipe, then flopped into a green velvet settee.

"Henry, what do you intend to do about this John Tanner?"

"What do you mean?"

"He is, without exception, your greatest detractor. His cynical comments about your abuse of your office have stripped us of respect and stirred up half the citizens of the Sault. He has sullied your good name."

"No more than your carousing, James. You seem not to care who knows of your exploits. It is an embarrassment to me and I wish you to stop."

"Nonsense. Few know of my private life."

"And your poor wife? Does not Anna Marie count in all of this?"

"Anna knows not what I do when away."

"What? Come to your senses, man. You think she is blind?"

"She understands."

"You need stop your philandering, James. If not for her sake, then for mine. Betwixt you and Tanner, half the town seems to be turning against me."

"Half, yes. But those are the troublemakers who dislike government of any kind. The others tend to support your work here."

"Yes, half are in my henhouse and will be as long as I keep pennies in their pockets and the wool pulled over their eyes."

"Or until Tanner, the white savage, finds the words to rile them. You must nip this in the bud, Henry. Rid yourself of him. I know a way."

"And what might that way be?"

"Of all the things he loves in life, his daughter, Martha, soars the highest."

"And?"

"Henry, take her from him. In fact, take all three of his children. It would destroy him to lose his little angels."

"And, how would you suppose I do this?"

"How? You are a territorial judge. I am your sheriff and clerk of your court. You saw to that. Tanner and his children live in a hovel, no more than a birch bark shanty. The four of them crowd around a fire on the dirt floor like savages."

"What would the people along the St. Mary's River say? They'd think me a despot. James, I have seen Tanner's home. 'Tis not as bad as you portray. Many of our villagers live worse. He lives as Indians have lived for many centuries."

"This life Tanner and his children lead may be fine for savages, but, Henry, simply put, it is not civilized. In the eyes of any reasonable Christian, his lifestyle is unhealthy and unsafe for his children. I say you must use your office to stop this abuse."

"How?"

"As your sheriff, I can put his children in my custody. As Judge, you could permanently remove them from him. It would be best for the children. Moreover, it would mark the end of John Tanner. He would become known less as Tanner the author and more as Tanner the abuser of children. Don't you see? His voice would be hushed. He would no longer have the ears of the townspeople. His pride would suffer. He would suffer. I believe he would go back to the wilderness from whence he came. We would be done with him, Henry, and I say good riddance!"

"James, I do not pretend to like the man. Still, this would seem far too harsh a treatment in the eyes of others. You and I know that his children are not being treated poorly. He feeds them well, keeps them in school, sees to it they attend worship service, even has Doctor Jones look after them when he cannot."

"Tanner defames you, Henry."

"Think of how this might affect his children."

"They'd be all the better for it."

"Would they? To have their father removed from their lives? To become wards of the state or the mission?"

"I say again, you are a fool, brother. Use his children against him and be done with him."

"No, James. I must mind public opinion. I refuse."

"But ..."

"Good night, brother."

Under a black, starless sky, James Schoolcraft made his way across town, a single lantern in his hand. Fuming over his brother's words, he paused at the path leading to his home, then passed it by. He soon climbed the back porch steps leading to the door of an attractive neighbor. Hearing a faint sound similar to that of the front door closing, he lifted the latch and entered her home smelling the faintest odor of pipe smoke. Schoolcraft lit a candle and blew out the lantern.

"Darling, are you awake," he said in a forced whisper.

"You've come earlier than you said, James. Did you argue with Henry again?"

"He's blind as a bat," he replied, climbing the stairs to her bedroom. "You should have been along to witness his foolishness."

"No thank you, James. I find your brother too haughty, too abrasive. I cannot tolerate the beast."

Schoolcraft peeled off his shirt. "He wants me to stop seeing you. Claims you are damaging his good name."

"He is pompous, stubborn, and arrogant, James. That is the reputation he should concern himself with. Certainly not his brother's affairs."

"Well said. Did you have a pleasant evening, dear?"

"Me? Oh, yes. I always seem to find ways to entertain myself in your absence."

"I should have come here, instead. My mind is still upset."

"You know, James, I would prefer you always be here with me. Some day, after your divorce, we will be together forever. No more skulking through the dark."

"How wonderful that sounds."

"Have you told her?"

"No, not yet. I've not found the words." James Schoolcraft slipped into bed, pulling the covers over them. "Perhaps tomorrow."

Behind the farm, a soldier slipped through the darkness away from the house, then followed the river trail back to Fort Brady. Lieutenant Bryant Gibsen opened, then closed the barracks door and found his bunk.

"Gibsen," came a voice through the darkness, "you are bound to be caught one of these nights. If not by the Major, then by some jealous suitor."

"Caught? By God, I got caught, alright," replied Gibsen. "But neither by army nor suitor. I found myself caught in an angel's embrace."

"Why not find yourself one of your own instead of the sheriff's wench? Wouldn't you be all the better for it?"

"Better? Better to have some schoolchild begging me to marry her? Some young lass after my freedom? Nay, I'll take this one. She has her eye on marrying into the Schoolcraft family. No talk of me as her groom. And, should a child result, well, it's not my nuisance, it is Schoolcraft's."

"*You* are the nuisance, Gibsen. You, Schoolcraft, and scroungers like you give good men a bad name."

"Bah! I only take what is freely offered."

"I shall not call you a dog. I like dogs. You are less than a dog."

"So you say. But it is I who now drifts to sleep with thoughts of an angel's embrace fresh on my mind. Now, goodnight. I hope your dreams are pleasant, sir. Mine surely will be."

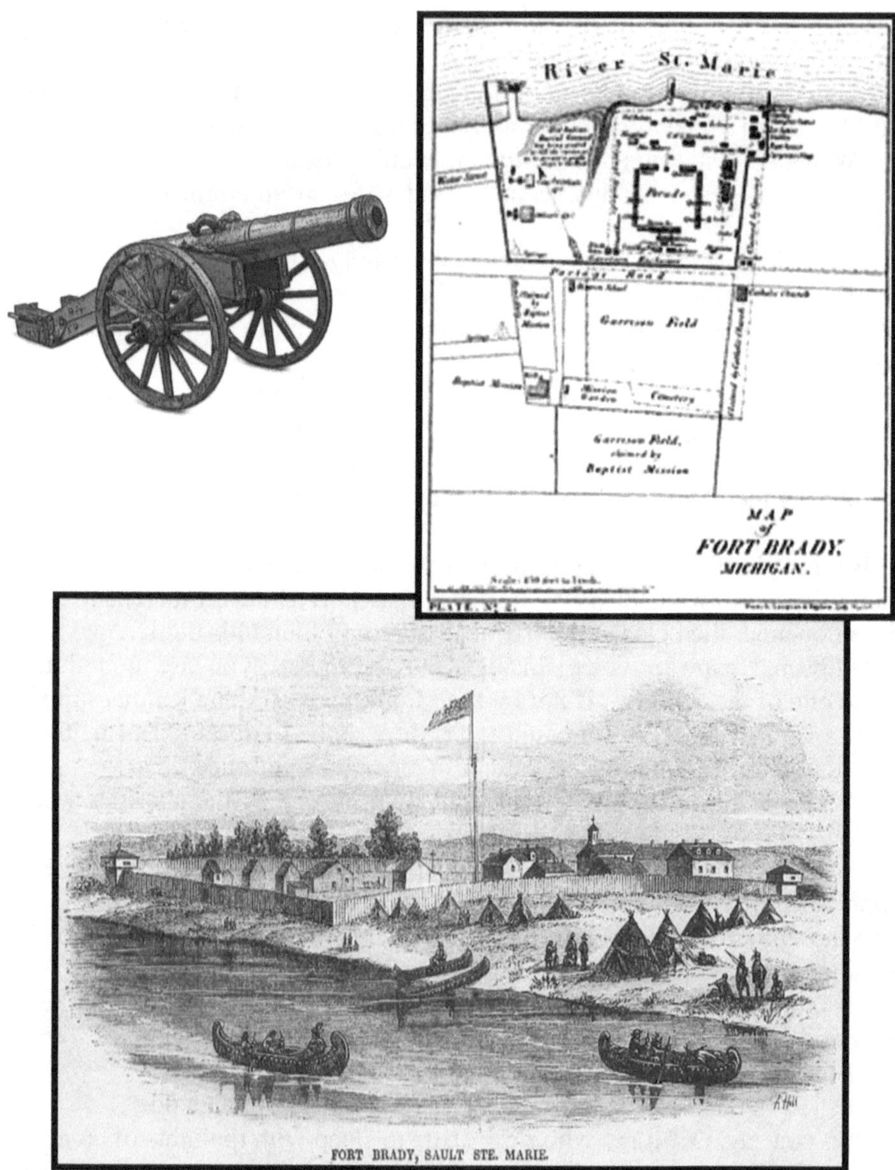

FORT BRADY, SAULT STE. MARIE.

Chapter 39
A Tangling of the Web

Henry Schoolcraft heard the knock. Resting his fork on his plate, he rose from the table, bumping his wine glass as he did. Wine splashed across the cloth as the glass fell to the floor, shattering.

"Blast it all!" he screamed. "Who in blazes calls at suppertime? I'll ring his filthy neck, I will!"

As the maid and the missus tended to the mess, a louder second knock sounded. Henry answered the door to find John Tanner.

"You! What is it, Tanner? What in blazes do you want?"

Taken aback by Schoolcraft's anger, Tanner shouted in reply. "I want my pay, Henry. You paid the others and you will pay me as well."

"You failed to complete the expedition. By law, that is known as breech of contract. It allows me to deny your pay—all of it! Now be off."

"You sink lower than the bellies of the wicked worms that will one day crawl in your casket."

"Leave, Tanner. I do not wish you near my home or family again."

"I will not allow you to refuse me my earnings. I demand you fetch me my pay at once or …."

"Or what?"

"Or I will make known your many clever connivings. I will reveal your true nature. You will lose your undeserved reputation. And, if I am successful, your position."

"Bah. No one will listen to your gibbering and complaining, the crazed ravings of some wild man gone mad from living like a savage. You, Tanner, have become little more than a sour malcontent, frantic with frenzy, rage, and hatred."

"We shall see about that, Schoolcraft. I came here only to ask for my pay. Now, sir, I will not accept it even if offered for I shall witness far greater satisfaction in seeing you suffer public humiliation and loss of your unwarranted appointments."

"Do what you will, Tanner." Schoolcraft slammed the door, cracking the window pane. "Blast it all!" he screamed again.

A month passed. Sheriff James Schoolcraft left his office and headed for the pier. He met the mail boat and carried the small mailbag to the post office, his only duty for the day. The postmaster sorted the mail in minutes, handing the Sheriff a single letter bearing only his name and the word, "Soo."

"That is all, Mister Fields? One letter?"

The postmaster checked again. "Were you expecting more?"

"Yes. A letter from Henry. He is in Detroit for a time as part of his service to Michigan."

"Perhaps next week."

"Yes. Perhaps."

With no work to do, the sheriff left for home early, but passed the path to his house and headed for that of his lover. Climbing the back porch steps, he entered, hanging his hat on a hook. As he removed his coat, he heard a man's voice upstairs. Schoolcraft stood listening for a moment, then pulled a flintlock pistol from a pocket in his coat. He checked the pan for powder, and crept, step by step, up the creaking stairway.

"Shh!" came a whisper through the open bedroom door. "I think I hear him coming."

Schoolcraft rushed now, taking the steps two at a time. He reached the top and burst into the bedroom to see a man pulling on his britches, a stripe down the side of each pant leg. Schoolcraft raised the pistol, pulling the hammer back.

"Please James! Don't!" screamed the woman.

"And tell me, dear, why I should not kill this intruder where he stands?"

The officer calmly continued dressing, pulling on his shirt and sliding his arms under the suspenders. "If you intend to kill me, Sheriff, do not do it for fear I stole from you. For what I took was freely offered."

"Who is this man?" Schoolcraft shouted. "What name will I see on his headstone?"

"I am Lieutenant Bryant Gibsen, if you must know. You, Sheriff, should thank me—I have been tending to your boudoir duties for months on end."

"Months?"

"'Tis true, James. I shared time with Bryant in your absence this summer. You were not there for me. He was."

"This summer? Am I to believe, all the while I was on the expedition this man shared your bed? Eleven weeks?"

"Sheriff, please, turn the pistol away. If shooting either of us was in the cards today, you would have already pulled the trigger."

Schoolcraft gently lowered the hammer and the pistol.

"James, darling, please understand that Bryant is not at fault. It is I who you need to blame."

"Sheriff, you must not take my coming here as an insult to your character. On the contrary, you should be proud! You have chosen a lover so eye-catching, so alluring, that other men envy you, envy you to the point of losing all sensibility."

"Lieutenant … Gibsen, is it? Don your boots and remove yourself from my sight at once. Should you return, you *will* hear the crack of my pistol."

"I will leave, Sheriff. However, should you lay hand to this fair woman, it is *you* who will hear *my* shot the same instant you feel my bullet pierce your heart."

Chapter 40
Quimby's Offer

Martha laid a fresh sheet of paper on her school slate. She dipped her pen tip in the ink and prepared to write. "All right, Papa. Say it right so I needn't have to start over."

John Tanner stroked his chin and began.

"Dearest Friend, Lewis Cass of Detroit

"I write to you in despair for, though I didst suffer eleven weeks in the company of Henry R. Schoolcraft during the recent expedition westward, I and only I have not been paid. Know you that upon return to Mackinac, he forbade me to publish my recollection of the expedition and when I refused to agree, he ejected me and now refuses me my due pay. Know you as well, that he has kept me away from my livelihood by hiring his brother-in-law and sister-in-law in my place as interpreter. He has made his brother, James, the Sheriff and Clerk of Court. No family takes more from your coffers than does this family of false servants of yours. Having no more to say, I bid you good-bye now and good health to you as well.

"Yours in highest admiration,

"John Falcon Tanner"

The reply from Governor Cass arrived by mail boat two weeks later.

"Dear Mister Tanner,

"I do hope this correspondence finds you and your children in good health, albeit your prosperity may suffer from the oversight you reveal in your complaint.

"I received your notice of non-payment of due wages for eleven weeks on the trail and have instructed Mister Schoolcraft to promptly rectify this misunderstanding. He will do so upon his return to Sault Ste. Marie from Detroit in three weeks time.

"I have discussed your other complaints with Mister Schoolcraft at length and I now conclude only that he has sought out and discovered the most qualified employees available for the positions they now hold. Although this may look inappropriate to some, I believe it is of paramount interest of our fair Territory of Michigan to employ the most capable to serve the citizenry.

"Most sincerely yours,

"Lewis Cass, Governor of Michigan Territory and War Department Secretary to the Honorable President of the United States."

Ongoing reading lessons from his daughter allowed John Tanner to sound out and speak each of the governor's words. Though he struggled to get through the message, he understood enough words to make it clear that Henry Schoolcraft would be spared any disciplinary action from Governor Cass.

"Even Lewis Cass turns against me," complained Tanner. How am I to carry on when all sides seem to suffer me one blow after the last? To blazes with the lot of 'em!" He crumpled the letter and tossed it into the fire. Immediately, he reached in, retrieved it, and swatted out the flame. Flattening the page, now charred along one side, he read it again, then put it between two of Martha's books where she would find it during her studies.

An hour later, James, Martha, and little Marie arrived from the mission school. John dished up four bowls of muskrat stew and the bread he'd baked over the coals earlier that day. After supper, Martha helped her father with the letter.

"What is this word, misun…?" he asked, pointing at the page.

"Misunderstanding, Papa."

"Ah, so the governor thinks that the wily polecat, Henry Schoolcraft, did not realize my ill-treatment. It is Lewis Cass who misunderstands. Schoolcraft is clever and cunning with his words and sly in his scheming. Well, we will see what clever words and schemes he has when he arrives from Detroit."

Doctor James continued transcribing John Tanner's recollections of the expedition. Night after night, they worked by a single, whale oil lamp. One evening, as they were completing another chapter, someone rapped on the door. Edwin answered the knock.

"Major Quimby, Edora, Elsie! Please, come in." The doctor turned to Tanner. "John, look who visits us! Do open a bottle of cider!"

"Well, Mister Tanner," said the major, "how nice to see you. Do we interrupt? We could return anoth…."

"Nonsense!" said Edwin "Yours is a welcome interruption, if an interruption at all. Your daughters light up the room, as always." Edwin bowed, lifting and kissing the gloved hands of the two young women.

"I agree," Tanner said, filling the cups. "Your visit shatters the tedium we suffer upon ourselves night by night. What brings you out this one?"

"What else but the women in my life, John? I have been assigned a mission."

"A mission, Papa?" said Elsie. "This is hardly a mission. Mister Tanner, I have been speaking with your daughter, Martha. We share the same classroom now and again. She tells me of your great progress in reading."

"John, I did not know," Edwin said. "This is wonderful! Think of it. One day you will be able to read books—your own narratives for Heaven's sake!" He offered a cup of cider to Edora with a smile.

"Mister Tanner," said Major Quimby, "my daughters and their ever-thoughtful mother wish to extend an offer."

Edora interrupted. "We wish you to use our library, Mister Tanner. We have a fine selection, all manner of books to help you along."

"And you could bring Martha and Marie if you want," added Elsie.

"Mister Tanner, my daughters, seldom denied their wishes as they are, will understand if you say no. However, know that we are sincere in this offer. We would be honored to have a popular author use our study."

Tanner filled the cups again. "Major, Edora, Elsie, I accept."

"Major," asked Edwin, "would you consider going one step beyond? Would you allow Mister Tanner and me to work on his next narrative in your library? It would be wonderful to have access to such rich reference books. Why, your maps alone could …."

"Say no more, Doctor James. My family would be delighted."

"Edwin," said Tanner, "we keep some very late hours."

"Fret not disturbing my family, sir. We have an outside entrance and you may come and go with no concern."

"This is so wonderful," said Edora. "We will look for you tomorrow, Edwi… Doctor James? Oh, Mister Tanner, you as well?"

"Miss Quimby, after supper I will deliver the good doctor to your door."

"And I shall serve the tea!" exclaimed Elsie.

James Schoolcraft woke early. Shaved, dressed, and fed, he slipped through the woods to the home of his lover. An hour later, he strolled along the river toward his office in the early morning light. No sooner had he left when Lieutenant Gibsen climbed the same steps, entering her home. Within seconds, he stood next to her bed.

"Bryant, you should not be here. James was sincere in his threat."

"He cannot keep my heart from longing for you. You must understand."

"I do, Bryant, I do. But remember, he is a Schoolcraft and, like his brother, too proud to be bested. You must be careful."

"There must be some way we can be together."

"Not in this life, I fear."

"In this life?"

"Bryant, he plans to divorce his wife and take me as his bride."

"Poppycock!"

"'Tis true."

"He says the same to Polly Wilson and half the chambermaids in Detroit."

"But he loves me. As much as I enjoy your company, Bryant, I fear you and I must remain apart. Our love cannot survive as things now exist. Now leave before …"

"No." Gibsen slipped off his suspenders.

"Please, Bryant, go and never return lest he slay you and I see your coffin every night in my dreams."

"Slay me? I think not," replied Gibsen, pulling off his boots.

Lieutenant Gibsen left by the back door, the way he came. He did not see James Schoolcraft who watched him slip through the woods toward Fort Brady. The sheriff stared at the second story bedroom window. Fuming, he walked to work, this time arriving at his office where he sat alone for the remainder of the day.

Over time, Bryant Gibsen's lust turned to love and his contempt for James Schoolcraft to jealousy. He often hid in the woods behind her home, admiring her from afar and plotting a way to remove Schoolcraft from their lives. A thousand ideas came and went. One returned over and over. Each time it did, Gibsen resolved another part of the problem, another fault with the plan, another oversight that might lead him to the gallows. As months passed, his plan matured until only one detail remained: Gibsen needed someone to assume blame for the murder.

The return of Henry Schoolcraft to Sault Ste. Marie happened on a Thursday. His brother met him at the docks with a horse and wagon.

"Tell me, James, does John Tanner continue to squeak and squeal, like the hungry piglet he is? Or has his disdain for me settled some?"

"I fear Tanner still complains of the name Schoolcraft at every turn in the road. Most here turn a deaf ear to him as they have tired of his whimpering."

"James, do you know that this impudent white savage had the audacity to send a letter to the governor? A letter intended to embarrass me? Belittle me? And this, after all I have done for him?"

"I dare say he has some cheek."

"He filed a complaint that I unduly withheld his pay due him for the expedition."

"Preposterous. Considering his behavior, he deserved no pay."

"Lewis Cass has ordered me to honor Tanner's claim for back wages."

"Will you, Henry?"

"I fear I must, though I have no funds in the budget. Thus, he will need to wait for his money."

"How long?"

"Another year."

"That should fix him."

"It will not. Tanner has his other income from that mediocre book of his."

"You know, there is a way, Henry. I told you of it months ago."

"Take the children, I know. After learning he sent that letter to Lewis Cass, I cleared a path."

"A path?"

"The Michigan Legislature has already approved of it. The children may be sent to Detroit to be put into the care of the Catholic missionaries serving the territorial government there."

"I see. Then as Sheriff, I will …"

"Wait. You will wait until I say, James. The timing must be precise."

Chapter 41
The Punishment

John Tanner resumed his gospel interpretations at Abel Bingham's mission school. This volunteer work along with his study of reading and evening work on his second book kept him occupied over the coming weeks.

His days started early and reached late into the night. Each morning, he would lead his horse to the mission school as daughters, Martha and Marie, and son, James, rode bareback. James, the eldest, and Marie, the youngest, attended classes. Meanwhile, Martha read Bible verses to her father who translated each into Ojibwe. Martha carefully wrote every word as her father sounded them out. Pages of text soon piled up on the table between them. One morning, Reverend Bingham interrupted.

"John, I must speak with you about your son, James."

"James?"

"He has become more of a burden to the mission than we can endure."

"My boy does have spirit. I will give you that."

"I fear his behavior is far less than the women of the school can tolerate."

"I will deal with James, Reverend. His conduct will improve."

"You do not understand. This morning, before class began, James set some pine needles afire that filled the school with eye-watering smoke. John, he could have burnt down the school. We cannot risk such behavior."

"James did this? James?"

"Your son is far beyond our control—so far that I feel I must expel the boy."

"Expel my son? Nonsense! He may have the spirit of a bobcat inside, yes, but expel him?"

"You will have to assume the balance of his education at your home."

"I stand before you in utter disbelief! Where was his mother in all this?"

"Therezia knows of his deeds."

"And?"

"She, too, has thrown up her hands in despair. Therezia claims that James is now your responsibility. She will have no more to do with the rascal."

"I see. Bring him to me. I will take him home and return him tomorrow. Then you will see a new James, a better James."

"As much as I would like to deliver him to you, John, I cannot."

"You cannot?"

"He's run off."

"My son, James, run off? Run off to where?"

"Who knows? He took your horse. I suppose he expected a thrashing."

"That James! My, he does have spirit." Tanner turned to his daughter. "Martha, I need to find your brother. Tend to your little sister."

"Yes, Papa," she answered. Then, "Papa, please do not beat him. James is good in his heart, even if at times he is as wild as a wolverine in his head."

By the time his father reached their lodge, James had come and gone. John followed the hoof prints down the road until they turned off toward St. Mary's River. The tracks led to a trail along the riverbank, then around a large muskeg swamp. John crossed the swamp, knowing this shorter route might allow him to head off his son. Midway through the muskeg, a fox shot out from between the cranberry bushes, ran ahead, then stopped to look back.

"O-saw wah-goosh, do you lead me? As a compass from Wenebojo?"

The fox turned and ran. Tanner followed, soon tripping over a large bone.

"Moose?" he asked himself. "Red Fox, why lead me to moose bones? Or is this one of *your* tricks, Wenebojo? A prank designed to stop me from finding my son? What is the reason I stumble on this?

The fox disappeared into the muskeg. A few steps later Tanner found another bone and a tattered buckskin shirt. Then, a single moccasin and more bones scattered nearby. He looked at the teeth marks on the bones. "Wolves have feasted on you, my friend," he whispered. "I hope you perished before they came upon you and not after."

Tanner pulled a pinch of tobacco from his pouch and chanted as the tobacco drifted down onto the bones. "May your life in the next place be a pleasant one." He turned, hiking the short remaining distance through the swamp, then up and onto the riverbank trail. There, he found the fox waiting.

"Again, you tease me, Red Fox. What is this foolishness? Do I misunderstand? Is this a test? What is your reason for this?"

The fox barked, then ran down the bank into the muskeg again. Tanner watched its white-tipped tail bob behind and vanish.

"Wenebojo, you confuse me. Will I ever know the meaning of this?"

Tanner sat, leaning against a large oak split by lightning, waiting for his son. When a horse and rider appeared far down the trail, he hid behind the tree. As James rode up, his father stepped onto the trail and snatched the reins from his son's hands.

"Pa?"

"You chose the wrong path this morning at your school. Now you steal away. Son, before a man leaves his home, he must settle his accounts. Is this how you settle yours? By taking your father's horse?"

"Pa, I meant no harm. I swear!"

"No matter. You need to stand tall for your actions. Every man does."

The boy hung his head. "I am sorry, Pa."

"Get down from my horse."

James dismounted, trembling, unable to look at his father.

"Please don't beat me, Pa. I am dreadful sorry for runnin' off. 'Specially with your rifle."

Tanner looked at the scabbard slung across the horse's rump. "You took my rifle?"

"I did, Pa. Don't beat the daylights outa me. It's an old rifle, Pa. That's all it is. Just an old, worn out musket. Don't beat me for it, Pa."

"You think this is about an old rifle?"

"I didn't think, Pa. Just up and left. Please don't beat me."

James watched as his father pulled the old flintlock from the scabbard. The rifle had fed his family and many others during his years in the Red River Valley. When fellow trappers struggled to find food, it saved them from starving. He'd killed bear and buffalo, deer and wildcats, caribou and elk with this rifle. The stock and ramrod showed their age and a nail from a thrown horseshoe held the hammer in place. Yet, the old muzzleloader was part of him. Memories flashed through his mind of many hunts, many times he carried it through blizzards and under blistering summer sun, of many long journeys when it lay in his canoe as he paddled lakes and streams.

John Tanner looked into his son's eyes. Then, with both hands clutching the muzzle, he swung the rifle around and around over his head and flung the rifle high into the air. They watched as the rifle, slowly spinning, sailed, then splashed into the muskeg swamp. Tanner turned to his son.

"James, you are worth more to me than anything. This is *not* about the rifle. It is about what you did at school. It is also about being a man."

James shook with fear. "Please, Pa. Don't beat me. Please!"

Tanner unfastened one of the horse's reins from the bit. "Turn around."

James obeyed. John doubled the leather thong and whipped the boy's behind. James shrieked and turned. Bawling now, the fourteen-year-old grabbed the leather with one hand and hit his father on the chin with the other. Tanner fell.

"I told you don't beat me! You do and I'll knock you down again."

Tanner rose to his feet, grabbed his son by the throat and began slapping him. The boy fell, squealing and shouting, "Please, Pa. Please don't! No!"

Though it seemed like hours to both James and his father, the beating was over in seconds. Tanner hoisted his bawling son onto the horse. James slumped onto the animal's shoulders, sobbing. "I'm sorry, Pa. Sorry I ain't like Martha and Marie."

"Just be honest, kind, and forthright, James. All a man needs to be and all a father can hope for."

John retied the leather thong to the bit and led the horse through town, James whimpering all the way home. As they passed the houses of neighbors, John saw curtains move as eyes witnessed the sobbing boy slumped onto the horse's neck, his hands clutching the mane. At their lodge near the edge of town, John Tanner pulled his son from the saddle, carried him inside, and flopped him onto the dirt floor.

"Lay quiet until I say, son. While you do, think of all that has happened today, for I shall be thinking of the same. James, you are not a bad person. You merely made bad choices. Tomorrow you will face another day and make more choices. Let us hope they are the right choices."

"I am sorry for what I done, Pa."

"Sorry is for the past. Think of the future. Tomorrow is a new day, a day given us by Gitchee Manitou. Unspoiled, James—free from flaws, free from evils. Our task is to not spoil its perfection with our selfish, wicked ways. It is not easy, son. Yet, we must try."

"I will, Pa. You will be proud of me, I know."

The next morning, John woke to voices outside. In the early morning light, Sheriff James Schoolcraft and two armed deputies called his name.

"John Tanner, I am here to arrest you for the beating of your child, James. Come quietly."

Tanner stepped outside. "I did nothing that my father or your father did not do, Schoolcraft."

"Come along, Tanner, or suffer the same as your son."

"Damn you, Schoolcraft! You know as well as I that your visit here has nothing to do with my son. It is your plump brother who put you up to this. Admit it!"

"Come quietly, Tanner."

"And who will tend to my children?"

"I will see to it they are cared for. Come along now."

"And what, then?"

"You will go before the regional judge."

"Judge Henry Schoolcraft? Your plump brother?"

"Yes. Judge Henry Schoolcraft."

"Schoolcraft, you forget who you are dealing with. Seize me and I swear it will be your undoing, one way or another."

"One way or another? What is meant by that?"

"Take it for what it is."

"I do not abide well with threats, John Tanner. Especially threats from some white savage, unable to make his way in a civilized fashion. Succumb to arrest or, by the Lord and the law, I will put my men on you here and now."

"Your men? I might have known *you* would not enter the fray. Has either one the courage to lay hand on this ... *white savage*, as you call me? Do they know that if I am truly a savage, as you say, the first man to do so might be first to lose his eyes? His nose? Even his scalp?"

"Arrest him!" ordered Schoolcraft.

Neither man moved.

"Take him, I said!"

The taller of the two men rushed at Tanner while the other raised his pistol. Tanner grabbed the tall man's arm and spun him around to the ground. The other man fired his pistol but missed. Tanner dove, knocking him into the Sheriff who stumbled backward and fell. Within seconds, Tanner had all three men disarmed and running for their lives.

Tanner shouted, "Return, James Schoolcraft, and you will soon face your maker. Tell your plump brother the same!"

Chapter 42
The Second Abduction

Sheriff James Schoolcraft left the office of his brother with a letter in hand. He stepped up into his buggy and set out for the Baptist Mission.

An hour later, Reverend Bingham arrived at Tanner's home.

"John, I have disturbing news."

"News? What news? Is it James? Has my son again done something wrong? Something wicked? I thought we were through with all of that. I thought …"

"Your James did nothing wrong. He is fine."

"My daughters? Are they all right?"

"All right? Well, yes. Yes, they are fine."

"What in the blazes is it?"

"Your children have been taken."

"Taken? What do you mean? Speak up!"

"Schoolcraft. Sheriff James Schoolcraft."

"What? Why? What gives him the right to steal my children? And for what purpose?"

"He showed me a warrant from the Michigan Legislature awarding custody of your children to the governor."

"Governor Cass? Lewis Cass? But he is a friend! Why would he do this to me?"

"My son, they feel you are not a fit father, that the children suffer in your care, that you beat them."

"What? My children live happy lives with their father. I never lift a hand to them."

"You beat your boy. Many witnessed you leading him through town on horseback afterward."

"I punished him for his wrongdoings. I did what every caring father does when his pup goes astray."

"There were complaints."

"Complaints? From whom?"

"The Schoolcrafts."

"I should have known."

"Where are my children now?"

"On their way to Detroit"

"Detroit?"

"By water."

"My God! Should I not have been told that I could kiss them goodbye?"

"It would have been better, yes. I am sure that the sheriff worried you would fly into a rage."

"Would not, should not any father?"

"John, I may have the ability to intercede."

"You? How so?"

"The church, my church, has taken in abandoned children. I could request your young ones be placed in my care again, as when you returned after being shot and left to die in Rupert's Land."

"Though I resented your laying claim to them then, I would welcome it now."

"I will write to Governor Cass. If he agrees, I will house and feed your children. I will do this for you."

"And for yourself, Abel Bingham. You never did wish them to leave your cluster of helpers—your mission maids and stable boys."

"I will forgive you this remark, but this time only. I will write to Lewis Cass on your behalf. I will also allow you to resume your work on the interpretation of the scriptures for the Ojibwe people. These things I do because I care for you and your children, my son."

"Detroit. My children have been stolen away to Detroit."

"I am so sorry to have brought you such news."

"And, what news! What terrible, terrible news!"

Stewing, John hurried to the office of his friend, Edwin James.

"Edwin, you must help. My children have been taken away by the Schoolcrafts."

"Taken where? What on earth do you mean?"

"Taken to Detroit! To the home of a turncoat, Lewis Cass."

"Our governor? Your friend?"

"Friend, indeed. He conspired with the Schoolcraft clan to steal them away. I am certain they did this to punish me."

"Oh, my, John. Can they do this? Can they swoop down and steal a man's family? I think not!"

"Ah, but they did. Henry Schoolcraft is a clever one. Sneaks in like a mosquito, then plumps himself up on your blood before you know it."

"What is it you wish me to do, John?"

"Write to Lewis Cass. Order him to return my children at once."

"I am hardly in a position to do so, John."

"Write a letter then, a letter that will show I have been wronged. Explain how Henry and James plot against me. Tell Cass I have still not been paid for long overdue wages. Will you do this?"

"I will."

"Tomorrow, I will ride the mail boat south and deliver it to Cass myself so he must look me straight in the eye."

"My friend, we shall write your letter tonight. Do not worry, John. You will have your say. And, if right is on our side, your children."

"Oh yes, Doctor. I will have them back. One way or another!"

John Tanner boarded the mail boat from the Sault to Detroit with stops at Mackinac Island, Saginaw River, and Port Huron. Reaching Detroit, he went straight to the Woodworth Hotel, the same public house where he slept two years earlier on his return from New York City. He plopped his pack onto the floor and sat at a table. A pleasant, fair-haired woman served him.

"I believe we met two years ago," he said, "though we spoke only for a few moments. I doubt you remember."

"You are wrong, Mister Tanner. I recall the talk we shared about your life in the frontier."

"So, you do remember. I am pleased. Though I have mentioned it to no others, I have thought of you often."

"I am flattered, sir. What brings you to our city?"

"You do."

"Me?"

"You and my poor children."

"I don't understand, sir."

"I have decided to remarry. My children need a mother and I a wife. My first choice was to come here in hope that you might allow me to court you."

"My word! You are to the point, sir. And what if I am already taken? Perhaps another suitor has my attention. What then, John?"

"If this is so, then I must lower my head in despair, slunk away, and search elsewhere. Perhaps I should leave now?"

"No. No, John. Stay. There is no other man in my heart, though I have long dreamt my man would one day come. Court me if you wish."

"And, what of the ties that bind you here?"

"My father will be upset, yes. But as long as he has his business here and there is profit to be made, he will find another to cook, clean, and make the beds." She placed a flagon of ale before him. "John, come sit with me. You tell me your stories and I will tell you mine. Perhaps, sir, this was meant to be."

The following day, Tanner walked through the busy streets of Detroit to the Governor's estate. There, he visited with his children before meeting with Governor Cass.

"John," said Cass, "please forgive me for not being forthright with you. The reports of your children being abused bewildered me and my fellow legislators to no end. We only acted to protect the children. Now that I have talked with them, I realize you may have been wronged."

"I assume Henry Schoolcraft told you these lies? Schoolcraft caused this grievous assault on my character and the happiness of my children?"

"Yes. But, I dare say, John. He is one of our most skillful and inspiring lawmakers. To the point, his words inspired this dreadful oversight."

"Oversight? You dare refer to this as an oversight? This is more likened to abduction, Lewis. No less of an abduction than I faced when I was their age. Schoolcraft and all who supported him should be jailed!"

"Settle your temper, John. No need to …"

"Governor! If a band of red men took three children, would these men not soon swing from your gallows?"

"Yes, but this was done by act of law, not by dark of night."

"Little difference when the outcome is the same, sir!"

"The same? John, your children will not be forced to live like Indians."

"Lewis, are you certain my children do not *prefer* living like Indians? Have you taken even a moment to ask them?"

"I suppose you are right. It is their lives we must consider, not our conventions, our way of life."

"Lewis, I came here to deliver this letter from my friend and the fellow who transcribes my stories, Doctor James."

"James? Edwin James? The surgeon who accompanied Major Long on his expedition to the Rocky Mountains?"

"The same." Tanner handed Cass the letter. "This should convince you of my reputation as a good, loving father and a dependable provider. It will also show how I am slandered, maligned, and vilified by the Schoolcrafts. They strive to make me look like less of a citizen simply because I prefer buckskin to wool. And all because your plump scalawag, Henry, does not wish me to publish my next book and his brother fears I shout too loud about his unfair appointment to the post of sheriff, sutler, and Clerk of Court by Henry."

"Publish your second book, my friend. Let nothing stop you. As for Henry's brother, I approved his appointment based on Henry's recommendation. I will reconsider it when next it comes to the floor for review. It is the best I can do."

"And must I wait until the next term to be paid my due wages?"

"What? You have not been paid? I instructed Henry to deliver your wages a month ago. Has he not?"

"Henry Schoolcraft has told me himself that you, Governor Lewis Cass, have said I need not be paid until next year's budget is approved. Do you deny this?"

"I do, sir! You were misled. Perhaps Henry did not understand my orders."

"More likely he feels he need not follow them."

"Nonsense. He knows who butters his bread."

"Governor, I feel it is only right that I inform you that, if I do not get satisfaction, I intend to go to Washington. Perhaps Father Martin Van Buren will lend me his ear."

"The president? Oh, my! You needn't go that far. I will write to Henry. He'd be a fool to not listen to me."

"And when he does not? Are you not then the fool?

"Your temper and insolence do you no favor, Mister Tanner."

"Lately, Governor, my temper and insolence are the only things that seem to gain attention."

John Tanner remained in Detroit two weeks, then returned to Sault Ste. Marie with his third bride on his arm and assurance from Governor Cass that his children would soon follow. With the villagers gawking, the newlyweds strolled down Water Street and beyond to John's birch bark lodge at the edge of town where his bride saw her rustic but well kept home.

"This is delightful, John! Fascinating! We will live the lives of those who came here first. You must show me all the ways of the Ojibwe women. Teach me that I might learn their secrets!"

"I will. Their lives, the lives of those who came before, are simple when compared with those of Whites. Yes. I will take you to the lodges of my many friends who live the Indian way. You will see. It is a good life. You will be happy with it. First, though, I will show you how warm and comfortable a buffalo blanket can be. Come inside my lodge—our lodge."

John's bride gave him a new look on life. Each evening, they walked through the town, his wife winning the friendship of everyone they encountered. Winter was long. The following spring, she gave birth to a son. They named him James Louis. James, for their friend, Edwin, and Louis, in honor of the governor. The child became their joy and obsession.

Then, one summer evening, John found himself confronted by a drunken Sheriff Schoolcraft at his door.

"John Tanner," he slurred, "you and that squaw of yours are nothing but a curse on our fair village. Go back to Prince Rupert's Land, savage—back to Winnipeg and your murderous people—your renegade Rainy River kin!"

"You are drunk, Schoolcraft. Go home. Leave us be."

"I will sleep best when you are gone forever. You are a savage killer of women and children. Of this I have proof."

"Pester me, Schoolcraft, and you will sleep forever and much sooner than you think."

"Your threats mean nothing to me, Tanner. I will see you gone, by God— one way or another. Do not think you can outwit me, savage. I am James Schoolcraft, Sheriff and Clerk of Court."

"You are nothing more to me than a woodtick waiting to be crushed under my heel and tossed into the coals of my fire. Go away, miserable drunken Schoolcraft."

"I'll go, but know that I will soon return to remove you and your Detroit wench from our village."

With both hands, Tanner grabbed the sheriff by the collar. "Speak rudely once more of my bride and I will slice your tongue from your gullet and stuff it down your bloody throat still quivering!" Tanner pushed him back and watched him sprawl onto the path. He closed the door and turned to his wife. "Shut your ears to this drunken lout. He cannot come between us."

"Is he right, John? Did you slay women and children?"

"No. Pay no mind to Schoolcraft. He is obsessed with ruining us."

"He said he had proof."

"A compliment, of sorts. It means someone read my book to him."

"So, you did not kill others?"

"No. My book tells of a time when, many years past, I was one of one thousand Red River Ojibwe who defended our hunting grounds from the Sioux. I fought alongside the Assinneboin and saw deaths on both sides but I would not raise my tomahawk. Those who died gave their lives for nothing. They fight still. Always have. They will fight until something more important brings them together as one. Now wash these foul words of James Schoolcraft from your mind. Rid yourself of this memory. Think, instead, of good days that lie before us. Many good days.

Chapter 43
The Tragedy of Little Marie

Work on Tanner's second narrative progressed slowly. One evening, between chapters, Doctor James pulled a letter from his coat pocket.

"John, I received a reply from Governor Cass. It is a copy of a correspondence from the Governor to Henry Schoolcraft. I believe you should take heed of these excerpts."

"Will my children be returned?"

"Hear for yourself, my friend. It begins, 'To the most honorable Henry Rowe Schoolcraft.'"

"Most honorable?" blurted Tanner. "Bah! Least honorable, lest you take into account his brother."

Edwin James held the note from Governor Lewis Cass to the candlelight.

Tanner's daughter has arrived [in Detroit] and is desirous of remaining with us. I asked her if her father was willing, and I understood that he was unwilling she should go. Whether he wished she should come here, I am desirous of knowing.

I am unwilling his daughter should remain, if he has any objections. Be good enough to let him know this view, and my feelings upon the subject. I believe him a very upright man, and I would not, on any account, do anything, he might conceive as injury.

He seemed to suppose that I had 'stolen' her, and also that *I* had discharged [him] from [his employment in your] office. I told him I knew nothing of his dismissal, but advised [him] to go to you and to apologize for all that was wrong and promise to do well.

Since then I have reflected upon his situation, and perceiving not the least feeling on account of [his anger and] the improper expressions he used, but attributing them to his grievance and perhaps some constitutional warmth of temper, I really pity him very much. He seems to me a forlorn heart broken man.

He wrote me also that he had four months pay due and speaks as tho I kept the money from him. But I find by your August account that he is unpaid, and conclude that your funds are exhausted. For the amount due to him please draw a draft in the usual form but leave the endorsement blank. But I beg you to pay him, even if you have to borrow money, on your own credits or mine, as I would not for any consideration, [wish] that the poor man should suffer for his money."*

"Yours in earnest, Lewis Cass, et cetera, et cetera," said Edwin.

*Precise words from Governor Lewis Cass to Henry Schoolcraft.

"Doctor, this *is* good news! My children *will* be returning!"

"Yes and no, John. I took the liberty of speaking with Henry Schoolcraft about this. He said he would allow them to be housed at the mission but no closer. He feels such would be more than a sufficient response to the governor's request and safer for the children."

"So. These wallowing swine, the Schoolcrafts, continue their persecution and harassment. It is time they learn that the hound chases the swine and not the other way around."

"Do not act out of anger, John. Perhaps another letter to the governor is in order. I will help you …"

"The time for letter writing is over. They paint me as a savage from the wilderness. Perhaps time has come for the Schoolcrafts to see how such grievances are dealt with by those who live in that wilderness."

A long winter soon set in, colder than most and fraught with heavy snowfalls. Life in Michigan's Upper Peninsula became difficult for all. But none suffered more than John Tanner's wife. By spring, the novelty of living the Ojibwe life gave way to a desire for a cabin with a cast iron stove and chimney rather than a birch lodge with a dirt floor and a fire ring beneath a smoke hole in the roof. She longed for the luxury of a table and chairs, a bed with a feather mattress, a window. John, unable to suppress his anger and frustration with the Schoolcrafts, paid little heed to her complaints.

"Husband, I can no longer endure living here in this … hut you call your lodge. When the wind howls, the snow blows in through the smoke hole faster than I can shoo it out. The wet walls drip on us night and day. The mud from the floor soils everything, even our food. Surely you can find us a better cabin."

"If you mean moving to Detroit, I will not have it."

"John, this life is not for me. Don't you see that? It is always damp in here. I am cold day and night."

Tanner tossed a log onto the fire.

"And that, Husband, is the last stick of our firewood."

"I will find more."

"The snow is too deep to find wood. You will have to climb trees to find dead limbs. Is this the life you wish to endure?"

"It is the life I have endured for many years. Many of those winters were harder than this. Yet, I survived. Wife, we will survive this winter as well."

"Please, John, we must find a better place, a better life, far from here. We must find a place where you are content, where you do not spend day and night thinking about …"

"You chirp like the hungry young crow demanding to be fed. When spring comes, I will find worms for you to eat."

Tanner pulled on his buffalo robe and stepped outside. He fetched his snowshoes from the snow bank, slipped his feet in the bindings, and trudged off toward the woods, pulling his toboggan. As he tramped above chest-deep snow, he could hear his wife crying in the lodge.

"Spring will come," he shouted, not knowing if she could hear. "Spring will come soon. You will be happy then."

Spring came, along with week after week of rain and cold. And, although the snow melted, the firewood they found in the forest was wet—too wet to burn. Cold and damp, John and his wife and child remained indoors, hidden from the rain. When the rain paused, John headed for the St. Mary's River where the walleyes were moving upstream to spawn. With no dry wood for a fire, they ate the fish he speared raw.

The cold, damp weather persisted. Young James developed a severe cough. They took him across town to visit Doctor James.

"Your son has a fever, but nothing to fear. I have seen many with the same cough this spring. As soon as the sunshine finally pushes away the rainy weather, your son's condition will improve. In the meantime, I have a shed full of dry firewood. John, you are welcome to all you need to get by until warm days return."

"I thank you, Edwin, but I cannot accept this. *You* sought, cut, and stacked that wood. It would be wrong for me to warm myself over your firewood."

"John, the wood is not for you. It is for your son. He needs to be warm and dry. Take it. Take all of it! Consider this not a gift from a friend but the order of your son's doctor."

John's wife hugged Doctor James. "You are a true friend in every way, Edwin."

"And a friend with much good news. So much, I know not where to begin."

"Good news for whom, Doctor?" said John. "Certainly not the Tanners."

"On the contrary! Tomorrow a ship will arrive bearing Martha and James, your children. Abel Bingham said so himself."

"Really? That is good news. But, what of little Marie?"

"The Reverend said she contracted the mumps. The ship's captain would not allow her on board his vessel. However, as soon as she is fit, she, too, will come. Oh, joy! The Tanners shall be reunited once more."

"Much to the chagrin of *King* Henry Schoolcraft and his court jester-brother, I imagine."

"Dear me, Husband! Must you always give over to your hatred for the Schoolcrafts? Can you not help but turn away good news?"

"A day will soon come when I will no longer care a fig about either of the Schoolcrafts. Nor will anyone else."

"Doctor, will John's children be confined to the mission, then? Away from the cold and damp?"

"According to the reverend, yes."

"I shall see about that," muttered John.

"Frankly, Husband, they would be far better off staying in Detroit."

Tanner glared at his wife, then turned to Edwin. "How much do I owe you?" he asked "And be sure to add in the firewood."

"Owe me? Why, that is the other good news! 'Tis I who owe you—the author, John Tanner! The mail boat brought another payment from Henry Cahill in New York. It seems he has now translated your book into German. John, it is selling very well there and in Austria as well."

"German? My book?"

"I cashed the draft just this morning. Here's your half of the poke, John." Edwin plopped a buckskin pouch heavy with silver coins on the table. "Thirty eight silver dollars, my friend. And there's sure to be more on the way."

John's wife grabbed the bag of coins. "How wonderful! England, France, Germany, where will it end?"

"And America," Edwin said. "Do not forget America. Our sales here are doing very well. By summer's end you two will have enough to purchase a home in town. Perhaps even across the river. There is some good land waiting there—and at a good price."

"We have a home," said John. "A home where we can be close to the earth."

"Close to the earth?" snapped his wife. "Need we be so close that it ends up in our food and on our clothes? A home in town—in *any* town—seems little to ask of an author with books selling on two continents."

Edwin nodded. "A home in town would be better for the boy's health, John."

"But would it be better for his mind? Life would be too easy. He would grow up to be soft and lazy."

"Husband, all who live in houses do not become soft and lazy. Nor do all who live in wigwams become hearty and strong. You know this."

"Hmm. I will ask the spirits. They guided me in the past. They will not fail me now."

"And what will the spirits say when I leave you, when I take our child to Detroit where we might live in better health?"

Tanner said nothing. The glare in his eyes spoke for him. Fearing his anger might turn to rage, he rushed out into the rain, shutting Edwin's door with a slam.

On a sunny, June day, Reverend Abel Bingham, unable to hide the pity and sadness in his eyes, sat across the desk from John Tanner. He reached out for Tanner's hand.

"My son, thank you for coming. I know this was sudden, but I have received the worst of news. I fear there has been a dreadful, dreadful … event."

"Martha? Is it …?"

"No, my son. Martha is well."

"Then ... James?"

"No. Please, let me continue."

"Marie? Little Marie?" Tanner tore his hand from those of Abel Bingham. "How? Will she be all right? Where is she? I must see her this very moment!"

"My son, she is with Him, now."

"Him?"

"God the Father."

"No! Not my sweet little Marie! Your god has no right! Where is my sweet Marie? I must see her this instant!"

"God called for her, my son."

"What?"

"A shipwreck in yesterday's storm on Lake Huron. All hands and passengers drowned. So much grief."

"No! You are wrong!"

"And this because she was ill and not allowed to sail with the others."

"No! I will not hear this!"

"I am so sad for you, my son."

"You must stop calling me your son. I am neither your son nor the son of your merciless god. Nor is my little Marie your god's daughter."

"You mustn't say that. My God *is* God. God of all gods."

Tanner came to his feet, the chair behind plunging to the carpet. "My god is Gitchee-Manitou and he is staring down at you now, wondering why you did not stop Henry and James Schoolcraft from sending her away! You are just as responsible as they. You, Abel Bingham! And do not tell me your god is above mine. For my god, Gitchee Manitou, does not send storms that sink ships and kill children. *Your* god, the god for whom you build your wasteful, luxurious cathedrals, the god for whom you reap money from those who have so little, the god in whose name you fight wars, he is the god who kills children. Not mine!"

"My son ..."

Tanner vaulted across the desk and clutched Bingham's throat with both hands. Squeezing with all his strength, he screamed, *"Do not call me that. I am not your son or the son of your ruthless god!"*

Gasping, the minister fell to the floor.

"Abel Bingham, your actions have resulted in the death of my sweet little Marie. Here is your penance. To atone for your selfishness, your sins against my children, my family, for your greed and the way you manipulate your mission for your own benefit, you will, henceforth, care for my remaining children as though they are your own. Like your children, mine are no longer to toil in your kitchens or scrub the floors of your school. They will not empty your chamber pot each morning. James will no longer muck out your stable or toil in your garden. Martha will no longer wash your filthy laundry.

"Both will eat at your table, morning, noon, and night. Their food will be the same as yours. As they grow older, you will see that they are educated and offered employment until the end of their days or yours, whichever comes first."

"I cannot do this, John," Bingham said between gasps."

Tanner pulled his knife from his sheath and held it to Bingham's throat. "Perhaps you should reconsider."

"All right!" he gasped. "I will obey your wishes."

"Yes, Abel Bingham. You will. For if not, know you that the Falcon will always be watching—waiting to swoop down on you with sharp talons. And long before your god has the good sense to do the same."

Chapter 44
Scrip, Mister Schoolcraft?

Tanner left the same day for the port at Saginaw River to search for his little Marie. He returned five days later, empty-handed. Little Marie was not among the few bodies that washed onto shore after the shipwreck. Like so many others before and after, Lake Huron would be her grave.

Until now, no one in Sault Ste. Marie ever saw tears in John's eyes. Nor had anyone seen him inebriated. But now he stumbled from tavern to tavern, chanting Ojibwe and Sioux songs of grief. One evening, he arrived home to find his wife preparing for a journey of her own.

"John, I was hoping to be gone before you returned."

"Gone? Gone where?"

"I am taking baby James to Detroit to live with my father. It is best."

"No. You will stay here."

"Another winter? Another season would be too long, too much to bear. I will not risk the health of our babe or my own. I am leaving."

"You are not!" Tanner dumped the contents of her satchel onto the ground, a score of silver coins scattered before him. He stared at the coins, then at his wife. "You steal my child *and* my money?"

"We will need money to live."

"Yet, you need little money to live here. I provide all you need. You will stay." He lifted a half-empty whisky bottle to his lips.

"Please. For sake of our child's health, John, let us go."

Tanner sorted through the clothes on the ground, gathering every silver dollar. He stuffed them into the pouch hanging on his belt. "You will stay. I have decided."

"Then, here. You may as well take these, too." She handed him a stack of scrip notes. "These were delivered here last week by Henry Schoolcraft's stable boy.

"From Schoolcraft? Are they poisoned?"

"The boy said these notes are good in trade at James Schoolcraft's general store.

"This is my back pay? The wages Henry owed me?"

"Yes. I used one to buy food. They seem to be the same as other money."

"But only at his brother's store."

"At least it is something."

"It is something, all right. Another twist of the knife into my ribs. Now get this idea of leaving me out of your head. I will not allow it. That is my decision."

Startled, James Schoolcraft looked up from his paper when the tall, lean, buckskin-clad John Tanner charged through the office door, slamming it behind.

"What now, Tanner? Another of your senseless complaints? Another waste of my time?"

Tanner stepped to the desk and slapped a stack of scrip notes in front of the sheriff.

"Scrip, Mister Schoolcraft? You pay me with scrip?"

"These notes are worth as much as any issued by the U.S. Mint, Tanner."

"You were told by the governor to pay my back wages, not give me these notes of promise."

"They are as good as money."

"Yes, but only in your store. I will not trade in your store. Therefore, they are as worthless as the Schoolcraft word and your lies to Governor Cass."

"See here, Tanner, you've no right to speak to me like that!"

"So! Now you wish to take away my right to speak the truth?"

"Get out before I throw you in my calaboose!"

"And how will our governor respond to that? Will he finally see that you and your brother spend all your waking hours trying to wound me? Malign me? Steal from me the respect of my friends and neighbors?"

"Respect you never possessed. Now take your damn pay and get out."

"Yes, I will take my scrip and leave. For, should I leave it, I know you would use it to sweeten your own tea. Better I send it to Lewis Cass along with my account of this."

"Wait! Perhaps I can resolve this by other means."

"Amuse me, Schoolcraft."

"To show you I am your friend and ally, I will allow you to use these as collateral toward a loan—assurance that you will repay. You would then have cash in your pocket to spend when and where you please."

"A loan, you say?"

"Yes. A loan from my own personal account."

"At what rate of interest?"

"A modest ten per-cent. Less than what is charged by the bank."

"I see. In other words, you will give me ninety cents on the dollar and keep the other ten for yourself?"

"Yes. Agreed?"

"You think me a fool? Well, sir, I am not. I am owed a dollar on the dollar. Your conniving does not change that. In fact, it only serves to further embarrass and condemn you for your treachery and deceit. I will let the governor know of this devious offer from the false-hearted brothers Schoolcraft."

"Wait!" shouted the sheriff as Tanner left, slamming the door.

An hour later, at Fort Brady, Henry and James Schoolcraft met in Henry's office. Seeing no one in the hallway, James closed the door. Speaking to his brother in a hushed tone, he said, "We must do something about John Tanner and soon."

"What now? Has he threatened someone anew?"

"He intends to send the scrip I paid him to the governor."

"Let him. It is proof that I paid him his back wages."

"We cannot allow him to do this. When Cass learns the notes can only be used at my store, it will surely convince the governor that this and therefore Tanner's other complaints are defendable. We cannot let Tanner write that letter!"

"I see. How do you propose to stop him?"

"Help me find a reason to arrest him. It must not sound contrived, trivial, or frivolous. It must be a violation that will condemn him in the eyes of the public. Help me."

"Public drunkenness! James, you can arrest him tonight when he leaves Major Quimby's home. He and Doctor James work very late. Though Tanner will not be drunk, who will know? Throw him in jail. Tomorrow, you can spread word he was drunk and slept it off in jail."

"Not enough. This is Sault Ste. Marie. Those villagers who are not stumbling drunk by midnight are already at home asleep. They won't see this as a problem worthy of jail. We need something better."

"Theft?"

"Still not enough. Wait, theft from the church, theft from Abel Bingham's mission! The villagers will be in a rage!"

"Theft of what? And who will do this for us? You?"

James didn't answer.

"And how? Are you willing to break into …"

"I have it! No need to break in when something can break out."

"Explain yourself."

"A cow, Henry. I can do this today. I will simply stroll from my farm through the woods to the mission pasture. There, I will set aside three fence rails, find, and lead a cow home to my farm. No one will think to look there. Tonight, by lamplight, I will have my stable boy butcher her and I will bury the hide in Tanner's yard. Everyone will think he stole the cow from the Baptists—a scheme sure to work!"

That night, in the Quimby family library, Edwin James and John Tanner finished another chapter in the narrative of the expedition to the Mississippi headwaters. John Tanner's wife looked on, holding little James. Edwin put the stopper in the inkwell. He closed the desk as the clock struck ten.

"Gentlemen, you finish early tonight," said Major Quimby. "Time for a toddy before you push off?"

"Certainly," said the doctor.

"Perhaps one," Tanner said. "I fear I had my fill last week. My grief got the better of my sensibilities and I drank far too much."

"I attest to that," said Tanner's wife. "My husband's behavior was unhealthy, shameful, and, I will add, embarrassing."

"Yet justified," said Edora. "I cannot imagine what the pain of losing a child must cause in one's soul."

"It does that," said Tanner. "No matter one's place in life, rich man, wise man, beggar, or fool, we all are emptied by the death of someone close. And more than ever when it arrives unannounced."

"Still, we must endure," added Edwin. "And few know more of endurance than the Falcon. The thousands of readers who now sit, eyes-wide, staring at his book know that well."

"Not *my* book, Doctor James. *Our* book. Your name adorns every copy."

Edora passed around glasses of brandy. "And this next book," she asked, "how is it coming along?"

Tanner grinned. "Miss Quimby, we finished a month past."

"Sir?"

"My dear, we noticed that we had not finished the entire lot of the Major's brandy. Thus we felt a duty to return." Tanner drank his brandy, returning the empty glass to Edora.

"My word!" said Edwin.

"Hair of the dog, Doctor."

"I beg your pardon?"

"Hair of the dog what bit you."

"Make sense of yourself, Mister Tanner."

"I often heard this said in New York. I believe it to be a frequent phrase of many Easterners."

"Hair of the dog?"

"It is often said early in the morning."

"Those Atlantic Seaboard people are a bit odd," added the Major.

"Speaking of early next morning, I fear we must depart." said John's wife, wrapping the blanket around the infant.

Edwin stuffed the manuscript into his satchel, bowed to Edora Quimby, kissing her hand, and followed Tanner outside. Edora shut the door.

"Papa," she said, "I am going to marry that man one day. I know it."

The major looked at his daughter out of the corner of his eye. "Which one?"

"Papa! You know very well which!"

By moonlight, John Tanner crossed the Fort Brady parade ground, carrying his infant son. With him strolled his wife and Doctor James. They ambled down Water Street until Edwin went his way and the Tanners theirs. As they walked, John heard a horse-drawn cart approach from behind. Nearing their home, they saw a man step onto the road ahead, a lantern in hand.

"Edwin?" shouted Tanner. "Edwin, is that you? Did you forget something?"

The man ahead didn't reply. Tanner glanced behind to see the cart nearing.

"Who is there?" he yelled. "Who is it? State your name!"

"'Tis me, John," came a familiar voice, "your old friend, Sheriff James Schoolcraft."

Tanner again looked behind at the approaching cart, then turned to the man ahead.

"What do you want?"

"Only to speak with you a moment, John."

"Speak? Of what?" Tanner yelled.

"A problem we seem to share, John."

"Explain!" Tanner shouted. The cart behind them stopped.

Schoolcraft approached, exposing a pistol with hammer cocked. "Unless you wish to die here and now in a pool of your own savage blood, you will come with us."

"Us?"

Two soldiers climbed from the cart, each with pistols pointed toward Tanner. His wife screamed as one grabbed the child from John's arms and the other pulled her away.

"Come quietly," said Schoolcraft. "This cart will carry you, whether alive or dead. No matter to me. What say you, Tanner, alive or dead?"

"Please, John, for our child's sake, go with them. Please!"

"Alive or dead, Tanner," repeated the sheriff.

"Alive, that I can one day repay you, and your plump brother. However, I will not repay you in scrip. No, it will be real payment, full payment, and permanent."

CHIPPEWA COUNTY
COURT HOUSE

Chapter 45
From Bad to Worse

Two days after being jailed, Judge Henry Schoolcraft called his court to order.

"John Tanner, also called by the Ojibwe name, Shaw-shawwa na-baysay, you stand before me accused of the theft and butchering of a cow belonging to Abel Bingham's Baptist Mission. What say you?"

"I say you and your brother hatched a clever plan this time, your plumpness."

"Dare you insult this court again and you will be fined, jailed, or both, John Tanner. Now, did you steal the cow from the mission?"

"You know very well I did not, as does your brother."

"Mister Tanner, the hide from the stolen cow was found buried near your hut. Do you deny this?"

"If you found it there, then why would I deny you found it there? However, what I must deny is that I buried it nor even knew it ever existed, other than on the poor cow. What I also deny is your innocence in all this. You and James want me gone, one way or t'other. Everyone in this room and in this village now knows this."

"John Tanner, is there anything else you wish to say before I declare my verdict and pass sentence?"

"Yes! I wish to ask but one question of the court."

"Go ahead, then. Ask your one question."

"Where is the meat?"

"What?"

"Where is the meat?"

"The meat?"

"A half-ton of beef."

"Well, perhaps …er …"

"Perhaps? Perhaps it could be stuffed away in salt barrels in your brother's barn, waiting to feed his slovenly children."

"Preposterous! What makes you think such a foolish thought?"

"Words from your brother's very own barn boy, Chester McNutt."

"What's this?"

"While at the river angling for our breakfast meal three days past, I saw him washing blood from his hands. Chester told me he'd been up butchering a cow all night. Might that cow be one in the same as the one you say I stole?"

Flustered, Schoolcraft hesitated, then shouted, "Of course not!" With a flip of his hand, he motioned the sheriff to the bench and whispered, "I thought you said the cow's carcass would be taken to Tanner's lodge. Where in the blazes is it?"

"In my barn," came his brother's hushed reply. "But surely he is guessing. How could he be certain?"

"It matters not how, James. What matters is that he does or, at least, suspects as much. Have you any solution for this, James?"

Mouth agape, the sheriff offered no answer.

"Go home to your farm this minute and dispose of that cow's remains. Be sure no one sees you. Go!"

As his brother left the courthouse, Henry looked at the roomful of villagers, then at Tanner. "Ahem," he said, banging his gavel. "I am declaring a recess while the sheriff seeks out more evidence. My court will resume in …"

Tanner shouted, "So, Henry Schoolcraft, is this how you conduct your court? When you cannot find enough rope to hang an innocent man, you send your little brother scampering off to find more rope?"

Ripples of laughter rolled through the crowd.

"Shame be upon you, Henry Schoolcraft. Shame!" As Tanner sat, Doctor James stood.

"John Tanner is dead right, Henry! Clearly, something is afoot, here. I, for one, will not tolerate this in my community."

"*Your* community? How dare you! You are out of order, Doctor James. Sit down."

"I shan't! For months, now, you and your brother have done all possible to discredit this man, to ruin him in the eyes of his friends and neighbors, all these people here attending. You Schoolcrafts have danced your devious dance for too long. Time's now come for you to pay the piper his due."

Cheers rose from the room.

Schoolcraft slammed his gavel. "Sit down, Doctor James! Sit before I eject you from this …."

A man in the back row stood. "Then you will need to cast me out, too, Judge!"

"And me, Henry," cried out another as he came to his feet.

Within seconds, all in the room stood in support of the defendant.

Henry sighed. "John Tanner, in light of … missing evidence, I will, in due time, release you from custody of this court. However, Tanner, take heed that any further mischief or misconduct on your part will bring you before me again. And, next time, I shall be far less generous. As for you, Doctor Edwin James, I advise you to steer clear of ne'er-do-wells who might sully your reputation and thus erode your livelihood."

"Henry," shouted Edwin, "were I inclined to avoid ne'er-do-wells, I would never again set foot on the same soil as you!"

John Tanner beamed as a roar of laughter and cheers rose from the villagers, overpowering the repeated slapping of Schoolcraft's gavel. He knew then he had friends once again. He could not know for how long.

As ordered, John Tanner was released. Doctor James and several others met him outside the courthouse.

"Edwin, my wife and son were not in the courtroom. Have you seen them?"

"No, not since we parted the other night."

He asked the others. "Can anyone here tell me where my wife is?"

"I dare say I can, sir," said a short man. "The poor woman sailed off."

"Sailed off?"

"By schooner early today."

"Schooner? What? Which pier? Point, man. Point!"

"There, sir. Pier two."

Tanner raced down the pier to the porter's bench.

"Young man, the ship that sailed early today, where's it bound?"

"Detroit, sir."

"Can you show me the manifest?"

"Why, yes sir. Here, sir. Can I help you find a name?"

"Yes. Mrs. John Tanner and son, James."

He followed the names down the list. "Here, sir. They are on board."

Moments later, John Tanner had both Henry and James Schoolcraft cornered in the Sheriff's office.

"What of my wife and child? What part did you have in their leaving? Tell me!"

Henry spoke first. "Abel Bingham was concerned for their health and safety. He arranged passage to Detroit. I had nothing to do with this. Nothing!"

"Believe my brother's words. Your wife and child left under the advisement of the church, never to return."

Tanner's eyes narrowed. "Why do I doubt you speak the truth? Something in your voice tells me you were involved in this, Sheriff."

"Nonsense," said Henry. "We'd no hand in it. We are innocent."

"Innocent? Your maker may soon explain the term to you both, if Satan does not claim you first!"

"You dare threaten us? We, officers of the court?"

"Why is it I cannot turn around that some Schoolcraft is not plotting another vengeful deed against me? Are you two possessed? What must I do to stop this hostility? Will it take the death of one of you? Or both, perhaps? Must I add to the list your wives and children as did people I knew along the Rainy River? What will it take?"

"Another threat!" said the sheriff. "Henry, shall I arrest him again?"

"And have the citizenry upon us?" He turned to Tanner again. "Tanner, you have challenged the wrong adversary. You know not my power."

"Nor you the rage of the spirits you gather by your deeds and deceit, spirits beyond mortal control, spirits who warn you to sleep with both eyes wide that you may see your own death stalking."

"Out, Tanner," shouted Henry. "Get out before I send you back to my jailhouse!"

John Tanner left, his anger surpassed only by his sadness. Heartbroken, he found his way home where, outside, he saw dishes scattered on the ground. He cursed his wife, thinking she left them there in her rush to leave. Entering his lodge, his eyes slowly adjusted to the dim light. Before him, strewn around the room, lay his few belongings, the remainder of his wife's clothing, books loaned him by Major Quimby, and worse—his pistol missing. His money gone. Tanner's heart sank lower. For only the fourth time since childhood, tears welled in his eyes. Then, hidden under buffalo robes left by the thief, he found his new rifle, musket balls, and powder. Clutching his rifle with both hands, John Falcon Tanner looked up at the blue sky beyond the smoke hole and screamed, "Wenebojo! Wenebojo! Show me my next path and spare me this infernal suffering!"

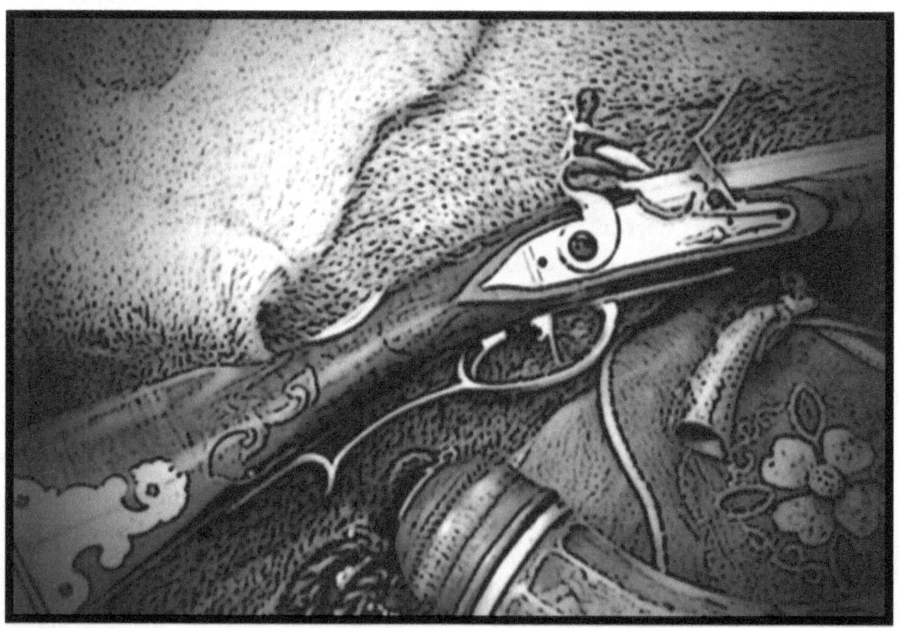

Chapter 46
The Murder

The spirit of Wenebojo is everywhere, in everything, and in everyone. All have power to call upon him. Few know how. Net-no-kwa, the much-respected ogimaa of her large village of Ottawa people, taught Shaw-shawwa na-baysay well. Her Swallow knew how to summon Wenebojo—how to draw strength from him. Softly chanting, John Tanner stared at the sky beyond the smoke hole in his lodge. As he did, within his eyes, certain objects in the room seemed to glow as though bathed in moonlight. He began collecting only those few glowing things, objects of greatest importance.

His rifle, powder, flint, musket balls, pemmican, sage, and tobacco soon filled his rucksack. A map carried by those in the Mississippi expedition slid in next. Deer sinew and needles, a skinning knife, a fire kit, a steel trading ax, his last four silver dollars, a copy of his book. He looked around. Everything remaining could be replaced, would be replaced if need be.

He looked again beyond the smoke hole at the blue sky. "Wenebojo, because of you, I have lived long, sung many songs. I saved many lives at Fort Douglas and in the Rainy Lake wilderness. I have helped my brothers and sisters, both white and red understand the language of the old ones. I have taken three good wives and fathered nine young ones, though but six remain, if that. You, Wenebojo, helped me become known far and wide as White Falcon. You spared me from death many times. For all this I thank you. As always, I am ready to do your bidding. I am John Tanner, the White Falcon. Whether you choose for me to die now or live another life, I accept your wisdom."

His rucksack over his shoulder and rifle in hand, Tanner left his lodge. Silently slipping his canoe into the St. Mary's River, he crossed to a small island where he had a clear view of the port of Sault Ste. Marie. There, he watched, chanting his songs, waiting for advice from the spirits, confident Wenebojo would guide him. He listened as the water of Gitchee Gumi passed by the island through the night. In the pre-dawn glow, he watched a dragon fly emerge from a nymph. It slowly opened its wings, stretching them wide. As the morning light grew warm, its wings began to flutter. Suddenly it flew into the air, hovering before him for a moment before disappearing into the sky.

"Thank you again, Wenebojo. I know now what I must do, which path I must follow. It is time I emerge anew, stretch my wings and fly." He slid his canoe into the water and paddled for shore.

A hushed call came through the window of the Indian dormitory at the mission school. "Martha! Awaken, Martha. Awaken! It is I, your father."

"Papa? Papa, what are you doing here?"

"I came that you might help me."

"Help you how?"

"I must send two letters and have neither pen and paper nor your talent with them. Please. Come outside. Will you do that for me? Will you come help your poor old father?"

"Of course, Papa," she whispered as she pulled on her dress.

"Oh, thank you, daughter. This will be a letter you will long recall. Come. Hurry."

Martha found paper, quill, and ink, then climbed out the window.

"How is Reverend Bingham treating you?"

"Fine, Papa. I know not what so abruptly causes him to pamper me so. I have become like an angel in his eyes."

"He merely treats you as the angel you are. And James?"

"Likewise! And this even more perplexing for, as you know well, James is far from angelic. Why, only yesterday did Reverend Bingham bestow on him a pair of his old shoes that James could attend Sunday service not bare-footed. Neither James nor I can make sense of this conduct."

"Martha, are you prepared to write a most important letter?"

"Yes, Papa."

Sitting on an overturned milk pail in the early morning light, young Martha Tanner dipped her quill in the ink. As her father spoke, she wrote the following words:*

> Father Mr. Van Buran, President of the United States
> Sir
>
> I take opertunity this day to reach my words to you with tears, calling upon you for help, because of my long Sufferings by the hand of Mr. Henry Schoolcraft.
>
> It is 7 years past since he [hired or] lays his hands upon me. Governor Cass placed me hear to be a Interpreter for Government and Mr. henry Schoolcraft took the office away from me on purpose to give it to his Brother in law George Johnson And He took my Daughter[s and son] away from me also and stript me alone and throw me down to the dust, and I was agoing right down to Washington to make Complaint to the President but Governor Cass stopt me there in Detroit.
>
> And my Wife was taken out of my hands by force by two Soldiers. Fort Brady. I was walking along in the street leading my Wife along in love on visiting with my Daughter and a young Child in my arms which was only months old and which was very dear to me and 2 soldiers came running in the street and one went between me and my wife and took her out of my hands by force and the Soldiers ran off with her and I saw them Carrying her in the baptist Mission house and I went up to the house and lookt for my wife but I could not find her Mr Elder Bingham minister shut her up in upstairs room and next day Mr Bingham

---

*Precise words from John and Martha Tanner to President Van Buren, 1846.

and Mrs Bingham & Mrs Davis & Miss Rice all the Bapttist Missionary family walkt down with my wife to the shore and sent her on board the vessel in the hand of Mr Schoolcraft and sent her away. Mr Bingham and Mr John Hulburt and Mr Ashman and several Soldiers and they all gave mony to my wife sending her away So I dont know now what is become of my Child if it is dead or liveing I know not.

Mr Bingham said to me two or three times a strong word your wife is in my hands you shall never see her again as long as you live, and moreover they Cast me in prison without any Cause and they kept me in prison and my [house] was broke open and my house was robed very bad a hundred Doll[ars] - worth of my property was destroyd. Now Father if you please to get my family out of these mens hands and restore them up to me so I may live if not I am sure it will be my end. my family is Dear to me more than my own life I lost three of my Daughters by the hand of man. one was killd by Ojipiway Indians she was shot with a gun she was 20 years of age and I lost another one on Mackanaw island she was 16 years old and I dont know what is become of her and all this brings my heart down weak. since my wife was taken awy from me my tears never stop running one day not one night yet. and I call upon you to do something for me for my liveing I cant do any kind heavy work because I am cripple by Ojibyuay Indians when I was a prisoner among them only interpreting thats only one thing I could do. if you pleas to excus our bad hand writing this is my little Daughters handwriting. thats all I say to you Father.*
John Tanner

A second letter, this one to Michigan Governor Lewis Cass, included a one-dollar scrip note good only for general merchandise and food at James Schoolcraft's store. Tanner knew this damning evidence would support his claim that the Schoolcraft brothers were persecuting him. Both letters would be posted later that morning by his daughter.

John Tanner hugged his daughter, then crossed by canoe to the island where he'd spent the night. There, he hid, waiting, watching and wondering why Wenebojo wanted him there. Late in the afternoon, he began to understand as he watched a soldier, slink along the river's edge.

Silently, Tanner slid his canoe into the St. Mary's River and followed him.

James Schoolcraft locked the office door and left for home on this pleasant July 6, 1846, evening. With the moon rising above the eastern horizon, he walked the same path as always through the woods to his farm, unaware of two men watching. He was startled when one called his name.

<hr>

*Precise words from John Tanner to President Van Buren, 1846.

He turned. "Who's there?"

No answer came.

"Who calls my name? Show yourself!"

Still, no answer.

"Who's there! What do you want?"

Tanner, hidden in the shadows, watched as the man in the bushes who had called Schoolcraft's name raised his rifle. Before Tanner could react, a bright flash lit the evening shadows and the crack of the musket shook the air.

Shot pointblank in the chest, the force of the blast drove Schoolcraft backward. Lying on the path, he tore open his shirt and stared at blood gushing from his chest with each heartbeat.

"Who did this?" he gasped. "Who shot me? Who has murdered …?"

No answer came. The soldier fled. Tanner approached, finding Schoolcraft dead, his shirt and the ground soaked with blood. He ran to his canoe and shoved off, paddling downstream. Tanner soon beached his canoe and swiftly made his way through town to the home of his friend, Doctor James. The second knock brought the Doctor to the door.

"Edwin, I fear I am in grave trouble and in need of your help once again."

"John! Oh, John. I was so worried when I heard."

"Heard? Then you already know?"

"The entire town knows."

"But, how?"

"The smoke brought many to inspect the remains of your home."

"My home? My wigwam? Burnt up? When?"

"Today, John. You mean you did not know? Is this not why you came?"

"No, Edwin. I fear the reason I am here is far worse."

"What is it, John? Tell me!"

"Not a half-hour ago did I witness a murder."

"Murder? My word! Who?"

"James Schoolcraft."

"James? No! Who did this?"

"Gibsen, from the post. Lieutenant Gibsen"

"I know him to be a rough fellow, but …"

"Edwin, I saw him steal along the waterfront under the piers. I followed. Gibsen waited in ambush not ten feet off the trail, then shot Schoolcraft through the heart."

"I must tell the Major."

"Wait. I fear I will be blamed. I have been mistreated by the Schoolcrafts. Fought with them. People will now think me the murderer."

"Yes. You are right. I believe you will be held responsible."

"Gibsen surely knows this. He must have planned it. Planned for me to hang for his crime. Gibsen almost certainly burned my home to make it look like Schoolcraft did it. All fingers will point to me. People will think I could take no more misery and sought revenge by killing James Schoolcraft."

"But, how can we prove otherwise? Gibsen covered his trail with care."

"Edwin, look to the bullet in his chest. That may be the noose around Bryant Gibsen's neck."

"John, you must turn yourself in. Stand your ground. Your surrender will reveal your innocence."

"No. Henry Schoolcraft will lynch me. I have dreamed of this."

"And, if you take flight? Will people not further suspect you?"

"I have no choice. My dreams are seldom wrong. I must go now."

"But you will be hunted down by the United States Army. They will not stop until they have you or you are dead."

"I know of places where they will not look. Perhaps, Canada. The soldiers cannot follow there without consent from Montreal. By then, I shall be …"

"No! You mustn't tell me where you intend to go. I may be forced to disclose your plans if Schoolcraft brings this to his courtroom." Doctor James crossed the room to his desk. He opened a compartment and pulled out a buckskin pouch. Handing it to Tanner, he said, "This money is from your book. There's enough here for good start somewhere new, my friend."

"But that is your share,. You gave me mine."

"Yes, but, here. Take it. When more royalties arrive, I will be paid back."

Tanner put his hand on the doctor's shoulder. "Edwin, we may never again meet. If more money comes, take out your share, then see to it my children are cared for well. Will you do that?"

"Of course, John. Now, if you intend to flee, you best be gone for Henry Schoolcraft will surely be at my doorstep minutes after news of the murder."

"Yes. I must go. Edwin, of all those who I have known in my five decades, I treasure your friendship most."

"Journey well, my friend. I will do my all to see that Gibsen and Schoolcraft do not cast blame onto you."

A quick bear hug and Tanner left. Edwin James watched as the twilight mist concealed his friend's escape from Sault Ste. Marie.

By light of a lantern, Doctor James made his way across town to Fort Brady and the home of Major Quimby as the clock in town struck nine.

"Why, Doctor James," said Edora, "Such a pleasant surprise! More late night toil on the new book?"

"Oh, how I wish for that to be the circumstance, Miss Edora. No, I fear I have some shocking news for your father. I must see him."

Major Quimby stepped into the parlor. "Edwin, what is it?"

"Trouble. Dire trouble—a shooting—a murder, I believe."

"My word! Who?"

"If I understand correctly, one of your soldiers laid plans to ambush our Sheriff on his way home tonight. Now the body of James Schoolcraft lies along the trail near his home, chilling in the night air."

"No! James Schoolcraft dead? By the hand of one of my men? Who?"

"Lieutenant Gibsen."

"Bryant Gibsen? Ridiculous! No man of mine left this post tonight."

"Oh, how I wish I was in error, Major. But I fear this to be true. You see, I heard this from a man who stood witness to the murder."

"Some drunken sailor? Some stumblebum?"

"A man you know and respect, sir."

"Who? Tell me!"

"Never mind that. We need to verify the death, then inform James Schoolcraft's wife and brother."

"Do you mean to say no one has told them?"

"Other than me, you are first to know."

"Yes. We must tell them. Where is Schoolcraft's body?"

"At the wood's edge behind his farm. We will need more lanterns, Major."

"You still have not told me who witnessed this, Doctor."

"'Tis because I am so reluctant to say."

"You have no choice, Edwin. To keep secret his identity would put you in the midst of it—accessory to murder, if murder is found to be the cause."

"I know. Still, I suffer deep anguish in disclosing the fellow's name."

"I demand it, Edwin. His name. Now!"

"John Falcon Tanner."

By the time Doctor James, Major Quimby, and three soldiers left Fort Brady for the Schoolcraft farm, Tanner had begun his escape, a moonlit ascent by way of the St. Mary's River toward Gitchee Gumi. His destination was not Canada. He whispered to the wind as he paddled.

"Wenebojo, many times you have helped me find my way. Now guide me to a place where I can begin a new life, where I can live as another, a place where there are no Whites. The Doctor was right when he said the soldiers will search until either they find me or believe me dead. In their minds, then, John Falcon Tanner must be thought to be dead. Yet, how can I make them think I am dead when here I am, very alive?" His paddle cut silently into the dark water, casting reflections from the moon in ever widening circles. He stared at the moonbeams breaking over the water and noticed three ravens roosting in a pine. "Aandaag, I have a song for you." In Ojibwe, he whispered a new chant. "In their minds, John Tanner must die. In their minds, White Falcon must die. In their minds, Shaw-shawwa na-baysay must die.

What magic must I use, ravens? What songs must I sing to make the world think I am no more? How do I do this?" He sang again. "In their minds, John Falcon Tanner must die."

As Tanner paddled west, a young soldier knocked on the door of Henry Schoolcraft's home. Soon, Schoolcraft stood over the body of his brother, consoling Anna Marie, his sister-in-law. In tears, she asked, "Henry, who could have done such an evil deed?"

"I will tell you who. This is the work of John Tanner. He has threatened my life and the life of my dear brother again and again. Now the coward has carried out his warning to get back at me. I will see to it he hangs for this."

"I think not," Doctor James said. "You will notice, here, the wound bears the mark of a military rifle."

"How so?"

"Buck and ball, Mister Schoolcraft." Edwin wiped blood from the victim's chest revealing one large and three small entrance wounds. "I beg you to have your surgeon, Doctor Houghton, confirm these were made by a soldier's rifle, most likely from the Fort Brady armory."

"Preposterous!"

Major Quimby nodded. "Doctor James is right. One musket ball and two buckshot for good measure. Buck and ball. Standard throughout the Army." He turned to the soldier behind him. "Sergeant Hancock, set out for the armory, post haste. Inspect every rifle, then report back to me immediately."

"Yes, sir," the sergeant said with a salute.

"This is folly!" shouted Schoolcraft. "Other than the occasional exchange of money for goods at his general store, my brother had no dealings with your soldiers. We need to be after Tanner 'fore he slips away."

"Henry, you are wrong," Anna Marie said. "My husband had words with a soldier. Strong words."

"Words? Bah! How strong? Over what issue?"

"Another of his trollops, I suppose."

"Nonsense!"

"Henry, my husband, as you know, was unfaithful. Both he and a soldier from Fort Brady had designs on some harlot. I know not who, nor do I give a whip. But I know it to be true."

"Nay, this is Tanner's doing. As Territorial Judge, I am ordering an immediate search for the murderous coward."

"What soldier, Anna?" asked Major Quimby.

"Bryant Gibsen. He and James hated each other. I never thought it could come to this."

Incensed, Schoolcraft bellowed, "I will not allow this! I am not about to see the Schoolcraft name disparaged and the reputation of a good soldier dragged through the mud. This was Tanner's doing, I tell you!"

"I disagree," countered Doctor James. "'Tis true Tanner was at odds with the Schoolcrafts, however, that is not reason to convict the man."

"At odds Doctor?" bellowed Schoolcraft. "Is that how you term it? Tanner has been a burr under my saddle ever since he began that blasted book of his. Neither my brother nor I have felt safe with him on the prowl. He must be hanged for this. At odds, Doctor? Indeed!"

Sergeant Hancock returned, out of breath. He approached Major Quimby.

"What did you learn, Sergeant?"

"As suspected, sir, all muskets on the rack were charged with buck and ball and ready to fire—save one."

"And?"

"Sir, by the smell of the muzzle, the rifle had been discharged tonight and returned without cleaning or reloading. The quartermaster will confirm this."

"Did the quartermaster have a record of who this rifle was assigned to?"

"No record of any rifle going in or out since the morning inspection, sir."

"There!" exclaimed Doctor James. "Precisely as I explained. A military round shot from a rifle taken earlier tonight from the post armory. This and an eyewitness account of the deed. What more do we need?"

"I will tell you what we need," bellowed Schoolcraft. "Your witness! But he will not appear because he is the true murderer. You will not find him lollygagging hereabouts. My supposition is that he has already taken to the woods, and is making his escape. If so, his flight proves guilt beyond doubt. Oh, Tanner is our murderer Doctor James. And that, sir, is the opinion of the judge who presides over this region—Henry Rowe Schoolcraft!"

"Mister Schoolcraft," said the Major, "this is not your courtroom, nor is John Tanner, your adversary, your foe, on trial."

"Tanner is guilty of murdering my brother. He shall hang for it!"

"A conviction without an investigation? A death sentence without a trial, sir? I shall not let your rash, premature verdict be reason for Tanner's lynching, Mister Schoolcraft." He turned to Anna Marie. "Madam, I am going to instruct Doctor Houghton to extract these bullets that we have them for evidence. Will you so consent?"

"Of course, Major."

"I protest!" huffed Schoolcraft. "I am the authority here, not you, Major."

"Mister Schoolcraft, any misdeed possibly involving my soldiers or my armaments requires my attention. I warn you, sir, do not interfere with my investigation."

"Quimby, you offer no choice. I shall ask Colonel Boyd to intercede."

"For what reason?"

"Reason? Why, both you and Doctor James are friendly with John Tanner. Too friendly, in my estimation. Perhaps the colonel will not be so blind."

"Do as you will. But, mind you, be prepared for your own trial should Tanner suffer death at your hand without a fair trial. Meanwhile Schoolcraft, stay out of my way."

Chapter 48
Return to Sturgeon Lake

We know what we have left behind. The great mystery lies beyond the next bend.

Each stroke of Tanner's paddle was strong and steady. His canoe glided silently along the shore, casting only a gentle wake. He headed westward along Lake Superior's southern shore, finally knowing where his journey would end—a journey that began with a dark, dark vision.

He'd come to the Sault a solitary traveler and so he would leave. A man of vision, he now better understood the differences between the Indian's life and the white man's way. He also understood that more and more white men would come to the northern waters and woodlands just as his people, following another vision many years earlier, traveled beyond Gitchee Gumi. His journey would take him to the part of Michigan Territory called Ouisconsin, a place with many lakes and rivers filled with menoomin, the good grain that grows in water and gives life—wild rice. He'd return to a place he saw twice on earlier treks, Lake Namakagon, the lake of the sturgeon.

With each silent stroke of his paddle, the horrible events in his wake now seem to dissolve and vanish like the small whirlpools of cold, Gitchee Gumi water spinning behind. As he paddled, he heard Wenebojo whisper, "Thirteen days you must travel westward along the southern shores of Gitchee Gumi. Only there will you find your peace—only there."

As his canoe glided swiftly along the shore, two eagles watched from the top of a tall white pine. "Is that you, Wenebojo?" he asked the eagles.

An otter followed him, diving and surfacing again and again, curious about this rare sight of man and canoe. "You, Otter," he whispered. "Your cousin once saved me. I do not forget this. Now you follow me. Surely, you must be Wenebojo in disguise."

A doe and two fawns stood on the shore, motionless as he passed. "You don't fool me, Wenebojo. You are keeping your eyes on me to be sure I find my way. For this I give you my gratitude."

Thirteen days after leaving Sault Ste. Marie, John Tanner paddled west along the south shore of Gitchee Gumi, distancing himself from his troubles. Nearing the Odanah at Bad River, he turned inland, then followed the White River southwest, retracing his previous journeys. A long portage brought him to Lake Kagy-nogum-aug. Nine miles south, he portaged, paddled, and portaged again to the river flowing out of the lake of the sturgeon—Lake Namakagon.

"Namakagon," he said as he entered the lake. "Namakagon. It is a good name. Yes. This place I will make my home. I will build three lodges here and take the name Namakagon as my own. My other names are now lost to me. Those few who I might encounter will know me only as Namakagon, now the chief of a village of one."

In the north of the lake, Chief Namakagon found a large island. "I have seen this in my dreams many times," he said to himself as he paddled by. "It will be my new home. I will keep a canoe at each end and one in the middle. Like a deer, I will have escape routes in every direction." He continued around the island. "And, here I will construct my first wigwam—the birch lodge of an Ojibwe."

Three evenings later, a fire warmed his home and a sturgeon smoked over the coals. The sole resident of the lake stepped out onto the sun-warmed beach, freshly decorated with the first leaves of autumn. The late afternoon sunlight sparkled off gentle waves far out in the bay.

Namakagon wondered if he would see his children or his friend, Edwin, or the Quimby family again in this life. His thoughts then drifted to his former homes and the many people he'd known over the past five decades. He gazed at the first star of the evening, realizing the visions sent to him by Wenebojo meant he, Namakagon, had much more to do with his life. He knew, too, Lake Namakagon was where he would spend the rest of his years.

A loon called from far out on the lake. Namakagon smiled, closed his eyes, and sang a song of gratitude to Gitchee Manitou. Then, another to Wenebojo before returning to his lodge for the night.

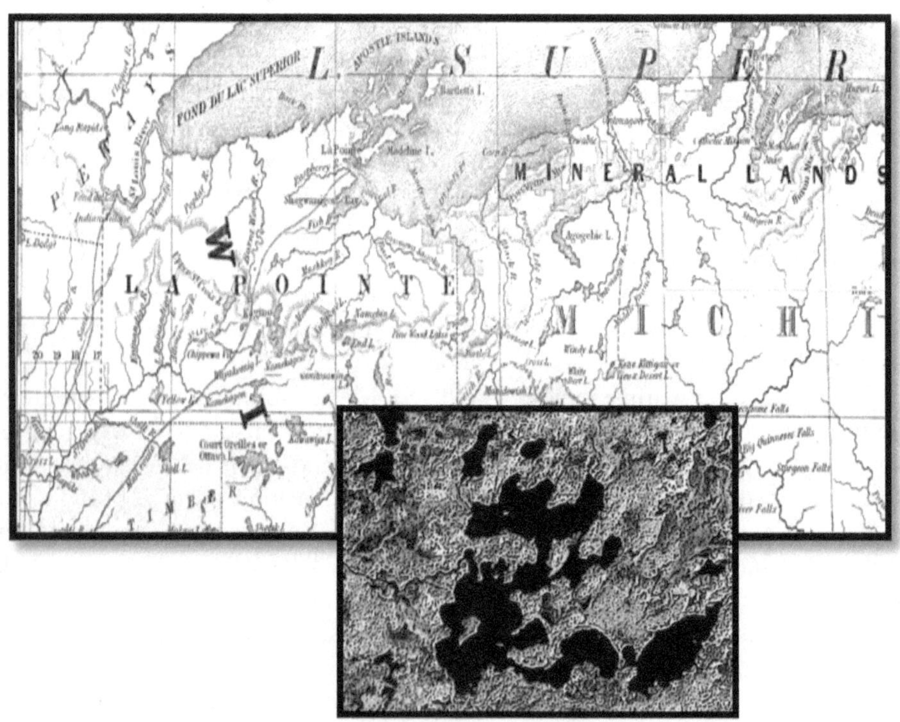

Chapter 49
Three Ravens

As the mystery of what lie ahead for Chief Namakagon began to unfold, so did the search for John Tanner begin its slow stretch across time. It soon crossed the territories of Michigan, Wisconsin, and into Prince Rupert's Land.

Notices bearing Tanner's likeness, posted from Fort Douglas to Kentucky and east to New York, brought no response. In spite of Henry Schoolcraft's incessant accusations, the residents of Sault Ste. Marie slowly grew to believe John Tanner innocent. But Tanner would never learn that public opinion eventually favored him and the search for him was to be abandoned.

The nearly completed manuscript for John Tanner's new book disappeared from the home of Doctor James, confiscated by the court as possible evidence in the James Schoolcraft murder investigation. The three-hundred pages never again surfaced, though they strongly influenced Henry Schoolcraft's book on same subject, the Mississippi headwaters expedition of 1832.

Tanner's first book grew in popularity, resulting in numerous reprintings in several languages. Edwin James distributed the royalties as promised, ignoring all questions regarding the arrangement.

Lieutenant Bryant Gibsen, never charged for murder, joined in the search for Tanner. Rumors soon spread that Gibsen located him in Canada, murdered him, and hid the remains to assure there would never be a trial. Infuriated by the rumor, Schoolcraft badgered Colonel Boyd to seek reassignment for Gibsen. Not long after, Gibsen was one of many called up to serve in the Mexican War. After the war ended, Gibson was involved in the murder of a Mexican citizen. Word soon spread that he was tried and sentenced to hang. Gibsen received a last-minute pardon by a general wishing to protect a fellow officer. Gibsen later died of natural causes. Residents of the Sault learned that, on his deathbed, Gibsen confessed to the murder of James Schoolcraft, a confession Henry Schoolcraft refused to accept.

Although search parties had scoured Sault Ste. Marie and the surrounding woodlands looking for John Tanner, they'd always returned empty-handed. Then one day, two hunters hiked the riverbank along the St. Mary's River. Near a large oak tree, split by lightning, one man saw something move in the muskeg swamp. He raised his shotgun and pulled back the hammer.

"Bah! Only ravens," said his partner. "Don't waste yer shot."

"Looks like they are feeding on something. Deer, maybe? Or moose?"

"Could be him."

"Who?"

"Tanner."

"The one who kilt the sheriff?"

"That's hogwash. Tanner never kilt nobody. Never. But there's money to be had if it's him them birds is peckin' at."

"We best see for ourselves."

As the men waded through the marsh, three ravens flushed, circling overhead.

"Here! Look here! Bones! And a moccasin, and a shirt, to boot! Think this could be him? Tanner?"

The ravens continued their circles above.

"If 'tis, we are due a fine prize from old Henry Schoolcraft."

"Look! Over there! A musket!"

"By gad! Will ya cast yer eyes on that!"

They slogged closer to the gun.

"Look! There's a J and a T carved right in."

"Must be Tanner's, all right. Our good fortune, I'd say."

"Let's be off to the fort with it."

An hour later, they delivered the musket.

"See, Mister Schoolcraft? His mark, right here on the stock. Been chewed some by mice, but it's his, all right. Carved plain as day. A J and a T. Mister Schoolcraft, you'll find his bones a-layin' in the swamp along the river."

"Looks to me like you finally got your brother's murderer," said the other hunter. "Now, how 'bout that reward money?"

"An old musket means nothing. Show me the bones. If I declare them to be from the body of John Tanner, you will get your reward, as will I."

"You? But, we thought the reward was for the man who found Tanner."

"My reward is knowing the white savage who murdered my brother is dead. Dead and soon to be forgotten."

That same day, Henry Schoolcraft reluctantly paid the men their small reward, though not thoroughly convinced the corpse was that of his foe. However, the villagers *were* certain. The search for John Tanner died. Henry Schoolcraft would forever doubt he'd found the remains of his adversary, the White Indian, John Falcon Tanner.

Chapter 50
The Best Path
1887

The wind outside Diindiisi's lodge diminished and then grew quiet. She stepped outside. Tor followed. Late afternoon sunshine now streaked through the clouds. For a long moment they stood, silently taking in the sun's glow on the newly fallen snow.

"Tor, you should go home now. It will soon be dark."

"Before I leave, you must help me understand what you have told me."

"Yes?"

"Your father, the man I call Chief Namakagon, came here to hide from the soldiers? Hide from this Indian agent? This judge? Henry Schoolcraft?"

"Yes. Though he killed no one, Father hid here like a criminal. But he also lived the life he loved best, the life he had lived as a young man—the life of an Anishinabe. He took a new name, the name you know him by, Mikwam-mi-migwan, Ice Feathers. He took this name because, on the coldest of days, the frost grew on his beard like feathers of ice."

"Did he ever learn about the true killer's confession?"

"Yes. Many years later. But Father did nothing different. The train they call the Omaha came here thirty-four years after my father did. With the train came many Whites to change the rivers and take the timber away."

"Like my pa and my uncle."

"And you, Tor."

"Yes, like me, I suppose."

"One man who came on the train was the newspaperman, George Francis Thomas. He came here to write about this land for his newspaper in Chicago. The stationmaster told him about my father—that he was the only Indian here who could speak English. Thomas sought him out. Father spoke with him but was not willing to give up his true name. Even when Father learned that Lieutenant Gibsen had confessed on his deathbed to the murder, he said nothing."

"How did he find out about Gibsen?"

"To practice his reading, Father would walk to town and read the newspapers left in the depot. One day he saw his old name, John Tanner, in the paper. He read that Gibsen confessed and then died. I asked my father if he would now go find his other children, my brothers and sisters in Michigan and Manitoba. He said he would not. He did not want to upset their lives again. He did not trust Henry Schoolcraft, either. Father said he never knew a man more obsessed than this Schoolcraft. Even after the soldier confessed, Schoolcraft refused to believe it was the officer who murdered his brother."

"But, Gibsen murdered another man, too?"

"Yes. When war broke out with Mexico, he was one of many soldiers who marched into Mexico City. This ended the war. Gibsen and other soldiers were celebrating. They were drunk. Ran out of whisky. Wanted more. Robbed a store. The storekeeper was shot and died. The papers said Army judges sentenced Gibsen to die but a general spared him because he was an officer. The other soldiers with him that night were not so fortunate. They were hanged.

Gibsen did not live long after that. Before he died, he confessed to slaying the sheriff. Henry Schoolcraft would not believe this and did all he could to raise doubt about Gibsen's confession. You can see why Father was not willing to change back into John Tanner."

"You're right. He chose the best path."

"Even after learning that Henry Schoolcraft died, Father did not want to upset the lives of others who thought him to be dead for so many decades. Today, few of his kin know of his life here in Wisconsin. His was a great life. Perhaps, one day, his story will be known by all."

Tor put his hand on Diindiisi's shoulder. "I will not tell others of this, Blue Jay. It is not my place. I knew him only as Mikwam-mi-migwan, Ice Feathers, and Chief Namakagon. Should I ever be asked about a man called John Tanner, I will tell them this: I was once a close friend of a wise Anishinabe elder named Namakagon. And I believe he once knew the White Falcon, John Tanner, better than anyone else."

"And when someone persists? Asks you to explain?"

"I will say they must search elsewhere, Diindiisi. For I, Tor Loken, will never unveil the secret of my friend, Chief Namakagon."

I stared at the diamond-shaped silver medallion in one hand and the county map in the other, planning my day. The map contained the final clue I needed to find Chief Namakagon's silver mine. According to the 1898 plat book, a forty-acre parcel homesteaded by a J. L. Tanner was only a short drive away. I knew now that Grandpa Tor's friend and mentor, Chief Namakagon, and John Falcon Tanner, the author, war hero, adventurer, and, eventually a murder fugitive, were one and the same.

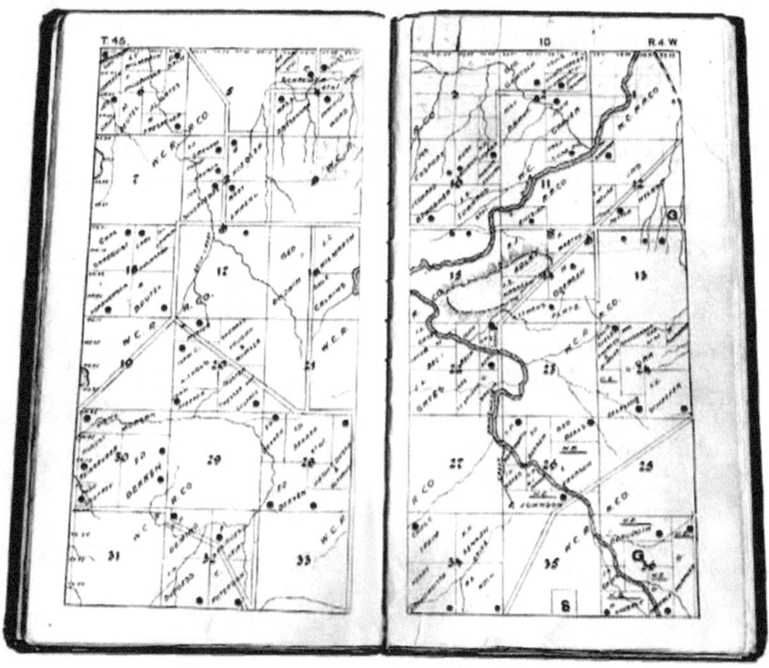

Yes, Namakagon was, in fact, the White Indian. In his four decades here, he had walked many, many times along the Marengo Trail, passing right through the silver and gold country. Thirty-some years before any miners placed their claims, he was there. But did he know of the silver? I was sure he did. After all, I had discovered only one *Tanner* in the original Ashland County plat book. With my own eyes, I saw the name, Tanner, signed on the deed in the land records office. The Marengo Trail cut right through his forty-acre homestead. That signature proved beyond doubt that John Falcon Tanner, also known as Chief Namakagon, owned land smack-dab in the middle of the richest silver and gold mining region in Wisconsin.

I also understood that, because this was now public land, someone someday would search that forty until they found the source of Namakagon's silver—silver he had traded for medicine in Ashland in the 1880s—the act that most certainly led to his death at the hand of another in 1886. Yes, someone was going to find that silver. Perhaps today. Perhaps me.

As the loons in the bay raised their usual springtime ruckus, I fried up some bacon and eggs. Sipping my morning coffee, I wondered how it must have been for John Tanner to completely cast off his former life in 1846, to survive alone far out in the Wisconsin wilderness for four decades, to live the life of a hermit hiding from the law. Did he wonder, each morning, if this might be the day when soldiers would descend on him? Capture him? Hang him for a murder he didn't commit? I could not fathom the day-after-day, year-after-year torment that Chief Namakagon endured.

I stepped out onto the porch of the old lodge, wondering what to do with all I had learned. Three ravens flushed from a tall pine and circled above the yard of the old lumber camp. I watched them as they watched me for the longest time. I thought of the three ravens that led two hunters to John Tanner's rifle in 1847, ending Schoolcraft's search. Those ravens obscured the truth, concealing Tanner's flight to Wisconsin. Those three ravens made it possible for John Tanner to become Chief Namakagon and eventually come to know Tor Loken, my grandfather. They also made it possible for Shaw-shawwa na-baysay to share his vast knowledge with Grandpa.

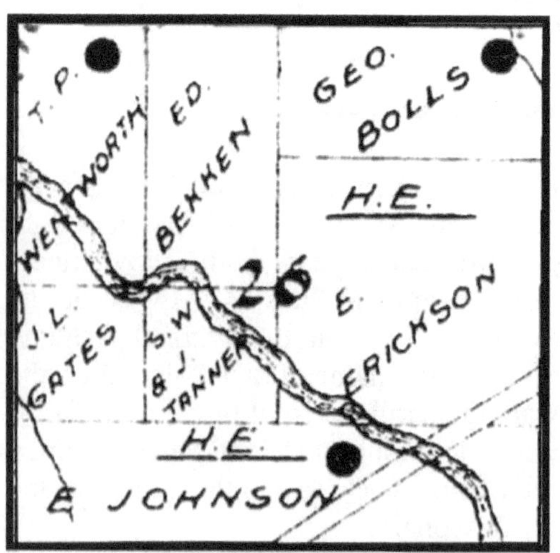

I looked up at the three ravens circling overhead, then stared again at the silver medallion in my hand. As the ravens flew off, I wondered how long Wenebojo would want me to protect what I'd discovered—the knowledge of Namakagon's silver treasure, my unlocking of the previously unsolved 1846 disappearance of John Falcon Tanner, and this new comprehension of the amazing secret of Chief Namakagon.

Suddenly, I knew what I must do.

Glossary to accompany the Chief Namakagon series

Aft: Toward the stern or rear of the vessel.

Anchor: 1. A large, heavy weight designed to hold a sailing vessel in place when lowered to the bottom. 2. To lower a weight, thus stopping the vessel.

Aandaag: Raven

Animosh: Ojibwe word for dog.

Anishinabe: *a-nish-i-NAH-bee*. The original Native American people who lived north and south of the western Great Lakes region. Primarily Ojibwe but also Algonquin, Pottawatomie and others.

Barber chair: Slang for what is created when a tree is improperly notched prior to cutting, resulting in a tall splinter rising up from one side of the stump that makes it resemble a chair.

Bark eaters: Slang for lumberjacks.

Barn boss: Oversaw care and feeding of the animals.

Blackbird: A slang term for a log driver who was skilled at walking on the floating logs.

Blackjack: Gingerbread. A sweet cake made with ginger and blackstrap molasses.

Blaggard: Undesirable person. Scoundrel.

Boom: A large raft of logs that were held together by a ring of logs connected by chains. Boom companies were formed on parts of some rivers to sort logs and direct them toward the right mills.

Boozhoo: *Boo-ZHOO*. Hello. Possibly from the French term *bon jour* meaning good day. Probably from a contraction of Wenebojo and a greeting that acknowledges the omnipresence of Anishinabe culture and the strength of Native American camaraderie

Brakeman: Railroad worker whose job is to set and release safety brakes, among other jobs.

Breakup: The spring ice melt when logs could again be driven to the mills.

Bow: The front of a sailing vessel.

Bull Cook: A worker who did many camp chores including the feeding of some animals, bringing in firewood, keeping the stoves filled, fetching water for the kitchen, clearing paths through the snow, plus many kitchen chores. Not well-paid.

Calaboose: Jailhouse, prison, the brig.

Calked boots: Leather boots with spiked soles that helped men walk on the floating logs.

Camp dentist: He sharpened the saws and axes.

Cant hook: A tool for rolling logs. Made of a stout, wooden handle and a C-shaped hook. Like a peavey.

Caught in a bear trap: Lumberjack slang for getting into trouble.

Chain-haul team: The men who used horses or oxen and chains to load the logs onto the sleighs.

Chautauqua: *sha-TAHK-wa*. Traveling entertainment troupes that would set up large tents and then offer lectures, music, comedy, burlesque and theater before moving on to the next rural communities.

Chequamegon: *she-WAHM-a-gun. A large bay on the* south shore of Lake Superior. Also a national forest in Wisconsin.

Chippewa: Originally pronounced *CHIP-ah-way*. Now usually pronounced *CHIP-ah-wah*. French slang for Ojibwe. Also a river in Wisconsin.

Choppers: Heavy leather mittens.

Clydesdales: The largest of the big workhorses.

Cookees: Assistants to the head cook.

Corks: Calked (spiked) boots.

Creel: A basket on an over-the-shoulder strap that's carried by a trout fisherman.

Cross-haul: Loading the logs onto the sleigh by using a horse or ox to pull a chain that would roll the log up a ramp mounted on the side of the sleigh.

Cross-hauler: The man who loaded logs onto a sleigh using horses or oxen and chains that crossed over the load. Chain-hauler.

Crosstree: A cross-member on a mast from which a sail is hung. Runs perpendicular to the mast.

Cruising: Inspecting and estimating the value of standing timber. Timber cruisers were also called land-lookers.

Deacon's bench: A pine board attached to the ends of the bunks. It ran the full length of the bunkhouse (sleep shanty) and was usually the only seating, other than on the benches at the cook shanty tables.

Deadhead: Make a trip to deliver cargo with no prospect of returning with other cargo.

Diindiisi: Blue Jay

Donkey engine: A steam engine used to haul full logging sleds up steep hills.

Double Eagle: Twenty-dollar gold coin.

Double sawbucks: Twenty dollar bills.

Double-bit ax: An ax with two cutting surfaces so it will last twice as long between sharpenings.

Dray: Hauling service.

Dressed:, Gutted. Entrails removed. Cleaned.

Engineer: The driver of the train.

Fireman: Railroad worker whose job is to move firewood or coal from the tender car to the boiler, keeping the steam pressure up.

Flaggins: Dinner carried into the woods for those men who were working too far from camp to eat in the cook shanty.

Flintlock: A muzzleloader using a flint to ignite the powder in the pan.

Foremast: The mast nearest the bow of a ship or boat when more than one mast is present.

Foresails: Sails supported by the foremast. Near the bow of the ship or boat.

Fortnight: Two weeks.

Four bits: Fifty cents.

Galley: The ship's kitchen.

Gabreel: A long tin horn used to call men for meals.

Gandy dancers: Slang for railroad construction crews. They earned this name from the repeated, rhythmic stomping on their Gandy brand shovels when tamping crushed rock under railroad ties. This shovel-tamping technique appeared similar to dancing a jig.

Gang saws: Powerful, multi-bladed saws that, in one pass, could cut many boards from a single log.

Gee: A signal used to train horses to turn to the right. *Haw* turned them left.

Gitchee Manitou: *GI-chee MAN-i-too*. The Great Spirit.

Gray backs: Body lice. Common in the camps.

Grippe: Any of several flu-like illnesses.

Hay burners: Work horses.

Head push: The camp boss.

Hoar frost: White, often thick crystals of frost that cover objects when the air is moist and warm and those objects are below freezing.

Hull: The bottom of a boat.

Iron Belt: The iron-mining region of far northern Wisconsin and Upper Michigan.

Jam crew: A team of log drivers that specialized in breaking up logjams.

Keep and ear to the rail: Slang for staying aware of or looking for. Rails transmit the sound of an oncoming train. By putting one's ear on a rail, news of a train approaching comes faster than listening in the conventional way.

Kerf: The groove cut by the saw.

Kith and kin: Friends and relatives.

Lac Courte Oreilles: *la-COO-da-RAY*. A major Ojibwe village and a lake in northwest Wisconsin. Also an Ojibwe tribe.

Latrine: A pit or ditch used for human waste.

Liniment: A paste, salve, ointment or tonic usually rubbed on a wound or sore area to relieve pain or somehow heal the injury.

Locomotive: Train engine. Steam powered till 1950s.

Log drive: Logs were floated down rivers in the spring. Men would drive the logs to the mills downstream much as cowboys drove cattle to market.

Lumber baron: A wealthy, powerful businessman who prospered from the timber industry.

Mainmast: The primary, usually tallest mast on a ship.

Mainsails: Sails supported by the mainmast. Near the center of the vessel.

Makade: *ma-KAH-day*. Black

Makwaa: *MUK-wa*. Bear.

Mash-Kikii Kwee: Healer

Megwitch: Means "You are too kind," the equivalent of "thank you" in Anishinabe.

Midewinni-shamen: Spiritual leader. Mystical healer.

Menoomin: men-OO-min. literally, good grain. Wild rice was plentiful in many Wisconsin waters before the logging boom altered the lakes and rivers.

Métis: MAY-tee. Mixed blood people, often having a Caucasian father and an Anishinabe mother. Predominately found from N. Michigan to Montana.

Mikwam-mi-migwan: *MIK-wam-MIG-wan*. Feathers of ice.

Mizzenmast: The mast nearest the stern of a ship or boat when more than one mast is present.

Namakagon: *nam-eh-KAH-gun*. A large lake in northwest Wisconsin and headwaters for the Namekagon River.

Namekagon: *nam-eh-KAH-gun*. An outstanding northwest Wisconsin river. On early maps, some cartographers spelled the river Nam*e*kagon and other map makers spelled the lake Nam*a*kagon. These different spellings remain today.

Nokomis: no-KO-mis. Grandmother.

Ogimaa: *OH-ga-ma*. Chief.

Ojibwe: o-*JIB-way*. Sometimes spelled Ojibwa. Correctly pronounced with the long *a* sound. The French fur traders called most Anishinabe people who lived in the western Great Lakes region either Ojibwe or Chippeway.

On the up-and-up: Honest. Truthful.

Pac-wa-wong: *pa-QUAY-wong*. A rice-rich lake formed by a widening in the river downstream from Cable. An Ojibwe village sat on the west shore until a lumber company dam raised the lake, killing the rice.

Peavey: A tool used for moving logs. Composed of a stout wooden handle, a C-shaped steel hook and a steel point.

Pemmican: A mix of grains, dried fruit and dried meat. A high-energy food, easy to carry and resistant to spoilage, making it ideal on the trail.

Percherons: Purebred French work horses.

Picaroon: An ax handle fitted with a short, sharp, steel pick rather than a blade. Used to stab, and then pull or turn logs.

Pinery: The great stand of virgin pines that once stretched from central Wisconsin to Lake Superior, into Minnesota and Michigan. Until 1890 it was, by far, the richest range of white pine on Earth.

Pinkertons: A Chicago detective agency distinguished for investigating and preventing train robberies in the late 1800s. In 1885 the Pinkertons had more men and more weapons than the U.S. Army.

Port: The left side of a marine vessel when facing ahead (toward the bow).

Portage: A land bridge between waters (n) or the act of carrying a canoe across such a bridge (v).

Rack bar device: A T-handled box containing a magneto that could generate an electrical charge. Used to detonate explosives.

Rail: 1: Railroad worker. 2: The safety rail around a large boat or ship. 3: Lengths of heavy steel, designed specifically to support a train. Used atop crossties to build a railroad track.

River Pig: Log driver.

Road monkey: A worker who maintained the ice roads, trails and tote roads.

Rut: The deer breeding season when does are in heat and bucks often lack normal caution.

Sand man: The worker assigned to slow down a timber sleigh by throwing sand in the track. Straw was also used.

Sault Ste. Marie: *SOO-saint-marie*. A settlement and military post on the eastern end of Lake Superior.

Sawyer: A logger who felled trees using a crosscut saw. Also mill workers who ran saws.

Schooner: A fore-and-aft rigged sailing vessel having at least two masts, with a foremast that's usually smaller than the other masts.

Scrip: A certificate that guarantees certain value. A type of promissory note, usually mass-produced.

Shaving the whiskers: Wisconsin's pine was often compared to being *as thick as whiskers*. Clear-cutting a forest was compared to shaving the pine *whiskers* from the landscape.

Shypoke: Slang for a Green Heron.

Sky pilot: Clergyman.

Silver cat: A stiff sapling bent over by a fallen tree. When the tree is moved, the sapling can snap up, injuring or killing a logger. Differs from a widowmaker in that it comes from the ground up, not down from above.

Slats: Lumberjack slang for ribs. Barrels were made of thin, curved wooden slats that were held together by metal hoops. The rib cage was compared to a wooden barrel by some.

Sleep camp: Another term for bunk house.

Sluice: *SLOOSE*. A channel built to control which way a log can travel.

Slush bucket: Large metal scoop pulled by an ox and used to move soil, create road grades, and excavate.

Slush out: To remove soil and rock using a slush bucket and oxen.

Snow snakes: Mythical creatures that hid under the snow, waiting to steal the lumberjack's tools. Often blamed for this.

Stamp hammer: A hammer used to mark the lumber camp's name on the end of each log.

Standing part: The unattached end of a rope or chain.

Starboard: The left side of a marine vessel when facing ahead (toward the bow).

Star load: A huge load of the biggest and best pine.

Stern: The back of a sailing vessel.

Stove lids: Lumberjack slang for pancakes or flapjacks. Inspired by the heavy, circular, iron lids found on old, wood burning cast iron cook stoves.

Sutler: Civilian storekeeper for a military post. Also trades with others.

Swamper: The saw crew member who trimmed branches from downed trees and cut any brush in the way of the sawyers and teamsters.

Switchman: Railroad worker who, by throwing a manual switch, shifts the position of the track, thus changing the train's direction.

Tender: The train car immediately behind the engine that carries the fuel for the boiler.

Three-master: A boat or ship with three masts. They are the foremast, mainmast, and mizzenmast.

Thwart: Canoe Cross-bar. Attached to both gunnels. To portage a small canoe, the porter lifts the canoe by the thwarts, flips the canoe hull-side-up, and carries the canoe overhead, one hand on each thwart.

Top loading: Guiding the logs onto the sleigh while standing on top of the pile. AKA the sky-hooker.

Travois: *Trav-OY*. A device used to drag heavy items. Usually made from lashing saplings together.

Trestle: *TRESS-sil*. A large railway bridge

Two-man crosscut: A 5 to 9-foot-long saw blade fitted with a handle on each end. Perfected in the 1870s, it replaced the ax as the primary tool for felling trees. This greatly accelerated the harvest.

Union suit: One-piece underwear. Longjohns.

Waabishki: *wa- BEESH-key*. White.

Waffled: Refers to scars resulting from being kicked by calked boots during a brawl.

Walkin' boss: A woods boss who managed several camps at once by walking to each.

Wannigan: *WAHN-i-gun*. Company store. Also a portable kitchen that was used to prepare food for workers who were too far from camp to return for dinner at midday.

Wash: The turbulent water behind a vessel.

Wenebojo: *we-ne-BO-ZHOO*. A key spiritual character to many Native Americans, His father was a man. His mother was the west wind. His grandmother the Earth. Wenebojo is often depicted as a half-man, half-spirit, who delights in playing tricks on and confusing people, both to demonstrate his talents and wisdom and to protect all plants and animals. Able to perform miraculous feats, but also vulnerable and capable of making thoughtless errors. He may take the form of animals, rocks and plants. Sometimes called Wenebush. Wenebojo is, to many Native Americans, what Jesus is to many Christians—the worldly manifestation of the great spirit.

Whiffletree: The rear wooden component of a horse team's rigging that connected the team to the load. and evened out the force of the pull from two horses. Also called an evener.

Widowmaker: A dangerous tree or limb that may injure or kill a logger when it falls.

Woods Boss: Foreman of the crews that worked in the woods.

Yellowjack: Cornbread. Also called johnnycake.

Enjoy this book? If so, please tell your friends and your local library. Secure online ordering is available at BadgerValley.com. See excerpts, illustrations, and special prices at BadgerValley.com. We ship free and pay your sales tax, too!

A Note to Treasure Hunters

This popular pastime can be fun and rewarding. Before you go, check with your state's Department of Natural Resources and the U. S. Forest Service for regulations. Some areas, such as U.S. Park Service lands, are off limits. **Artifacts can't be removed from some public lands.** Though panning for minerals is usually allowed in public waters, any bounty found may be the property of the adjacent landowner. **Trespass regs must be honored, too. Ask permission.**

Be sure to tell someone where you are going and when you expect to return. Consider consulting a treasure hunter's association website for more advice.

Know before you go in order to make your treasure hunt safe and successful. Good luck!

Recommended Reading

Readers interested in further study of John Tanner, AKA Chief Namakagon, might consider an Internet search of J. E. Bayliss's *River of Destiny, the Saint Marys*; G. L. Nute's, *"Border chieftain,"* and Maxine Benson's writings. The historian John Fierst has published several in-depth accounts of Tanner's life. You will find more on Tanner in the *Dictionary of Canadian Biography Online* and the *American National Biography Online.* The Manitoba Historical Society has several documents about John Tanner and his descendents. Another excellent account is <u>Sketch of John Tanner, Known as the "White Indian,</u>" by Judge Joseph H. Steere of Sault Ste. Marie.

Perhaps the best place to start your research is in Tanner's own book, *A narrative of the captivity and adventures of John Tanner, (U.S. interpreter at the Saut de Ste. Marie) during thirty years residence among the Indians in the interior of North America.* Though the words are Tanner's, his friend, Dr. Edwin James, did the writing. Revised often and reprinted, the original 1830 version may be the most difficult to read, yet the closest to Tanner's actual words. Several versions are free online.

George Francis Thomas, Herbert Wagner, Kim Wallin, and Eldon Marple each studied and wrote about Chief Namakagon. James Brakken has contributed three historical fictions on Chief Namakagon. He also published an annotated version of Ben Armstrong's 1892 memoir that Brakken believes verifies that Armstrong knew Chief Namakagon, received silver from him, and took him out to see the silver mine, but turned back so as not to show dishonor to the Great Spirit. Good luck in your research!

James Brakken's Illustrated "Up North" Short Story Collections

THE MOOSE & WILBUR P. DILBY
Plus 36 Fairly True Tales from Up North.

Thirty-seven short stories straight from the heart & the heart of the north. All fairly true, more or less. Some are sad, some shocking, most are hilarious. Small town tales of baseball, fishing, hunting, tavern tales, family situations, jokesters, murderers, gangsters, and flimflam men. Lost treasure, lumberjacks, and legends of the north. **Features *two* 1st place award-winning stories.**

BILLYBOY, THE CORNER BAR BEAR
Plus 36 Fairly True Tales from Up North.

Thirty-seven *more* short stories straight from the heart & the heart of the north. Some are sad, some shocking, most are hilarious. But, like the tales in *Moose,* all 37 of these are fairly true, more or less. Includes 6 Corner Bar yarns, 5 "gangster" tales, several Warden Snook Wilson yarns, and many more stories from days gone by. A *must* for your "up north" bookshelf and a great gift for all ages.

BOOK 3!   *45 FAIRLY TRUE TALES FROM THE OLD CORNER BAR*

Ah, the good old days---when the rivers of time flowed slower and taverns served as public meeting places. Though these tales could've come from most any watering hole, they originated in the old Corner Bar in Cable, Wiscconsin, a quiet village not far from Lake Superior.

While names and some of the "particulars" have been changed, these stories are based on true events as told to or recalled by James Brakken, Bayfield County's award-winning author of historical novels and short stories.

So, come on in! Meet the gang. Lift a glass and join the fun. These "fairly true" tales will leave you laughing or shocked or sad or utterly flabbergasted when you learn how clever some patrons of the old Corner Bar can be one minute, yet how dimwitted the next!

Step into the past in the old Corner Bar. We've been waiting for you!

DARK—A CAMPFIRE COMPANION

56 very scary short stories & delightfully frightening poems for dark & stormy nights or under the blankets with a flashlight! Spine-tingling tales of ghosts, dragons, ne'er-do-wells, and monsters—each waiting to raise goose bumps. Every story is morbidly illustrated by long-dead master artists of the macabre. Chilling, yet thrilling fireside reading. A "must-have" for every cabin bookshelf and home library.

About the Author ...

Bayfield County author, James Brakken, began writing in college when "Muskie Madness," his story of a fishing trip with his father, appeared in *Boy's Life Magazine* in 1974. More articles followed in *Sports Afield, Outdoor Life, Field & Stream, School Arts,* and other publications.

His first novel, *The Treasure of Namakagon (2012),* features a boy in an 1883 northern Wisconsin lumber camp and Chief Namakagon's legendary lost silver mine. The suspicious 1886 death of Namakagon and the 1846 disappearance of a Sault Ste. Marie murder fugitive led to two more novels, *The Death of Chief Namakagon* (2013) and *The Secret Life of Chief Namakagon* (2014), where Brakken solved a 168-year-old cold case when he proved Chief Namakagon was actually John Falcon Tanner, the adventurer who vanished in 1846. Brakken's *Annotated Early Life Among the Indians* (2016) documents Chief Namakagon's silver mine and offers many great 1800s Northern Wisconsin stories.

Treasure won 2nd place out of 10,000 worldwide entries in the 2013 Amazon Breakthrough Novel Awards. Brakken also received the 2013, 2014, and 2016 Lake Superior Writers Award and the coveted Wisconsin Writers Association Jade Ring for his short story collection, *The Moose and Wilbur P. Dilby plus 36 Fairly True Tales from Up North* (2015). *Billyboy, the Corner Bar Bear* offers 37 more "fairly true" up-north tales to have you rolling with laughter one minute, in tears the next.

Brakken earned statewide recognition for conservation with his *Saving Our Lakes & Streams: 101 Practical Things You Can Do Today* (2016). Brakken offers discounts of this book to conservation clubs and lake associations. *Alias Ray Olson* (2017) is a true-crime thriller that exposes the truth behind the June 1939 homicides in Sawyer County and Wisconsin's largest-ever manhunt. It's a close look at the *perceived* guilt of a man convicted in the press and hunted by hundreds. Brakken's *INFAMOUS (2019)* is another true-life, north woods crime novel from the 1930s. It chronicles John Henry Seadlund's rise to Public Enemy #1 in only 4 years.

DARK: A Campfire Companion (2012) is an illustrated collection of 56 of the author's delightfully frightening short stories and poems. It's ideal for dark & stormy nights or for reading under the blankets by flashlight.

45 Fairly True Tales from the Old Corner Bar offers hilarious tales of life way back when. It's a must-read for anyone who's ever hung out in a tavern "up north."

Thornapple Girl (2021,) Brakken's most recent fact-based novel, chronicles the life of Myra Dietz, a young woman caught up in her father's 1910 struggle against lumber barons who denied him his earnings.

The Heroine of Cameron Dam (2021), is Myra's long overdue "lost" 1929 memoir, prepared for publication by Sybil Brakken.

Of Brakken's writing, *Publisher's Weekly Magazine* and *Amazon Books* said, **"Difficult to put down. ... A great read,"** and **"the flow of words is like an old fashioned song."** All James Brakken books are illustrated. All are intended for adults but great for young readers, too.

Find **special pricing** today at **BadgerValley.com**, where **shipping to USA and APO addresses is free** and Wisconsin sales tax is paid by the author.

Enjoy this book? Then please tell your friends & your local library.
Free shipping and secure online ordering is at at BadgerValley.com.
See special offers, excerpts, and illustrations at BadgerValley.com, too.

9 780099 762499 1